The Sand Fish

The Sand Fish

A novel from Dubai

MAHA GARGASH

HARPER

NEW YORK • LONDON • TORONTO • SYDNEY

To my parents

HARPER

HarperCollins books may be purchased for educational, business, or sales promotional use. For information please write: Special Markets Department, HarperCollins Publishers, 10 East 53rd Street, New York, NY 10022.

FIRST EDITION

Designed by Aline C. Pace

Library of Congress Cataloging-in-Publication Data
Gargash, Maha.
   The sand fish : a novel / Maha Gargash. — 1st ed.
       p. cm.
   ISBN 978-0-06-174467-9
   1. Women—United Arab Emirates—Social conditions—Fiction. 2. Young women—Social life and customs—Fiction. 3. United Arab Emirates—History—20th century—Fiction. I. Title.
   PR9570.U543G377 2009
   823'.92—dc22

                      2008054423

09 10 11 12 13   OV/RRD   10 9 8 7 6 5 4 3 2 1

Author's Note

All the places and communities in this novel are of the author's imagination but are based on the various societies that lived in the region that today makes up the United Arab Emirates and the Musandam Peninsula of Oman in the early 1950s. The author has chosen fictitious names for the towns, villages, and communities for two reasons. One is that some of these places and communities no longer exist. The other reason is that she wanted more liberty in bringing them to life.

1

They'd arrived. The strangers who had come to her home to seal her future.

From inside the stone hut Noora could hear them clearly, clucking their complaints like chickens fighting for grain. They were tired and irritated; this much Noora knew. After all, they'd crossed her waterless mountains in a journey that must have lasted the better part of the day.

"Bags of brittle bones, Sakina, that's what we are."

"Yes, Gulsom, I've rattled so much on that donkey I still can't stop shaking."

There they were, the voices of the matchmakers. Gulsom's was thick and hoarse, Sakina's thinner, with a soft quiver that seemed eager to please.

Noora shuddered now as she listened to her brother's voice, calming their exhaustion with an offer of water and dates. She would have liked to throw her arms in the air and scream, let go in rib-shaking sobs. Instead, she made fists, let her nails dig deep at his betrayal. Her own brother, the playmate of her childhood: Sager, just a year younger than her seventeen, and half a head shorter—and he was giving her away. Just like that.

Noora hugged her chest and felt the ripeness of her breasts. Soon, a man, a stranger who would be her husband, would crush that softness. What else would he crush? She hunched her shoulders and curled back into the dimmest corner of the hut. On the outside she was a woman, but her insides screamed for the loving protection a child craves.

"Right, where is the girl?" Gulsom's thunderous voice demanded.

Noora sat up straight and pulled her *shayla*, or head cover, low over her face. Through the transparent, black weave, she watched the matchmakers shuffle into the hut. After the customary greetings, they slumped heavily in front of her and introduced themselves as sisters who were talented in preparing brides for a married life.

"You're a very lucky girl," Gulsom said. "Not everyone gets the chance to please a man as rich and prominent as the one you're about to marry."

How easy it was for her to say that. She wasn't the one who'd have to leave her home and sail to some distant village. She wasn't the one who would have to share a stranger's mattress. Noora could not join in Gulsom's enthusiasm. So she stared ahead and waited silently for what was to come.

"Now, dear, I want you to stand and walk a little," Gulsom instructed.

Noora rose and, wrapping her *shayla* tight around her chest, took a step toward the entrance.

"No, no, lift your dress. I want to see how your feet move."

Noora pulled her dress up, revealing the loose *serwal* pants that tightened at the ankle, and continued with a few uncertain steps. She threw a glance over her shoulder, caught the sisters nodding their approval. With burkas covering most of their faces—forehead, nose, mouth—they looked like hawks about to peck the flesh off a kill.

"Very good." Sakina's voice quivered with glee. "*Masha' Allah*, God protect—no limp, no ugly twists."

"You can sit now," Gulsom said, "right where you are, close to the doorway."

"Keep your face to the light, dear."

Noora sank to the ground as the matchmakers shifted toward her on pear-shaped behinds, creating a neat triangle. Gulsom took a deep breath and pulled up her sleeves. "Now, let's look at you." She tugged at the *shayla* and it slipped onto Noora's shoulders.

The sisters slackened their necks and let loose an erratic dance of daring inspection. They jerked their heads from side to side, bobbed them up and down. Within the angular slits of their burkas, their eyes darted in dizzying directions, and under their silent gulps of scrutiny, Noora felt the heat rise to her face. That's when she detected the crinkling bags underneath their eyes. They were smiling.

Sakina giggled and said, "The pomegranate has lifted to her cheeks, sister."

"Another shy bride," Gulsom said, reaching out for one of Noora's auburn plaits, fingering the tips. "Soft but neglected. See, sister?"

"Yes, sister, but that's all right," Sakina said, stroking Noora's broad fringe, which, according to the custom, was trimmed high to show her full forehead. "It's good hair. See how this bit shines. A little jasmine oil will nourish the rest." Noora flinched as Sakina's calloused fingers crawled down her face and traveled back up a cheek. She stopped at the ears for a firm tug—first one, then the other. "Fine, clean, nothing there."

Gulsom's hand reached for Noora's chin, and as she yanked her face to the light, Noora narrowed her eyes. She knew what would happen when the light hit them. They would glow with the blaze of emeralds. That's when they were their most attractive, and she hoped Gulsom would miss it. But Gulsom was bold and thorough. She plucked Noora's eyelids open and took in all that shine, humming her approval before rubbing Noora's cheeks with two of her thick fingers. "Skin is a bit rough," she declared, "but a nice mixture of cardamom and milk will soften it. Humph." Her grunt felt hot on Noora's neck. "I don't like that," Gulsom said. "That scar under your chin. What happened?"

"I fell and hit a rock when I was small," Noora said, surprised at how spiritless her voice sounded.

Gulsom's tongue danced in a fountain of clicks. "Well, there's nothing we can do about that, is there?" She inserted a thumb and two fingers to unfasten Noora's lips and checked her teeth. "Solid, except for this chip here."

"It's from that same fall," Noora said, hoping the handicap might somehow dishonor her, make them lose interest in her. But they had already moved to other parts of her body, kneading and handling her as if working a piece of dough to the right consistency. One pair of hands clutched the back of her neck; the other rubbed her back.

She flinched as Sakina's lumpy fingers dug into her shoulder blades. Her touch was stronger than her voice. "She doesn't have the fat of the pampered. Too bony." A few presses later, she concluded, "But her bones are strong, *masha' Allah*, not sick. Good for housework."

Gulsom pawed her midriff. "This is good, well rounded. Excellent for childbearing." She circled her palms on a thigh and squeezed her way in rounded grips to the knee. "Hmm," she sang with satisfaction, "the legs are solid, strong enough to carry the weight of a pregnancy."

"So much work to be done," Sakina trilled.

"Yes," agreed Gulsom, "but we can prepare her. We'll make her neat." She scanned the interior of the hut, as if seeing it for the first time. "It's good you keep a clean house, but do you know how to cook?"

"Yes, *khalti*, aunty," Noora mumbled.

"Poor soul," muttered Sakina, and for the first time Noora noticed some sadness in her eyes. "Stuck here with no mother and a gone-to-who-knows-where father."

"No time to feel bad, sister," said Gulsom, a confident flurry of excitement ruffling her husky voice. "We have a mission: to take this child and turn her into the respectable wife of an important man." Turning to Noora, she added, "We'll get you ready, *insha' Allah*, God willing. We'll take over the role of your mother and teach you all that you need to know."

"And there are two of us." Sakina giggled. "So you're twice blessed."

"There's so much you need to know and very little time."

"Women who have followed our advice have made the best wives," said Sakina, her voice warbling with pride. "Not one husband has complained."

It was then, when Noora watched the sisters beaming their silent congratulations to each other, that she understood. She had passed the test.

What followed was their knowledge, committed to memory through their many years as matchmakers. The sisters inhaled the blissful air of success before unraveling a list of instructions designed to ensure a happy husband.

"Remember, you are going to become a part of your husband's home," began Gulsom.

"Cooking and cleaning . . . ," said Sakina.

"Mind you, all the while looking beautiful."

"And smelling nice: rose essence behind the ears, incensed clothes and body."

"No more of your wild ways in these mountains," Gulsom cautioned. "If he wanted someone like that, he would have chosen a savage from the jungles of Africa."

"You have got to be demure now," Sakina said, a soft quiver rattling her speech.

"For the first year, he mustn't see you chew."

"Just move your mouth like this." At once, the sisters paused to demonstrate. Their mouths remained concealed behind the awkward shifts of their burkas. Little by little, Gulsom's string attachment that held the burka in place loosened, and the burka tilted to one side, exposing the edge of a tiny nose that lifted in an elegant swoop. Noora raised her brows with surprise. That fine nose was a sharp contrast to Gulsom's brusque temperament.

Gulsom cleared her throat and, adjusting her burka, continued, "One important piece of advice: when you spit the pit of a date into the tray, make sure it doesn't make a sound."

Noora wondered how that could be done.

Sakina laughed nervously. "No one believes it can be done, but it can." She turned to her sister. "You remember that Al-

Miqbali girl, when she thought she couldn't do it. And with a little practice, *masha' Allah*, she managed to make the pit land on the tray with the softness of a grain of sand."

Gulsom shook her sister's lighter mood to one side. She hadn't finished. "Don't smile," she warned Noora.

"If you have to, just look down and smile in your head," Sakina explained. "No moving the mouth."

"Don't talk too much."

"Ooh no, no," Sakina squeaked. "Never, never talk too much. He'll think you're easy."

The two women paused, even though Noora kept nodding them on. The quicker the inspection could finish the better.

Then Gulsom coughed—an important cough that cleared the air—and Noora guessed she was about to give out the most vital piece of information.

"Now," said Gulsom, "what I am going to say next is for your benefit, and I advise you to follow it."

Noora glanced at Sakina for some hint, but Sakina had cast her eyes down to the ground and was silently drumming her knees with her fingers.

"Look at me," Gulsom ordered. "Word is that you're head-strong, that you want to do everything your way. Is that true?"

"No, *khalti*." Had Sager said that about her? She felt her eyes sting with the betrayal that her brother kept throwing at her. Where was he now? Was he listening from outside? Was there a smug grin on his face?

"You can't afford to be proud, my girl," continued Gulsom, her voice rumbling with meaning. "It's not good. You are poor, but you will be getting the privilege of living well. Remember that and appreciate it. If your head grows big and you become spoiled, your husband might throw you out. Out! And then you'll have nowhere to go."

Sakina's voice trickled back into the conversation. "Poor girl," she said, her eyes blinking rapidly. "We are very rough on her."

"We're telling her for her own good, sister!"

"We can't even blame her," Sakina said. The sadness had swallowed the chirp of her voice. "To think, all her life growing up alone, so far from other people. It's not fair. What were your parents thinking, dear?"

"They should have married her off when her mind wasn't formed yet," Gulsom said.

"Yes, as soon as she'd ripened," said Sakina. She was twittering again.

"Even earlier, just so that she could get used to her husband's house for a little while before he could touch her," Gulsom said. "But it's no use thinking about what was. Now we have to concentrate on what will be. You're a lucky girl. You got yourself a rich man. Be thankful."

"Yes," Sakina confirmed. "Thankful."

The sisters continued to instill in Noora the necessity of modesty of her sex and the timidity that comes with poverty. Their voices thickened with every word as they wove their conjugal web of constraint, until Noora felt they had shred any strand of hope that lay hidden in her heart.

The matchmakers were entering her life with the force of a spiraling dust storm, leaving behind only the taste of grit in her mouth. And she had to swallow it. Now, as they rose to leave, Noora wondered what had happened to the eagle in her. When had the frail chick staggered to take its place?

She was too tired to fight. Too much had taken place in too

little time: the sting of betrayal, the hurt of false promises, the pain of loss. And now, as she sat alone in that hut of tightly packed stones, as she faced banishment, she tried to pinpoint when it had all begun. And almost at once, she remembered the sand fish.

2

In her mountains, at the tip of the Arabian Peninsula, the earth was more often thirsty than not.

Noora Al-Salmi climbed to the top of the ridge that rose above her home and walked to its edge. She ran her eyes along the barren cluster of fractured peaks. In the west, the same clouds she'd spotted every day for the past week were gathering once more, taunting her from afar. On this dawn, they were darker and she could tell there was rain in them.

She licked her lips and swallowed the dryness in her mouth. She was desperate for the rain they carried. This heat, the heat of 1950, had lasted a full nine months, the longest she could ever remember. The sky had dried at the same time as her mother's death through a mysterious illness, which ate up her strength and shrank her to skin and bone. Now, the water in their well tasted brackish. And soon it would dry up completely.

Noora sighed and turned away. And just then a sudden gust blew her *shayla* off. She chased it as it danced and twirled in the air, rushing with the wind that carried it, feeling that hope was running along with them, too. That wind could blow those bloated clouds over her home. It could build up into a mighty storm, and the rain that fell out of them would somehow find its way into her family's well.

Her *shayla* floated along the side of the ridge and landed on the tangle of branches of a lone acacia tree. It was then, just as she plucked it off the tree's thorns and placed it on her head, that she spotted the skink, basking on the gravel to one side of the tree.

She thought she'd seen every creature in her mountains, but this one was different. More snake than lizard, it had no pronounced neck, only a thinning of the body at both ends: a long wedge-shaped snout with eyes on the side and a short tail that tapered to a fine point.

"Sager," she called, and when her brother did not answer, she called him again.

He arrived just in time to catch it slither onto a small rock that rose between the acacia and the ridge. It moved like a snake, too. "It's a sand fish," he said.

"A sand fish?" said Noora, rounding her eyes at him with a slight jealousy at his knowledge. "What kind of name is that?"

When he did not answer her, she turned back and examined the skink again. It was slightly larger than her hand, its body covered with smooth, shiny scales. Even in the muted dawn light, its back shone a brilliant yellow, with black-brown bands along its length.

"I don't know what it's doing here," said Sager.

"Warming itself, of course."

"No, you don't understand. There are no sand fish here. They live in the desert."

Noora snorted. "Sand fish, what names you make up."

"They're called that because they leap in the sand and swim in it," he said, making moving humps with his hand. "Wait, I'll show you."

"Don't . . ."

But it was too late. Sager was already stooped under the acacia. His *ghitra*, turbaned so neatly, got caught in the tree. Out tumbled his curls—and they got caught, too. Those fine ringlets: more and more, they became the only softness she could see in him. He was built as solid as a boulder. His skin was coarse and had none of the gold that lightened Noora's complexion. Instead, what gold he had speckled his eyes, just like their father's. But the tiny dots in Sager's eyes were mostly hidden in the shadow of his protruding forehead.

Noora began giggling as she watched him spit curses at the acacia. The more he twisted and wrestled, the tighter the tree embraced him. "Sand fish, really."

"Why am I even bothering?" he said, finally managing to free his hair. As he crawled out, his mouth curved into a squiggle that pulled with it the fine line of wispy hair that was waiting to turn into a mustache. "Why am I wasting my time with you when I have so many responsibilities?"

Again, that big word. That manly word. *Responsibilities*: how important it made him feel! More and more, he liked to throw it at her, like a spear aimed to pierce her throat so she could not answer back. "There's still our father," she said. "He is still the head."

"Not always," Sager said, tightening his *ghitra* back onto his head and brushing the dust off his dishdasha, the loose-flowing robe men wore. "Now that his mind is more out of this world than in it, I have to think for this family. I have to make all the important decisions."

She was about to answer back when another blast of wind blew into them. It shook the tree and startled the skink. The sand fish dove into the wall of the ridge and hit its snout.

Noora gasped, and suddenly she and her brother were making a dash to either side of the acacia to see what they could do, which only made the sand fish panic more. Again and again, it tried to escape in the only way it knew how. Stuck in a place it shouldn't be, again and again it smashed its nose—and Noora felt its pain: a dull pinch just below her navel, in the deep of her belly.

"We've got to do something," Noora called to him.

"It won't make it," Sager called back. "There's nothing we can do."

There were ribbons of blood, fine as silk thread, streaking its nose and a gash in the shimmer of its yellow back. Noora was sure it would lose its tiny toes as she watched it scrape the hard rock. It was trying to swim through!

"Do something!" she ordered.

Sager pushed his arm between the tree and ridge and tried to grab it. Once, twice, his hand closed on it, but it slithered out of his fingers, and finally the sand fish dove into the acacia.

Noora shrieked. It was twisting in midair, unable to land— trapped—its tail pierced by one of the tree's thick needles. Sager thrust his arm through and finally caught it.

"There, there, there." Noora cried, pointing him farther up the valley, where the earth was crumbly, easier to sink into. "Take it there."

But the wriggling, bloody sand fish would not stay still. It slipped out of Sager's grasp and clambered onto his chest, taking a leap in the air in what Noora was sure would be its last. She cupped her mouth to stifle her squeal.

In the air, it spun and twisted. On the gravel, it landed with a smack. The impact ripped off a section of its tail, which flew to one side and started to slice the air blindly.

But the sand fish was alive. The sand fish was hobbling up the mountain.

"Come on, let's go," Sager said. "We have to go get the water."

After the trauma it had been through, Noora wanted to make sure the sand fish reached the softer earth. "Let's just see . . ."

"Look," Sager said. "As long as we're around, it'll try to escape, try to hide in that same way. It'll ram its head till it kills itself. Let's just go."

3

They set out with the first arrow of light. Noora was carrying a goatskin bucket with a long rope attached to its handle, and just like her brother, she had slung two water skins over her shoulders. They flapped against her waist as she led the way up the gentle slope of their mountain. All the while, she tried to spot the sand fish.

"How do you think it got here?" she asked once they'd reached the broad, flat plain at the top.

"I don't know," Sager said, remaining a few steps behind her.

She stopped and turned to face him. "I mean, the desert is so far from here."

"It's not important," he said, his face as rigid as stone—a young face trying so hard to look old. "And who cares anyway."

He did care though. She had seen the anguish on his face as he'd tried to save that wretched creature. His features had crumpled as if he had squeezed the juice of a bitter lime into his mouth. But now he was putting on another face, one that could hide his emotions, one that would prove him a man.

Noora watched the loose stones tumble under his feet as he stomped past her. That march, so determined, was telling her he was leaving his boyhood frivolity behind.

He's so serious with me nowadays, thought Noora, as she followed him. She understood that Sager worried about their family, his sense of duty, now that their father was slipping into another world. But why he was pushing her away, she could not understand.

"We are so alone, so isolated," she muttered to herself. "That should be enough to keep us always close."

"What?" he said, throwing a cool glance at her over his shoulder.

"Nothing."

They stopped at a sharp decline, which overlooked a cluster of desert acacias. There, behind the trees, was their hidden water source: an ancient cistern hollowed out of the rock.

Sager pulled his dishdasha just over his knees and knotted it at the waist before zigzagging his way down. Then Noora did the same with her dress and prepared to descend sideways. It was the safest way.

As she stretched her leg down, her *serwal* ripped, exposing her knee and shin. She twitched her brows into a scowl, as if her tightened face might somehow pull together the gash, make whole the little, pink flowers that sat on the washed-out blue fabric. It was then that she spotted Sager's disapproving look.

"Hide your legs," he ordered.

"It's a rip," she cried. "I'll fix it when I get back, but I'm not pulling my dress down. It might get stuck under my feet. Then

I'll trip and fall." She started to mimic the irritation in his voice. "And anyway, why are you looking at my legs, being disrespectful like that? Just turn away. Don't look." She caught the rush of blood to his cheeks before he dropped his eyes to the ground—and Noora snorted her joy at having ended his bullying. Sager turned to the trees, but she hadn't finished yet. She slid down the crumbly bits of gravel at the end of the descent and slammed into her brother's back.

Sager stumbled and fell, his head just missing the thorny limbs of the acacias. Noora gasped and slapped her mouth. She hadn't intended that. It was meant to be a playful shove. When she bent over to help him up, he elbowed her away.

"The problem is you don't know when to joke and when not to, what you should take seriously and what you shouldn't," Sager said, as he got up.

"I didn't mean to push you like that."

"It doesn't' matter. This . . . this . . . the way you are, it just won't do."

"What do you mean?"

"Look at you . . . ," he began, waving all five fingers at her. Then he paused and the pout of his mouth was filled with mortification, a shamed aversion to what he was about to say. "You've got curves," he blurted. "Everywhere!" He swung his arms in the air. "You're not a girl anymore; you're a woman. Those curves are there to remind you to stop running and jumping, for you to slow down and turn domestic. So start acting like a woman."

Noora gaped at him. "And if I am a woman, what does that mean? What happens now?" She pulled her *shayla* over her face and let it drop to reveal only her eyes. She knew Sager would not see the humor in her exaggerated act of vulnerability, but she continued anyway. She fluttered her lashes, slowing the movement till it turned into a demure glance at the ground.

"You see? I can't even talk to you," he said. "You look a mess. You don't even comb your hair in the morning. You're like a savage that fell in mud."

Noora felt her ribs shake with the rattle in them. The first light of day was quickly turning into a dawn of confrontation. "Well, what do you want me to do then?"

"Stay at home more," he said. "Do all the things women are meant to do; leave the hard work for us men."

"So," she said, her eyes narrowing, "what are you saying? Are you saying you'd rather carry four water skins filled with heavy water all the way back, instead of two? Are you strong enough?"

"I'm saying you should change your ways. This drifting all over the mountains like a tribesman, it has to stop."

"Why?"

"Because . . . because it has to. You've got to start carrying yourself properly. You don't want people seeing you and thinking you're a crazed woman."

"What people?" She looked up at the violet tips of the mountains. "Do you see anyone?" Noora knew they were quite alone. The closest community lived a full morning's walk away, in Maazoolah. As for passing caravans, she would have spotted the flickering stars of their fires on her walk up, and if it were the rare, lone traveler who happened to venture into the uncertainty of her mountains, he would have followed the unwritten laws of peaceful intentions by quickly making his presence clear: arriving when there was light and setting up camp in an exposed part of the mountain. That was the best way of avoiding a surprise attack, which could take place at any time and from any one of the many isolated tribes of the Hararees, the name loosely given to the mountains which likened the rugged tips to silent sentinels.

Few persons traversed the hostile peaks they lived in the middle of, preferring to take a more roundabout way on their journeys from desert to coast and back. They dreaded coming face-to-face with the ancient residents of the Hararees. The approach of strangers was discouraged through long howls that reverberated, bouncing off the sides of the sheer cliff faces, to give the desired impression of an aggressive army ready to attack from hidden positions. Little did the traveler realize that the mountain men had only one dread, a dread born through the need to protect their water.

Sager snarled and grabbed the water skins and the bucket. "I'm not going to waste my breath on you," he said.

"You don't have a right to tell me anything," she said. "I am older than you."

He didn't answer, only squatted under the umbrella crowns of the acacias to make his way through.

"Only *abbah* can tell me what to do," she called after him, the defiance in her rising the farther away he got. "He's our father, the leader of this family."

She heard Sager snicker before disappearing into the darkness of the hollowed rock face.

"I'll carry myself the way I want," she shouted at him. "I'll walk the way I please and sit any way I like." And with that, she slumped to the ground and, supporting her weight on her palms, kicked her legs out in front of her. It wasn't very feminine, but she didn't care.

She heard her brother grunt, and she knew he was shoving the large stone that covered the cistern. They always pushed that stone together, but this time Noora was not going to help him. "Let him do it on his own, the big, strong man," she muttered.

Why did Sager care so much about the way she looked or carried herself? With the exception of his recent rebukes, no one else bothered. Her home was a paradise of informality with no rules and no society to draw that fine line that separates acceptability from shame.

She heard the thud as the stone shifted, and then the crackle of the smaller rubble under its bulk. And her fury rose. He was managing without her. "And besides," she shouted at him again, "I've tried. You know I've tried, and it didn't work."

Sager didn't answer.

She was nodding to herself forcefully. It was true. She really had tried.

Once, many years ago, when she had first shown signs of womanhood, her mother had tried to instill in her some of the softness and modesty of women thought desirable by society. Fatma had told Noora to take smaller steps when she walked, to talk in a gentle voice, and, rather than laugh, to look down and giggle discreetly. Fatma had explained that when, one day, Noora got married, she would have to follow the rules of her husband's household.

Noora had found her mother's list of advice fascinating, and for a while, she had put her heart into her walk and her voice, preparing for her future matrimonial life. When she fetched the water, she would lift a corner of her dress and proceed with tiny steps up the mountain. The journey took her twice as long to complete. Then she had tried to call her brothers for lunch with her most delicate voice, but they never heard her. And so, she would twist that same little corner of her dress and tiptoe down to find them. That took longer than usual as well. Finally, there was the laugh. She practiced averting her glance to the ground and letting out a shy giggle. But by looking down, she missed all the funny expressions her father made, which left her frustrated and angry. *These women must be angry all the time*, she had thought.

And then, her mother introduced another set of instructions, concerning Noora's looks. Noora was to undo her plaits three times a day to comb her hair and keep herself neat and dust-free.

"But it doesn't need so much care, *ammah*," Noora had objected.

"Yes it does," her mother had answered. "You take care of your eyes, don't you, lining them with kohl like the rest of us. So why not your hair, too? You don't want it falling off, do you? To keep it strong, you must take care of it, rub sesame oil in it."

"And what am I supposed to do about the dust? It is all around me."

"Make sure you shake it off your clothes more often."

And so, Noora had combed her hair, drenched in sesame oil, every morning, noon, and evening. In between, she wiggled in her dress to shake the dust off. All the while, she felt the silly walk, soft voice, pitiful giggle, flyaway hair, and treacherous dust made her life more complicated than it needed to be. To make matters worse, her efforts fell on blind eyes. She received no praise or encouragement from her father or brothers.

Finally Noora gave up and returned to her old ways. She decided she would follow the rules of modesty when the new husband came along. Till then, she was content in knowing what needed to be done. Fatma seemed satisfied as well. She had done her duty as a mother, and now she could forget the subject altogether. Like Noora, it seemed she had decided there were more important concerns.

Yes, she had tried.

Noora yawned. She was calming down now. She felt another rip as she stretched her arms above her head. This one was smaller, a mere hole along the seam just under the arm of her flowered red dress. She sighed. The only part of her mother's lessons of womanly ways that proved useful and that she excelled in was sewing. Her fingers moved quickly and precisely when she sewed, leaving behind a strong line of stitches neater than a trail of marching ants.

The bucket tumbled down the cistern, landing with a dull thump at the bottom. And then it journeyed back up—no spill, no overfill. As Noora listened to that sound, more rock in it than water, she felt her rage return. Why was she waiting for Sager? Without another thought, she rose and started climbing back up to the plateau to make her way home.

Let him carry all four water skins on his own!

4

That was how it went when boys and girls, brothers and sisters, grew up to become men and women. Their worlds separated.

By the time Noora reached the edge of the plateau, the sun had leaped into the sky, bleached the mountains, and crusted the earth. It was as hot as the fury she was still carrying.

Noora paused to look down her valley. There stood the four stone huts that made up her home: the two living-sleeping rooms, the goats' and chickens' shelter, and the store. How lonely they looked.

She ran her eyes farther down beyond the huts to the bottom of the valley, where a small hill rose. Its side was smooth, and stuck to it were the ruins that had once been her great-grandfather's dwelling. Under the dazzle of the morning sun, she could barely make out their outline. The rough oval blocks were camouflaged so effectively, swallowed, as it were, that they became a part of the barren hill to which they were attached.

She knew every chip and crack in the weathered blocks that made up those ruins. She and Sager had played there when they were younger. It was their childhood watchtower, where they made up their games: hiding and appearing, building and demolishing. They pretended the blocks of stone could shield them from all the big, dangerous creatures that roamed the mountains. There were wolves, which they sometimes heard but never actually saw. There were leopards, too, which they imagined slinking around the huts in the dark of night, and the snakes and scorpions, of course. Her brother was different then. He used to laugh and shout. They used to laugh and shout—together.

And now Sager was drawing a line that would keep them apart. He wanted to trace that same line found in every society of the Hararees. But why did he have to do that? They lived in an isolated patch of the mountains. They belonged to none of those communities.

Noora marched down to the huts. It was only when she saw the smoke spiraling from the outdoor hearth that she began to calm down. Her father was lighting the fire to make breakfast. Preparing the food was a woman's job, but her father, with his own set of rules, embraced the acts of brewing coffee and baking bread as if they were the most natural tasks for a man of the mountains. It had always been that way. Her father, Ibrahim, mixed up the male-female roles so that they were interchangeable. And that was how he had brought them up, long before the voices entered his head and made him unpredictable.

She noticed the change in him soon after her mother's death (even though she now suspected the madness had been in him much earlier). He was sitting in the middle of the valley, stiff as a stone, his mouth mumbling words she could not make sense of. She had felt invisible as she tried to get his attention. His eyes had remained glazed as he slipped into that other world to confer with the whispers in his head.

Noora skipped over the last bits of rubble and, stepping close to her father, looked deep into his eyes. She whispered God's protection, *"Masha' Allah, masha' Allah,"* and quickly decided he was alone. No voices ruffled the clarity of his hazel eyes.

How she loved his eyes, made lighter as they sat in the smudged black outline of his kohl. There were little gold specks in them that glittered the way water did when the sun fell in it. She preferred their energetic gleam to the murky green of her eyes, which were more like the sludgy mess left behind in the little ponds of stagnant water where the tadpoles lived.

"What is it?" he asked, when he noticed her staring at his face.

"Nothing," she said, and stepped back.

Little sparks flew into the air as he fanned the fire. "Hungry?"

She nodded, sinking onto her haunches and grinning. Sager could lecture all he wanted, but her father was still of sound mind, capable of taking charge of their home. Her gaze drifted toward the scurrying goats and chickens, released from their night shelter. The donkey was near her hut. It hauled out its teeth and yanked a yellow clump of grass lodged in the dry earth. She could hear her other, much younger, brothers, Aboud and Hamoud, playing in the ruins. The normality of the scene filled her with warmth—until she turned back to her father.

Ibrahim was gazing north, at a distant peak. She knew it well; that was Jebel Hnaish. The vertical dome spiraled upward just like the snake it was named after. Her tribe, the Al-Salmi tribe, used to live there. Now all that remained on its flat summit were the stone skeletons of their abandoned homes.

Jebel Hnaish was part of Ibrahim's tale of loss. He had narrated it to her when she was a little girl and had asked why she had no cousins, uncles, or aunts. "We are all that is left of the Al-Salmis," he had told her. "A long time before you were born, a vengeful drought came to the village our people lived in, up there on Jebel Hnaish. The well and underground sources dried up, and when their livestock died, the tribe could not do anything but wander out, to find water. The able set out, and for days they traveled long distances."

How intrigued she had been. In her little girl's mind, she had pictured the long procession of men sliding down the rough mountain face, journeying into the unknown. She had imagined the group staggering with thirst, having no option but to lick the dew off the morning plants.

She shook the memory out of her head, sprang up, and grabbed the earthen bowl off the low wall by the hearth. "*Abbah,*" she said. "Here's the bowl, take the bowl." She had to deter him. Whenever he spoke of their tribe's defeat and cowardice, it threw him into a trance that lasted for days, broken only by bouts of bitter remembrances and a sinking depression. She scooped a ball of dough and lifted it to his face. "*Abbah*, let's bake the bread."

He ignored her, kept his eyes fixed on the mountain. "The mountain can be deceptive," he said. "What may look like no more than plain rocks and stones could very well hold blessings—water, deep, deep down. But our tribe could not find it."

She swiveled in front of him, tried to break Jebel Hnaish's

hold on him. But it was too late. The golden specks in his eyes had stopped moving.

"Let me tell you what happened to our tribe." His brows furrowed with importance and he added a solemn nod. "Our tribe was destroyed by one man, one selfish man: Ahmad Al-Salmi—that was his name. He was their leader, and he led them to hell. He found a well and his thirst was so great that he immediately went toward it." Ibrahim paused to throw a curse. "God show him the flames of hell."

"He's gone now."

"That stupid, selfish man just helped himself to the water, without thinking of the consequences. Do you know what happens to people who take someone else's water, Noora?"

"Yes, *abbah*, they get killed," she said, and pointed to the fire. "Look, look, the embers are ready. We have to bake the bread, quickly before the fire dies."

Ibrahim would not look. "Ahmad Al-Salmi understood the law of the Hararees: the touching of someone else's water without permission only brings tragedy. Ahmad Al-Salmi did not respect the law."

Maybe if she hurried him on. "And then he was killed by the Al-Hatemi tribe, who owned the well, and so was everyone else who had touched that water. And the rest escaped and ran back to the village."

"They ran to the village like mangy dogs," he said, spitting at the mountain. The clump landed in the hearth with a sizzle. "But what was the use? Revenge was going to follow them. The Al-Hatemis arrived with angry eyes and raised arms that held sharpened *yirzes*." Ibrahim's arm was up now, clutching a make-believe *yirz*, the small-headed ax that all mountain men carried to chop wood or to use in battle.

"Instead of fighting, they ran." He waved his arm at Jebel Hnaish. "The Al-Salmis left their homes and ran. They were chased all the way to the sea. I hope they drowned in that sea—cowards, dirty dogs with no shame, filthy animals." His voice was losing its strength, turning into a croak that was drowning in humiliation. "They chose defeat over an honorable death in the name of protecting their roots. Imagine, Noora, they left their homes!" His arm remained suspended above his head and his jowls melted into his neck. The only movement came through the flicker of his eyes.

Noora thought he might collapse, so crushed did he look. "Why didn't the Al-Hatemis attack us as well?" she asked. Of course, she knew that part of the story, too, but she was trying to bring him back home, to the people who loved him: his family.

At first, she thought it worked. Ibrahim shook his head as if waking from an odd dream. "Because our home was so far away," he answered simply. "You see, the Al-Hatemis didn't think to look here. They didn't know that we were Al-Salmis, and they certainly didn't know we had our own source of water. By the time news reached my grandfather about what had happened, it was too late. The tribe was scattered. The Al-Hatemis were victorious." He pointed to the ruins. "You know my grandfather lived just over there."

"I know, I know. Aren't you hungry, *abbah*?"

"Hmm?"

"Hungry? Breakfast?" She shoved the bowl back into his limp hands. Yes, he was recovering now. Yes, he was going to bake the bread now. Or so she thought.

He let the bowl slip out of his hands and crash to the ground. And then he wandered away.

Instead of following him, Noora rushed to salvage what dough she could before the earth swallowed it completely. Two, maybe three, pieces of bread, she reckoned as she spread the dough onto a thin, metal pan and placed it in the hearth.

Grainy bread: that's what they would have to eat this morning.

5

She wanted the day to end.

No sooner had she stitched the tears on her dress and *serwal* than she plunged into a whirl of frustrated vigor. She felt her hand tug too hard as she milked the goats and sweep too broad as she cleaned the huts. By late afternoon, she was pulling out weeds from their plot. And still the sun blazed, casting a layer of wobbling haze over the rocks and stones of the valley. The heat made everything move slower. And Noora remembered her mother.

"The stones, it's all because of the stones." That's what Fatma had said over and over again, whenever she spoke of the madness that had plagued so many of her husband's ancestors. "All those scalding rays," her mother had insisted, "bounce off the stones and, over the years, burn the mind. It made them all live in their heads and share secrets with voices no one else could hear. Thank God, your father wasn't affected."

"Thank God he wasn't affected while you were alive," Noora mumbled into her chest as she raked the earth to root out a particularly stubborn weed. As a girl, Noora had not believed her mother. Now she wondered whether it was true. There was her father, farther down the valley, as still as the boulder he was sitting on. And there were the rocks and stones attacking him from every direction. The sun's hammering rays fell hot on her head, and in a sudden panic she rushed to take cover.

Noora shifted the panel of wood that sealed the entrance to the store and collapsed in a corner between the small bushels of maize and onions harvested from their plot. Half a sack of flour, a tin of ghee, and a basket of dates sat in the other corner, leaning against a few pots, pans, and earthen containers. Every few months Sager and her father made the journey to the coastal village of Nassayem for those supplies in exchange for the wood they collected from the mountains. This time Sager would probably have to go alone. And then her heart softened as she realized the duty that was beginning to weigh heavy on his shoulders. Besides, she couldn't stay angry at him forever.

A fat, green fly landed on her nose. She flicked it away and reached out to shift the sack of flour, behind which sat an oblong basket. Lifting the cover, she dipped her hand through the mass of cut-up squares and triangles of fabric used to patch the rips in their clothing. She ran her fingers along the bottom, feeling its rough weave, passing the blunt teeth of the comb she no longer used, and flinching at her reflection in the grainy surface of the hand mirror that went with it. She looked like a young woman, not the girl she still felt she was. From heightened cheekbones, her face extended into a slender nose that seemed to pull everything else to the sky. She wiggled it, and the pout of her peach lips quivered like the petals of a dainty flower in a breath of desert air.

She rummaged once more, finally finding the knotted bundle of stones she was looking for. It was her collection of pretty pebbles picked from the mountains by Sager, all especially chosen for her.

After undoing the knot, she tumbled onto her tummy and anchored her head on her palms for a leisurely inspection. Even in the dimness of the store, they shone. They were smooth, special, some pale, flashing lines of brilliant color—saffron, lime—others dark, speckled in gold and silver, dancing like a watery night.

Yes, she couldn't stay angry at him forever.

A yawn crept from the back of her throat. Her eyelids slackened, her head slumped into her sinking elbows, and she fell into a deep sleep.

It was the fat, green fly that woke her up with its hysterical buzz, or so she thought—until she heard the howl, which was eerie yet familiar. Then silence, but her eyes snapped open anyway. And no matter how wide they swelled, she could not see a thing in the deep black that surrounded her. Only the musty smell of dust and old fronds cleared her sleep-drenched mind. She was still in the store.

She stumbled to the doorway, wondering why nobody had woken her, feeling irritated that nobody had worried about her absence, when she heard the howl again. Softer now, a human sound coming from an animal—or was it the other way around?

Sometime during her nap, clouds had gathered and drawn a mighty blanket that swallowed the stars, the moon. Noora's eyes remained wide open as she walked past the huts and toward where the sound was coming from. And that is when she saw the shadow that was her father. He was down in the valley, perched rigid on the same boulder as before. How long had he been sitting there?

"*Abbah*, why are you out here?" Noora asked, when she was close enough to speak softly so that she would not jolt him.

The moan he made was part confusion, part grief, a whimper that reminded Noora of a pained animal. "Gone," he mumbled, "all gone now. I'm all alone here."

"No one has gone," she said, trying to pick out his expression in the darkness. "We're all here, near you. We have always been here."

Ibrahim crossed his arms and let his head drop to his chest. "Gone," he repeated, "all gone."

Noora touched his arm. "Let's go back to the hut, sleep."

Ibrahim's voice evaporated to a soft whisper. "You, you, you . . ." And his head began to sway from side to side, like a rumbling rock rolling down and up, again and again, along the sides of a smooth ravine.

"We're here," she repeated. "We're he—"

And she jumped back with a squeal as her father flung his arms in the air. "Why did you leave your homes?" he yelled. "Why didn't you defend your honor?"

A flare of lightning blanched the sky, caught the gold in his eyes. He looked haunted, hunted. He was struggling, she could see that, struggling against those devious voices. They tortured his mind, made him imagine things, made him forget who he was: her father, the one she loved, the one who pampered her when she was a girl, the one who let her do as she wanted as a woman. And he was straining to chase them away. And she had to help him now.

Noora stepped back, just out of his reach—just in case—and prepared to be brave. Once he understood what was happening to him, he would be able to fight those voices. With a thick swallow, she squeezed the fear out of her voice and said, "*Abbah*, it is the stones. That's what is making you so."

Silence.

At least he stopped waving his arms. "Your brains are tired," she persisted. "You see, the stones take the heat and point it at your head. And then this happens."

Ibrahim hunched his shoulders and pulled up his knees. Like a frightened mouse, he curled his body into a ball.

Encouraged, Noora took a few steps closer and continued with the firmness of a mother advising her child. "You have got to avoid the heat that comes out of the hot rocks. It goes right through your eyes and to the back of your head, where it does all kinds of bad things."

He was breathing quickly, rocking back and forth. How vulnerable he seemed.

She rested her hand on his shoulder. And that was when he turned.

Ibrahim grabbed her wrist. It was a crushing grip and she shrieked with the surprise of it. Before she could do anything, he leaped to his feet and seized her hair with his other hand.

"Who do you think you are?" he shouted, shaking her like an empty sack. "Talking to me this way?"

Noora tried to wriggle free, tried to unclasp his fingers from her hair. All she managed was to kick up the gravel under her feet. He was just too strong.

"I know you want to betray me, too," he sneered. "More Al-Salmis betraying their own people!"

"No," she bawled, when another flash of lightning caught those dots in his eyes, throbbing in furious circles.

"*Tuff!*" He spat at her. "You lie!" He pushed her onto the gravel and hollered at the sky. "Why is there so much betrayal around me?"

Noora knew she should escape, but the shock of his brutality numbed her. She turned away from him, coiled like a snail shrinking into its shell, and twisted the pain out of her wrist and rubbed the sting off her scalp, surprised to find her hair was still rooted in place.

She did not hear his return. She did not see him standing over her. She only felt his crushing grasp.

Noora opened her mouth, but no scream escaped. Shock and fear trapped her voice as she felt his powerful knuckles dig into the cage of her ribs. Scooped up in his arms, she pierced the air with futile kicks. Desperately, she tried to think. Instead, she gasped like a fish pulled out of water.

Then she felt a thud. Ibrahim had let her go, just as the third bolt of lightning ripped open the sky.

And the rain she'd been waiting for all those months finally fell.

6

She'd leaped to her feet like a hunted animal and scampered up the mountain. In the swell of the storm, Noora searched for a hole she could crawl into. She wanted to be alone to nurse her wounds—a hideous blend of pain and shame.

Under the dark, thundering sky, she roamed blind as a mole, slipping over rivers of running earth and stumbling over dodgy stones reeled in her path by the force of the wind. Where was she? For the first time, Noora felt lost in her mountains.

Someone was calling her. Or was it the wind hooting her name?

"Nooooooraaaa!"

The moon emerged as an island in the black sky—just for an instant, just enough to throw a cold, blue beam on a figure. She caught the flaps of a dishdasha and turned to run away.

"Wait. Come back. Where are you going?"

She recognized Sager's voice and realized that she had been circling blindly, close to home. He was waving his arm at her. She hurried up toward him and began helping him pull out all the containers, every pot and jug they could find. As they lined them up to collect the rainwater, the sky let loose a bolt of lightning that exposed the ache that throbbed in her face.

It took only a nudge of a question for Noora to let her agony pour out, fierce as the rain that pelted the mountains. By the time they staggered into her hut to dry themselves, all the shock and turmoil that had bubbled in her settled like frozen droplets at her fingertips. As for Sager, there was a fury in him. She could tell by the way he was rubbing dry his head.

"It is no use talking to him anymore," he said. "He hasn't just retreated quietly into his head; he has become dangerous. You know, I'd noticed things in him, angry things, and pretended I hadn't. There were these . . . these . . . wicked looks in his eyes."

Noora wanted to say something wise, and when she couldn't think of anything, she kept squeezing the wet out of her plaits. In the light of the hurricane lamp, their stretched shadows danced along the walls.

"I never imagined he would attack you like that," Sager said, continuing to flatten his curls with vigorous rubs. "And you know what else? It's just going to get worse. We have to do something . . ." Suddenly he froze, and his dancing shadow turned into a blob on the wall.

"What, what is it?" said Noora.

"I have an idea. I think I know someone who might be able to help him."

"Who?"

"Zobaida Bint-Sheer."

"Zobaida? She can't help him."

He nodded and his wilted curls awoke. "Yes, yes, she can."

"How can she help him? What is she going to do? Ask for advice from the jinn?"

Sager stopped nodding at the mention of the mysterious jinn, those invisible spirits, made of fire, which lived in their own world but sometimes managed to slip into the human world.

Noora sneered at him. "You really believe she can talk to them?"

"Maybe . . . I mean, every Muslim knows they exist," Sager said, and coughed to shake the quiver out of his voice. "It's established in the Holy Koran."

"Well, I don't see how she can help *abbah*," Noora said. "I mean, she's just interested in cheating people out of their money."

"No, she's not. She is a healer. People come from everywhere to see her. They travel from the far deserts, the sea towns. They come for everything: broken bones, aging pains, stomach cramps . . ."

Noora began shaking her head, resisting his idea, even though it was beginning to make more and more sense. Why was it that whenever he suggested anything, she always felt like disagreeing? Why couldn't she just agree?

". . . exorcisms, the evil eye, mystery illnesses—just like the one that is making our father mad. Zobaida is famous for her healing powers."

Noora continued to shake her head. "Anyway, *abbah* won't even meet her. He says she is just a witch who deals with the devil."

THE SAND FISH {39}

"Maybe she has ways to make him listen to her," said Sager. "Or maybe she'll mix a potion or two to cure him." He flung his arms in the air. "I don't know. All I know is that everyone says she is a miracle maker. And that's exactly what we need: a miracle."

Finally, Noora began nodding—slowly—while she thought about it. "But he'll never agree."

"He doesn't have to know yet."

"He hates her."

"It doesn't matter." Sager raked his hand through his hair. "Look," he said, "let's just go and see her, find out what she says."

Noora let out her acceptance in an exhausted sigh.

By the time Sager returned to his hut, the hammering drops had softened to a light drizzle. Noora lolled on her mattress, listening to the fill and spill of the containers outside, as runaway raindrops slid off the roof and plopped into them.

She stretched her arms over her head and tightened her feet to a point. She rolled her neck from side to side to let the strain of the grueling day dissolve. She had to get some rest. She and Sager had agreed to visit Zobaida at first light.

With the late night hours, the sky cleared and a full moon bathed the interior of Noora's hut with its sapphire glow. The night crickets rasped their lullaby in an intoxicating air, so cool, just right for a peaceful sleep. But Noora remained awake, struggling between an icy rage and burning tears.

All night she had been trying not to hate her father, trying to pity him instead. But she could not. Anger and frustration continued to grip her, tight as a murderous fist, as dagger-sharp images of how he had flung her and crushed her exploded in her mind.

And then the purple predawn darkness swallowed the night. Noora heard the crunch of the donkey's hooves on the rocks. She sat up, eyes alert. *It's time*, she thought.

7

Aow-wah! Aow-wah!"

The familiar howls echoed in the valley. To Noora, it was a welcome respite after her long walk with Sager, a silent walk in a light mist, in which she had remained wrapped in her thoughts. Not that Sager was feeling chatty. He had put on his stern-man face.

"I think we've been spotted," Noora said. She squinted, but all she could see was Maazoolah, perched on a slender neck of the mountains from which terraced plots stepped down.

"Aooo!"

"Just like baby wolves."

Sager's tight mouth finally loosened into a smile. "The little ones must be practicing," he said.

The little boys of Maazoolah dashed out from behind the rocky outcrops lower down from the village, descending in tumbles and hops toward them in a jumble of sizes. They squeaked their greetings like kids bleating for attention.

"*Marhaba* Sager. *Marhaba* Noora."

"Let's play, let's play."

"Can we ride the donkey?"

"You scared us silly with those howls," said Sager, and cleared the *yirz*, water skin, and tin bowl off the donkey's back.

"Yes," added Noora. "We were about to turn around and flee. We thought some nasty tribe had taken over your village."

"Don't think we saw you just now," said a plucky little lad. "We spotted you a long time ago and followed you before letting out the alert."

"We thought we were going to be attacked," said Sager. "Thank God, you don't have any weapons with you."

"We've got our weapons, but we take them out only if we need to," said the brave one, pulling out a coarse branch from behind his back. "We wouldn't charge unless we were prepared." He turned his head toward his army of ragamuffins and, raising his hand, signaled the confirmation. They pulled out their arms—twigs, stems, leaves—from under their tattered dishdashas.

As the procession headed up to the village, Maazoolah's little girls joined them. They held Noora's hand and followed Sager, who was trying to control the boys. "My poor donkey is going to collapse," said Sager, as each lad used his strength to bully the other off the beast's back. The donkey brayed its complaints.

Sager tried again. "That's three of you on its back. Get off, Salem, you are too big. Besides, you have stayed on too long. Let little Omar have a turn now." Other boys were clambering onto his shoulders, choking him with stubborn grips, knocking his *ghitra* off. Sager bent over to pick it up and chuckled with pleasure. "You're smothering me."

By the time they reached the high settlement, Sager and Noora were walking in a sea of bouncing youngsters, howling and squealing with excitement. It wasn't every day that visitors came to their village.

Some twenty stone homes made up Maazoolah, forming a crude circle on the flat plain at the top of the mountain. The women were scurrying in and out of their homes, busy with their household tasks, and working the plots, along with the rest of the men, were Sager's friends. They had watched his noisy arrival and were now heading toward him with smiles.

"*Salam Alaikum*, peace be on you!" they called.

"*Alaikum As-Salam*, and on you be peace." Sager returned their greeting, followed by a heaving of syllables, which released each of their names with the customary tone of masculinity adopted by the young men of the mountains: "Saif! Abdullah! Mohammad! *Marhaba!*"

At once, Noora felt shy. After rounding up the girls to one side, she lifted the edge of her *shayla* and, holding it just under her eyes, watched her brother extend his nose to touch his friends' noses, one by one, in the traditional welcome—three light sweeps of the tip: left to right, right to left, and a middle press. This nose kiss was the unwritten etiquette of greeting for the men of the region.

News of their arrival had reached the village long before they had heard the children's howls. Although there were no watchtowers at Maazoolah, the community's roving eyes were sharp. And so, old woman Moza Bint-Falah, a distant cousin of their mother's, had readied breakfast for them: Arabic coffee, dates, and bread, sprinkled liberally with energy-giving mountain ghee laid out on the round, palm frond dining mat just outside the hut for the boys. Noora would join Moza indoors.

She was waiting for them at the door of her two-room hut. Her silver plaits rested on her chest, on a loose orange *thoub* with yellow dots, so sheer and light it was like a haze covering the red dress that was underneath it. Sager kissed the old woman's head and hand, then Noora did the same.

"*Masha' Allah*, how you've changed, how you have grown," said Moza. She held the wide sleeves of the *thoub* tight under her *shayla* and squinted at them through the generous slits of her burka. "I haven't seen you in such a long time."

Sager's and Noora's eyes met in a knowing glance. "No, *khalti* Moza, you saw us recently," said Sager.

Moza swept her head toward them and nudged out her ear. Remembering her dampened sense of hearing, Sager spoke louder, "We came when our mother died."

Noora, her father, and brothers had carried Fatma's body all the way to Maazoolah on a stretcher so that a large group of people could recite the prayers of the dead before burying her. It was the proper way. It was the Islamic way.

"Your mother?"

Talk had it that Moza's memory lapses had begun three years before when her husband, as sometimes happened with other mountain men, wandered off into the mountains and never came back. The villagers had searched for Sultan Bin-Zahran for weeks before giving up. But Moza had refused to lose her faith in his return. After all, Sultan, with his pointy beard and darting eyes, was Maazoolah's enterprising drifter. With his bandolier of ammunition crossing his chest and circling his waist, he scaled the mountains and the desert beyond, collecting wood, honey, and even mountain radishes and herbs. Then he would sell or barter what he could. Everything he brought back, Moza locked away in a tin chest that she kept in her bedroom.

"Have you forgotten, *khalti*?" said Noora.

"We buried her in the graveyard over there," Sager said, waving his arm over his shoulder.

"And then I stayed with you," Noora added, waiting for a hint of recollection in Moza's lazy eyes.

Throughout the three days of mourning, the scent of damp breathing and heavy sighs had filled Moza's hut as Maazoolah's women arrived to pay their respects to Noora. There were waves of moans and groans of regret (or perhaps body aches, since it was always the old women who initiated this road of sorrow). And then, they let out their pleas:

"The sorrow! Let it out so you don't feel it later."

"Cry, child, cry now!"

Then silence.

They had wanted her to release her heartache quickly so that she could get on with the act of living. Conditioned from very early, they knew it was senseless to let a loss disturb the emotional balance of life for too long. There was enough severity in their world. The unforgiving sun, the callous rays, the incessant dust, the lack of water—all of it stretched the line that separated life from death, stretched it so thin it could snap with a blink of the eyes. That was the way to look at things—the only way—in the Hararees. The old women moaned once more, before urging Noora to remember that death was small, that dwelling on it was pointless: "The world is for the living."

"Don't let the sadness rot in your head. Just move on."

Moving on! Wasn't that what their life—all of them—was about?

Finally, when all else had failed, they had surrendered to their accepted wisdom.

"Nothing we can do about it; *Allah* is the decider."

"What are we, except His subjects and slaves?"

What a grief-stricken lot they were, slumped all around her with those long faces. They had tried so hard, but how could she snivel and whimper in front of those strangers?

Noora signaled Sager to join his friends and, ushering Moza into the hut, tried again. "Don't you remember how full of women your house was?"

Finally, Moza's sluggish eyelids turned taught. "Ah, ah, ah, I do. Now I do." She tugged at her silver plaits with the recollection. "You stayed with me, yes. But you didn't stay long, did you?"

"Ten days," Noora said.

"Ten days?" Moza's eyes went blank.

This time Noora did not explain—and the old woman seemed to forget just as quickly. As they settled around the breakfast mat, Moza asked, "What news?"

"No news, except the news of rain," said Noora. "Lots of rain, *masha'Allah*, yesterday—all in one go."

"Ah, the rain always comes," said Moza, staring at the air. "When it leaves, you think it's gone forever . . . but then it comes."

The beauty that came with the occasional rain was all any of them knew of the gentleness of nature. And now, the boys were talking about it, too. Noora had to lean back to see them through the open entrance of the hut. They were eating, bent over the palm-frond mat. Mohammad said, "We've had a whole week of it. It just stopped yesterday."

Noora took a large bite of bread and, as she chewed, fought a sudden pang of jealousy that rose in her. How unfair! Maazoolah had a full week of rain and her family had received only one day. *Even the clouds blow sweeter away from our home,* she thought, and pushed the rest of the bread into her mouth.

"Yes," added Saif, pouring some coffee for Sager. "It came late, but it came a lot. *Masha' Allah*, look at how green our plots have become."

Sager swallowed the bitter brew in one gulp. Then, jiggling the tiny bowl-shaped cup lightly between his thumb and fore-finger (an indication that he didn't want a refill), he glanced over his shoulder.

Noora stretched her neck and followed his glance, catching a view of the tapering terraces. From the edges of the mountain rim, they narrowed downward, each surrounded by low, stone walls. With a base of barren rock, the Hararees yielded less grazing than the sandy deserts of the interior. The mountains held just enough soil to make the scanty cultivation possible. But Saif was right; Maazoolah's cramped parcels of land were a shocking green.

"That was a wonderful downpour," said Abdullah.

"A blessing," added Mohammad.

"A true blessing," echoed Saif. "We even slaughtered two goats to celebrate. And then we performed the *nadba*."

The *nadba*: nobody quite knew who had made it up, but whenever it took place, every man and boy rushed to join in.

"You should have seen us," said Mohammad. "What a manly chorus we were around old man Abdul-Rahman. He held that goat's skull high up and barked away."

"*Masha' Allah*, he still has the best voice of all," said Saif.

"Yes, I could feel the blood rush up and tickle my face every time he shouted *hao*," said Abdullah.

The other boys let out a series of coordinated yaps—"*Hao, hao, hao*"—before collapsing into a frenzy of laughter that shaped a sad smile in Noora's head. It was a long time ago, but those eerie cries of togetherness remained vivid in her memory. She leaned forward and chomped more of the gooey bread. It was the second piece, and still her empty stomach would not fill.

Noora was just a little girl, young enough to be in the company of men, when her father had held her high on his shoulder to watch the *nadba*. The circle of men was tight around the cheerleader, a man whose voice was particularly strong. Clutching the blanched skull of the goat they had just eaten, he raised his arm above his head and barked his appreciation. As he repeated the curious howls, he was echoed by the group.

The tribe had bonded further with an upsurge of raised fists that pulled Noora into the performance, too. Her voice had risen high, shrill as a yowling kitten, over the men's deep grunts. It went on and on till she thought it would never end. But then the coughs of exhaustion brought it to an abrupt halt. Their voices had turned hoarse.

Why did good things always have to end? Suddenly, Noora didn't want to go home, where her father could turn on her again, where Sager's scorn would only grow more bitter and ugly. She yearned to stay here, where there were people, people who did things together, who cared for one another. She wanted to watch the children play. She wanted to listen to Moza's watery voice.

Her windpipe felt clogged. She took a mammoth gulp, but there was too much bread in her mouth. She choked. Tears streamed down her cheeks as she coughed and coughed.

"There, there," said Moza, patting her back. "Why are you eating so quickly?"

Noora spat the lumps of bread into her palm.

"Here, drink some water," said Moza. She had trouble lifting the earthen jug, tilting it over the tin cup she held in her other hand. And when Noora stared at her swollen joints, she said, "Old woman pain. It's not just the fingers that won't bend well; it's the knees, too."

"I know that, *khalti*, don't you remember how I rubbed them for you? Every day, I rubbed them for you."

"When?"

"Never mind," Noora said. She pulled Moza's hand and began kneading the pain out of her joints.

The old woman shut her eyes tight and moaned. "Will you stay with me a while, give me such relief every day?"

Noora did not hesitate. *"Insha' Allah*, I will, *khalti."*

From outside, one of the boys shrieked. "Ha ha, keep dreaming, my friend." It was Mohammad, and now he let out a boisterous laugh. "That wicked woman won't even come to our village."

"That's true. She complains it's too far."

Now this was a new voice. Noora kept rubbing Moza's hand and leaned back to see who it was. There was another friend who had joined the boys. Although he had his back to her, she could tell he was older. His shoulders were broader and his voice thicker.

"It's cruel that God gave her the healing hands," said Saif.

"Yes," said Mohammad, wiping away his tears of mirth, "healing hands that work only for paying hands."

"Well, I'll have to get a lot of wood," said Sager, smiling. "And if that doesn't bring enough money, I'll just have to stay longer and work in a few this-and-that jobs in Nassayem."

"It won't work," said the new voice. "Zobaida Bint-Sheer does not need your little coins." A cluster of flies circulated over the food and his arm floated over the mat. In one self-assured swoop, he shooed them away.

"Why?" asked Sager. "Surely any coin is a good coin."

The man (for Noora had decided he was no longer a boy) tilted his head slightly. She could see the side of his jawbone. It had none of the roundness of the other boys' faces. It was sharp, just like the jagged peaks of their mountains. Clinging to his chin were the dense beginnings of what promised to turn into an attractive goatee. "News says she has been busy with a new client," he said. "A rich new client."

"He has come from a distant coastal village," continued Mohammad, "nowhere near our mountains. Ten days it took him to get here."

"So who is he?" asked Sager.

Noora wanted to know, too, but just then Moza snapped open her eyes and asked where she and Sager were journeying to. Noora bent forward and quickly told her how her father's behavior had turned erratic recently. She did not mention the attack; that would have just ruffled the mildness out of the old woman. "So, we decided to find Zobaida and see what she can do to help him."

Moza inhaled deeply. It was clear she had not heard every little detail. She was about to ask something when Noora tugged her thumb. The old woman shut her eyes again and exhaled her relief.

How much of their talk had she missed? Noora stared back out into the sunlight, thankful for the dimness of the hut, for if the boys (and the man) could see her, she would have looked ridiculous, with her spine curved like an old woman's, her neck twisted like that.

They were whispering now, their turbaned heads drawn close together. Noora fought the wind, which threw their voices the other way, but could pick up only the droppings of their conversation: ". . . private troubles . . . tried and tried . . ."

"Zobaida, you say?" Moza's voice sounded like it was coming out of a hollow well.

"Yes, *khalti*, yes," Noora said, and pressed her palm harder.

". . . desperate . . . wish-wash cure . . . between the legs . . ."

Mohammad and Saif began giggling.

"After a good rain, the bees get busy," Moza said.

Noora nodded her away just as the boys broke into a ripple of laughter—all of them, except Sager (just like him, not to enjoy a joke).

"Honey, that's what you should be looking for, sweet girl," said Moza.

Noora sat straight. "What?"

"I said honey. That's the only way you'll be able to sweeten Zobaida's tongue."

8

Who was the man they were talking about? What were his problems? Sager and his friends had whispered an intriguing tale. Their faces had been stamped with shock and disbelief. The burn of curiosity sat at the tip of her tongue. But she had to wait for the right time, when she was alone with her brother, before she could ask.

With the next dawn, Sager and Noora set off, following the trail to Nassayem. Halfway into the journey, they veered north, pulling the donkey into a broad valley in which rose an abundance of trees. This was Wadi Sidr, and here they could find the best wood.

Acacia and *sidr* trees rose in groups of five or six in the middle of the *wadi*; others stood alone at the sides, where the mountains slanted vertically from the valley floor. It was when they paused to drink some water that Noora put on her most casual voice and asked, "So who is he, that man you were talking about?"

Sager's answer was as abrupt as a slamming door. "It's man talk, not for you to hear."

Noora pushed on. "Just tell me what his problem is. Anyway, I heard most of it."

"Well, you shouldn't have," Sager said and, picking up his *yirz*, strode to a handsome acacia. Its solid trunk sprouted out of the ground and split into an explosion of sturdy branches.

So that's how it was going to be. She watched him clutch a branch and begin chopping. Ten hacks later, he pulled it off. "Well, aren't you going to help?" he said, looking over his shoulder at her.

Noora stretched her arms above her head and, mid-yawn, said, "I don't know. If you don't want to tell me your man talk, then maybe I shouldn't be doing your man work." She shot him a smug look, but he only shook his head and turned back to the tree.

Chop, chop, chop! Noora sank to the ground and, easing back onto her elbows, smiled at the one thing Sager had failed to notice. Every hack was a wasted effort. Every bough he broke off the tree was useless. Let him tire himself, the clever-big-man. He was chopping wet wood, wood that he wouldn't be able to sell.

Noora yawned again and stared up at the mountains, a disheveled carpet of gleaming old rocks and bright, young shoots. She took it all in: unruly scrubs with tips bursting into tiny, red flowers; fluffy, white dots on stout bushes; bizarre purple clusters that crowned stunted cacti. No matter how long or short the burst of rain, the speed of the bloom was quick and urgent. And so was the wilt that would soon follow.

Chop, chop, chop! Sager was tackling the next tree. A breeze bathed her face and she closed her eyes, losing herself in the noises that followed the rain. In the distance were a bubbling brook and a murmur that came and went. *Was it the wind?* Nearby, frogs croaked, crickets rasped, and, every now and then, the scampering whoosh of some small animal clattered the pebbles.

"Well? Are you planning to fall asleep here? Get up and help."

Noora opened her eyes with a start. She had drifted off. There was a huge pile of chopped wood, and Sager had just picked a branch and was beginning to scrape the thorns off with his *yirz*. She got up and marched toward him. "There's no point," she said, pulling the branch out of his hand. "This wood is useless, look." She ran her finger over the pale inner layer. It was moist. "You see? The rain has made the wood all watery inside. You've tired yourself for nothing."

"It doesn't matter," he said, through clenched teeth.

"It won't burn well," Noora said. "It will make smoke, and then they will come looking for you, saying that you cheated them and sold them bad wood. You know all this!" She hit her head with the soft base of her palm. "Why didn't you think before you started?"

She smiled at his flustered face, at the tiny dots of perspiration that lined his upper lip, sluggish and clammy, like the sticky sap of some of those plump-leafed mountain bushes. And then her smile seeped out and turned into a huge grin.

Sager kicked the pile of wood, startling a toad into a mighty leap; it landed with a plop in a puddle nearby. "You let me chop and chop, and you said nothing? Why?"

"Because you won't tell me anything. And because you're always in a bad mood. I watched your friends giggle and laugh, but not you. No, your face dropped as long as an oar. Why are you always such a sour face?"

Sager glowered. "All right, you really want to know?"

The whites of his eyes were turning pink. She wasn't sure she did want to know, but she threw him a defiant bob of the head anyway.

"I was just thinking, sweet sister, about your dilemma," he said. "Getting so old now, and not married yet—all because our selfish father wants you near him. And it made me sad. And, I think, that's why my face grew as long as an oar." He crossed his arms high on his chest. "Yes, so sad I was, sister, to want good things for you and not be able to give them to you. I thought how nice it would be for you, to have someone who would be able to take care of you, like that rich man we were talking about. Imagine! To live in a real house, with many rooms; to eat well—dates from Basra, mangoes from India, pomegranates from Persia—to be adorned with the finest gold." He sighed and clicked his tongue. "But now, I see, it was all wasted thought."

They had to start over.

Noora followed her brother deeper into the valley, where the mountains drew closer together, to find dry wood. Soon they were walking through a steep-sided gorge that reminded her of the rift between them that was deepening with every passing moment. And it was all because of her. Why had she let him go on chopping that wet wood, tiring himself like that? He had spoken from his heart—she was sure of it—and she had played with his seriousness.

The air vibrated in a constant murmur as it funneled through the passage, as if whispering to her to make amends. She tugged at the donkey and called to him, "You know, we don't really have to find wood."

He didn't answer, only climbed over a heap of rubble in their path. It was a section of the mountain that the rain had dissolved and sent crashing down.

"We should be looking for nests," she continued. "*Khalti Moza* told me that Zobaida loves mountain honey, that she would take it as payment." No sooner had she clambered over the broken piece of mountain when Sager stopped and tilted his head at an angle. "Well, what do you think about—"

He raised his arm to hush her. "Listen," he whispered, and pointed up at the scarred peaks. "There, there."

"What?"

"A bee, there it goes." His finger danced in the air. "There is a nest up there."

She shaded her eyes with her hand and stared at the blue of the sky. "What, I mention honey and suddenly you spot a bee? I can't see a thing." She was sure he was getting back at her.

"There! It lifted east, then dipped south." He hurried to the donkey. "I saw it, I saw it," he mumbled, and grabbing the bowl and the *yirz*, he scrambled up the mountain with an urgency that infected her.

Whenever he wanted to, Sager could outdo her. His powerful legs catapulted him up the steep climb. His square build lost its rigidity as he twisted, skipped, and leaped, lithe as a mountain cat. There were no trodden paths in this part of the mountain and Noora struggled to keep up. With her *shayla* clasped tight under her arms, she pulled the donkey into a terrain strewn with jumbles of weathered boulders, folded and crumpled into bizarre shapes. Was he making it up, seeing the bee and all, so that he could tire her? "Maybe you're wrong," she called up to him. "This could be a waste of time."

When he did not reply, she decided to say no more. Let him take charge and play his game if it made him feel good. Even if there were no nest, she would not make much of the matter. And he would continue to feel fine. Those were the thoughts that filled her head. And yet, she kept scanning the air for a bee or two.

The dense concentration of rocks opened into a gravelly ascent, speckled with fragile grasses and tiny, yellow flowers. When Sager stopped and cupped his ear, she did the same. Holding her breath, she strained to pick up the telltale buzz of a nest. Instead, the wind blew another sound.

Was it the cry of a child? Puzzled, she twisted her head toward the sound, but the wind changed direction àgain. This time, it threw the hum of bees. The surprise was as jolting as a splash of cold water. He was right!

There was the dance of the bees. They flitted out of a shallow crevice at the top of the mountain, catching the light in chaotic twists and twirls. The nest was impressive: a long triangle, which distorted into a lumpy ball on one side at the bottom. It clung to a broken branch that had somehow wedged into the ground at a slant.

She wanted to share the danger but held back. Better to let him feel in charge again. Maybe then he would lose that long face. Sager was already crouched next to the nest, his eyes peeking through his *ghitra*, which he had wrapped around his face. She watched him extend an arm and woo the jumble of striped bodies away from the nest. They parted, but the middle of the hive was dry and empty. The bees had consumed this part of the comb.

Sager flicked a bee off his arm and tried again. With the fat of his palm, he brushed the bees on the lump at the bottom.

This part of the nest glistened with moistness. Sager wasted no time and cut a clean slice with his *yirz*, letting the lump slip into his bowl.

The bees objected in a furious buzz. They lifted to the air in a dense cloud of frantic movement around his head. Noora could tell he wanted to run, but they both knew that that would just excite the bees more. She followed his wary steps away from the nest, feeling both the urgency and control a thief must feel in a house with sleeping residents. The bees pursued him, carrying their final protest in spasms of flight. They delivered more stings, but Sager's elation could not be dampened as he hugged tight their gold.

It had worked. His mood was transformed. Even though he was holding back his smile, it seeped out of his eyes and made his face glow. He covered the bowl with a muslin cloth and roped it securely to the donkey's back. Noora was about to compliment him on his bravery when they heard the hollers of children from not too far away. They looked at each other, puzzled.

"I thought I heard some children's voices earlier," she said, nodding west. "It came from the other side of that mountain."

Her brother cranked his head this way and that, trying to get his bearings. "I think we are right by Nassayem. You see, it makes sense." He drew the direction vaguely in the air with his arm. "We continued through the *wadi* and then took a shortcut when we climbed this mountain."

Before he could continue, Noora pointed up. Once again, they'd been spotted by children.

9

The boys of Nassayem were pretending to be an army. Their mission was to escort Noora and Sager safely along the slant that led to the edge of the village.

"Avoid that bush; it's full of snakes," ordered the leader, a spindly limbed boy with generous lips, taller than the rest. The group, now following him in single file, walked around it, careful not to touch the unruly tips.

"That's Faraj Al-Mugami," Sager whispered to his sister. "He's Sheikh Khaled's youngest son."

Noora nodded and tugged the donkey along. "I guess that's why he's barking his commands like the chief of a warring tribe."

Faraj gave his next command. "This way, this way, not too close to that big rock. If it tumbles down, we'll get crushed under it."

No sooner had they avoided the ominous curved arm of rock that jutted over them than Faraj stopped. His fleshy lips parted. "Look," he said, pointing down the valley. "There she is—the witch." He lifted his arms and the boys took cover, crouching behind what stones they could find. "And what are you two waiting for?" Faraj hissed, signaling to Noora and Sager. "Take cover before she sees you."

"Now this is too much," Sager grumbled, though he let Noora pull him behind an ocher slab of stone. She kept hold of the donkey's reins so that the animal didn't wander off. Then they watched.

Of course, the witch was Zobaida, a black-clad bundle hobbling up a distant hill. Perched on top of the hill was her hut, looking friendless under two dried-up palm trees.

"When are we going to see her?" Noora asked.

"As soon as this stupid game is finished," Sager said.

Noora yawned and let her gaze drift to the boys' peering faces. What a mixture of sorts they were. Her father was never impressed with Nassayem's people. He called them "bastards, untrue to their origins." They were made up of sailors from distant ports and towns who had stayed behind, dwellers of the nearby hills, and mountain men who preferred to stay close to the opportunities the sea brought. With the years, they married each other, and now the population was a concoction of many races and colors: black, brown, olive, and white faces with straight, wavy, and frizzy crowns. Nassayem accepted them all, but her father would not. He always told her that when tribes mixed, they got mixed up. They lost their goodness and purity.

"What do you want with her?" Sager called to the boys, as Faraj signaled the boys to rise from their hiding places. "She's just the same as us."

"That's what you think," squeaked a mousy-haired lad. "She talks to invisible people all the time."

"Yeah," added a pink-cheeked boy. "And she has got smelly things in her house."

"Not only that," Faraj said, his voice beaming with knowledge. "She turned her son into a dog."

Noora rolled her eyes with exaggerated surprise. "A dog?" The waves of the sea certainly lapped a strong imagination into their minds. She was about to laugh when she noticed Faraj's bottom lip flip to his jaw in a scowl.

"That son! From outside he looks like a person but inside he's really a dog. She even took away his tongue."

Finally, Noora laughed. "Oh, a dog that can't speak or bark."

Now the inside of Faraj's mouth bloomed into a gleaming hoop. "Laugh if you want," he said, "but we've watched her. She's the master; he's the dog."

"Dur-Mamad the dog!" the pink-cheeked boy mocked. "When she wants water, she raises her arm and he runs to get it."

"And when . . . ," began a third boy before Faraj signaled him to be quiet.

"There he is," whispered Faraj.

Noora and Sager followed his glance. Dur-Mamad was farther up the slant they were on. His nest of grizzled hair disappeared behind a rock as he stooped to pick something up. Noora turned back to the boys and sighed, amused at their childish minds, wondering why they had dropped to their knees like cautious mountain cats.

"Attack!" cried Faraj.

His voice bounced off the sheer cliff faces, and the boys darted toward Dur-Mamad screaming insults. Noora and Sager were about to run after them when they heard the donkey's bray of panic. It lashed the air with a sharp kick and dashed the other way.

"The honey," Sager cried and leaped at the donkey, clamping his arms around its mane. Noora plucked its ears and hissed a soft word of comfort. But the donkey would not listen. It kicked once more and pulled them with its weight. They staggered and let go.

Noora's mouth dropped open as she turned back to the boys. They'd turned into an army of ruffians, closing in fast on Dur-Mamad. They were hurling stones at him. One caught his calf; another chipped his arm.

She and Sager rushed to help him, a middle-aged man who had braced himself for what was to come. He curled into the ground as the jumble of boys landed on him. Noora cringed as she watched them pull his hair and pound his back.

"Get off him." It was intended as a bold shout, but Sager's voice cracked between heaves of breath.

She ran as quickly as she could but had to stop when a thorn lodged deep in the softness between her toes. All the while she kept her eyes glued to the unfolding cruelty. Faraj was trying to flip Dur-Mamad over, to create a hollow into which his bullying army could wiggle, pinch the man's cheeks, and poke his nose or eyes.

But Sager was there before they could do that. He seized Faraj by the shoulders and, pulling him up, slapped him across a cheek. Faraj fell onto the gravel.

By the time Noora reached them, the boys had wilted into submission as Sager dared them to take him on, confirming his strength with a thrust of the chest. "What devil stirred you?" he said, and walked back to Faraj. "Are you a creation of God?"

Faraj looked up at Sager, shook his head, and spat. "He's a freak. And, anyway, he likes us to play with him."

"You call this playing?" Noora scolded, and turned to include the other boys. "Throwing stones at the man, punching him, pulling his hair like that? Look what you've done to him." She threw her arm toward Dur-Mamad, but he wasn't there. She scanned the mountain. Nothing. Dur-Mamad had slipped away as quietly as a spirit.

Faraj pointed an accusing finger at Sager. "You slapped me!"

"And he'll slap you again!" Noora snapped, and puffed her annoyance at the boys' rounded eyes of anticipation. There was no guilt in them. She wasn't sure what was infuriating her more: Faraj's rude boldness or the boys' eager whispers of cheer for their leader's bravery.

"He has no right to slap me. He's not my father," shouted Faraj.

Noora ignored his whine and turned to the boys. "You are cowards, all of you."

Sager joined her. With his chest pushed out, he took a few menacing steps toward them. "You should be ashamed of yourselves," he growled.

The boys retreated with bulging eyes.

"Get out of my sight before I twist your ears one by one until they fall off."

A small boy cupped his ears and scampered past Sager and Noora. The others followed, fleeing toward the village. Faraj scrambled to his feet and, with a tear-stained face, scampered down the mountain.

Sager and Noora kept the scowls plastered to their faces as they watched the boys kick up a trail of dust in a panic of skids and slips. Noora wondered what joy they had gotten out of terrorizing the wretched Dur-Mamad. Wasn't the harshness of their mountains enough? Maybe her father was right. Maybe they had turned wild from all that mixed blood.

She could hear their shrill objections long after the dust had settled, long after they were tucked safely in the village. Only Faraj had stopped at a safe distance from them just under Zobaida's hill—by the donkey. "I'm telling my father on you," he yelled. "And he'll beat you up and never let you come to our village again." And with that, he wrenched the *yirz* out of its rope holding and threw it as far as he could.

Sager and Noora gasped and dashed down.

He pulled free the water skin and emptied it into the dry earth. Then he flung it in the air.

"Stop it!"

Faraj would not. With a final tug of revenge, he pulled loose the bowl of honey. He dipped his paw and clutched the comb, raised it to the air like the blanched skull of the *nadba*. Then, with a final smirk of defiance, he howled his victory: "Aooo!"

Noora groaned. "No wood, no honey," she said, and bent over to pick up the water skin. "We've made this journey for nothing, haven't we?" She looked up at her brother, his arm clasped tight around the donkey's mane. "I mean, what kind of children are these?" she said.

"They're the kind who just want to wreck everything," he mumbled, and a vein throbbed in his temple. "Spoiled, left to grow up like animals."

"Well, we can't just ignore it all," said Noora. "I mean, this Faraj boy, you said he's the village sheikh's son, this . . . this

. . . Sheikh Khaled. Isn't he the wise sheikh who is supposed to settle troubles? Well, maybe he should settle this trouble—a big one, I think, ganging up on that wretched man, throwing our things like that, stealing our honey. We must see this sheikh-father of his and complain."

Sager shook his head and let out a resigned groan. "What's the point? The honey's gone."

"You get stung and they gulp the sugar. That's not fair." She threw her arms in the air, opened her chest to the sky. She was about to screech her aggravation when she spotted Zobaida and the son peering from their hill. "They're looking at us," she whispered, and, dropping her arms, she began brushing the dust off her dress.

Zobaida disappeared into her hut, but her son rushed down toward them with the enthusiasm of a child. As he drew nearer, Noora thought he might pounce on them, and she instinctively stepped back. But Dur-Mamad stopped abruptly and began hissing his hellos, a large grin shrinking the whites of his eyes. His complexion was the color of soot. Dull as a foggy night, even the wobbly curls of his salt-and-pepper hair could not throw a shimmer into that face.

Dur-Mamad tried to communicate some information with haphazard flings of his arms. When she and Sager did not understand, he took a step forward and kissed Sager's shoulder. Then he kissed the donkey's forehead and tugged it up the hill, indicating that they should follow.

10

Dur-Mamad clutched Sager's wrist and led him in. Then he walked back out and indicated to Noora that she should follow. Once she was in Zobaida's hut, a whiff of rotting grass, old skin, and toenails assaulted her nose just as Dur-Mamad sealed the entrance with a thin board, leaving only a sliver of light.

"Stinky in here," said Noora. "Why did he shut us in?"

Sager shushed her. "Show manners—we're guests here."

She fidgeted and shifted on her feet when something scraped her forehead. Noora lashed at it. She had crossed from bright light to dimness and had to blink hard before she could make out the dried plants hanging upside down from the roof.

"Well, where is she?" Noora whispered.

"I don't know," said Sager, as he settled on the floor on folded legs. "Just sit and wait."

She sat. "What does she want?"

"I don't know."

They waited, and as Noora's eyes adjusted to the shadowy interior, she yawned and let her gaze drift to a row of jars and bottles lining the far wall. Were those squiggles dead sand-racer snakes? Her lips fell open in disgust. "Erkh. Did you see what's in those jars?" In another jar, she was sure she could pick out the tips of the tails of mountain scorpions squished together. "Erkh," she repeated. "This place gives me the shivers. Let's get out as soon as we can."

She heard Zobaida before Sager could respond. From the darkness the healer appeared, shuffling in on her bottom from a doorway that led into another room they had not seen. Her clothes rustled and there was a clicking sound from a mysterious necklace. She settled cross-legged in front of them like a dark queen about to attend to the woes of her subjects. With her head tilted to one side and her eyes half-closed, she waited.

Sager cleared his throat and said, "Your son brought us here."

"Yes, but you were coming to see me anyway, weren't you?" Her raspy voice flowed like a lethargic current.

"We were, but now there's no point. We can't pay you."

"Yes, because that rascal stole your honey."

What witch-blood ran in Zobaida's veins that she should know so much? Noora's head pulsed with the thought just as Zobaida shifted and stretched her legs. The beam of light from the doorway fell on her chest, on the source of the clicking sound. That was no mysterious necklace! It was her talismans, dangling from loops sewn to the edges of her *shayla*. Noora scrunched her nose at the teeth, claws, shells, and tiny bundles of cloth. She did not want to know what was in them.

Zobaida swiveled her head, and Noora dropped her gaze, only to be startled by Zobaida's deformed feet. From the ankles down, they curved into crescents that had none of the beauty of the moon.

"You know, my mother tried to straighten them when I was small, but it didn't work," Zobaida said, and snapped open her eyes. Both her seeing, black eye and her blind, blue eye joined in an intense stare at Noora. "She would pin me down with her knees and place heavy rocks on my feet. How it hurt!"

Noora felt the heat rise to her face. "I didn't mean to . . ."

"Never mind all that," Zobaida said. "*Masha' Allah*, you have done a good thing today. You are the first people ever to defend my son." She sighed and clicked her tongue. "So helpless, life hasn't been kind to him, giving him a tongue that moves without purpose and ears that can't catch the sound of the wind."

Sager muttered something about only doing what was right when she silenced him with a raised arm.

"No! What you did was something special. Dur-Mamad is my only son—as valuable to me as my liver. Even his father wouldn't have stood up for him the way you did. He abandoned us, you know, when Dur-Mamad was just a toddler." A growl crawled at the back of her throat, and she raised one of the clinging teeth to her mouth and blew a whisper over it. "To Moosa, you scoundrel, wherever you may be. May this tooth blunt your vanity and make you feel no better than a filthy dog." Then she burped and slackened her eyelids. "Now, how can I help you?"

Noora and Sager were too stunned to speak. And for a while, the only sound that filled the hut was their muffled breathing.

"Well?"

Sager coughed and released their predicament in a rattle of words.

"Yes, I understand." Zobaida nodded. "You have your home, but it's no fortress of safety now that your father has become mad." She had turned serene, almost motherly.

"We don't know what to do," Sager confessed.

"I can make you a potion, *insha' Allah*, that will make him gentle. But the madness will always be there, this you must understand." And with that, she pulled out two stones from behind her back and clapped them together.

The board slid open. Light poured in, and Dur-Mamad hopped into the hut. *Had he heard or felt her call?* Noora did not have time to mull it over, for she was struck dumb by the unfolding special language of mother and son, which left her open-mouthed and feeling useless.

There was Zobaida's head lifting to the roof. There was her tongue slipping out in three sharp thrusts. There was Dur-Mamad reaching out for the shriveled plants she had indicated. A punch of a fist into her palm sent Dur-Mamad scurrying to fetch a mortar and pestle. When he returned, Zobaida twisted her wrists in the air, shaping an imaginary bottle he had to bring.

She was about to make the potion. The meeting was about to end. Noora felt cheerful at the thought.

But then a change washed over Zobaida. She had just begun to pluck the crumbled leaves from their stems when the black and blue of her eyes rolled to the back of her head. She dropped the plants and stared ahead through milky orbs. How eerie she looked! Her shoulders began to shake in a succession of tremors that wiggled all the way to her calloused feet. Were the jinn crossing into her world? Noora looked to Sager for an answer, but he was sucked into Zobaida's trance.

"I've never seen you before," Zobaida said. "Am I right when I say that you have come from the deep mountains?"

Sager nodded, even though his eyes remained glazed as he followed the healer's swaying head.

"We are Ibrahim Al-Salmi's children," Noora said sharply. She had to break the daze her brother was in. "We live a day's walk away."

The tremors stopped and Zobaida's head fell to her chest. She began mumbling into her burka. Each word blurred the next, and just as Noora tried to pick out what she was saying, Zobaida coughed back to earth.

A flutter of blinks and the black and blue of her eyes bobbed back into place. Her head wobbled slightly, and she pressed the ground with her palms, as if making sure it was still there, before addressing Sager. "You have more problems than just your father, don't you?"

"Everyone has problems," Sager mumbled.

"But there is one particular problem that jabs at your heart, isn't there?" She fumbled for one of the shells and began stroking it. "You have now become the man of the family and your biggest concern is your sister."

Sager dropped his gaze and said, "It's true I worry about her. But then, what brother doesn't worry about his sister?"

Noora crossed her arms high over her chest and grunted. They were talking about her as if she wasn't there. Where was this leading to?

"She refuses to listen to you," Zobaida said. "One thing you must know is that she's different—headstrong, wild. But then, that's all right." She chuckled. "I'm different from other women, too."

Noora scowled at the witch's attempt to spin her humor on the seriousness that had gripped the air. "I'm not so different, *khalti,*" she said, and wondered whether she should be calling her aunty at all.

Zobaida stayed focused on Sager, releasing her eyes in an unremitting prowl over his face. "You see it was written that you would come for one problem but instead get the solution to another—the hidden problem that's eating up your mind." Zobaida touched her temple with a finger. "Your sister is growing too old—unmarried—and you don't know what to do."

Noora objected with a squeaky gasp.

Zobaida hushed her with a wave of the arm, as if she were no bigger than a mosquito, and continued to address Sager. "You want the best for her, but of course it's unthinkable that you try to find a husband for your sister. It's just not done, to throw her name around like that. Shameful, wouldn't you say? I mean, it's the man who picks the wife, not the other way round. But I can help. You see, I was told what's best for her. I was given the solution."

Did she say solution? Noora wanted to storm out of the hut, end this strange visit without giving it any more thought. But her breath thickened with curiosity and her limbs felt heavy. She remained where she was, stuck in a clammy air of anticipation.

"She must get married," Zobaida declared.

It was time to stop all this! "You don't know anything about us," Noora said. "You don't know what we want."

"Let her talk," Sager insisted.

How easy it was to fool Sager. What would the witch say next?

The witch threw in some praise. "I think you are lucky to have a brother who cares about you so much. *Masha' Allah*, he is a brave and gallant brother."

Noora shifted her weight as a renewed urgency to flee washed over her. She gulped at the sluggish air and said, "But this meeting has nothing to do with me. We came for our father, not me." She turned to Sager. "Tell her, Sager."

"If you don't want to hear what she has to say, you can wait outside," he said.

Tiny tingles nipped at Noora's face, and the damp stench in the hut seemed stronger than when they had first entered. "Maybe I will," she said.

Noora got up and marched to the doorway. There, she paused to throw one final glance at them. Sager was waiting patiently, a blank stare fixed to the ground. The witch, on the other hand, was watching her intently, with a gleam of triumph in her eyes—both the seeing and unseeing.

11

S weet girl," Moza called. "Come here."

Noora marched into the bedroom. Just like the living room, the floor was covered with palm-frond matting. Two mattresses were rolled in one corner, and above them, on a nail wedged into a gap in the wall, hung one of Moza's dresses. In the other corner sat Moza's padlocked tin chest.

"Time to ready the mattresses," Moza said. She had a sleepy voice that always sounded as if it might lead to a yawn.

Noora blew her frustration into the air. A full week she had been staying at Moza's hut, and still, Sager had not come to beg her to return home. The images flashed in her mind once more: Sager would find her missing; Sager would worry; Sager would search for her all over the mountains; Sager would not be able to find her; Sager would be sorry.

Moza extended her arms and, pushing her bottom into the air, bent over at half speed.

Yes, only when Sager saw that she was missing would he appreciate her. How would they manage, her father and brothers,
without her? Who would mend their clothes? Who would cook
and clean the huts? Who would haul the water? Hah! Yes, only
then would they know her value.

Noora spotted Moza's fingers twiddling the edges of the first
mattress (preliminary attempts to the firm grip she needed)
and sprung to her aid. "Here, I'll do it," she said, and grabbed
the edges out of Moza's fingers, which were still looking for
that firm grip. Noora rolled one mattress out and then did the
same with the other one. Once she shifted the mattresses next
to each other into the middle of the room, she looked up. But
Moza was not where she had left her.

With rare speed, the old woman had stepped to the other
side of the room and was now sitting in front of the chest. She
turned to Noora and crinkled her mouth into a smile. Her hand
fumbled in her pocket and she pulled out a red strip of fabric,
at the end of which hung a key.

"This key opens the lock," Moza said.

It was a welcome diversion. "What is in it?"

"Oh, lots of nice things, all useless for an old woman like
me," she said, handing the key to Noora. "It's full of things my
husband brought back from his wanderings. Open it and take
everything out, so you can see properly," she insisted.

Noora clicked open the lock and pulled out a small knotted
bundle from the top. She untied the knot, liberating a handful
of colored silk threads. She cupped the bobbins, her eyes lighting up with the variety of colors.

Encouraged with her first find, Noora proceeded, removing
the rest of the contents. Once she had piled them between her
and Moza, the old woman looked proudly at her possessions:

six pieces of cotton and silk fabric in typical strong colors for dresses and *serwals* and a piece of rigid, indigo-stained cotton for making burkas. There was a basket of smaller pieces of fabric to patch rips; a pair of blunt scissors; two bronze hand mirrors; a bottle of jasmine oil and another of amber essence; four wooden combs; and a dagger and two knives, their handles embellished with silver filigree.

"*Masha' Allah*, this is quite a treasure," said Noora.

Moza ran her hand over one of the thicker cotton fabrics, sky-blue with broad, emerald stripes. "Look at this piece. Why does my Sultan waste his money so? Every time he'd bring something, I would tell him I am too old for all this." Her droopy eyelids turned taut. "I wonder what he will bring back with him this time."

Noora grabbed the fabric and fluffed it open. "Why are you storing all these things?"

Moza swept her head toward Noora and pushed her ear out.

Noora spoke louder. "You shouldn't store things. You should use them."

"I can't sew and I don't like the way the village women . . . well, their stitching is so crude."

"Why don't you let me sew them into clothes for you? My stitching is clean."

"*Masha' Allah*." Moza's eyes rounded with surprise. "Who taught you?"

"My mother."

Moza's decision was quicker than her movements. "No longer than here for my dresses." She pointed to just above her ankle. "Otherwise, I might trip on them. And don't forget to put gussets along the length on both sides—so pretty that way. And not too much embroidery around the neck—it scratches me, you see."

As for the *serwals*, they were to follow the traditional cut: baggy around the waist and tapering into tight ankle bands that could be fastened with cloth buttons that Noora had to make.

"As much embroidery as you want on the ankle bands," Moza instructed. "Use all those colored threads, and choose any pattern you want: lines, squares, triangles, zigzags—whatever you like." She paused and spread the fabric with emerald stripes on Noora's chest. "Ah," she said. "Exactly the same color as your eyes. You must take it."

It was a generous gift. Noora tried to refuse—just a bit.

"No, no, no," insisted Moza. "In my house, you must have a new dress."

Creating the dresses filled Noora with enthusiasm. This new undertaking would fill the monotony of her empty day hours, and she wasted no time in starting. She snipped the fabric to the right size. And then her fingers sped along the seams, piercing the material, tugging the thread in quick, coordinated yanks. Within two days, Moza's first dress was ready.

With the exception of the early morning hours, when she went to get water from the well, Noora spent her days in and around Moza's hut, cooking the food, washing the clothes, brushing the layers of dust out of the rooms, and taking care of Moza. The rest of the time she sewed.

Later, with early evening, came the soft dance of small feet outside the hut. The children of Maazoolah snuck out of their homes to peer at her, the visitor in their midst, through tiny gaps between the stones of Moza's hut. There they remained until their mothers' stern voices called them back. For the first time in her life, Noora was living in a community. And yet she still felt like a stranger. The togetherness she had longed for weeks earlier was just not there.

As darkness wrapped the village, the wind carried the last noises of the night: a man clearing his throat, a baby sobbing its distress, the bleats of a goat or two from this side or that. Only when the soft crackle of the night crickets embraced the stillness of the village did the thoughts she had been ignoring all day trip over one another in her head.

Why hadn't Sager come to get her? How much of that witch talk had he believed? And what about her father? Night after night, Noora lay next to Moza. And night after night, as Moza snored, Noora struggled to sleep.

A yawn swelled at the back of Noora's throat. Was sleep coming? She closed her eyes and waited. Moza's snore was taking shape once again: the light sniffle gained momentum, a sharp puff marking its peak. A croak gurgled deep in her chest and, bit by bit, grew into a husky roar.

It was no use. Noora curled toward the wall, bending her knees into a square. She stared at the moonbeams—cool, cobalt—falling in thin shafts through the gaps of the stone wall. Then something else: movement.

Three tiptoes and a flutter of fabric that broke a moonbeam.

Someone was outside.

She heard a sharp intake of air, as if pulled through clenched teeth. There was a hiss of pain in it, and she was sure that whoever was outside had stepped on a thorn. She waited for the muffled cry that would plausibly follow, but Moza's steady snores filled the room once more. They were growing in confidence, with longer pauses in between: a thick drag, a gap, and a burst of air in the exhale. She imagined each pause getting longer than the one before. What if the old woman suddenly stopped breathing?

She heard the footsteps again. They were careful and anxious, the kind that tried hard to stay silent, but the crunch of the gravel stole away their discretion.

She rolled off the mattress and pressed her eyes to a tiny gap in the wall, but all she could see were the tapering terraces of the village, wrapped in the indigo of the moon. She knew the person was still there though, standing very close to the wall. She counted three cautious intakes of air before she heard a hesitant shifting of weight as the person slinked away.

Her visitor came the next night and the nights after that. By the fifth visit, Noora had found a loose slab of stone in the wall. By the sixth visit, she pulled it out. Through the oblong gap, she spotted the telltale sign of his dishdasha as it glided past her: it was a man.

She snapped the stone back in place and, overcome with a peculiar shyness, tumbled back onto the mattress, her heart thumping with intrigue. Why did he linger outside Moza's hut every night, standing so still so that all she could hear was the flow and pause of his breath? The sound of his breath was steady, but every now and then she detected a light tremor that further fueled her curiosity. Who was he?

The next night she decided she had to put a face to this man. As she stared out through the gap, she caught the moon's gleam on the hump of a tiny beetle crawling close to a tree stump that was rooted next to the wall. Surely, she would be able to see more. From the sound of his breath, she could tell he was close and standing a little to the side of the gap. She felt the strain in her eyes as they grew larger and rounder. She heard her neck crack as she twisted it as far as it would go, but it was no use. The man remained wrapped in the shadows of the night as still as a rock, with only that touch of apprehension in an otherwise steady breath.

He must be someone from the village, she reasoned. Why did he come only at night while the village slept? Did he come for her or for some other reason? What did he want? She shook her head to erase the questions. There was time for them to linger in her mind later, once he had left and she was lying alone with soft tingles racing through her limbs and only her active mind as a companion.

There was a soft clatter of shifting pebbles and she assumed he was leaving, for he never stayed very long. But the footsteps grew louder. A hot panic rushed through Noora as she realized he was walking toward her. She glanced quickly at Moza, who remained deep in her rhythm of sleep. When she turned back, the man stood in front of her, not more than three steps away.

A half-moon hung behind him, bathing his shoulders with its calmness, but his face remained in the darkness. On this, his seventh visit, Noora could not hold back her curiosity any longer.

"Who are you?" she whispered.

"Someone," he said.

"What's your name?"

"I can't tell you, Noora."

"That's not right." What else could she say? "You know who I am. I need to know who you are."

He crouched next to the wall, and she began tracing with her eyes the sharpness of his cheeks, the sure bridge of his nose. Something about him was familiar and she tried to see more, but the shadows lingered in the dips of his face.

"I feel bad for you," he said.

"Why?" She could smell his breath, a warm mixture of earth and grass. It hung between them, heavy, holding the suspense of this very new experience.

"With what's happened to your father and all."

How did he know so much about her? "Well, don't feel bad," she said, her lips tight with disdain. "I'm all right."

"No, no, I don't mean to look down on you," he said. "I am just saying you don't deserve what you have gone through."

He was probing her insecurities; she wanted the tangible, the facts: his name, age, family. Why was she accepting this stranger's concerns? "I can't talk to you unless you tell me your name," Noora insisted.

"I just worry about you. I want to help you."

Once again he had drifted onto another road, avoiding the important questions. She had to merge their paths. She was about to try again when a cough floated into the still air. It came from the village; someone was awake.

"I must go," he said.

"But who are you?"

A light breeze ruffled his dishdasha, scattering the moonbeams into puddles of luminous blue that caught his teeth glistening in a smile. *Why did he look so familiar?* He bent closer to her and whispered, "Rashid. That's my name." His palm inched its way into the opening, his fingers brushing her clutched knuckles. "Meet me at the far well tomorrow after lunch, when the village rests."

She blurted the first concern that came to mind. "How?"

"Just say you want to go for a walk."

"But ..."

He smiled again. "You don't need to be with the old woman all the time, you know. You can move about. It's not a prison. No one will even notice."

Noora felt the heavy weight of duty lift off her shoulders. In its place settled the anxiety about the taboo meeting he was suggesting, a meeting she already knew she would keep.

"Just go to the close well, the one we use. Then pass it, turning west. Keep going straight, and I'll find you."

It was all happening too fast. She needed to know more. What landmarks should she keep an eye open for? What should she say to anyone who saw her?

But Rashid had already risen, fading into the shadows of the slumbering village.

12

Moza consented with a nod and a yawn, after which she stretched out for her nap. Noora walked out of the hut and set off under a sky blanched by the early afternoon sun. At the well, she veered west, just as Rashid had instructed her to, and then crossed a flat plain on the top of a ridge: an easy walk, and yet she felt her pounding heart sink into the softness of her belly. She was walking to a meeting of uncertainty with a man she did not know.

Now the ridge began tapering downward, narrowing into a coarse path with massive boulders rising on each side. She heard the clatter of shifting stones down below as a speckled goat came into sight. Quickly, Noora slipped into a dent between two rising slabs of rock. Its owner could be close by.

She sat down, and, clasping her knees, waited, keeping watch over the goat as it tugged at a sumptuous fountain of grass growing at the base of a palm. Her ribs were beginning to shake with a renewed flood of anxiety.

Why was she following such a dangerous mission? She knew she would be disgraced if she were found out. She began wondering how the villagers might punish her. Would they lock her up? Would they beat her? Or would they simply send her back to her brother, let her carry her shame to her home? Naturally, nothing would happen to Rashid. It was always the woman who bore the humiliation.

Noora frowned at the risk she was taking. Yet she did not think of turning back. The more she imagined Rashid, the more she was intrigued. He had stood there, looking so strong under the moonlight. He had been so concerned about her well-being. Noora nodded. Yes, she was sure there was a special goodness in him that would shield her from any troubles that might come her way.

She scanned the valley of closely packed boulders. Every now and then, a draft grumbled its way through the gaps. She heard the sporadic bleats of more goats. Satisfied that she was quite alone, she let her *shayla* slide onto her shoulders and began raking the part in the middle of her hair as if, with all the anxiety she'd been carrying, it might have shifted to one side. That's when she heard the flapping of fabric from somewhere above her.

"Up here."

She pulled the *shayla* back onto her head and looked up. There was Rashid, once again in silhouette, towering on the edge of the ridge above her, the wind billowing his dishdasha.

"Come up here."

There was no more time for reflection. She brushed the dust off her emerald-striped dress, just readied the day before, and clambered up to join him. By the time she reached the top, her face was flushed from both the climb and her nervousness. And there was Rashid, tall and composed, staring at her with almond-shaped eyes.

Noora did not know what to say. So she dropped her gaze to the ground and muttered a sentence he did not hear.

"What?" Rashid asked.

"There are goats down there," she said, feeling silly as soon as the words dribbled out. Such a feeble attempt at crafting a fluid conversation!

Rashid nodded and said, "They're mine, but they don't matter." His arm cut the air in a broad stroke. "What matters is that you're here, with me, in this special place."

Noora looked around her and wondered what was so special about the ridge they were standing on. There were no plants or trees and very little shade, just rocks and stones—a whole jumble piled behind him.

An awkward silence followed while she thought carefully before uttering her next words. Finally, she asked, "What do you want from me?"

He started, as if awakened from an intense dream, and coughed. "It's hot. Why don't you come and rest here by these rocks?"

He dropped to one side of the heap and she sank to the other, trying to fit as much of her curled body in the thin sliver of shade. Down below, the goats plodded on and she wondered how long he had been watching her before he called out to her.

She snuck a peek at this person who had lured her to this meeting. She had never seen anyone with such long lashes. They rested in a thick arc just under his eyes as he looked down at the ground, picking up a twig and scraping the earth in front of him, drawing random squiggles that looked like baby snakes. His *iqal*, the black head rope, was tilted slightly over his *ghitra*, giving him the distinguished look of a young sheikh of a tribe.

He looked older than her brother (and certainly more handsome). His goatee gave him a certain maturity Sager did not possess. She was sitting next to a man, not a boy, and it was that thought that twitched her memory. It was Sager's friend, the one who had joined the boys for breakfast with his back to her, outside Moza's hut. The realization both excited and scared her.

Rashid let go of the twig and sprang up, expanding his chest into a stretch. The sudden movement jolted Noora, and she dropped her gaze onto the safety of the ground in front of her, wondering what he would do next.

"Come with me," Rashid said, and he began to shift the clutter of stones between them to the side, unearthing a small opening that widened into a dark crevice, large enough to squeeze into when standing up. "I want to show you something."

Noora hesitated. Was she ready to take this unusual adventure a step further?

"Don't worry. My intentions are noble. I just think you will like what's inside."

Noora stood up and looked over her shoulder, as if searching for someone to tell her what to do. Only the goats answered her silent call, with bleats she could not translate. She looked back at Rashid, who stood patiently, his thick lashes fanning the pleas in his eyes.

With her nod, Rashid warned, "Now, once you get in, keep your head low and follow the wall with a hand. It gets dark, but just walk after my light."

"What light?" Noora asked, but he had already stepped into the opening.

As she followed him, coiling her shoulders through the narrow entrance, she saw the glow: a hurricane lamp, which he lifted to light the way through a tunnel that was barely wider than her hips.

A few steps in she noticed that the roof dipped lower farther on. Still, she followed him till they were staggering, mostly on bent knees, and soon Noora felt she was sinking into the mountain's stomach. Her hands clamped brittle walls and, with every step she took, the air cooled and her nerves heated up.

She was about to turn around and run, back into the light, when she was caught by the soft rhythm of his breath, breaking the rustle of his dishdasha. That magical breath! It roused the memory of his secret visits, the ones that had kept her awake with anticipation night after night.

She sighed and continued, feeling the crumbly surface of the wall dampen and the scent of moist clay cool her nostrils. The passage was widening and their shadows grew longer and crawled up the expanding roof.

She was walking straight now, her eyes round with expectation. The tension in her touch lightened and she skimmed the walls with her fingers. Something trickled on the tips. "What's that?" she gasped.

Rashid's laugh echoed in the hollowness. "It's just water," he said. "Walk slower and test the earth here. Don't slip. Some bits are wet."

"Wet? What are you talking about? There's nothing wet in these mountains."

Rashid didn't answer, but she was sure she felt him smile. Then she heard them: one, two, three, four. And more.

Plops of water on water. The tunnel opened into a spacious cave with a dark pool in the middle. Her mouth fell open. It was a sight like she had never seen. The pool could easily fit ten standing adults!

Droplets seeped through the roof, piercing the darkness of the pool with subtle sparks of luminous green on its surface. She walked over to the gravelly edge and, sinking to her knees, scooped up a handful to taste. It was slightly bitter but pure and chilled. She spotted trails of tiny bubbles pulsing to the surface. The pool was also being fed from somewhere deep below.

"What do you think?" Rashid said.

"I can't believe it. It's beautiful." She sat down and stretched her feet into the water.

Rashid joined her, resting the lamp between them. He said, "You know that deep, deep green on the top of the water? It's the same color as your eyes."

Noora laughed and wondered why she was nervous to begin with. He was a decent person, and although the fluttering in her stomach continued, she was beginning to feel a little more comfortable with him.

He smiled and continued in a mumble, "They're very beautiful eyes, *masha' Allah*, and you shouldn't hide them."

"I don't. I mean, I use them—to see."

"No, I mean you look away a lot. You shouldn't."

"I don't," she said, but she dropped her gaze to the ground. Such talk tickled her insides.

"You see? You're doing it again."

Noora pushed her feet into the grainy bottom of the pool. The water wrapped her calves and the pebbles kneaded her soles.

"You know, a lot of people think I'm not worth much, but it's not true," said Rashid, his voice as rich as velvet in the hollow of the cave. "There is more value in this place than in all the gold in India."

Noora looked at him and nodded. In the glow of the lamp his eyes shone like wet pebbles. They were fixed firmly on her feet as she pushed them in and out of the water, breaking its stillness, sending green swirls to the deeper middle. The water lapped the ankle bands of her *serwal*, leaving a wavy line on the hem.

"All right, we have to go," he said, losing the smooth resonance that had just embellished his words. "It's better not to get back late. I don't want people asking where you were."

Noora sighed at his concern and dipped her hands in the water to rinse her face, as if the pond might disappear abruptly. *He really cares about me*, she thought.

13

They met at the cave every day at the same time, returning to the village just before it awoke for the afternoon prayer. It was easy to follow time in Maazoolah, sliced, as it were, into sections defined by the muezzin's voice as he stood at the edge of the mountain and made the call for prayer. Noora always wondered why he faced the valley and not the homes. Then Moza told her that his voice had to reach all passing travelers as well as the villagers.

When Moza had asked her where she went during the hot hours when she should be resting, Noora had blinked away the guilt that grazed the green of her eyes and told her that she was used to taking long walks at that time. She did not like to lie to the old woman, but what else could she say?

Sweet Moza! She had been convinced quickly and had passed that information out to the other women of the village when they came to visit, bringing Maazoolah's news in neat parcels of information, arranged according to importance. One day, Hessa Bint-Ali came to visit and brought along her niece, Aisha.

Aisha was a short, chubby girl, slightly younger than Noora. She spoke little but smiled a lot. That's when her cheeks ballooned and tightened her eyes into slits. Aisha was promised to Hessa's son.

"Any day now," said Hessa, her coal-black eyes beaming through her burka with pride. Her voice was particularly strong, a raspy crowlike call that traveled far. "And what a lucky boy my son is. *Masha' Allah*, Aisha is like the rain, full of goodness. She sprinkles her happiness on everyone."

They were sitting in a circle in Moza's hut sometime between breakfast and lunch. Aisha was wedged like a chunky piece of meat between her aunt and her mother, Khadeeja. She peeped through the lines of her eyes, her dimples deep craters under her bloated cheeks, and let her aunt tell her tale.

Hessa was narrating a detailed account of Aisha's recent illness. "We were hot and cold every day, and shivers in between. No sleep. Sooo much coughing." She pinched Aisha's well-padded ribs and added, "Look how thin we've become."

"God bless her," Moza said. "And to get so ill when she should be fattening up for her marriage."

"We'll have to start eating more, won't we?" said Hessa, rubbing Aisha's back with affection. Then she sighed and her eyes drifted to the folded *serwal* Noora had just finished sewing. "That's new, isn't it?" she said, pulling it up and flapping it loose, holding it in front of her face to make sure the proportions were right. She tugged at the seams. When the *serwal* would not come apart, she let her fingers run up and down along the wavy lines of embroidery on the ankle bands. Satisfied, she declared, "This is very good work."

"*Masha' Allah*, Noora made the whole thing," said Moza. "Sweet child."

"It's nothing compared to your generosity, *khalti*," said Noora, lifting the old woman's hand and kissing it.

"*Al-Hamdulillah*, young one, *Allah* be praised," said Moza. "It's all His doing."

By the next day, news of Noora's sewing expertise had spread to every household. Maazoolah's women had neither the patience nor the interest in the art of clothes making. They were not shy to use Noora's talents. Ragged dishdashas, torn dresses, and *serwals* arrived for repairs in small bundles at Moza's hut.

And so Noora settled in to sew for the whole village. She did not expect to be paid for it. After all, what did these people have? Maazoolah was no different in its neediness from all the other mountain villages. In truth, Noora looked forward to the extra work. It justified her need to sit by the doorway of Moza's hut in full view of whoever, man or woman, passed by. She knew there would be no malicious gossip at such indiscretion because everyone understood that she needed the sun's light to be able to thread the needle and sew her neat stitches.

There was another reason Noora chose this particular spot. Moza's hut was slightly raised, so that she had a good view of the plots and, more important, the men working the earth. Rashid was always there. In between stitches, Noora would sneak looks at him, taking in his erect back and strong shoulders in greedy gulps.

As her needle pricked the fabric, she stifled the deep guilt that came with keeping a secret that was breaking society's laws. Instead, she drifted into pleasing reveries flooded with Rashid's words and gestures. Her meetings with Rashid at the cave continued, as did his night visits.

A few days later, Hessa came alone to talk to Noora. Her black eyes seemed impatient and she hugged a knotted cloth. "You are looking so radiant," she said. "What are you doing that is making you look as golden as a pot of honey?"

Noora felt her cheeks color. It was not like Hessa to throw compliments at her.

"Let's go in, before the sun makes us black," Hessa said.

Noora rose and followed Hessa into the hut.

"Now," she said once they were settled, "as you know, my son is marrying Aisha. He doesn't know it yet, but he'll never feel sad once she becomes his wife."

"When is the marriage?"

"Soon, *insha' Allah*, soon," Hessa whispered mysteriously. "We have to prepare everything first." She proceeded to open the bundle she had brought with her. "I want you to make these pieces for my future daughter-in-law, as part of the bride-wealth. You can sew two dresses, two *serwals*, and one *thoub*."

Noora fingered the most attractive piece: fine *dagh* silk of a fiery-red. She lifted it up in front of her face and looked through the translucent fabric. Clothes for a bride, how special they felt. "She's lucky to be getting such a lovely piece," said Noora.

"Nothing is too much for our adorable Aisha," said Hessa, "even marrying the son of a Bin-Ghanem, which to anyone else would be a real privilege."

"Bin-Ghanem?"

"Yes. Don't you know? My husband's ancestors were the original inhabitants of Maazoolah."

Noora didn't know. Nor did she understand why that made

the Bin-Ghanems special. As far as she had noticed, all the villagers shared the same poverty. The exception was Moza, whose husband had showered her with gifts in their long union, all stored in that tin chest.

"The red one you are holding, that is the bridal dress. So you will need to make it look special."

"It's beautiful," said Noora, fluffing it open. "I know exactly what to do: rich embroidery with silver thread on the chest, and little silver stars all over the rest of it, so it will just shine and shine. I'll put large gores under the arms. Moza has some scraps that would suit—bright blue, I think." She let the excitement of preparing the bridal dress carry her. "And then, to make it all perfect, I'll let it trail into a soft tail." She looked up, about to say more, when she noticed Hessa's sure manner had melted. A tiny flicker of light bounced off her sharp eyes, trying to penetrate their dead blackness, give them a soul.

Was it hesitation? Was it pain?

Hessa opened her mouth, but then clamped it tight again. Its edges quivered with some shadowy emotion.

"I will have these clothes ready for you very soon," said Noora.

"Oh, I know," said Hessa, and coughed away the croak that lingered at the back of her throat. "It's not that. It's something else. I always worry a girl, not of us, will steal my son."

Noora mouthed a silent "ah."

Hessa recovered the caw of her voice. "For my son to be deprived of Aisha's goodness would be a tragedy. You understand that, don't you?"

Noora nodded.

"A man must get married to his own people, his kin. If he doesn't, he would just be asking for trouble." The flicker that had grazed Hessa's eyes just moments earlier was gone, and now she was staring at Noora with the cold blackness of night.

Noora nodded again.

"And the woman who doesn't take account of this simple rule is not worthy of respect."

That afternoon, as they sat side by side at the edge of the pool, Noora told Rashid about her meeting with Hessa. "It was the strangest thing. She complimented me first, said my skin was like honey, and then she suddenly changed and gave me these nasty looks."

"Well, women can't be expected to be as reasonable as men. Their minds work differently."

Noora twiddled her toes in the water and searched for the hidden wisdom in what he had just said.

"And a mother's feelings are always different. Special."

That she agreed with, but she still wanted to know why Hessa had thrown those accusing looks at her. "It was as if she were blaming me for something. And I didn't know what it was. Have you heard of any rumors? Do you know this woman?"

Rashid's laugh sounded forced. Still, it brought a smile to her face.

"It's not funny," she teased.

"No, but you're funny. You probably imagined the whole thing."

"No—"

He cut her off. "Look, I don't want to talk about who said what and why. I hear that all day. I want to talk about you and me."

"What's there to say?" Noora had told him all the details of her life already.

"Well, you know how I feel about you."

She kept quiet. Talk like that brought out the weakness in her. Dunked under the pebbles, her big toes squished the smaller toes.

"I think about you all the time. I can't eat properly or do anything."

She did not enjoy the lack of control she experienced when he spoke that way, but there was nothing she could do about it. She fingered the edges of her *shayla* and twirled complicated shapes into it.

"I dream about you every night after I leave you. Then, when the sun comes up, I can't wait to see you again."

She pulled her knees to her chest, trying to control the tiny tremors that were spreading from her inside to her outside. She had to speak quickly, change the subject. Fixing her eyes to the middle of the pool in front of her, she said, "*Masha' Allah*, you people are so lucky. You don't need to worry about water."

Rashid grunted and flopped on an elbow. "No one knows about this place."

"Yes, but if there's a long drought, you'd share it."

He grunted again. "This is my place and I show it to whomever I choose."

"This is God's place and His blessing, and it should be shared."

"There is no need. There's enough water in the village well."

"Yes, but with all this water that's always being filled, you can build a *falaj* system. Just think, all those carved channels to feed your crops. You'll never go hungry. And not just that, you can grow so many other things."

"No!"

"You're just saying that," she persisted. "You don't really mean it."

"Stop talking about water! It's here and it's mine. And that's it."

All the little shakes and quakes that had spread to her limbs dissolved. How could his sweet words turn bitter so quickly?

Then his gentleness returned just as abruptly. "I don't want to talk about water," he said. "I want to talk about you—about us."

It was better to stay quiet, just listen.

"I care about you."

Her fingers sat stiff on her thighs. Under the pebbles in the water, her toes felt cold.

"I care about you," he repeated. "I want to marry you."

For the next few days, Noora was busy preparing Aisha's bridal dress. Using the silver thread, she embroidered the front with subtle loops of foliage. She streaked the petals and leaves with the full-raised stitch and filled them with the lace-web stitch. She lined the cuffs in silver piping and pierced so many delicate stars into the rest of the *thoub* that it looked like a fiery night sky.

Then she began working on the ankle bands of the *serwal* that was to go under it. Cashews: that's the motif she'd decided to embroider on the sun-yellow fabric. Circling the bands, leaf green cashews in the background set off the brighter lime green cashews in the foreground.

Noora curled the outline of a cashew and looked down at the terraces. There he was, dwarfing the other men he was working with, looking as princely as can be. Soon she would be receiving her own bridal gifts.

"I want to marry you." That's what he had said. Such small words, but what important words.

With their newly defined futures, Rashid had grown bolder in their meetings, often holding her hand and stroking her palm. She liked the touch of his rough thumb. It made her feel protected. Did he feel her fingers wilt when he held her hand?

One time, he had teased a strand of hair that had escaped both plait and *shayla*. Her daring had surprised her as she had closed her eyes and plumped her lips in little tremors, waiting for that same rough thumb to sneak down and calm the quiver of her mouth's desire.

Moza peeped through the doorway. "*Masha' Allah*, it's looking very beautiful—so clean and neat," she said, patting Noora's shoulders with approval. "And your face. How it glows. Are you happy staying with me?"

"I am," said Noora. She wanted to drop a hint of the real reason for her elation, how it seeped into her face and brought the pink to her cheeks. But Rashid had instructed her not to tell anyone until he spoke to Sager and asked for her hand formally.

Soon, Noora thought, happily counting the row of cashews she had just finished.

Noora hopped over the familiar plain under a still, white sky. Rain was coming, but even that could not keep her away from the cave. With Rashid's proposal, she felt their meetings now held the legitimacy they had lacked. She belonged to him, and it was only a matter of time before she could make it public.

It wasn't until they were sitting side by side, holding hands at the edge of the water, that a niggling insecurity surfaced as she remembered Zobaida. What if Sager refused to give his consent?

"Soon, you'll be talking to Sager," she began, and squeezed Rashid's hand, hoping he would connect with her thoughts.

"Yes," he said. His thumb felt rougher than usual as he began to stroke her palm.

"But what is your plan? How are you going to ask him?"

"I know how to talk to Sager. He's my friend."

She gripped his hand harder. "And what if he doesn't agree? Then what?"

"Why wouldn't he agree?"

"Well, he's a funny boy, my brother. Sometimes, he lets other people influence his mind." She shrugged. "I don't know. Maybe he wants me to stay with them."

"To do what? Grow old and ugly, and die alone?"

"I don't know." She sensed he was not comfortable with the subject and decided to change it. Smiling, she looked up at his face and said, "Our first will be a boy. We'll call him Salem. Salem Bin-Rashid Bin . . . What?"

"Same as my name, of course."

"And that is?"

"Rashid Bin-Abdullah, you silly girl."

"That's your father's name. What about your family?"

"Why are you so bothered about my family? I will be your family." He sounded impatient.

Every time she wanted to talk about their future, he acted defensive. "And where will we live? At Maazoolah?"

"No, we'll live in the desert."

She looked at him agape.

"In a tent, and we'll move from place to place. And we'll bring up camels, too. And that's not all . . ." A snicker crept up his throat before he could continue. The laugh that followed sounded strained.

He was trying to lighten the mood by teasing her. "Don't joke," Noora said. "I am serious."

"Why do you worry so much?"

She wondered whether that was true. "I don't know why."

"Well, you can't help it I suppose." He sniffed. "You have had a lot to worry about in your life, living all alone, like a savage out there."

She yanked her hand out of his and slapped him repeatedly on his arm with the back of her palm. "Savage?" she cried.

"No, no," he said, with obvious glee. "I meant living so far from people. Being isolated all your life in faraway mountains, that's what makes your ways rough." He lifted his hands to protect his face. "Don't injure me, angry woman, strong woman! I can't defend myself."

It was an invitation to use both hands, and Noora attacked him with her full heart in loving slaps and punches to his chest and stomach. He curled into a ball and she tried to roll him over to expose his more tender parts, but he was too heavy. Shifting her weight to her thighs, she shoved him using her full body, uprooting him with the first thrust, surprised at her own strength. He tumbled onto his back.

With the speed of a hungry dog, she punched the cavity, feeling her fist rupture the softness of his belly. His gasp reverberated in the hollow of the cavern. She had hit him too hard.

Rashid was quick to react. His arms coiled to his chest and shot out. She felt the thump ram the air out of her chest.

Noora landed at the pool's edge, half in, half out of the water. Her *shayla* slipped onto her shoulders and spread around her, sucked in the water and went limp. She sat awkwardly, arms lodged behind her, her bent legs wobbling as she tried to regain some poise. She blinked away the tears that were welling in her eyes and watched him rise, shake the dirt off his dishdasha, and blend with the darkness.

Noora coughed to test her voice before speaking. "There's no need to be so rough."

"You started it."

"But I am only a girl. You're a man. Much stronger than I am."

"If you can't handle the joking, you shouldn't joke."

"That push wasn't a joke," she mumbled. She pulled the *shayla* back onto her head and crept toward the middle of the pool. The deepest point reached just below her chest. She closed her eyes and, holding her nose, dipped her head, immersing her hurt into its darkness.

She held her breath for as long as she could. Then, resurfacing, she gulped the air. Her eyes wandered to the hurricane lamp. It remained in the same place, but Rashid was not in its light. She stood very still and waited to hear his footsteps, but only the sound of trickling water, as it slid off her head and into the pond, filled the cave. She remained frozen in place for a long time, till those same trickles weakened and collected to form individual drops. With each plop, she felt her brooding anger dissolve, and just as she was about to move, she spotted him.

Rashid emerged from the shadows like a lost ghost. He waded into the pool, setting off ripples that lapped her chest. Noora felt her heart quicken, and she was suddenly aware of the way her clothes were clinging to her skin. Even though she knew that it was too dark for Rashid to be able to see her properly, she felt exposed. She started tugging at the fabric to create air pockets that could hide her sodden outline. Wet pops echoed in the cave, and that made her more conscious of the strange desire that was seeping out of her.

He stopped in front of her, his face a hand's distance away, and pulled the *shayla* onto her shoulders. Even though she felt more exposed with her head uncovered, she did not resist.

"I didn't mean to be so rough," he whispered. "It just happened. You hit me so hard, I just pushed without thinking."

Noora crossed her arms tight over her chest to squash the swell of it, and smiled. "It's over now."

"Forgive me?"

"I forgive you."

She turned to walk back when he clasped her hand and tugged her toward him.

"Don't go," he said and pulled her into an embrace, their faces almost touching.

The water they were in suddenly felt thick and her dress heavier. She was aware of the force of his pulse beating against her ribs. She tried to root her feet in one place, but her nervousness kept them sliding and tripping over each other. So she tightened her knees lest she collapse.

He was shivering and yet he felt so strong. He was blowing hot breaths onto her face. She knew she had to pull away, but her halfhearted attempt to ease out of his grip prompted him to hold her closer.

"You are my life," he whispered. "I want to hold you, hold you so close that we melt into each other."

His voice sounded as liquid as the water they were in. She tried to see the passion in his eyes, but they remained in the shadows. The air felt thinner, warmer. Her strength was being squeezed out, like water from a sponge. *Must stop this*, she thought. Her arms fell limp to her side, her knees softened, and she melted into his embrace.

His taut ribs crushed the suppleness of her chest. He nuzzled his head into her neck, took in her scent in long inhales. *Must stop this.*

He began stroking her back and kissing her eyes—small moist pecks that lingered, sticky as ripe dates. His warmth made her tremble, and she felt a part of him hardening. She did not know what this meant but, right away, sensed the danger in it. It was time to break this deep, deep embrace.

"I have to go," she squeaked, and heard the shake of panic in her voice.

"Just a little longer and—"

"No," she said, louder, with authority. "I have to go now!"

She heard him take a massive lungful of air. His grip eased and he dipped his head into the water.

Noora frowned at her stupidity. She was soaking wet. What was she going to tell the villagers? She followed Rashid out of the tunnel, squinting at the sudden light, when the answer came to her in one of God's acts of mercy.

The sky was still white, but the rain had come and gone. Deep puddles filled the various dips and crevices of the mountains. Noora smiled and said, "You know, it's the first time I've ever missed a downpour. And it was all for you."

Rashid tried to hug her again, but she squirmed out of his grasp and climbed down the ridge, sure that he was watching her. As usual, he stayed behind to avoid arriving at Maazoolah at the same time.

Noora couldn't wait to ponder what had just happened. The strength had returned to her limbs and she ran along the plain, carrying the weight of a dress thick with water and a mind brimming with the feel of him. She felt energetic and exhausted, confident yet awkward. So many different things at the same time: happy but guilty.

How bold of him to touch her in that way! And how shameful of her to accept! Instead of punishment, God had rewarded her with the excuse of rain. And how had she repaid God? She let a man who was not her husband touch her, arouse her in a way that was most sinful.

As she reached the village well, she vowed she would not let Rashid touch her like that again until they were married.

14

Early the next morning, news crept into Moza's home on whispering tongues. Noora was in the bedroom folding the bridal gifts when three older women entered Moza's hut. She heard them say that Hessa had had a fight with her son when he confessed that he did not want to marry Aisha. Their murmurs grew bolder as they released the details of the confrontation.

"I heard the smacks of the cane clear from inside my home," said one woman. "And I couldn't hear him raise a hand back; he just stood there and took it."

"He's big and strong, but don't forget she is his mother after all."

Moza's slow voice quickened a pace. "And now what?"

"Nobody knows. He has disappeared. Gone!"

It didn't take long for Hessa to visit. That same day, just before the afternoon prayer, she flew into Moza's house, her *shayla* flapping behind her like the wings of some giant bird. Then the heartache surged out of her.

"He thinks he's a man," she said, "all big and powerful, throwing his cruel words at his defenseless mother—a widowed woman—breaking her heart, shaming her in her own home." Her voice started cracking at the edges and she paused to regain control. "He doesn't understand that to be a man, he needs to honor his word."

Moza blew a sigh of compassion, and Noora's mind drifted to all those beautiful clothes she had made, stacked so neatly in the other room. She had put her heart into that bridal *thoub*, created in it a red night sky with all those glittering stars. And what about those smiling cashews, identical in size, on the ankle bands? How cheerful they looked: lime green on leaf green. Yes, smiling they were, unless Hessa flipped them upside down. What would become of all those clothes now that the marriage was off? Would Hessa take them anyway, or would she rip them to shreds?

Hessa's head slumped to her chest. "My poor sister," she mumbled. "I had to tell her that my son had lost his mind."

Moza craned her neck toward Hessa. "What was that?"

Hessa's head snapped back up. "I said, I had to tell my sister that my son had lost his mind. Imagine, he said, 'I don't want to get married,' said, 'Aisha is like my sister.' Is that the talk of a man? Giving his word and then taking it away?"

Moza fidgeted before throwing a general message of consolation. "Boys are young in the head. They say things, but they don't mean any of it."

But Hessa would not loll in Moza's puddle of sympathy. "Well, this boy is not young in the head," she cawed. "He's stupid in the head." And then she turned to Noora and took in bits of her face and figure. Suddenly the slits of Hessa's burka seemed too large, somehow showing too much of those hard eyes.

Hessa's eyes flitted, hawklike. There was a sizzle of blame dancing on their surface. Did the strong woman think Noora's stay at Maazoolah had brought bad luck to her family? Noora looked away, only to hear Hessa click her tongue. She wasn't finished.

"Then, when my sister's sweet daughter found out," Hessa said. "Well, what can I say? That young flower just won't talk to anyone, or leave the house. She won't eat! That angel—soon the youth of her cheeks will disappear." She shook her head. "And all because of that selfish son of mine."

A shadow broke the beam of light falling in from the entrance. Hessa snapped her head toward it and called, "Mohammad! I saw you!"

His head peeked through. "Yes, Mother?"

"Think again. Where could your brother have gone to?"

"I told you I don't know, Mother," said Mohammad. His lips spread into a cheeky grin. "Maybe he went to marry someone else."

Hessa bent over by the door, scooped up her slipper, and threw it at him. But Mohammad was too quick.

"You must calm down," said Moza, rising. "Let me get you some water."

Hessa nodded a stern thank-you and leaned back on the wall. Moza hobbled past her and out of the hut. Clamping her mouth shut, Hessa stared ahead, over Noora's shoulder, at the wall. She seemed to be searching for something—or maybe, for once, she had nothing to say.

Noora felt she had to console her. It was the right thing to do. She opened her mouth but then held back. Let her stay a while in that deep thought, her brows jammed together like that and her eyes, so clouded with concentration, turning blacker than the kohl on them.

Then, like a sleeping snake awakened by the squeak of a mouse, Hessa twisted her neck to the side and shot Noora a venomous stare. "If you ask me, some green-eyed devil must have played with his mind, don't you think?"

"I don't know, *khalti*," said Noora, surprised at her quick answer. "The devil is always around us, and it's up to us to make sure we don't follow his path." A trickle of shame lodged a sour taste in her mouth. Hadn't she followed the devil's path to those forbidden meetings? She swallowed hard. She had to retain that guiltless authority that had just filled her voice.

Hessa grunted. "Well, my boy has always been respectful toward his mother. And so, I wonder whether something . . ." She paused. "Or someone—has made him act this way."

Her thoughts were finally spilling out, but Noora was determined not to let Hessa play with her doubts. She tightened her lips against Hessa's hard stare.

"How come you are home at this time of day?" Hessa persisted. "I thought you would be out, on one of your long walks."

How much did Hessa know? Did she have her followed? A cold sweat leaked along the length of her. "Well, I'm a bit tired today," she mumbled, wiping her clammy hands on her dress.

"How long do you plan to stay here?" said Hessa. "Doesn't your family miss you? When will you go back to them?"

"Soon, *khalti*, very soon," said Noora.

Hessa's sooty eyes lightened with the thought. "Well, I'd better go," she said, rising in one sure move. "*Allah* will make things right, and we, the Bin-Ghanems, are strong."

Noora dropped her gaze to the ground.

"And who knows what I'll find once I get home," Hessa continued. "*Insha' Allah*, God willing, my Rashid will be back, full of regret at how he upset me."

Noora looked up, but it was too late. Hessa had already stepped out of the hut. She did not look back. And it was just as well. She would have surely picked up the tremors that shook Noora's breath, the twitch that seized the side of her lips, and the trembling fingers she hurriedly tucked under her thighs.

Was it the same Rashid? Was Hessa's son *her* Rashid?

15

Noora clutched the scissors and held the tips at a cashew. Just one snip—that's all it would take to send the
threads twirling loose. When hurt and fury bite at your
insides together, you want to do all sorts of destructive things.

Rashid Bin-Ghanem! Of course. His name, his family
name—held back from her, concealed in the shadows of the
cave. What did it mean? What were his intentions as he embraced the warmth of her chest, wooed her heart, kept her all
to himself? Was she to be the second wife?

She felt the handle of the scissors bore into her thumb.
There was the gleam sitting on the blades. A heat spread into
her fingers and she nicked a cashew. Still, she remained giddy
with confusion. She wanted him, but oh, the trust, it was
blunted.

The blades were parting once more. There was a creak of
rusty metal. Another cashew destroyed.

He had disappeared without a word. She knew he was not at the cave because she had gone there, walked along its length only to find it empty. Was he on his way to see Sager? Rashid had broken his promise to marry Aisha, but did she want him at the expense of another?

That gentle feminine side of her that had surfaced in the cave seemed far away. Here, she was another creature, bent on destruction. More threads sprung loose and when the cashews resembled a garden of weeds, she reached out for the red bridal *thoub*. She fluffed it open, letting the front of the gown settle on her crossed knees. Tremors played around her mouth, and she sliced the fragile twirls of silver thread, de-rooting those same stems, leaves, and petals that she had meticulously embroidered.

Hope and deception. It was a dizzying mix, and Noora could not separate the two. The madness that whirled in her head tormented her. With eyes as hard as stones, she stared at the silver stars sprinkled on the full length of the *thoub*. It was her idea, her design, of a fiery night sky. And now, it had to be thrown into chaos, too. She snipped and scooped out every single one, until she was satisfied that this most special of gowns was transformed into a furious crimson nightmare.

The moon looks the same at the beginning of the month and at its end: a smiling crescent that tilts to one side, keeping you guessing whether it's finishing the old or beginning the new.

It was such a night when Rashid reappeared.

"Who's that?" Noora whispered, even though she recognized the familiar breath outside Moza's hut.

"Me," said Rashid.

"You're back." She crept to the wall, pulled the stone out, and asked, "Where were you this past week? What happened?" Her eyes were open so wide they burned. She wished that crescent could expand, throw some light on his face. But it remained as it was, curved in a warped smile, hiding the struggle on Rashid's face, the struggle she heard in his breath.

He sighed and whispered, "It's not possible."

"What? Why? Did Sager say no?"

"I didn't go."

"Why?"

"Because there's no point. It's just not possible."

"Why is it not possible? What about us? We were to marry."

He threw his excuses at her: "Duty . . . the proper thing to do . . . can't break my mother's wishes."

Noora protested with all the strength she could muster. So stunned was she by his hasty submission that she forgot to scold him for having disappeared on her, for having lied to her. The emotions in her rumbled so violently that they clogged her throat.

She swallowed and heard him repeat what she did not want to hear: "Duty . . . the proper thing to do . . . can't break my mother's wishes."

What ridiculous words! She wanted to break them, destroy their meaning. She wanted to grab his shoulders and shake the passion back into him. But her limbs went numb, and the tears snuck out of the corners of her eyes. "What about me?" she managed to whisper. "How can you leave me like this?"

That's when she caught the rustle of his dishdasha as he stepped away into the dark. And then she stared at the nothing in front of her. For that was what she was left with: nothing.

16

She had to get away. Only then would the ache that throbbed in her dissolve.

With the next dawn, Noora peered out through Moza's doorway. She extended her arm, but all she could see were her fingertips, floating in the milky opaqueness of fog. When had this curtain drawn? She shook her head with disbelief. Of all the days, it had to be this one.

With all those sudden drops along the way, the mist would make her journey treacherous. The landmarks she relied on would be impossible to use—all those bizarre-shaped boulders, deep ridges, and shaggy trees would be concealed under the thick fog. She would have to rein in all her directional talent and intuition.

"You'll just lose your way," she heard Moza's sleepy mumble. "Why don't you wait a little, till the sun comes up?" The old woman remained burrowed under her blanket.

"I can't, *khalti* Moza. I've stayed so long already," said Noora, gathering her few belongings into a bundle. "I know they need me back home, and the sooner I go, the faster my mind will settle."

"But alone, my dear?"

"I've walked everywhere alone, all my life." There was nothing else she could do. She had to leave immediately.

"At least take the lantern with you," said Moza, shuffling onto her elbows as she prepared to rise.

Noora struck a match, lit the hurricane lamp, and was kneeling next to Moza just as the old woman staggered to sit up. *Move on!* It was the only thought that filled Noora's head as she bade Moza farewell with a warm hug. "If *khalti* Hessa asks, it's over there," she mumbled. There was no contempt, no satisfaction in what she had done, only a cheerless numbness at the thought of all those beautiful fabrics that she had destroyed.

"What did you say?"

"The bridal gifts," she said. "They are wrapped and ready. I put them in the corner." Shame washed over her, but Noora did not dwell on it. She had to hurry away.

Once she set off, she let the slopes and dips, twists and turns, of the mountains take up all her attention. It was a slow trek. Even so, she slipped on the crumbly surface a few times and bumped her elbow on the jutting arm of a rock. More than once, she wondered whether she had walked too far. How many hills had she crossed? Still, she continued. Was she going the right way? She questioned her keen sense of direction. At one point, she wasn't sure of anything except that her eyes were bulging out so much she would have to rub them hard to ease them back into place.

It was only when she found herself in the middle of a broad *wadi* that the mist eased. Noora paused to get her bearings. A damp breeze nipped her ears, and as she pulled the *shayla* tight around her head, she looked up, finally spotting the moon. It sat on a slumbering peak: a struggling, silver scar in the clotted sky. It sent its last glimmer before a veil of fog swallowed it whole. And then the mist rushed into a roll and whiffed its blanketing form in fast-moving patches, which appeared and disappeared.

A smack of pride jolted a quiver of a smile to her face. She wasn't lost after all. She recognized this *wadi*, strewn with so many *ghaff* trees. It was halfway to her home. It would be an easy walk now. Everything would be all right.

With a flash of confidence, Noora sat on a rock to slacken the strain out of her limbs, to rub her eyeballs back in place. And that's when the ache of Rashid's rejection washed over her once more. How to deal with it? This hurt was like nothing she had ever felt. It began with a sting, poking and jabbing, sharp as a needle thrust deep into her skin. And then it dulled, turning into a maddening hole of nothingness that was impossible to fill.

"Move on, move on," Noora mumbled into her chest as she felt her head slump. She jumped up and hastened along the valley, swinging her lantern, kicking the curling mist off the *wadi* bed.

Just keep moving and all that hurt will disappear! That's what she kept thinking. After all, wasn't that the way of things? Wasn't her life (just like everyone else's in the Hararees) so full of uncertainty and deprivation that she could overcome anything just by moving on?

The moon had vanished, the mist had lifted, and the first rays of light punctured the last weary threads of fog clinging to the peaks. There were the huts, looking so familiar, like some long-lost friends. She yearned for the predictability of her routine at home. Only then would she feel fine again. Only then would she find peace of mind.

But none of that happened. There was no normalcy, and certainly no peace. After a quick and nervous greeting, her brothers let her know the bad news. Their father had gone missing soon after she and Sager had left to see Zobaida. Just like Moza's husband, he had wandered off into the mountains and hadn't come back. Although her brothers had searched and searched, eventually they had given up.

All that shame and pain that she had chased away on her walk came crashing down on her. Rashid and her father: both gone! It was just too much. She wanted to snuggle up in the corner of her hut and sleep, sleep, sleep. And that's what she did— for the next three days.

She hardly ate the food her brothers prepared. How kind they were, rooted in a circle of worry around her, with tender pleas for her to take a bite of the bread they had baked, sip some of the broth they had cooked. How could she explain that all she felt was the numbness of loss? By the fourth day, she unfurled from the corner of her hut, driven by guilt at not helping out with the chores. Still, she remained listless as a wispy cloud as she roamed from one task to the next.

It was only a day later that the anger snapped into her with the sharpness of a brittle twig—and all because of Sager.

He called her in the late afternoon and softened her with tender words of reassurance. "It will pass; time will make it pass." They sat by the store and the afternoon sun cast an amber glow that fell on his shoulders.

How encouraging he was. She felt the green of her eyes lighten with the affection he was showing her. How kind he was. It was only when he showered her with his gifts that the claws of suspicion gripped her insides.

"A new *shayla*?"

"Well," he said. "The other one is so old it's not black anymore. Look at it. It's the same color as gunpowder."

She slipped on the leather slippers (her first pair), a little short on her feet. "Where did you get all these things?"

"From a passing merchant at Nassayem."

She slid the three thin rings (designed to be worn together), a little loose, on her middle finger. "But this is gold."

"Well, you know, you are my sister, and if I can't spoil you, who can I spoil?" he said with a smile.

She opened the tiny bottle of amber essence and sniffed. "Well, that's nice, but where did you get the money?"

"Well, let's just say that when you do the right thing, better things come your way. We saved Zobaida's son, and so, she helped us in return."

"Ah, that greedy fake," said Noora.

He frowned. "I think you are too harsh on her, too suspicious of her."

"Next, you'll be telling me that she gave you the money." She mocked him, but Sager would not smile. She watched his brows knot and stiffen into an expression of genuine hurt. And Noora began to feel a dread settle in her stomach the way mud stuck to the bottom of the ponds that formed after the rains. Fish could slither in it and toads could kick it up, but in the end it just sank back, firm and sticky.

"Well, in a way, she is the reason I was able to afford all this," he said. "You see, there's a man, a rich pearl merchant who's come to see her. And Zobaida's hidden sources told her what she had to do."

"Invisible sources? You must stop believing her rubbish talk. The jinn said this, the jinn said that!" She raised her arms and made claws out her fingers. "Whooo!"

"They do communicate with her, you know. The jinn told her to arrange a match for the pearl merchant. Of course, being so rich, he would have to pay a handsome bride-wealth.

"And naturally, she would take some of that—for her services and arrangements?"

"Of course."

Triumph lit Noora's eyes. "You see? That act: the rolling eyeballs, the shaking. In the end, all she wants is money. So what did she do, give you some of that money for saving her son?"

"No, no," said Sager. "You see, it was the first time anyone had helped her son. Zobaida was so happy that she gave me . . . well, gave us . . . another gift." He paused. "She gave us the gift of a better life—for you."

"Me?"

"Yes, you. I have been thinking. This is no life for you, stuck with us men in the middle of nowhere. You deserve better."

What was he talking about? She wanted to stay where she was. She wanted to fetch the water, milk the goats, cook the food, collect the wood. She wanted everything to return to normal—especially now.

"Finally, you can have your own home with your own family. And the man is rich. So rich you don't need to struggle anymore."

"What man? What are you saying?"

"I'm saying, the match is you."

He might as well have thrown sand in her face or punched her in the belly, because all she managed was to spit and gasp.

When she tried to speak, her tongue would not move. It sat in her mouth, dry as a thick piece of leather.

"Zobaida thinks you are worthy of such a special match. I think that's something, don't you?" He nodded and his ringlets bounced along from under his *ghitra* with his enthusiasm. "I mean, she's sending her matchmakers to approve you and turn you into a praiseworthy bride." He paused. "And she's even paying them from her fee."

When did it happen? When had Sager and Zobaida conspired against her? Was it just after she had stormed out of Zobaida's hut or later? Had Sager stayed longer at Nassayem and met the witch again and again?

"His name is Jassem Saeed Bin-Mattar, and he lives in a big house. He has got two other wives, but don't worry, it will be good because they'll be like caring sisters to you. They'll guide you in all those womanly things you were deprived of living here in this nowhere place with us, your ugly brothers." He managed a nervous titter. "Then, when your blessed children arrive, they would turn into additional mothers. First sisters, then mothers."

There he was acting like a thoughtful brother, pretending he worried about her. Finally, Noora found her voice. "Since when do you care about me? I disappeared and you didn't even bother to find me."

"I knew where you were," he said. "You'd gone to *khalti* Moza's. Where else would you have gone? And I didn't come to get you because I thought it would be good for you to be with other women for a bit. You know, learn their ways and all."

"How could you go and plan my life behind my back?" she yelled, punching her anger into the air with her fists. "You are so easy to fool. That witch played with your head, and you let her. All she wants is money. Don't you see?"

But Sager did not see, would not see. "The witch, as you call her, also said that you would need to curb that spiky tongue of yours. No man wants a wife like that."

Noora took a deep breath and mustered all her strength to control her rage. "Well, you can speak and plan all you want, but don't expect me to be that bride you're talking about."

17

Noora stretched her arms over her head as she lay on a slab of rock a little way down the slope of her home. A light draft of cool, early-morning air caressed her face and rustled the bushes around her. She rolled her head lazily to one side, spotting a gecko with vivid, silver stripes. It hopped onto the smooth edge of a boulder and lapped an eye with its tongue. Then, with a quick bob of the head, it dipped into a crack below. *At least it knows where it's going,* she thought.

Where was she going? Somewhere uncertain, somewhere faraway. Sager had described it differently. "Somewhere better," he had said, "where you will live like a princess."

How quickly he had mapped her life. And now, just a month after her return from Maazoolah, the plan was about to take effect.

Noora bit her lower lip. The betrayal! First Rashid's weakness and lies, now her brother's.

She had tried everything to make Sager change his mind. When reasoning failed, she'd incited quarrels that went round and round in heated circles.

"But I don't want to go away," she had yelled. "I want to stay here, with you, and Aboud and Hamoud."

"Is that the thanks I get for thinking of you? You are so ungrateful."

"Well, I'm not marrying him and I'm not going away. I am staying right here where I am."

"I can't allow that."

"Why?"

"Because I don't want you getting old between these rocks with no children and no future."

"But you're staying here, and Aboud and Hamoud, too."

"We are men. It's different."

After a while, he had ignored her, only waving her arguments to the side with a curt statement. "I'm responsible for you. I decide."

She had cried and bawled tantrums and, like a spoiled child, threatened to run away, even though she knew there was nowhere she could go.

When everything failed, she had turned down his gifts and sulked. For a long time, her lips fell like dejected petals on a forlorn face she carried everywhere she went. Still Sager would not back down. "I have given my word," he'd said. "It would be dishonorable to break it."

Now, as she lay on the rock, bathed in the morning glow of the sun, she wished her father were here. He would have protected her. Even with his madness, he would have wanted to keep her close. He might have even asked her what she wanted to do. Her opinion might have meant something.

She heard Aboud and Hamoud and looked up. She had even tried to convince them that they needed her, but somehow, while she was in Maazoolah, they had grown into small men, mindful of the decision-making powers their sex granted them. There they were, farther down the valley, a little past the ruins. They no longer hopped as boys did. Instead, they strode over the rocks, carrying frowns of importance. Every now and then, they swung the canes they carried, slicing a bush or scattering a clump of earth.

There was nothing more she could say. There was nothing more she could do. Noora dangled her legs off the edge of the stone and squinted up at the sky: big, blue, brilliant. The matchmakers would be here soon to seal the arrangement. With sharpened senses, they would scrutinize how clean her home was, whether she had two eyes or three. Noora sneered at the thought and yawned away what little resistance she had left.

18

I t's time," said Gulsom.

For seven days, Gulsom and Sakina had prepared Noora for her new life: they had bathed her; lined her eyes with kohl; softened her hair and body with jasmine oil; scented her with an incense of *ood* peelings, amber and musk; perfumed her with rose and sandal essences; and smoothed henna on her palms and on the bottoms of her feet. And now, she was ready.

Sandwiched between the matchmakers, Noora stepped out of their home layered in clothing. Covering her dress was the silk bridal *thoub*, a transparent bottle green, festooned with a splash of silver embroidery, and on her head sat her *shayla* and the *abaya* body cover. A toddler jumped into her vision, wailing his protests at a goat that had just snatched his piece of bread. She had not seen him coming and nearly tripped out of the too-short slippers Sager had gotten her, because the burka blocked the sides of her face. It was one more confinement she had to get used to. Now that she was a married woman, she had to wear it in public. It trapped her face like a moist, second skin.

The formal agreement had taken place just the day before. Early in the morning, Faraj's father, Sheikh Khaled, who was Nassayem's religious authority, had entered the hut along with Sager, two witnesses, and Noora's future husband, Jassem. Normally, her curiosity would have prompted her to steal glances from behind the veil at the man who was soon to become her husband. But some shyness and an odd sense of obligation kept her eyes fixed to the ground. Sheikh Khaled had asked her if she accepted Jassem as a husband and she gave her verbal consent. The process was straightforward. "The girl agrees," Sheikh Khaled declared. There was no fuss, and as the men retreated from the hut, Noora had remained frozen in place, both numbed and astonished that she had lost the courage to refuse.

As they walked through Nassayem's tight-winding streets, Gulsom released a meat-and-rice burp. Its pungent smell curled under Noora's burka and stayed there. Then Gulsom's voice boomed, "Don't crowd the bride!"

But there was no crowd at Nassayem, just a few girls who paused in hanging their washing on the flat-roofed homes to watch the three women shuffle by. Where had the villagers gone? Where was the commotion of the night before when Jassem had ordered the slaughter of fifteen goats for the special bridal feast? Her feast—the feast she only heard of on the excited tongues of the women, the feast she could not attend because, as a bride, she had to remain hidden till her husband took her.

It was only when the village mosque came into view that she heard the bridal trills. Women and children waited by the slope that marked the end of the rocks and the beginning of the sandy shore.

Gulsom grunted her satisfaction. She shouted her enthusiasm as they swarmed around Noora. "Make way. Give the bride space to breathe!" The women rounded their mouths and vibrated their tongues once again. And that is when Noora's panic began.

Within the trills and swirl of well-wishers and the heat of excited children tugging at her *abaya*, she felt her stomach twist and a sour taste stick to the back of her throat. Her journey was coming to an end—or was it just beginning? Whichever way she thought of it, it was not talk anymore. It was happening—to her—and it made her head feel light.

"We're nearly there," Sakina whispered to Noora. "Time to cover." She loosened her arm and veiled Noora's face with the *shayla*.

Through the slits and weave, the sun dimmed and the mountains turned gray, and Noora caught her first glimpse ever of the sea. So much water! It stretched out as far as she could see, so blue, till it was darker than the sky. This was a never-ending pool of mystery. She tightened her clasp around Sakina's arm.

"Don't be scared," Sakina said, her voice trembling with emotion, like a mother who was about to lose her daughter. "Just look straight ahead and one step at a time, even in life."

"But that water," Noora mumbled, as the grainy sand seeped into her slippers. "I have to ride on it, and it just goes on and on."

Sager waited with the new husband by the rowboat that was to carry her to the larger *jelbut* vessel. When Gulsom had described Jassem the pearl merchant as a "mature man," Noora assumed he would be her father's age. But he looked at least ten years older—fifty years old or so. There he was, shining in his white dishdasha and neatly turbaned *ghitra*. He stood straight, his chest and tummy pushed out, full of the confidence of the rich.

As their slow plod drew them closer to the shore, she saw a third man, bending over to steady the rowboat against the laps of the waves. Under his *ghitra*, his hair hung in silky strings around his chin. He looked a few years older than Sager, perhaps twenty or so.

A flurry of waves rocked the boat. "Hold it steady, Hamad," Jassem instructed the young man. "Now, let's move on. We have to take advantage of this wind that's picking up."

What terror! She had to climb into that tiny boat. The thumps in her chest muffled the voices around her, and under her veil, she wheezed and panted like a weary dog. It was worse than when her father had attacked her! At least she knew then that she feared his madness. But what was this dread? Was it from the deepening water in front of her or something else? As Jassem and Sager reached out for her hands to help her onto the boat, she pulled back.

"What's wrong with her?" said Jassem.

She felt Gulsom's arm hug her waist and nudge her ahead. "Don't be silly!" Gulsom whispered. "Keep your dignity! Haven't you learned anything from us?" Her voice had the sting of a bee.

Noora glanced at the puzzled faces of the crowd around her. She hated that she was making a scene—it showed weakness. But she couldn't help it. An alarm she could not understand was keeping her from boarding that boat. Or was she clinging to some last hope that someone might save her?

Gulsom's arm shoved her forward. And that's when Noora flopped into a bundle, buried her face in her palms, and rooted her weight to the sand. They would have to lift her to get her on that boat.

"I come all this way and this is how she acts?" said Jassem. "Doesn't she know how fortunate she is that I'm taking her away from all this . . . this . . . wretched poverty?"

Then her brother spoke. "Let me talk to her."

Noora felt him kneel down next to her. His fingers made their way to her chin—so soft, so gentle—and raised her head.

He pulled the *shayla* off her face, but when she tried to fix his gaze, his eyes would not stay still. They bounced up toward Jassem, then flitted to the crowd that huddled around them. He, too, seemed uncomfortable under their scrutiny. "You must go," he said, turning back to her. "It's all arranged. It's done."

Hope vanished. She searched for some regret in his face, some emotion she could carry away with her, to think about when she was alone.

"You are his now," Sager whispered. "I can't help you. Nor can anyone else. So . . ." He paused. "Stay safe." He lowered his gaze to the ground and stamped a hasty kiss on her forehead.

She closed her eyes tight and whispered into her burka, "Mustn't expect much, mustn't expect much." With a light touch, she let the *shayla* slip back over her face. The sun dimmed again and she murmured, "Must be thankful, must be thankful."

As she willed herself to rise, she heard the sighs and mumbles around her. And the matchmakers' words flooded her mind: "Must be obedient, must be obedient."

❦ ❦ ❦

Noora gripped the sides of the rowboat as it bobbed over the bay. In the middle sat Hamad, with each stroke rowing them into deeper water. His eyes were large and serious, as if all the problems of the world were swimming deep in them.

She sighed and let her eyes drift over Hamad's shoulders to the other end of the boat. There was her husband, lifting his nose at the sheer cliff faces that clawed Nassayem's bay. The sides of his nostrils hung like wings. Prickly hairs cascaded through the dark crevices, as if aching to take in the crisp morning air. What an off-putting nose! Under the sun, its thin point gleamed, and balanced on the tip sat a pair of round, metal-rimmed spectacles.

She clutched the boat tighter and dropped her gaze into the water. Even through her veil, she could see all the way to the shining pebbles at the bottom. How deep was this water? Could she dip her arm and pick them up?

A school of yellow fish quivered along the bottom, their pink stripes catching the light before they chased one another around a mossy rock. It was a world she was seeing for the first time, just like the one she was heading toward in a place called Wadeema.

19

The *jelbut* glided smoothly out of the bay. Noora listened to the muffled splatters that slapped its sides from the musty room belowdecks. She sat on a mattress that was to be her bedding, between two sacks of rice, a tin of ghee, and a couple of baskets of dates. It was the storeroom, and she was sharing it with Lateefa Bint-Majed.

Lateefa was Jassem's cousin and first wife. She had accompanied him on this journey to approve his choice of a new wife, and after just one visit to the matchmakers' home, Lateefa, with a voice full of the dull rasp of two stones rubbed together, declared, "She will fit nicely in our household."

She must be roughly her husband's age but looked a little older because of the pouches under her eyes and the chicken skin of her chin. All her youth lay in her thick hair, dyed orange with *henna*. The tassels at the ends of her funnel-shaped, gold earrings tinkled as she twirled the mass into plaits. "I think it will take us seven days or a little more to reach home." Her spittle broke the specks of dust that floated in the air.

"Yes, *Ommi* Lateefa," said Noora.

It was the first thing Lateefa had insisted on, that Noora call her *Ommi* Lateefa, Mother Lateefa. And Noora guessed that that's how she saw herself: a mother figure to Jassem's younger wives. Noora was the third wife. Lateefa had told her that Jassem's second wife, Shamsa Bint-Juma Bin-Humaid, was about twenty-two years of age and that he had married her three years earlier.

It was Jassem who had decided on their living quarters. They were to stay belowdecks, away from the crew's curious eyes. They were to come up on deck for some fresh air for an hour in the morning and another at dusk.

The *noukhada*, or skipper, shouted from above, "Coming to open sea!"

Noora heard the stomps of the crew and wood creaking on wood, lumbering rumbles like old bones coming to life. The lateen sail whispered and fluffed into place, ready to take on the drive of the wind. The boat rose slightly, then dipped with a thump. Its gentle sway on the bay's flat water was changing.

Again and again, it lifted and fell until Noora's stomach started to do the same. She breathed deeply through her nose, but the smell of old timber, dust, and salt made her stomach heave and rumble some more. When she tried breathing through her mouth, the damp and dust mixed together and stuck to her tongue.

Now the boat was rocking from side to side like the hips of an old mule. Every now and then, it catapulted toward the sky and dropped hard with a thud that shook the *jelbut*'s wooden hull. Noora swallowed repeatedly, but the sour trickle of nausea would not go away. It snaked up her throat until she felt she could not control it anymore.

"I'm going to be sick," she said.

Jassem made a sour face and decided the living arrangement had to be changed. His wives were to be moved above deck, to the front. "Inconvenient, but necessary," he said to Lateefa and, turning to Noora, added, "Lucky you didn't mess up on the food. Up there, you will be all right. You must suck on a lime and let the wind cure you." Jassem instructed Hamad to bring their mattresses up and to secure a low awning on one side. For privacy Jassem erected two wooden poles that were to hold a stiff piece of muslin. This was the screen that was to separate his wives from the crew.

Once in the open air, Noora ignored Lateefa's bickering about the bother of moving and concentrated on feeling better. She sucked on a lime and faced the wind. As she gulped the salty air, she felt the queasiness slowly lift.

The wind stung her eyeballs, and she moistened them with a flutter of blinks before guiding them along the coastline of sheer cliffs and fragmented rocks that tumbled into the sea. Then she looked to the open blue, where sunken mountains rested, the first of which loomed large in front of them. Its rim seemed too thick to circle.

She heard Jassem call out from the other side of the screen, "Devil's Rock! Hold on tight, women!"

Noora shivered with a new wave of anxiety. Lateefa had told her about that rock, how there were devils that lived under it to shake any passing vessel that squeezed its way through the passage between the cliffs and the monolith. Noora sank to her knees and mouthed a prayer. As they entered the passage, she felt the boat shudder. Certainly, something lived in that deep water, something invisible and horrible. An underwater twister was spinning them as if they were no heavier than a feather. And yet Lateefa remained unruffled. She sat as still as a mountain, cross-legged under the awning, her full body covered with a light blanket. She looked like a tent, her head the central pole and her thighs holding the ends of the weave taut.

The lateen sail lost its shape, flapped and jerked, protested the wind that now seemed to be blowing from all directions. A gust lifted Noora's *abaya* and sucked it over the barrier sheet and, right away, her plaits flew into chaos.

From under the blanket, Lateefa shouted at her, "Tame that hair. You look like a wild animal."

So she could see! "It's the wind, *Ommi* Lateefa," Noora cried, holding her billowing *shayla* with one hand and bunching her unruly plaits (which the wind had loosened) with the other. "I can't control it. My hair's flying everywhere. And now, my *abaya* has gone, too."

"And speak properly!"

It was not the first time Noora had heard those words. Ever since that one time Lateefa had met her at the matchmakers' house, she had insisted that Noora drop her mountain accent.

The tent hollered again. "Why do you talk funny anyway, clicking your words like that?"

How could the older woman be thinking of straightening her words at a time like this? "That's how we all talk, *Ommi* Lateefa."

"Well, you'll have to start talking our way, you know. Otherwise every one will think you are stupid."

Noora didn't answer. She was watching what those hidden

devils could do. They were pulling the boat toward the rock. She tasted the sting of sickness once again as the boat grumbled, twisted, and creaked. Its sail jerked and she heard Jassem call, "More left steer!"

Noora could not watch anymore. She curled into a ball and swallowed and swallowed. This was no time to get sick.

Then, miraculously, the boat steadied and swayed forward. It seemed they had passed the grips of those devils and she could look up again. Peeking through her fingers, she spotted Lateefa's blanket. Even it had slipped off with those last shakes, lying in a mass around the older woman's hips. Lateefa was staring at it, her mouth a pout of displeasure. "How much of me must I sacrifice for others?" she said. "How much of me will be left in the end?"

Noora didn't answer. It was better to keep swallowing.

The muslin sheet flapped open from behind her. Jassem peered and said, "Calm now. You can move about." She looked up at him and caught his nostrils rising high. What a sight she must have been with her hair tangled and sneaking out from under her *shayla* to cover a sweaty face that was surely greener than her eyes. Still, he stretched his arm to her. "Come," he said, "you can stand up now, and wash your face."

And for a moment, she forgot to swallow. With her hand clasped in his, she vomited on him.

The wind eased, the boat steadied, Jassem went to get cleaned up, and Lateefa was once more under the blanket, watching the world through its rough fibers. She said nothing about the mess Noora had made on their husband, only continued to complain about her discomfort. "They call this a blanket? It's so worn-out I can feel the wind through it. And this mattress under me, so thin I feel my bones are sinking into the wood." Lateefa grunted. "Now I'm beginning to feel sick, too. Limes, water, now!" she cried. "Ehh, Bin-Surour!"

As if expecting her order, Hamad's arm popped through the corner of the sheet with a handful of limes and a porous pot of water, which he blindly hung on a beam. Lateefa pulled off the blanket and immediately started rinsing her mouth over the side of the boat. And that's when Hamad's arm entered their space again. This time, it was holding Noora's *abaya*.

Noora reached out to take it when the wind played its mischief again. It blew off her *shayla* and snatched the sheet out of Hamad's fingers, flinging it into the sky.

She faced him off guard and unveiled. She knew she had to look down, but her eyelids remained taut, holding the intensity in his unblinking eyes—sad and tender all at the same time. The moment was brief, but Noora felt it stretch like a sleepless night. It was only when she heard Lateefa's thunderous hawk and spit over the side of the boat that she flinched and lifted her hands to her cheeks, blinking at the russet circles of bridal *henna* dyed in the middle of her palms. She was a married woman staring shamelessly at the face of another man.

Noora was curious. Why had that Hamad boy stared at her so? She thought about his face, the pleas in his eyes. He was a stranger, and yet she felt connected to him in some way. He had that same look of desperation she was feeling. Maybe it was because his life belonged to Jassem, too. Listening in to the sailors on the other side of the sheet, she gathered that Hamad was Jassem's apprentice. Did he feel as trapped as she did?

She spotted a rip in the lower corner of the sheet, close to edge of the boat, and quickly decided she could take advantage of it. She guessed that if she reclined on her side with her back to Lateefa, she could pretend to be sleeping. Her head would rest on her arm, and that way she would be at the same level with the rip. Then she would only have to fix her eye to the hole in order to watch what was going on with Hamad and the rest of the crew.

She waited for Lateefa to lie down for a nap before testing her assumption, prepared to make adjustments, like propping herself on an elbow or even making the rip bigger if need be. But, just as she had predicted, there was no need for any alterations. It was easy, and her first glimpse was one of feet with hardened soles. Big feet, small feet, all deeply browned and roughened by the sun and wind.

For days, as the sea opened generously and the mountains gave way to rocky hills, Noora tried to catch a glimpse of Hamad. But he remained well out of her vision. Then, one morning, as Noora stirred out of sleep under the early sun, feeling its warming rays on her back, she heard his voice close to the barrier sheet. It took an instant to shake the sleep out of her head and to settle to look through the rip. She felt her eyelids quiver as she strained to spot him, but all she could catch was a view of the side of his dishdasha just before a sudden burst of wind slapped the sheet into her eyeballs. She pulled back. The burn was sharp. Her eyes watered. She rubbed the sting out of them and was back at her post within moments.

Hamad was gone. Now it was Jassem who was in her vision, steering at the other end of the *jelbut*. Some of the men had paused in the middle of their tasks to listen to what he was saying. It seemed as if Jassem had just finished telling them a funny story. His eyes crinkled and his nose flattened as he released a hearty laugh. Noora crumpled her lips and nose till they stuck to each other. How happy he looked. And why wouldn't he? He had never felt the pangs of deprivation.

"Jassem Saeed Bin-Mattar is a fortunate man." That's what Lateefa repeated to Noora day after day. "His father was a pearl merchant and so was his grandfather before that. So, you see, with such an impressive lineage, he was born richer than the rest of the village, and certainly luckier. He can afford to dress well and eat rich and varied meals. But he doesn't do any of that." At this point in her description of their husband, the man she so obviously revered, she always nodded solemnly. "You see, he is a humble man."

The sea rocked the boat into a gentle lull and the wind changed direction, blew Jassem's voice to Noora's ears. His words carried that unique weight of privilege as he trumpeted words filled with the pearls of wisdom that the rich carry. "It is a necessity of life to live in a simple manner. Isn't that right, Hilal?"

"Yes," said the *noukhada*, and joined the men, who seemed content to prolong their break by doing no more than listening to what Jassem had to say.

Jassem's voice rose above the wind and broke the flaps of the sail. "You see, if you live the simple way, you can still live happily if one day you lose your riches. And the reason is that you never indulged your desires to begin with. Why do you need to pay more for food? I don't, and believe me, I eat well." He chuckled and stroked his tummy. "Why does one need all those expensive spices? We should all be eating the food of the modest: rice and fish. Yes," he continued with conviction, "you don't need cardamom, turmeric, dried limes, or any of those annoying spices—which, by the way, are there more for show than anything else—to make rice and fish taste delicious. All you have to add, to give it a little zing, is the squirt of a fresh green lime."

The sailors were beginning to fidget as the sun's sharp rays settled on their heads. Noora watched them and wondered whether they could leave him in the middle of his story, just look the other way and carry on with their duties. They remained where they were, and Noora could not decide why. Was it because they depended on him for their livelihood and were compelled, out of duty, to listen to her round-bellied husband, or were they really enjoying his story?

"And you have to make sure that that same lime will be used to boost the taste for a whole week," continued Jassem, pausing to smile, before adding with finality, "A couple of squirts of lime a day—yes, that's all you need."

20

B y the next day, the rocks softened into large, saffron
dunes. And the day after that, the humps paled and
flattened, replaced with a swampy shore from which
seabirds lifted, their feathers gleaming under the sun, to flap
alongside the lateen sail of their wind-driven boat. And then
they followed a coastline of dazzling, white sand.

Noora had gotten used to the lift and fall of the boat by now,
and whenever Lateefa dozed under the blanket, she passed the
time by watching the eight-man crew through the rip.

"Not a week has passed and already she's sick of him." That
was Khamees, a sour-faced diver with lanky limbs.

"All over him." And that was Sangoor. He was blessed with
a velvety voice that had been dipping in and out of tunes since
they had begun the journey.

And now he was humming again, and she knew it would
lead to a song:

"With romance falls the black veil of night,
Bittersweet memories fill my mind with might.
I remember the gleam of her milky complexion,
And a tear sneaks from my eyes but I cannot mention,
I'd be ready to sacrifice my all,
Surrender my life for her sweet call."

The tent moved. "That donkey's bray again," Lateefa muttered and fumbled out from under the blanket. "Now, where are we?"

As Lateefa squinted at the dazzle of the sun, Noora asked, "Am I in trouble?"

"Why would you be in trouble?" Lateefa said.

"You know, with my husband." She paused. "I mean, our husband, after I soiled his dishdasha. He hasn't come to see us since."

"Pah! What do you think? You think he has nothing better to do than nurse your unsettled stomach, that he is not needed to guide this boat?"

"So . . . I'm not in trouble?"

"Pah!"

And with that second *pah* Lateefa covered her head once more, and Noora knew she was not going to get an answer. So what if he stayed away? So what if everyone stayed away, including that Hamad boy? It was only his arms, brown with the sun, that she glimpsed, as they emerged on her side of the sheet, to deliver this or pick up that. Still, even with that thought, she shuffled back to the rip. Why shouldn't she look? Instead of Hamad, she spotted Jassem snapping open his timepiece. "Half past three," he declared. He sniffed the air as if he had just picked up the scent of rotting fish and pointed ahead. They had arrived at Leema.

* * *

Khor Marmar—the marble creek: Lateefa had told Noora about it, describing it as a hundred shades lighter than the open water. Some merchant, a long time ago, had named it so because it reminded him of the marble of the mosques in Persia and India.

And he was right, that merchant. Even from under her veil, Noora had to squint at the shimmering piece of sea that emptied into a balloon-shaped creek around which the town of Leema rose. The water was a luminous milky white, deep enough for boats to float on. But not always—at least that is what Lateefa had said. "For a few days every month, the sand sucks in the water and leaves just a little bit in the middle. And when that happens, you can walk across from one side of Leema to the other." Noora could not imagine it. "And picture this," Lateefa had continued, "when there is no water, the boats have to sit on the sand, leaning to one side, waiting for it to come back and lift them up again."

What stories she made up! Noora looked ahead. Khor Marmar was full of water. And on it were all shapes and sizes of boats. Some forty dhows with sails wrapped around high masts were moored to the rough coral stones that made up the dock on the eastern side of Khor Marmar. Around them and in between, smaller boats bobbed. Some were carved out of a single palm tree trunk; others were a collection of palm fronds secured with rope. Then there were the tiny wooden barrels, pretending to be boats, half in half out of the water, always carrying a child or two.

It was a grand sight after the lull at sea. So many people! Men crouched on the sandy banks fixing nets, bent over crates and lifted them up, rowed across the lagoon, stood at the shore polishing hulls, even swam.

So much to see! Her eyes drifted to the houses on both sides of the creek. They were nothing like the stone huts of her mountains. These had smooth walls, golden as the sun—solid squares crowned with low towers.

"Wind towers," said Lateefa, with a nod of knowledge. She had removed her blanket and was now adjusting her veil, making sure it hung neatly over her face. "They trap the wind and funnel it through, into the house. Cool, cool air."

What genius thought of such an invention? With her head full of cool, cool air, she began counting the wind towers: thirty lining the eastern bank and another twenty on the western bank.

"Only the rich have wind towers," said Lateefa, the pride of the prosperous warbling her voice. "We have two in our house."

"Which one is your house?"

Lateefa waved an arm in the air. "We're a little way away, in Wadeema. You can't see our house from here."

Perhaps Sager did know what was best for her. Perhaps this would be a better life. For the first time, Noora dared to hope. Was it because of this new place so full of the throb of life? She was infected with the sudden bustle around her after so many days listening to the sigh of the sea.

Once she was off the boat, her spirit rose further when she saw that Jassem wasn't angry at the mess she had made days ago on his dishdasha. He didn't raise his nostrils at her, nor did he scold her; he was cheerful, insisting that the women accompany him and Hamad to the souk, Leema's market, before carrying on to his house.

He looked as happy as a child with a pocketful of sweets. His *ghitra* flapped along his shoulders as he led the way, followed by Hamad and the women. They passed a row of murmuring women sitting cross-legged, their wares spread on pieces of cloth in front of them. Odds and ends, that's what they were selling: bottles, tins, scraps of rope and thread, small bundles of herbs, needles and buttons. And that's what Noora was examining. Hamad's eyes did not interest her anymore. They dissolved into an air bombarded with the cries of men who uttered words she could not understand. Persian, Indian, and African tongues mingled with the Arabic, along with the bleats of goats for sale held tight by their masters.

Even Lateefa was excited, clutching Noora's arm firmly, forgetting her fragile bones for the moment. She pulled Noora along with a startling strength and agility, dodging a donkey's swishing tail, shifting to one side as the cartwheel it was pulling, laden heavy with sacks of rice, rumbled past them. "Rice, green limes, onions, lentils, and radishes," Lateefa listed, making sure her voice was loud enough for Jassem to hear. When he did not respond, she added, "Some special foods, too."

Jassem stopped and looked back at her.

"You know what I mean, husband, like pomegranates and bananas."

"Pomegranates? It's not the season," said Jassem.

"Yes it is. They always come at this time from Persia."

Jassem waved his hand impatiently. "What do you want pomegranates for, woman?"

Lateefa stuttered. "Well, you know, for you and your new wife—as a treat."

"A treat? No, no, no, no. Too messy. When that red juice gets on your clothes you can't wash it off."

"Bananas then?"

"No bananas. You pay so much for them and they finish so quickly. Mush-mush in the mouth and they are gone." He let out a generous chortle. "So quickly you can't even remember what they tasted like." He tapped his temple with a finger, as if deep in thought, and added, "I think it is mangoes we should get. Pure, sweet—that is the fruit for pampering." His arm swung generously in the air. "Yes, mangoes. As many mangoes as we can find."

Only Noora heard Lateefa sigh and whisper, "But it's not the season for mangoes."

Noora smelled the souk before seeing it. As they entered the dimness of the narrow lanes, the sharp scent of spices rocketed up her nose and settled on her eyeballs. A piercing combination of pepper, ginger, clove, and cumin misted her eyes before the cooling scent of cardamom, cinnamon, coriander, and anise seeds dried them up again. Only then did she notice the tawny shafts of light that pierced their way through the palm-frond awning. They fell on the ground and lit up the shuffling feet that compressed the sandy lanes, sharp beams carrying bits of floating dust.

Since Jassem maintained that spices were a waste of money, they breezed through the spice lane and turned into a street filled with blacksmiths' embers. The heat clung to the air, which was ringing with the sharp clangs of hammers on metal. More noise but fewer people here. The street forked and they veered right, where Noora heard the buzz of saw on timber. She sneezed as she caught the whiff of fresh wood through the fine shavings that flew into the air.

Then the tailors' street: quieter, with just the start-and-stop hums of sewing machines. A man emerged from the dimness of the third shop, his hair slicked into place with so much coconut oil that its scent trailed out of the open-fronted stall. He waved his hand at Jassem. "*Arbab*, master, you back? What I hear? *Masha' Allah*, you marry?" He seemed to have a way of using only the important words and losing the rest in an accent twirled through the curl of his tongue.

"Ah, Kumar! *Salam Alaikum*." Jassem waved his greeting and kept walking.

"Why run so fast? Come drink tea, good strong Indian tea. You married now, stop! Shop for new wife. Why no buy presents from my shop? Bestest fabrics from Bombay. Number one quality, must sell." He smiled and wagged his head.

Jassem laughed and paused to say, "You Indians, always wanting to make more money." He turned and continued a few steps before stopping again, raising his brows with recognition at a fragile man with a pointy, white beard coming toward them. "Ah," Jassem said. "*Salam Alaikum*, Juma Bin-Humaid, what are you doing here, so deep in the market?" Jassem greeted the old man with a nose kiss and Hamad kissed his hand before stepping to the side.

"A visit over there," said Juma, pointing ahead. "God knows I shouldn't wander so far from my shop. This damp gets into my skin, makes my bones crack."

Jassem chuckled. "The damp? The damp is everywhere, my friend. It settles on these roofs, seeps through your dishdasha, wets this packed sand you're standing on. The sea, my friend—when you are by the sea, the damp crawls all over the place." He let out a hearty guffaw while his friend raised a palm to greet Lateefa and ask how her health was. That was all it took: a casual query about health for both Juma and Lateefa to start pouring out a whole list of ailments that they had endured and continued to suffer from. There were back pains and headaches, heart throbs and indigestion, itches, and dizziness. Their problems seemed endless, and Noora shuffled from one foot to the other wanting to move on, envying Hamad as he stole away to the other end of the street. She couldn't do that. She had to remain where she was.

Then Jassem coughed—a serious cough that ended Juma and Lateefa's animated conversation. "That other woman is my new wife!" he declared.

"You are blessed, Jassem," said Juma, his beard fanning out slightly in a smile that Noora thought looked more nervous than it should. A cane dangled through the quiver of his bony fingers, looking strangely out of place. A cane belonged to a strong man. Juma Bin-Humaid could hardly be called that.

"Just so you know," Lateefa whispered to her, "Juma Bin-Humaid is Shamsa's father, a merchant—and rich like our husband."

The other wife, thought Noora. That explained his restlessness. He must hate me! She watched the old man curl his fist around the cane, but instead of steadying his grip, his hand shook more. So he crossed his arms high on his chest and began raking his beard with his fingers. They were dull and brittle, reminding Noora of the dying twigs she would often spot in her mountains, clinging to the trees that had nourished them. The smile had left Juma's face, and he looked as if he had something he needed to say.

Jassem placed an arm around Juma's frail shoulders. "So, *masha' Allah*, how much money have you made since I was away?"

"The usual. No more, no less."

"Good. Well, we better go now. We have to get some supplies for the house before heading home." He winked at Juma. "I must distribute some food at Wadeema to honor the arrival of my new bride. A full day of meat and rice they will have."

"Wait!" said Juma. "Before you go, there is something you need to know."

Jassem's eyebrows lifted above his spectacles. His nostrils rested serenely as he waited to hear the old man's news.

But Juma was faltering, clutching his cane to his chest. So fragile he was that Noora feared it might stamp his skin, leave behind a nasty bruise. "It's as if there's more damp air today," Juma muttered. "It's as if it has come to eat at my bones. Do you feel it?"

Jassem looked around at the invisible air. "I think you might be feeling under the weather. Why don't you rest a little? Go home and lie down."

Juma finally unlatched his arms. "Home, yes, that's it. It is home I need to talk to you about." He coughed a weak cough that suited his frame. "I'm very happy for you, for your marriage. But I am not happy for my daughter."

Jassem grunted. "Not to worry, she will get used to it."

Just as Noora wondered whether they, the women, should be listening to this delicate subject, Lateefa tugged at her *abaya* and guided her a few steps back to Kumar's stall. She picked up a piece of fabric and said, "What do you think of this one, Noora? See how soft this cotton is?"

Kumar hopped back to the front of his stall. "No, no, no, *Ommi* Lateefa," he said, his mouth a curl of displeasure. "For new wife, silk only." He turned to Noora and flapped open a piece of silk, luminous in saffron and coral stripes. "See? This latest style. This called *Bu-Glaim*."

Noora inspected the fabric, but her ears continued to pick out Juma's airy voice. "I don't know if she'll get used to it. It's as if she is made of fire, that daughter of mine. She is very upset."

"What? You mean she told you?" Jassem sounded surprised. "How did she know?"

Lateefa's whisper was sharp and urgent. "Not good, not good." She cowered and moved toward some plain white cloth at the corner of the store.

And Kumar—he had unfolded three more bolts of fabric, all rich in texture, smooth to the touch. "*Bu-Glaim* no good? Here, more number one fabrics: green, red, purple. You like, you like, you like?"

But with his last "you like?" Noora had already looked away, over her shoulder, at the two men. "Don't be upset," Juma was saying to Jassem. "I think it's Lateefa who told her before you went away—you know, to prepare her."

Noora spotted a blaze in Jassem's eyes as he stared past her, at Lateefa. But his voice was steady when he asked Juma, "And? What else did your daughter tell you when you went to Wadeema to see her?"

"Oh no, I didn't go to Wadeema. She came to me."

"What?" he barked, and Noora spun back to the fabrics, bumping her head to Kumar's. He was leaning out of the store, the curiosity launching his neck into a series of furious jiggles.

"Oho," whispered Kumar. "Only trouble come when bringing more women in life."

"Yes, she came as soon as you left, a few weeks ago," Juma explained. "She is at my house now."

"And what did you tell her when she came home to you?" Jassem had lowered his voice, but the rumble in it remained.

"What can I tell her?" said Juma. "I told her she could stay till you came back, but then, she must go to Wadeema. After all, she doesn't belong to me anymore. She's yours."

Jassem grunted. "You are a good friend and a good father," he said. "But now I have got to sort this mess out. Let's go and fetch her."

Jassem's arm bore heavy on Juma's fragile shoulders as he marched him out of the tailors' lane at a speed that seemed too fast for the old man to cope with. Noora was concerned. Juma's neck stooped and he dragged his feet. Twice, his knees fumbled into a trip, only to be straightened with a sharp tug from Jassem's arms. How long could he continue under her burly husband's embrace? The cheery mood of earlier had evaporated and Jassem's urgency of setting things right had taken its place.

Noora and Lateefa followed the men as they turned left into the potters' lane and continued to the end. There, it opened into a large square, hemmed in by the rising walls of town homes. That's where Hamad was waiting, and as Jassem's purposeful steps came to an abrupt halt, Juma seized the opportunity to wiggle out of his clutch.

Al-Barza square: it was so full of people it jolted Noora after the calm of the inner streets. She dropped her gaze to the side, where a book binder had set up the tools of his trade on top of a trunk. His face carried the dust of faraway places. The afternoon sun cast a soft glow on his shaved head as he fingered the yellowed pages of an old Koran, patiently shuffling them into a neat pile. Next to him, a long-necked man sat on a wooden stool facing a barber, who was busy neatening his beard.

"This place just gets messier and messier," said Jassem, raising his nose so high it looked like the beak of a large bird. He swept an arm over his forehead, wiped off the beads of sweat that clung to it, and turned back to them. "Now keep close here," he said, nudging his way to the sides of the square. "I don't want you getting lost." He twisted his shoulder away from a tin container swinging on a pole balanced over a water seller's shoulders before adding, "Or hurt."

Hamad held Juma's arm and Lateefa tightened her hold on Noora's. Two by two, they followed Jassem, weaving their way along the edges of the square, past the calls of the porters. "Two *anas* and I'll take your load wherever you want!" Perched on their see-saw carts as they waited for work, they looked like vultures.

Next to them, sitting on neatly folded legs, were the Bedouins with their camels and supplies of coal for sale. They gawked at the crowds, their faces fierce with the harshness of the desert. Noora spotted an older boy biting his lip as a bone setter twisted his broken thumb back into place. Through the din, she heard the crack and cringed. The souk was losing its appeal quicker than she had anticipated. She felt as vulnerable as a worm crawling in an open valley. Anything could fall on her. Anyone could kick her or step on her.

The dust that rose from the ground in a haze carried the stink of sweat and urine. Through it, she glimpsed children and beggars, blind men and cripples—and always a madman or two. "Pah," Lateefa blew into her veil. "Nobody knows what to do with them. So they wander the streets like strays." She waved an arm at a madman who was dancing toward them. "Pah! Pah! Be gone!"

The madman opened his arms in a generous bow and winked through a dust-lined eye. "Spare an *ardee* for a good cause. I am a good cause." A scar of a previous skirmish drew a line just above his left brow and his bald head was speckled with sores.

Finally, they reached the other side of the square and entered an empty street. Just as Noora gulped a cleaner breath, she noticed that the madman was still tagging along, twirling in circles behind them, begging for an *ardee*.

Jassem snapped at him. "Be gone!" He turned to Hamad and ordered him to get rid of the fool.

Hamad gripped the madman's arm and tried to lead him away. "Come on, be reasonable. Stop bothering us and go your way."

But the madman was not about to be reasonable. "But what will it cost you to help me? I'm not asking for a shiny rupiah. Just an *ardee*—a teeny, battered, rusty *ardee*."

"We don't have any money for you, so go away," Hamad said, nudging the beggar's chest.

The madman hung his head and dropped his lower lip. "Just an *ardee*," he squeaked. "Only one *ardee*." The madman had changed his voice to that of a child—he was trying another strategy.

This time, before Hamad could turn to push him away again, Jassem stepped in. His face was the color of the pomegranate Lateefa was deprived of. The thought made Noora want to chuckle, but she knew better than to do that.

"There are ways to deal with people like this man," he said to Hamad. "Let me show you."

The madman raised his shoulders to his ears and hauled out a set of neat, yellow teeth, each strangely in the right place. It was a silly grin, like that of a child about to be rewarded.

"Once, twice, you tell them to go and still they persist."

The madman swayed and flapped open both hands.

"It's all right. I'll handle him," said Hamad.

"You don't have the stomach," Jassem said, and grabbed the cane from Juma's limp grip. He slapped the madman: four flicks on the palms—quick, sharp.

The madman gasped and dropped to his knees. He looked up at the pearl merchant, his face frozen with the shock of the cane's sting.

"I spit on you and the people who created you!" Jassem raised his arm high and let loose another lash, stronger. Noora felt the air vibrate with the cane's force as it landed on his palms once again. Why were his begging hands still open?

This time he screamed and cushioned the sting under his arms. His head dropped to his chest and he shrank into a ball.

Noora was breathing hard now, sucking in her *shayla* with an open mouth, blowing it away again. She wanted to do something, but what? Could she throw herself in the middle, try to hold Jassem back, take the whipping instead? She dragged another breath and the *shayla* stuck to her tongue, its weave coarse in her dry mouth. The thought of getting too close to the beggar made her cringe.

They simply watched, helpless as infants. They were in an empty street, these two women and two men, their thoughts linked in a decision not to interfere. Juma had sandwiched his frail body between her and Lateefa, his face twitching with every lash. Next to him, Lateefa held her head high as if she were floating above them. And that

Hamad boy! What was he doing standing to one side, useless like that?

Noora traced the shape of his arms, easily ten times stronger than Jassem's. One whack—that's all it would take to send Jassem into a daze. He was clutching and loosening his fists, as if pumping some power into them. And Noora started to hope. She lifted her eyes back to his arms again and waited for their strength to show. But they just hung there, limp as a tattered cloth.

Jassem's arm was up again. He took a deep breath and whacked the madman two more times on his back. They heard no more cries this time, just muffled sobs.

Finally, the red drained out of Jassem's face and his nostrils settled back into place. "That should teach you a lesson," he said. The lesson Jassem had demonstrated was quick, not long enough for a crowd to gather. Only two men watched from the far end of the street. "And what are you staring at?" Jassem yelled at them. "He needs to know that when he is asked nicely he should listen."

"But he's a madman," called the first man.

Jassem handed the cane back to Juma. "Even a madman can feel pain."

"But a madman can't understand," said the other man.

"I don't have time for this arguing about whether a madman can or cannot understand." He cracked his neck. "All right, let's go."

Together, they left behind the whimpers of the madman, who remained in the same position—a turtle with its limbs pulled in. Without Jassem to pull him along, Juma fell behind them and Noora could hear his quivering breath. "You will treat her well," he called to Jassem. "I mean, you're not going to

THE SAND FISH {153}

hold it against her that she came to us." He was begging now. "I mean, it is her home, too, and she should be able to come and see her family. I mean, I am her father."

"Of course I'll treat her well," replied Jassem, as if annoyed that he had to look over his shoulder to answer. A few steps farther on, he stopped abruptly, looked up at the sky, and spun slowly to face them.

Who would be the next to get caned? That's what Noora was wondering. But Jassem did no such thing. Instead, he tromped back to them, toward Juma, whose wiry beard was once more held captive under his arms. "Look," began Jassem, "I don't want you to worry about anything. Am I not a good Muslim? Isn't she my wife? And doesn't Islam require us to treat our wives equally, in every way?"

The old man nodded, although he seemed to be confused whether to smile or not. When he tried to sigh, it came out as a half-sigh, an emptying of the lungs that stopped short.

"I treat all my wives well. Each one has her own bedroom. To me, they are all the same. It's just that some are new and others are not."

Finally, Juma released the rest of his sigh. "Yes, I mean, what has Shamsa really done? Nothing shameful, nothing criminal. All she did was come to visit her family while her husband was away."

"I need to get all the women home now." Jassem spoke slowly, and Noora raised her brows at the softness of his voice, a pleasing tone with the gentleness of a bubbling brook. But when he turned to Hamad, the bubbling brook that had moistened his throat dried again. "Well, what are you looking at? Don't you have something to do?"

"I thought you wanted me to come with you."

"For what? Get going and bring those supplies for the house. I'll take the women home."

Hamad faltered. "What should I buy?"

"Can't you think for yourself? Can't you carry out a simple task on your own? You know what we need. Now go!"

"Why that Bin-Surour boy chooses to make him angrier, I don't know," Lateefa whispered to Noora. "He knows what our house needs: rice, green limes, onions, lentils, and radishes."

21

With the memory of Jassem's attack on the madman still fresh in her mind, Noora felt as timid as a rabbit. Her husband was not a man to be meddled with, and quickly she decided it was wisest to stay silent till she got to the house.

They had picked up Shamsa and were now trotting on their donkeys into Wadeema just as the sun paused over the horizon, its rim oozing into the sky. Through the slits of her burka and the weave of her *shayla*, Noora followed its line of glitter over the sea, watched it spill at the shore and blush pink the white dunes that rose on the other side.

In between dunes and sea, Wadeema unfolded in an elongated oval that began with a mosque and a small shop and ended with a large house. Sandwiched between these landmarks were the *barasti* huts, their coarse palm-frond walls drawing the twists and corners of the streets.

They passed the pearl divers and fishermen who stood along their path lifting their arms in greeting to Jassem. Women and children peeked through the doorways, trying to glimpse her. After all, she was the new bride who was arriving from far-away.

Noora heard their talk, too: "Which is the bride?" She knew it was hard to tell. She looked the same as Lateefa and Shamsa, tented from head to toe in their *abayas*, faces hidden under their *shaylas*, both legs dangling on one side of their donkeys. She also knew she was a bride who was not arriving as a bride should. There was no family to deliver her and not a hint of celebration. But she did not care. She just wanted a chance to be alone so that she could ponder the design of her new life.

Shamsa had been the pampered bride. On their journey at the front of the *jelbut*, Lateefa had gone into an elaborate description of all the special care Shamsa had received when she married Jassem three years earlier. For forty days before her wedding, Shamsa had been isolated in a special room in her home while her family prepared her for her new life. They had fattened her through a daily diet of milk and eggs, and her skin had been pasted with indigo and *warss*, a plant mixture of shocking green that whitened the complexion. Her hair was sculpted into an elaborate design using nourishing *yas* leaves. Then, as if that were not enough, her scent was enhanced with a sprinkling of a sweet-smelling powder of rose petals, saffron, and nutmeg. All that beautification had taken place behind closed doors while the villagers concentrated on everything else that needed to be done.

Noora wondered whether the villagers felt let down at her arrival, cheated out of their celebration. When Jassem married Shamsa, the town had joined to celebrate the event in a glow of collective joy that had lasted a full week. Now she was the bride, and she was entering the home of the richest man in Wadeema in the quietest way possible.

Then, as if reading her thoughts, Lateefa spoke: "How different this is. No special wedding dress to store in the memory this time." Her voice wobbled with the quickening pace of her donkey as it trotted next to Noora's. "Ah, Shamsa's bridal *thoub*," she continued. "What a blaze of color it was: every stripe of the rainbow with cascades of braided silver thread. And if that was not enough—ah, ah, ah, the gold that covered her. So much she had a hard time keeping her back straight!" She chuckled. "You know, all the women of Wadeema joined in sewing it, *masha' Allah*. No pay for them, just lunch for the whole week."

Noora rounded her eyes with surprise. Was she allowed to talk? Lateefa was ignoring Jassem's sulk, which had been traveling with them like a dense fog ever since he found out that Shamsa had left his home without his permission. What would he do to her, this older first wife? Would he cane her as well?

It seemed Lateefa didn't care. Her cheeriness raced ahead of the plodding donkey as she continued, "And that hair: two thick plaits, *masha' Allah*, falling along her cheeks with tinkling gold ornaments attached to them. And the rest: a headful of plaits—twenty, thirty, maybe more—all glossed and shiny. And when she moved, hayh . . ." She wagged her head with the remembrance. "That's when the plaits tumbled like this, hayh . . . hayh . . ."

Lateefa paused and waited for Noora to answer, but Noora stuck to her vow and kept her tongue tight in her mouth. The air had suddenly stopped moving, and she felt smothered within the embrace of the layers of fabric that covered her. Was this the sticky touch of the sea?

Lateefa's voice grew bolder. "Then there were goats to be slaughtered, rice to be cleaned, grain to be ground—all that, they did here at the village. Ah, all that chanting between the thuds of their paddles, crushing that grain in those massive containers. Then the cooking of the *hareesa* porridge. No pay for these men and women, either, mind you, just lunch for the whole week."

It seemed Jassem didn't mind Lateefa's sudden chattiness after all. He did not even look back at her. Noora watched him trudge on ahead, silent as a sack of rice. *Just as well*, she thought. She was not ready to handle any more ugly incidents.

"Then there was the scent of incense everywhere. And singing and dancing," Lateefa said. "How wonderful, how noisy it all was."

A little girl pointed and called, "The bride! She's the second one in the group." For a moment, Noora was baffled. How could she tell? Only when she followed the girl's finger did she realize that it was the henna, faded to a weak brown but nevertheless sneaking up from her soles. The henna had given her away.

"You're here!" The shrill voice of a child called from behind the heavy teak door of Jassem's home, and for a moment Noora was taken aback. She had understood that Jassem's house was childless.

The small, arched door framed within the heavy, main door creaked open, and under a graceful porch stood a girl-woman who looked not more than a year or so younger than Noora, with skin more blue than black in the flicker of the hurricane lamp she was carrying. Under her *shayla*, her frizz was restrained in two tight plaits, and she opened her mouth into an exaggerated grin and repeated, "You're here, thanks to God. Finally, you are here."

"Yes, Yaqoota, we are here—all together, and one more as well." Lateefa kept her voice low and controlled. Noora understood she was trying to direct some restraint into this excited person, but Yaqoota did not (or would not) understand. Her teeth gleamed as she shrieked a bridal trill.

Now Shamsa spoke: "You silly slave. Can't you see we're tired? Out of my way!" She slid off her donkey and shoved past Yaqoota, half-walking, half-running into the house, the thick bangle on her wrist slamming into Yaqoota's ribs as her hand slipped out of her trailing *abaya*.

"Oof!" Yaqoota's mouth shrank to a dot. She doubled over in an exaggerated droop but jumped back up right away. And then she let the full white of her eyes pop out. "Shall I go and see what's wrong with her, *arbab*?"

The *arbab* spoke. "No, leave her."

Lateefa puffed her irritation into her burka and muttered, "Never mind her. Come help me get off this silly ass."

Yaqoota reached for her hand and, supporting Lateefa's weight on her shoulder, eased her off just as the muezzin's voice floated into the air. It was time for the sunset prayer.

"I'm going to the mosque," said Jassem. "Make sure all is in order by the time I'm back."

"You heard him," said Lateefa, her head nodding toward Noora. "Take the new one to her room. Let her wash and pray."

"Yes, *Ommi* Lateefa," said Yaqoota.

"Show her our ways. Everything. You see, she doesn't know how we do things here, in a proper house."

"Yes, *Ommi* Lateefa."

"And then come and rub my back." Lateefa lumbered to her

room. "I don't have any strength left. I don't know if I'll ever be able to stand straight again."

"Do this, do that," muttered Yaqoota, once Lateefa had left them. "That's the life you get if you are a slave." She indicated for Noora to follow her as she stepped into the square patch of sand that made up the open courtyard. They heard a whoop and a chuckle and stopped to look up the *sidr* tree that rose in the middle. There was a mynah bird swaying on one of its shaggy branches. The sky, luminous with the last of the day's light, caught only the shine of its orange beak and glossy black tail. "Strange," said Yaqoota. "What is it doing up so late? Mynahs never come out at this time."

It chuckled once more and flitted away. Yaqoota shrugged and swung the lantern to the far corner of the house, to a door under an *L*-shaped arcade. "That's the house *majlis*, the living room, where we sit in the summer." Her voice had turned sober, lost its piercing edge. She lifted her arm up to the rectangular tower rising above. "You see that? It's a wind tower. It pulls in the air and blows it into the room." Yaqoota's face glistened in the still air. "Of course, it is not working now because the *arbab* has blocked it up for the winter so that the rain and dust don't damage it." She flapped the air in front of her face. "Mind you, it feels like summer tonight." She swung the lamp to the other side of the house. "You see, there's another one over there. That one brings air into the men's *majlis*."

Noora nodded from one wind tower to the other, as if willing it to funnel through a breath of air. The clammy humidity was like another skin.

"Anyway, let's get you ready." Yaqoota turned and began walking back to the entrance, waving an arm over her shoulder toward the two rooms on the other side of the wall between the wind towers. "*Arbab*'s room, *Ommi* Lateefa's room." Then, the facing wall. "Shamsa's room."

They stepped into the room next to Shamsa's by the entrance of the house: Noora's room. On the far wall was another door that led to a smaller room. Pressed in the corner was a high, four-poster bed. Next to it sat a hurricane lamp on a wooden chest, but still everything remained dark.

"How can you see through everything that's covering you?" said Yaqoota. "You don't need to keep all those clothes on you when you're in the house. Take it all off."

Noora had quite forgotten that she was still covered. She peeled off her *abaya* and burka, let the *shayla* slide onto her shoulders.

Yaqoota gasped and tipped Noora's chin up. "So pretty, *masha' Allah*. Your face is like a princess. Now, tell me, princess, what is your name?"

"Noora Al-Salmi."

Yaqoota squealed. "What kind of accent is that?"

Noora flinched. What boldness!

"Tell me, Noora Al-Salmi," Yaqoota said, now laughing. "Does everyone talk like that where you come from?"

"Like what?" Noora was not comfortable with such quick familiarity. She was not sure how to react to this girl-woman, so full of childish abandon.

"Come on, say something else," begged Yaqoota. "Please, please, please."

"What do you mean? You understand what I'm saying, don't you?"

Yaqoota dropped to her knees and bent over into a shudder of mirth.

They heard the pounding on the wall and Shamsa's voice

barking her anger, an anger that caused it to crack with strain. "Enough! Can't you see we need to rest?"

"Shh," said Yaqoota, raising her hand to her mouth to stifle her laugh. "Don't make any noise."

"I'm not the noisy one."

Yaqoota continued to giggle. "I want to laugh loudly, but I can't. There's too much anger in this house right now."

What a strange reception! Noora waited for Yaqoota's next eruption. Instead, Yaqoota swallowed her glee and said, "It is just that your accent is so funny." Then she stood up and listed all the other sections of the house, raising her arms in broad sweeps: "A privy in the house at the far corner of the courtyard, way back behind the men's *majlis*!"

"In the house?"

"Yes, the only house with one. Everyone else in Wadeema does their thing by the sea or in the dunes."

Before Noora had a chance to ask more, Yaqoota described it: a raised platform with a cemented hole that opened to the ground. "The hole is covered with a piece of wood so that you don't accidentally fall in. Believe me, you would not want to fall in that!" Again she hugged her arms and snorted, and Noora wondered how much gaiety bubbled in this girl.

Yaqoota wiped the mist from her eyes and continued. "Of course, for washing and bathing, you just go in there." She pointed to the attached smaller room. Noora peeked through the doorway. It was a low-ceilinged washroom. A large earthen container of water sat on a cemented floor that was slanted, so that the water could slip easily into a corner hole.

"Where does that hole go?" Noora asked.

"Into the street. This house is very special. It makes living easy. Water for bathing comes from the well."

"Should I go out and bring the water to the house every day?"

"Bring the water? *Masha' Allah*, this house has its own well." Yaqoota swept the air with her arm in a bold stroke of importance. "Outside by the kitchen."

A well in the house, too! *These people don't need to work*, thought Noora.

"But the house well's water tastes bitter and old. So we drink the water from the village well."

"Should I bring that?"

"No." A squiggle of puzzlement broke the taut skin on Yaqoota's forehead. "Yusef the water seller takes care of that."

"Well, what are my duties?"

This time Yaqoota did not laugh. Instead, she looked deep into Noora's eyes. "Don't you know? Your duty is to make a baby."

Noora sank to her knees in front of the only window in her room and peeled open the shutters. Thick bars covered the opening, which overlooked the courtyard, and she wondered at the logic of it. If the bars were to keep robbers out, shouldn't they be fixed on an outside wall? If they were meant to keep her from escaping, where would she run off to anyway?

From somewhere outside came the howling rivalry of tomcats. She groaned and let her gaze drift up along the *sidr* tree till it reached a sky depleted of its vitality: a piece of charcoal trapped in the square of the courtyard, the jittery dots of the stars struggling to give it light. She hugged the softness of her chest, felt the crush of her arms, and remembered Rashid, how he had held her that one time in the cave. He had given up on her, chosen to follow his mother's command. And instead of fighting for him, Noora had let her pride get in the way. What could she have said? Would it have made a difference? She sighed. What was the point of thinking about it now? It was too late: she belonged to another man.

The household was still. She wished she were moving, on a boat or a donkey, even just walking. In this house the only sound came from the kitchen, where Yaqoota was preparing dinner. The smell floated through the bars on the window—fish, maybe something else, too, but the pungent odor of fish was always victorious, as it masked all other scents.

She rose, suddenly wilted with fatigue, and sat on the bed. Her head drooped to her chest and she felt the sway of the sea. She had no appetite now that the weight of her new life was sitting heavily on her shoulders.

She smelled onions. In her mountains, their scent would have floated into the open air and watered her mouth. The onions would have signaled the coming of some tasty meal. Here, they bonded with the fish and clung to the air in an oppressive smell that would not dissolve.

Lateefa glided, silent as a ghost, on the other side of the bars, followed by a dense trail of smoke. She entered, and Noora was about to hop off the bed in respect to the older woman when Lateefa raised an arm. "No, don't get up. Sit, sit." Lateefa placed an incense holder and a bowl filled with what looked like yellow mud on the trunk. "Are you settled, dear?" she asked.

Noora nodded and caved back into her position, occupying her mind with the upsurge of howls coming from outside.

"Pah! Those cats," said Lateefa. "All night, all winter, they fight and scream at one another. It is hard enough to sleep without that noise." She grunted. "Never mind, *Allah* be thanked, we are home safe. Now, let's get you smelling good."

Noora's back stiffened as Lateefa lifted her plaits and inserted the incense holder. The smoke wrapped them with its amber scent, dancing snakelike toward the roof, and for a moment it swallowed that stale stench of fish and onions being fried in the kitchen.

"There, that's better," Lateefa said, placing the incense holder back onto the trunk. She dipped three fingers into the yellow mud and ran it along Noora's middle part. "Saffron, to make you smell nice, to make you pleasing." Then, another dunk of the fingers before she streaked a line on each cheek "I know those matchmakers prepared you well," she said, "but you don't need to follow every little thing they said when he comes to you tonight." Her voice sounded concerned, almost motherly.

So it was to be tonight. Noora's dangling feet quivered like fish slapped onto the shore. No more waiting. She counted in her mind the list of instructions that Sakina and Gulsom had made her memorize. She knew Lateefa was not talking about the date-pit trick. "Which part should I ignore?"

"It's all fine what they told you," said Lateefa, frowning with gravity. "But the part where you struggle, well, you don't really need to do that."

It was a point Gulsom had insisted on. By holding back as much as possible on her first night, a bride highlighted her dignity, her self-esteem. She was proving she was not to be had so easily, that she was not to be taken for granted.

"What should I do?"

"Ah, that's easy," said Lateefa. "Just lie back and do nothing."

There was a victorious cat outside, for the screeches suddenly stopped. Noora's fingers writhed into a tangle of complicated twists. She wished she could shrivel into a dry leaf that would crumble with the first touch of this man, this stranger, this husband, who was to come to her once the charcoal sky turned black.

22

Noora stood outside the doorway of Jassem's room. In the shadow of the arcade, she picked up the beginnings of a tune she knew too well. She had heard it almost every night for the past two months. It started softly as a series of broken hums that promised to lead to a structured song. But then the melody twisted wily in another direction, its notes falling one after another into a long line of purrs—cat purrs of pleasure. These simple spur-of-the-moment creations were his tunes of lust, the ones that stained the air every time he desired her.

He will come to me tonight, she thought. He will carry his lamp and full belly, and come into my room for some intimacy. Her stomach churned and the sourness itched the back of her throat. She swallowed hard. The sickly feeling trickled down. Again and again, she swallowed to push it down farther. For the moment, it was subdued, just as she had learned to subdue much of what she felt in her life by the sea.

She leaned on the wall, closed her eyes, and whispered, "I must be thankful. I must be thankful I'm married to him." *Thankful*: it was a peculiar word and, more and more, she repeated it to herself, desperate for it to fog her thoughts and trap some numbness in her limbs so that she couldn't feel him anymore once he came to her.

It never worked. The word hovered for the shortest moment and passed through her mind like an invisible breeze. Should one be thankful for basic physical necessities or emotional needs? It was a riddle her young mind could not answer.

She coughed and called to Jassem, "Supper is ready." The tune stopped abruptly and he grunted, and she understood that he would join them shortly.

Noora walked out of the protective darkness of the arcade and crossed the courtyard to join the other wives. They were sitting on the ground by the kitchen, their legs stretched out, as they supported their weight on elbows rooted to a couple of firm cushions. A palm-frond dining mat lay in front of them with a small bowl of dates on one side and a platter of radishes and onions on the other. The hot food was still in the kitchen, being kept warm in a pot till the *arbab* of the house could join them.

"Well, where is he? Did you call him?" asked Lateefa. Her burka shifted from side to side as she crunched a piece of radish. Unlike Noora and Shamsa, Lateefa wore her burka in the house.

Noora sat and stretched her legs straight in front of her. "He's coming," she said, and let her gaze drift to Shamsa's face, creamy as milk, with no blemishes, no scars. Noora's skin had none of the refined softness of Shamsa's, the smoothness that came with a life of indulgence. She could not help but admire its whiteness, so full of the shine of the moon even in the soft glow of the lantern. Over a fine nose, Shamsa's brows dipped and connected. Now she lifted one up and the other followed.

"What are you looking at?" she said to Noora. "You know, if you do what needs to be done, he won't ignore us like this."

Noora waited for more. It was the daily dose of Shamsa's contempt. One day, she hoped she would be able to let Shamsa's anger breeze through without affecting her, without reminding her that she was in this house to conceive.

"It's up to you to give him that baby," Shamsa said. "But you can't even do that. What do you think he brought you here for?"

Noora wanted to speak out, throw an accusation back at her. Why hadn't Shamsa fulfilled her obligation? After all, she had been his bed companion for three years.

"Just you wait, mountain girl! No baby means you"—she flicked her thumb toward the door—"into the street!"

Lateefa leaned forward and began pressing her knees. "Keep it quiet. He will be here soon, and you know how he hates the bickering."

Shamsa threw a sidelong glance at Noora and sat up straight. She peeled her cuff to her elbow and raised her hand to her forehead to rake her fringe in place, not that she needed to. Like Noora's, it was a short fringe, after all, sitting high on her forehead, a broad line from the edge of one temple to the other. It never got messy, that style designed to show the beauty of her face and complexion. No! She was showing off again, and not just the ivory sheen of her arm.

The chunky gold bracelet with thick spikes slid down her dainty wrist. There was the luxury she was born into displayed once more. And, every time, it worked to make Noora feel small.

Every time it ate at what confidence she had left. Noora twirled the three thin rings on her middle finger and burrowed both hands into the hollow between her thighs.

Shamsa snorted. "I don't know what he sees in her. I mean look at her feet, thicker than leather. All her life jumping on the mountains barefoot, I guess at the end of it they would have to turn hard as hooves, which is all right, I suppose." She sighed. "After all, she's just another goat from the mountains."

"When I say enough, I mean enough." Lateefa pressed her knee harder. "How many times do I have to exhaust my voice with you? How ungrateful you are. When I was your age, I had to endure the arrival of two other young wives." Lateefa paused to breathe in that special wisdom she had collected in her long matrimonial life. "I didn't bicker like this. When those poor girls passed away, God rest their souls, I kept my husband as happy as he could ever hope to be. I didn't nag him; nor did I trouble him with such pettiness." She closed her eyes and waited for a response.

"Yes, *Ommi* Lateefa, a difficult life you have had," Noora mumbled, and tried to ignore the smirk Shamsa was beaming at her as she crossed her legs to hide her toughened soles.

Lateefa's eyelids quivered and she opened her eyes, misty with emotion. "You don't know how lucky you are. All you have to worry about is trivialities. When I was the only one, I did all the housework, ignoring all those aches in my back, knees, and everywhere else." Her voice strengthened. "No complaints. I cooked, cleaned, washed. I had only Yaqoota's mother to help, God rest her soul, but she was withered and I did most of the work. At least now, you two have Yaqoota to help you out, young and strong that she is. Not that you have so much hard work to do."

Noora heard the clatter of pots in the kitchen. Why wasn't Yaqoota with them so that she could have said something (the truth!), revealed how Lateefa did no more than boss her mother, how it was Yaqoota's mother who had cleaned, washed, and cooked for years and years. Maybe Yaqoota would have taken Noora's thoughts and hurled them back at Shamsa, too. Somehow, Yaqoota could say whatever she wanted, and although Lateefa and Shamsa might shout at her, they never thought her important enough to argue with. She was the family slave after all, like her parents and grandparents before her, to be owned and worked but not argued with. "You see, her mind is not like that of the free!" Lateefa always said. "So one has to make space for her silliness."

As they heard the creak of Jassem's door, Noora watched the color rush to Shamsa's lucid cheeks. Ever since their arrival at Wadeema, Shamsa continued to receive stern looks from their husband. Jassem ignored her and refused to visit her bedroom. It seemed he hadn't forgiven her for having taken refuge in her father's home while he was away. Shamsa slapped her palms to the floor and rose with an indignant huff. She kicked her dress in front of her and marched to her room.

Lateefa shook her head and clicked her tongue. "Again? Why does she do that to herself?" Once more, as every night, Lateefa would give her a chance to spill some tears before sending her dinner to her room. Then, with an abrupt clap, Lateefa said, "Still, that's how it is now, and she will just have to learn to accept it."

As they watched Jassem cross the sandy courtyard, Lateefa leaned close to Noora and whispered in a solemn voice, "Now, listen to me, young Noora. Tonight, when he comes to you, lie very still." She paused and held Noora's gaze, as if she were dictating a secret recipe, before continuing. "If you do that, the seed will get rooted in your belly, and only then can it develop to become the baby we all want."

That night Noora waited for the familiar footsteps, those sliding toes with a duty that would carry Jassem to her room. She wished the baby would come soon. Only then would he give her less attention.

Her back caved and her legs wilted over the side of the bed as she waited for his arrival. She heard a sniffle from the next room: Shamsa's sobs, coming not so much out of love but out of failure. Failure to produce a child or, perhaps, out of losing her place as the new wife, the favored wife, of the house.

How quickly she colored, thought Noora. Her delicate complexion was not made to handle sadness. In the mornings, she would emerge with puffy eyes and a crimson nose, and Noora always wondered how many tears were stored within those eyes. Sometimes Noora wished she could cry like that. But her eyes had dried a long time ago, when Sager had sent her away, when she began her new life in this house of chalky walls. Now only the sharp sting of indignity prickled them.

There they were: the soft plods of passion, pausing at her door. She heard the door creak, and Jassem coughed and entered the room. She could not understand why he still insisted on clearing his throat every time he came to her. Did he think she hadn't heard him? She kept her head down, waiting for him to raise it. Wasn't that the way a wife should be? Patient, subservient, just as Gulsom and Sakina had explained. Her eyes followed his shadow as it floated along the wall. She held her breath.

She felt his pudgy hand on her chin, raising her face till their eyes met. A gleam ran along the rim of his spectacles (he always kept them on), and from behind the lenses his expression was serious, as if this were the most important event of the day. His hands slid to her shoulders in a firm press, the signal to lie down.

With a heavy clearing of the throat, he proceeded to perform his duty. He spread her legs in a triangle and pulled the hem of his dishdasha up, clamping it into his mouth. Then he lifted her dress and tumbled onto her.

Noora stared at the ceiling and the wooden rafters that held it up. How well she knew those muted brown logs. In between their supportive lengths the stone was crumbling. She watched the thin specks of dust drizzle down. They coated the back of Jassem's head and floated onto her eyeballs. Her eyes grew moist and she resisted the urge to blink away the irritation, chose instead to blur this moment of private embarrassment.

Her friend of the night emerged. The little lizard scurried out from under one of the wooden beams. It froze and twisted its head and, for a moment, fixed her in a stare. Then it shot its tongue out, slapping dead an insect she could not see.

The flame glowed on the trunk next to the bed and threw their shadows onto the wall. There was her head, the curve of her nose pointing to the ceiling. The rest of her blended into the lump of roundness that rose and fell on top of her.

She heard the moths bump into the glass cover of the hurricane lamp, adding their hasty clicks to Jassem's grunts. Then there was the sizzle and smell of their fragile wings as they dove into the heat of death.

Maybe this time it will work, she thought, feeling the quickening of his rhythm. A baby would not only put a stop to his nightly visits but fill her empty hours, too. She closed her eyes and concentrated on conception just as he groaned and shivered—the end of the act.

23

ff

I f she stood very still, she might catch a waft of air. Noora crouched under the wind tower in the family room and waited. But no breeze funneled through. The cooler days had long since evaporated, and summer was announcing its sizzling arrival.

Noora hopped over the burn of the sand and crossed the courtyard to the inner door of the men's *majlis*, the one that opened to the house's interior. It was still early in the afternoon and Jassem's daily visitors would not be there yet. The floor of the men's *majlis* was high, reaching the base of the large outer windows, and with the wind tower, too, there was always a stronger breeze in this room.

The door was ajar, and she was surprised to hear voices coming from inside. She stole a look and spotted Hamad, a pot of coffee clutched in one hand and cups stacked in the other, standing between the seated Jassem and *noukhada* Hilal, the skipper who had guided the vessel that had brought her to Leema. He was unfurling a whole list of niggling problems to do with the coming Big Dive.

"And the men," the *noukhada* was saying, "they need money—cash advances—so that their families can manage till they get back from sea."

"Of course they do," Jassem grumbled, "like every year."

Money! It had the power to warp Jassem's face. Noora spotted the side of his mouth turning into a squiggle that lifted up to his nose. His eyes stayed hidden behind his spectacles, which were half-fogged with humidity.

Hamad poured a drop of coffee into the top cup of his stack and handed it to the *noukhada*. While he waited to refill it, he started leaning toward the wind tower. He, too, it seemed, was seeking that elusive breeze.

"How many need money this time?" Jassem asked.

"All of them," the *noukhada* answered, and twiddled his empty cup back to Hamad.

"What?" Jassem removed his spectacles and wiped them on his dishdasha. Now Noora could see the frown and surprise in his eyes. "I knew some of them would need money, but all of them? How many are they altogether? Twenty divers, another twenty haulers? Most of them haven't even covered last year's advances. What do they think? That it's easy to make money?" He groaned and squinted at the outer door, the one that opened to the sea, as if impatient for the arrival of his daily visitors, as if willing them to walk through and change the subject. But it was too early in the afternoon.

Noukhada Hilal tried again. "You know, *arbab*, it hasn't been good lately. It is getting harder and harder to find pearls. I really don't know what's happening."

"Well, what do you want me to do? Put my own pearls in the oysters? You are losing your grip with the men." His voice turned harsh. "You should be stricter. Ration those divers, man, ration them! Work them harder so that they can endure more. If you don't push them to their full capacity, they will lose their strength, turn wobbly like old women. Let them stay down longer, so they have a longer breath the next time, and the time after that. Only then will they be able to look for more and more oysters."

Noukhada Hilal sighed. "Yes, I know what you are saying, but if I push them to dive more than the seventy or eighty times each day, they would just get sicker than they already are."

"We are not here to nurse them!"

"Already, the sea is harsh with them, dimming their sight, troubling their ears, weakening their lungs, and the madness when that evil spirit enters them, sometimes I don't—"

"Yes, yes, yes," Jassem cut him off. "I hear what you are saying." He grunted and set his spectacles back in place. "But I have to worry about stocking the boat and feeding them. Then, at the end of the trip, I get empty oysters? Would you say that's fair?"

"No, I wouldn't," replied the *noukhada*. "But I know, *insha' Allah*, with God's will, this time it will be different. I am planning to look for new reefs."

"New reefs? Is there such a thing?" Jassem fluffed the back of his dishdasha, trying to dry the moistness that wrapped the nape of his neck. "For hundreds of years we have collected the oysters from all over the gulf. I don't think there are any secret reefs in these waters."

Noora watched the *noukhada* nod and hoped that that would be the end of this conversation. She wanted them to leave. A trickle of a breeze was ruffling a trailing piece of Hamad's turbaned *ghitra*, and she wanted to sneak in and take his place. She heard Jassem's belly let out a long lament. His digestion was starting to play, she knew that by now. If the talk continued along the same trail, he would start burping as well. And there were other transformations that she had become all too familiar with. Whenever he had to pay, Jassem would get irritable, lose patience over the smallest things, and pull a long face for days and days.

"There is the pearling boat, too," said *noukhada* Hilal, his voice barely over a whisper.

"What's wrong with it?"

"I mentioned it to you before. It needs some repair work."

"Yes, yes, yes. How much work?"

"General maintenance, and there is a small leak in the hull, which is not that serious, but all the same I would feel safer repairing it before we set out." He let the words out quickly, as if the speed would cushion Jassem's distress.

"Everyone wants to dig into my pockets, take a piece of my generosity," Jassem said.

"*Masha' Allah*, you are all goodness."

Jassem burped. "Look," he said, "I'll have to see how much I can give, check my account book. I'm not that rich, you know. And besides, I am making my own trip to India. That needs money, too."

Noora's jaw dropped. Her husband was traveling! It was the best news she had heard since her arrival at Wadeema. She would be left alone—at last.

24

For days, Noora felt a vigor she thought she had lost. She swept flat the sand of the courtyard and dusted the rooms, milked the goats and brewed the tea, kneaded the dough and lit the coffee hearth. Although Jassem had not announced it yet, she looked forward to the day of his departure.

Late one afternoon, she rolled out some pink cotton material one of the women villagers had dropped off. Thanks to Lateefa, who had spread the word on what she called "the merits of the new member of the family, our third wife—goodwife," the whole village found out early about Noora's talent. Lateefa had described Noora as an accomplished seamstress. It was a skill she had added to the other two "most important skills" every new wife should have: well-shaped hips for childbearing and long, soft hair.

It was quiet in the courtyard. Jassem still had not returned from his shop in Leema, and Shamsa and Lateefa were out visiting. Noora was about to start cutting the material when she heard the familiar bleats of the goats at the entrance of the house. They always came back at this time after having wandered through the village all day. She sauntered to the door and let them in, shooing them toward the wire enclosure by the men's *majlis*. That's where they spent the nights, along with the chickens.

"Food for you," she said, surprised at the singsong that embellished her voice. She poured the water from the boiled rice from lunch into their tray and added some grasses.

"Come, come and look!"

Noora had forgotten about Yaqoota. "What is it?" she retorted, regretting immediately her impatience at Yaqoota's brusque interruption. There was no need to snap at her like that. Yaqoota stood by her whenever she could. Despite Yaqoota's loose tongue and unpredictable ways, Noora liked to think of her as a friend of sorts in this household of agony. "What is it?" she said, gently this time.

Yaqoota grabbed Noora's palm and pulled her toward Jassem's room, swung her to the side of the half-open door, and bonded her finger to her mouth. "Shh . . ."

Noora was surprised she had not heard his return. There he was, sitting on the carpet, which filled the room with its spectacular colors and patterns that curved into leaves and flowers. He had his back to them, settled cross-legged in front of his rosewood cupboard. How well Noora knew that large, three-door cupboard. She scrutinized its every detail whenever she dusted it. Branches of delicate blooms tumbled out and over the sides of two elaborately sculpted urns crowning it. That's where he hid the keys to it.

She watched Jassem run his fingers over the cupboard's

edges, along the delicate floral pattern with thin vines that entwined and blossomed into flowers of grace—roses, chrysanthemums, jasmine. He, too, seemed gripped by its loveliness, until he caught his reflection in its deep, brown luster. He leaned back and neatened his thinning hair. Then he stroked the stubble on his chin before letting his hands drop to his thighs.

Yaqoota shot a quick hiss of words: "He bought it in Bombay and nearly died trying to save it when a storm hit the boat that was carrying it."

Noora tapped Yaqoota's mouth shut, caught it before it could loosen into a trill of giggles.

Jassem touched the faceted crystal handle, unlocked the middle door, and pulled it open. At the bottom was a metal safe, which he clicked open.

"Let's go," Noora whispered.

"No, stay. I want you to see what's inside," Yaqoota murmured, her eyes deep with knowing.

Jassem tunneled his hand into the safe, pulled out two knotted cloths, and placed them on the floor. He took a deep breath and twiddled his fingers, as if about to touch a hot pot, before untying the larger bundle. The knot loosened and a cluster of pearls tumbled out. He sank his hand into the puddle of luminosity.

Light and shadow twirled on the pea-sized pearls as they raced off the tips of his fingers. Then he opened the second pouch and let roll his more precious pearls: ten large *danas*, which sat like refined queens, dwarfing the smaller pearls.

"Three of the *danas* belonged to his grandfather, and then were passed on to his father," Yaqoota whispered. "After that, they were handed to him, the lucky fatty. The others he collected."

Jassem picked up a *dana* and held it high. It released a discreet blush as the light seeping through the window fell on it. Noora's mouth fell open. She could not look away from the multitude of polished shades. So gripped was Noora that she did not hear the creak of the entrance door, only felt Yaqoota yank her arm and pull her into Lateefa's room. Someone was coming.

A line of drool snuck down the side of Noora's mouth, which she quickly wiped away, as they watched Hamad cross the courtyard and enter Jassem's room.

"Under the spell of the pearls, huh?" said Yaqoota.

"What nonsense," said Noora, feeling foolish at the way she had been gaping all that time. "They are only pearls, pearls that men risk their lives to pluck from the deep of the sea, pearls that make men like Jassem rich." Secretly, she wondered how much that *dana* was worth. Could she pocket it and buy herself another life?

"Don't think you can touch them." Yaqoota's ominous warning sounded like the rumble of a thundercloud "It's *haram*, forbidden, to steal."

Noora threw her a fierce look. "Steal? Are you saying I'm a thief?" They were just thoughts like all those other drifting thoughts that floated in her head. How dare the slave accuse her?

Yaqoota answered with a wink and three deliberate sways of her hips.

That's all they were good at, these darker people, moving like angels and speaking like devils. "I'm not a thief, you hear me?"

Yaqoota rolled her hip and lifted an eyebrow that drew squiggles on her broad forehead. And Noora had to grin. Yaqoota was just throwing words again.

Hamad was back, standing in the middle of the courtyard, staring at the *sidr* tree.

"Now what does he want it to do?" said Yaqoota. "Lean over and hand him some of its leaves?"

Noora was about to chuckle when Hamad punched the air and kicked up the sand. Even in the dwindling light, the red of his blood seeped clear through to his cheeks.

"What is wrong with him?" said Yaqoota.

"I don't know," Noora said.

The next day at breakfast Jassem made his announcement. He would be going to India, and Hamad would stay behind to take care of them.

Noora smiled into her chest. With Jassem's departure, her mind could rest at night. She would be able to listen to the sizzle of the sea in her moon-drenched room. She knew she would still have to deal with Shamsa during the day. But those nights! What blissful nights they would be. She would be able to close her eyes and fall into a deep sleep.

After breakfast, Shamsa and Lateefa headed to their rooms (they always rested after a meal), and Jassem went to his shop. That was the routine, and Noora, too, had her habits. She would enter the men's *majlis* and gaze at the sea through the outer window.

Hamad entered the house, carrying a sack of rice, as she crossed the courtyard. She caught the tiny shreds at the hem of his dishdasha and thought how easy it would be to repair them. All she had to do was open the hem and fold it in, hook it in place with a neat row of stitches. All he had to do was ask. But Hamad did not look at her, just walked straight to the kitchen with his mouth drawn tight.

She kneeled by the *majlis* window and stared out through the bars. Although it was still early in the morning, the air she breathed in was already warm and moist, as if it had been boiled over and over before being left to simmer. In front of her was the lifeless sky of summer, bleached by a sun that sat like a hazy blob. So much glare that she had to squint at the fishermen on the shore, repairing their nets, and the sailors bent over strips of canvas on the sand, shaping and sewing them into sails. Under an open-sided *barasti* that made up the Koran school sat the children, swaying back and forth as they recited a verse.

Noora joined them, whispering the verse into her chest. When they stalled, she did, too, until the teacher fed them a couple of words to set them back on track. It was just what her father used to do when he taught her and Sager the Holy Koran.

A lump expanded in her throat. How patient her father had been with her. Whenever she got stuck in her studies, he would give her a stern look and instruct her to concentrate harder. And yet, with Sager, Ibrahim had been different. He used a rough branch to punish him with a whack on his left palm. The few times Sager had objected with a child's weak protest, Ibrahim had let loose another whack on Sager's right palm.

Even at that young age of six or seven, Noora had felt her brother's pain. After the lessons, she would follow him wherever he went. But Sager always shoved her away. In the end, she'd stay at a distance and watch him. He would always find some dark crevice he could curl into. And Noora would wait for him to finish nursing his hurt.

"You are the flower he waters and I am the weed he lashes!" Sager's voice was always so full of spite. Could it be that that spite remained with him all along? Was that why he grew up into an angry and sulky young man? More and more, Noora wondered about such things, whether he resented her so much as to send her away.

She sighed and let her eyes drift to the horizon. Somewhere out there were her mountains, those summits of another time and another life. She squinted hard and pretended she could see them, imagined their jagged outline. Where was her father? Was he alive? And her brothers—were they managing without her?

She was escaping to her mountains once more, as she often did. What was the point? She shook her head hard to chase away that other life, to return to the up and down of the children's voices, to Wadeema's sounds, which were always filled with the slush of waves and the howling of cats. Her eyes grew heavy and she yawned. This was going to be a day just like any other.

That night, something happened. Jassem stopped in the middle of his lovemaking to talk.

At first, Noora thought she had imagined his breathy whisper. After all, she was numb to the movement on top of her. She was in some other place, engrossed with the acrobatics of the lizards (there were three of them now), counting the clicks of the moths (more suicidal on this night).

"Not working." That's what he whispered, and tumbled off and onto his back. "You are not working hard enough."

What did that mean? "I am, I am," she said, with urgency. She imagined standing at the front door early the next day with what few possessions she owned, kicked out of the house for not having been able to fulfill her role as a wife.

Jassem clicked his tongue. "She said there was a child. She said that."

Noora did not answer, did not watch his tummy rise and fall as he tried to control his breathing. She had turned to wood, a heavy log fixed to the bed. Who was he was talking about? Her fingers crawled to her dress and slid it down to her knees. Better not to stay too exposed.

Jassem rolled off the side of the bed and fluffed down his dishdasha. "Did she fool me? Now, what was it she said? Keep hope alive? How stupid." He was walking around the bed to her side. "What hope is there if you're not trying?" He picked up the lamp and held it over Noora's head, stared deep into her eyes. "Be patient and you will get your dream," he mumbled. "That is what she said."

Noora cowered. Her head felt so heavy she feared it might sink right through the mattress. She wished he would just go away. She swallowed hard and found her voice. "Who?"

"That ugly witch of your mountains! So many sacrifices I had to make, so many instructions she gave me, and I followed them all. I sat with shriveled plants hanging over my head and listened to her in that smelly hut filled with bottles and bottles of . . . of . . . dead things." He shivered. "In the end, what's my reward? Nothing."

"It's all God's will. He—"

But Jassem would not let her continue. He placed a fleshy finger over her lips and bowed his face closer to hers. When Noora closed her eyes, he ordered her to open them and stay still. She looked straight back at him but seemed confused. Finally he spoke. "I want the flame in your eyes that you hide from me."

✣ ✣ ✣

What did it mean? And what flame was he speaking of? He never said, and she never asked.

Instead, every night, he sat facing her on the bed, cross-legged, and unfurled all that was on his mind. He told her of his day at the shop: who came to visit, who he met at Leema. He asked her questions she didn't have the knowledge to answer. Why did his stomach grumble whenever he was upset? Why did the villagers expect so much of him? Why was he bored of Shamsa? Why did Lateefa nag so much?

It was a side of Jassem reserved only for her. He would speak in low tones, probably to make sure his voice did not travel through the walls. Once he had said all that he wanted, he would stretch his arms over his head, crack his spine, and sigh with relief.

Night after night he became more eager to talk than to perform his duty, and that suited Noora well. So she nodded him along, smiled in the breaks of light stories, frowned whenever the subject turned serious, even held his hand whenever he looked pained.

One night he brought with him a thick, black book, worn with use. It was his account book, and in it he recorded all the particulars of his expenses. It contained his pearl sales and cash advances to the divers. He explained to Noora what the detailed scribbles meant, showed her how to write the numbers, and explained the mystery of sums.

Adding and taking away was easy. But Jassem told her there were other things she could do with numbers. She could make them bigger or smaller using the tiniest sign.

While the house slept, he taught her. Soon she was writing with chalk on a small slate that he had brought for her. All the while Jassem scrutinized her progress. He nodded his approval when she made a correct calculation, groaned with good humor when she didn't.

It was only in the darkness that Noora saw her husband's nurturing side. Once the sun kissed the courtyard, under the scrutiny of the other wives, Jassem's stern face reemerged.

25

W hat? You got the habit again?" Lateefa shook her head with disbelief.

Noora sighed and shrugged, let her glance drift to the corner of the room to try to catch Yaqoota's eye as she paused in sweeping the floor. Only Yaqoota had the nerve to speak out, but right now the slave girl was too occupied, inspecting an army of red ants clustered around a crack in the floor.

"That's not good, not good at all," Lateefa continued, and lifted her head to catch some air. They were sitting under the wind tower of the family *majlis*. "Why did you get the habit?"

"I don't know," said Noora.

Yaqoota flexed her foot, took aim with her heel, and squished the ants in one go. Only then did she look over her shoulder at them. "That's why they call it the habit, *Ommi* Lateefa," she said. "It's used to coming for a visit, once every month."

How Noora had grown to love that voice, a high-pitched brew of innocence and abandon with a sprinkling of stinging sarcasm. Noora wanted to cheer her on, throw in a clever comment, but she wasn't quick enough.

Lateefa snapped at Yaqoota, "You hold your tongue before I cut it off!" With a force and speed that made her earrings jingle, she grabbed her slipper and hurled it at the slave girl. It slapped Yaqoota's chin and tumbled off her shoulder. Yaqoota yelped. "And if you continue in this way," said Lateeefa, "I'll throw you out to wander the nights in Leema. See if you can survive! See if someone doesn't pick you up and carry you off to the desert. See if you like being someone else's slave!"

It was a serious threat and Yaqoota's biggest fear. She had often told Noora of the Bedouins who came from the deep sands to steal other peoples' slaves, to sell them somewhere else. Yaqoota was not about to argue. She squeaked and ran out of the room, bumping into Shamsa in the doorway.

"What's wrong with that silly girl?" said Shamsa. "Always screeching with that rat voice of hers."

Lateefa did not answer. The pockets under her eyes were quivering with rage, and some other passion expanded the dark in them. Noora lowered her gaze. This was not the moaning *Ommi* Lateefa, not the mother to hope, not the gentle guide she always reminded them she was. This was someone else: an explosive *Ommi* Lateefa, whose patience seemed to have reached a boil.

As if it wasn't already hot enough. Noora felt the dots of perspiration tickle her upper lip as she dropped the corners of her mouth, tried to look affected by her failure so that Lateefa could return to that familiar, fault-finding grumbler.

"I'll tell you why the habit came again," Lateefa said to Noora. "Because you are not pregnant." She cupped Noora's chin and fixed her eyes, pulsing with urgency, to Noora's. "Jassem is leaving soon. He must plant the seeds before he goes." The crescents under her eyes slackened and she shut her eyes. For a long time she remained so, breathing deep, as she sifted through a stream of tangled thoughts.

They waited, both she and Shamsa, knowing that Lateefa always blocked her sight when serious matters needed sorting out. Then, with her first twitch, Shamsa was quick to drop to her side. She bent over and hugged the older woman's shoulders to show that they were united in their distress.

"I think *Ommi* Lateefa is right to be concerned about you, Noora," she said. "Where is that baby? What is taking you so long?"

Lateefa let out the sigh of the exhausted and reached over to the ankle band of her *serwal*, began fiddling with a thread that had loosened and coiled.

"Well," Noora said, "I have been completely cooperative. I have never said no."

"Completely cooperative?" Shamsa raised her hand to her chest. Today, she was wearing a necklace of thick, gold beads hanging on a red cotton cord. She began to twirl them, one bead at a time, as she held Noora in a defiant stare. "As if you have any choice!" she mocked. She was smiling now, waiting for Noora to avert her gaze (as she always did).

How much did they know? Noora thought, as the wilt washed over her. Her head felt heavy, her eyelids were beginning to close, making her lose focus on that shimmering necklace. Did they know that for over a month now Jassem was spending more time talking to her and teaching her numbers than planting his seeds? He thought her worthy of that. She was valuable to him. Did they know that she was beginning to enjoy his visits?

No! She would not look down. Noora snapped her head back up and stared at Shamsa, at those droopy eyes choked with kohl. Suddenly they were not as attractive as they used to be. They reminded her of a stupid camel. "Why are you always blaming me?" Noora said. "These things are in God's hands."

The thread broke and Lateefa looked up.

"And why are you picking on me," Noora continued, "as if you are so perfect? You haven't given him a baby, either."

"I could have," Shamsa said, "but he never tried as hard with me as he's doing with you." She was stuttering. Her mouth quivered at the edges, and for a moment Noora thought she might cry. She looked forward to that kohl melting with the tears and streaking black the white of her skin. But Shamsa didn't. Instead, she snorted and slapped the floor. "He eats with you and lets us wait. We have to eat after the two of you are belching your meals away. Is that fair? Is that what Islam says? Doesn't the prophet say that each wife should be treated equally? Jassem treats you like a princess when all you are is a cat-eyed pauper from the mountains."

"It's not true. I come from a tribe, the Al-Salmi tribe," Noora said. She remembered her father, how proud he was of their tribe, until that Ahmad Al-Salmi led them astray. "It was a strong tribe and honorable. Just because they didn't live in houses like this one does not mean they weren't important."

Shamsa pointed a shaking finger at Noora. "You, you . . . He visits you every night and ignores the rest of us, as if we were picked off the street."

"I never told him to ignore you."

Shamsa scoffed at Noora. "Oh? We have power over the *arbab*, do we?"

Noora watched the corners of Shamsa's lips twist down, and just like that, Shamsa's lucid complexion lost its beauty. Instead of the luminous ivory, Noora saw the pasty white of the sick. "No, not power," she said. "Just sense."

Shamsa's jaw clamped and her voice turned into a hiss. "Let me remind you who I am. I am the daughter of the most prominent merchant in Leema, richer than our husband." She freed a generous sweep of the arm. "I lived in a house two times larger than this one. I was fed milk when I was growing, pure milk from fat cows. I ate dates all my life of the finest quality from Basra." She rotated her tongue in her mouth and swallowed, mimicking the sugary taste of Basra dates.

"Dates are dates," said Noora.

"No they're not."

"Yes they are."

"You will never know what the dates I grew up on tasted like," Shamsa insisted. "All I am going to tell you is that they were nothing like the dates you were fed, full of sand and grit." She turned up her nose and sniffed. "You know which ones I am talking about, the ones you munched while you were running around with your starved herds."

Lateefa pulled another loose thread from her *serwal* with a snap and flashed the two women a sharp look. Using her first wife's privilege, she commanded them to stop.

"It's not my fault, *Ommi* Lateefa," Shamsa sang. "You can hear it for yourself. The mountain goat has a voice now. And she plans to use it."

Noora narrowed her eyes and was about to tell her that Jassem was teaching her numbers when Lateefa interrupted. "Not now!" she scolded. "You can lay blame on each other all day when you are alone. Now I want some peace and quiet." She flapped her hands in front of her face, tried to shift some air her way. "Why don't you two act the way you should, like sisters?"

She could have kept quiet, ended it right there and then, but Noora's mouth was watering with smugness. The wind of her mountains, so filled with support, was blowing. Jassem made the rules. He held the key to their fates. And right now, she was his favorite. She crossed her arms and let out her demand. "Shamsa should guide me wisely, not throw insults at me. I'm the younger one. It's not my fault that our husband wants to be with me. He sets the rules."

Shamsa yawned and stretched her arms. "Nothing stays the same forever. Enjoy what you have." She pulled her dress up slightly and twiddled her toes. There were her toe rings, sitting flat like shields with dainty loops, on both big toes. "Imagine, when he gets bored of you," she said, sighing with mock pity. "What will happen then? I can only pray that he does not throw you out. I mean, where would you go?"

"Hah," said Noora. "He'll never get bored of me." Shamsa didn't understand the intimacy she and Jassem shared. Shamsa did not hear what went on in the black of night, didn't know that whenever she and Jassem were alone, his feelings expanded like a bloated *wadi*. He whispered his worries and insecurities into her ears. Her ears only! And yet, the vulnerability seeped through. What if he did get bored of her?

26

J ust three days was all it took for Shamsa's prophecy to ma-
terialize. Like a thick fog, Shamsa's warning crawled into
Noora's room and stifled Jassem's murmurs of intimacy.

That night, as the house slept, Jassem arrived in high spirits and told her the story about his first trip to India. His father had taken him aboard a British steamer. "Ten days it took.
We were booked on deck class, a cost of nine rupiahs. We took
our food, pots, and bedding, and slept on deck." He chuckled.
"Every morning the deck cleaner would wake us up, force us to
move so that he could clean the deck. Ah." He sighed. "*British
India Steam Navigation*, that's what it was called."

"Britishin stim nashun?"

Instead of correcting her, he smiled and leaned toward her.
She now knew not to be afraid of him. She giggled and asked,
"What's wrong? What kind of name is that anyway? Can I help
it if those *Inglesi* people choose stupid names for their boats?"

Jassem laughed. "You of all people should be able to pronounce it. After all, with all those strange twists and clicks of the tongue, you mountain people should be able to pronounce anything." He opened his arms and let his warmth gush out as he wrapped her in a hearty hug. How protected she felt! She was sure he had never hugged Shamsa or Lateefa that way. With a hug like that, she was sure no one could force her to leave the house. No one could harm her.

But then he didn't let go. And the hug of protection began to feel more like restraint. Surely she was imagining it. She tried to slip out of his grip. When that failed, she wriggled, just enough for him to understand that he could now let her go. But Jassem would not. He kept his arms clamped firmly around her.

He began to shiver. It wasn't the shiver of feeling cold. This was a silent quake that was locked away somewhere deep inside—and it was coming out, vibrating in waves she could not explain.

"Are you feeling sick?" Noora asked, but he didn't reply, only sucked in the air with a hiss. Noora persisted. "Do you want some water?"

She felt his breath hot on her neck. And then he released her, pushed her away so hard that she bumped her elbow on the bed's poster.

"What weakness!" he exclaimed, and bounced off the bed. "You are playing with my mind, trying to make sure it melts whenever I am with you."

Noora rubbed her elbow and looked up at him. He was smoothing out the creases of his dishdasha, his arms zipped along its length in agitated strokes. What had she said? When his dishdasha could not get any neater, he began pacing the room. Noora watched his spectacles slip down the bridge of his nose with each step, until they clung to the little wings. Those nostrils that had stayed calm for so long now flapped with a blinding speed.

"When the heart takes you away, you do stupid things," Jassem said. He seemed to be talking to himself as he paced the six steps to one wall and back again. "You talk, say things you don't want to say." He stopped in the middle of the room and pointed his finger at Noora. "From now on, when I look at you, I want you to close your eyes. You have got witch's brew in them."

"I . . ." She was about to tell him it wasn't true, when he yanked off his spectacles. He had never done that before (even when he was performing his duty). She watched him squint and draw closer to her. His shadow loomed high above him. She must have been a blur to him, but to Noora his face was as transparent as the steam of simmering water. The warmth of their nights had evaporated just like that.

"I rescued you from poverty. Never forget that," he said. "I have given you so much that you should be kissing my feet, not making me speak worthless talk."

"I don't. I—"

"That witch said there would be a child. But there is nothing. Lateefa was right. What have you given me? What is your worth in the end?"

The cats were howling once more, and Lateefa scrunched her eyes and sniffed abruptly, as if catching their scent. Then she wiggled her foot away from Noora's kneading fingers. "You're useless," she said. "I can't feel a thing." She tapped the bottom of her calf. "Here, press here."

Noora dug her thumb into a tender spot.

Lateefa yelped. "What's wrong with you? Either too soft or too hard. Can't you do anything right?"

That voice! It hovered between the thick whine of a pained dog and the raspy bray of a mule. Lateefa grunted and rose to leave Noora's room. As she turned, Noora stuck out her tongue at her.

It was her fault! Her security was gone and it was Lateefa's fault. The only way she could get back at her was to frustrate her by making sure her much-loved rubs felt as torturous as possible. Every day for the past week Noora pretended she had lost her healing touch. She poked butterfly flutters on the hard skin and burrowed her fingers with full strength wherever she thought it would hurt most. And yet the older woman kept coming back.

Noora shuffled to the far corner of her room and began raking the wall, peeling away large sections of the gypsum till she reached the shells lodged in the coral-stone base. There was nothing else to do since Jassem had taken away her slate and chalk, so she tackled a plump shell with faded pink stripes that reminded her of the pebbles her brother used to collect for her.

"You will be living like a princess." That's what Sager had said. She grunted and dug at the wall with her fingers. Other shells, looking more like old toenails, tumbled to the ground, but the shells she wanted would not budge. Sager was convinced she'd be better off with the rich pearl merchant, far from the hardship and deprivation of their lives. How little he knew!

Her resentment toward Sager turned to bitterness, and soon she was lashing at the wall with such intensity that every poke and scrape was turning into an attack on her brother. How could he sell her off to some stranger like that? They were poor in the mountains, but all their worries were to do with things they could touch—food, water. Here, the worries were different and so complicated. She was always on her guard. In this house of rich people, you never knew what the next day might bring. Two of her fingernails tore. She yelped and shoved them into her mouth.

"There'll be nothing left of that wall if you keep on like that."

Yaqoota's voice at the doorway just irritated her, and she turned her attention back to the wall. "I'm going to use them to practice numbers," Noora said, ignoring the mess she was making.

"What for?"

"It will keep me thinking."

"Thinking? What's the use of that?"

"What is the use of anything?"

"Well, if that's your fun, soon there'll be no house for us to live in." Yaqoota snickered and hopped toward her. "You will have picked the walls down. No privacy for you and the *arbab*. And then what?" Yaqoota leaned over Noora and gaped at her. Her upside-down face was full of mischief. "As if there's any privacy now." She plugged her ears with her fingers. "He is making so much noise I can't sleep at night."

Noora pushed Yaqoota's face away. The slave girl never knew what to say and when to say it. It was true, though. Jassem was taking his duty more seriously. Every night he would order her to close her eyes (so that she couldn't bewitch him into talking), and he would liberate passionate grunts that competed with the yowls of the cats outside. So loud they were! It was as if he wanted the household to know that he was trying his best.

Noora pursed her lips and stared at the toenail shells around her. She did not want to talk about it. She feared she might weep if she did, so when Yaqoota did not pursue the subject, suggesting instead that they go and watch the village, Noora was so relieved that she jumped up and pulled the slave girl out of the room.

These were not ordinary days. There was the dash and hurry, an urgency that wrapped Wadeema as the divers and their families prepared for the Big Dive. Noora and Yaqoota peeped through the entrance of the house and watched children poke sticks at a sack they had filled with sand to become a make-believe shark in a make-believe sea. From behind the palm-frond walls of the homes, they heard the pressing voices of women as they prepared their husbands' belongings for the three-month-long voyage.

In the afternoon, those same women would come to visit Lateefa, as they did every day, to talk about the coming Big Dive. They would list heroic tales of accomplishment: whose husband had plucked the largest pearl, whose father had stayed down the longest, whose son had dodged an aggressive shark, whose brother had survived the most jellyfish stings. They were tales of glory, released in an excited flurry of words. Then the women would fall silent, sigh, and shake their heads. Every woman knew that her husband, father, son, or brother might not come back, might die in the sea. Every woman knew that if he did come back, he would arrive home sick and starved.

"It's the same every year," said Yaqoota. "They go and their women wait. And then, when the boat comes back, either it's good news or bad news."

Yaqoota's words made Noora's heart sink further. She sighed. "How much hope those women carry in their hearts.

How much hope is crushed in the end?"

"Nothing to be sad about!" Yaqoota slapped Noora's arm. "It's God's will. It is what He has written for them, and they have to accept it."

"You are heartless," said Noora.

"Look, pretty one, if we sit and wait, we will never get what we want. We have to do what we can to survive."

Noora raised her eyes questioningly. They were vague words but seemed full of the weight and value of gold. They were not words to come out of the mouth of a woman, and a slave at that. Was there some wisdom she had not seen in Yaqoota? "What do you mean?"

"Does it matter what I mean? A woman must do what she can for her peace of mind, that's all."

Peace of mind? Certainly Noora had none.

"She must find ways to make the passing hours tolerable."

Yes, Noora had many slow and miserable hours. "How?"

"You want me to show you how?"

Noora's pulse quickened and she nodded. Was there a secret that Yaqoota had discovered that could eliminate the dejection she consistently felt?

"You ready to start right now?"

Noora nodded again.

They set out straight away without too much thought on whether they would be missed. Covered from head to toe, they stepped over the mangled remains of the make-believe shark, which the children had abandoned. At first, Noora followed Yaqoota with nervous steps, turning her head this way and that, unsure as to whether anyone could identify her. She knew that as a respectable wife she should not be wandering aimlessly with the house slave in Wadeema's streets.

"Don't worry," Yaqoota assured her, guessing her fears. "No one will be able to recognize you, and we won't be gone for long, anyway." She paused, before adding, "Even if they look for you and don't find you, it won't matter. After all, you're not the favored one anymore."

The truth in Yaqoota's words stung, but Noora took in a deep breath and willed the nervousness to lift as Yaqoota led her along the edge of the village, where it was quieter. They entered a long and narrow street, lined on each side by *barasti* huts. Noora picked up bits of the conversations that were taking place within. Through the palm-frond walls, she heard a man assure his wife that he would come back safely, in a hoarse yet intense voice. The wife was quietly heroic, responding with a voice filled with dignity, telling him that she would accept whatever fate this journey would bring. Noora stared at the ground and slowed her walk, as if she were in a trance, listening to the somber mood, surrendering faith, and choked sobs that floated out from within the *barastis* along the length of the empty street. It was Yaqoota's shrill voice that shook her back to the moment.

"Women passing through!"

Noora looked up and spotted a man who had entered at the far end of the street and was walking toward them. In an instant, the man stopped, averted his gaze, and paused to the side. He pulled in his limbs so that she and Yaqoota could pass by without his touching them.

Yaqoota grabbed Noora's hand and pulled her along, and just as they drew close to him, Yaqoota yelled again, "Coming through!" with such force that he stumbled back into the wall of the *barasti*. His *ghitra* got stuck in the rough fronds and he jerked his head to the side. It slipped off, revealing an egg-shaped scalp.

Just as they hurried past him, Yaqoota bent her arms at her sides and flapped them. She bobbed her head back and forth and released a series of guttural clucks. From under her *shayla* and *abaya* Noora giggled, but the man could not see the funny side of Yaqoota's chicken dance. Worse, Yaqoota's foolishness revealed her identity.

"It's you! Yaqoota!" he said, as he fumbled with the *ghitra*, trying to pull it out of the fronds without ripping it.

Yaqoota laughed and rushed to the other end of the street, pulling Noora along.

"And who is the other one?" the man called after them.

They were running now.

"I'm sure you are a respectable woman," he continued, addressing Noora. "Listen to my advice. Don't go walking with that slave. She will spoil your manners, you hear? Her black blood will lead you to shame."

They kept running, past the mosque and the small shop at the end of the village, leaving Wadeema behind, until they reached a long and empty stretch of beach. "How did he know it was you?" said Noora, once her heart slowed and she could breathe steadily again.

"I am famous," said Yaqoota.

It was hot. Under the near midday sun, the water was luminous and the sand shone a fierce white. They removed their *shaylas* and *abayas* and bent over to unbutton the ankle bands. With *serwals* secured in tight folds at the knees, they lifted up their dresses and hopped over the scalding sand and into the shallows of the sea. The warm waves slapped their legs, and they began splashing each other and jumping over every breaking wave, laughing and giggling, giddy with frivolity. It was not long before their energy ran out and they flopped onto the sand to catch their breath.

Yaqoota reached out to pick something out of the sand and said, "This is the place to find them, not dig them out of the wall." She handed Noora a shell that was shaped like a beetle, its surface smooth, its color a pale pink with leopard spots. Noora placed it in the middle of her open palm and stared at it before raising her eyes to the rolling waves, which ended with soft slaps on the shore. She felt the distance between her past and present spread as wide as the sea before her. She began stroking the shell with her index finger and thought of Sager and the pebbles he used to collect for her. And it made her sad. It made her want to talk about her feelings.

"I hate him," said Noora. She meant Jassem but was thinking of Sager. "He makes me feel like I am his dog, to be ordered around. I hate the way he touches me, gropes me like—"

"Shh!" Yaqoota plugged her ears. "You can't be telling me these things. I'm unmarried, never been touched. If I listen to you telling me all these touchy-touchy things, you will make me lose my purity."

What was she thinking, trying to open her heart to this woman with a child's brain, to this woman who had just made fun of the shape of a stranger's head by performing a chicken dance? Such matters should not be shared with Yaqoota. In fact, they should not be talked about at all. Noora fell silent and stared at the sea once more, vowing to speak only of simple things.

"You know," she said, "I wasn't always this quiet. I used to have a voice louder than yours."

"Louder than mine?" Yaqoota said. "Not possible."

"Well, maybe not louder, but as loud. Whenever my brother bossed me, I would fight back. And my father always agreed with me. I did what I wanted. No one could force me into anything. Once, I got so angry at my brother Sager that I left him— just like that. And the poor troubled thing, I think he must have climbed every single mountain to find me."

"Hahh!" Yaqoota exclaimed.

Noora could tell Yaqoota wanted to know more of her true side, which no one in Wadeema appreciated. "Actually, I went and stayed at this village, high up on the mountain, with this kind old woman. The village was called Maazoolah, and by the time you climbed up the mountain to get to it, you could not feel your legs."

"Ooh!"

With Yaqoota's interest, Noora felt her worth grow. "Yes," she said, drawing up new memories as she continued, "I bet my brother almost died with worry when I disappeared on him, but I did not care. Everyone in Maazoolah valued me. I sewed for them, for the whole village. They loved me, and when I wanted to leave, they begged me to stay, especially this man, who . . ." Here, her voice trailed to a halt. Should she go on?

"A man? Who was he?"

"No one," Noora said, remembering Yaqoota's chicken dance again. "Just an old man whose dishdasha was in need of a lot of repair."

Reckless! That's the thought that sprang into Noora's head. Why did she have this urge to reveal so much? Perhaps it was Yaqoota's carefree ways and all that splashing in the water that was creating this need to unburden a load so big, a load that she would have to carry always. She must remember discretion.

Lateefa often commented that trying to understand Yaqoota and her erratic ways was a waste of time, that Yaqoota's mind worked differently. Noora always listened with skepticism. But now she wondered how much truth was there.

"Old men!" said Yaqoota. "Who wants to hear about old men?"

"You are right. No one wants to hear about old men."

"Let us speak of young men," Yaqoota said, shifting her eyes toward Noora in a conspiratorial look. "By the way, Hamad wants to talk to you."

It was a strange request for a man to ask to see a woman who was not his wife. And yet Noora felt indifferent. She had gotten used to seeing Hamad. He walked in and out of the house so often that he had become more invisible than the mist that the sea spread over the house every night.

"Let him come," she said.

27

Noora craned her neck out of her doorway. There was a plume of incense spiraling out of Shamsa's room. It cut through the bars of her window and out into the courtyard, where it hung like a cloud in the still air. These were the lazy hours of the day, when the sun cast its strongest rays and it was still early enough to be smelling nice, but Shamsa was wasting no time in preparing for the night. And that's how it had become. The *arbab* had swapped quarters, switched favorites, shifted his visits to Shamsa.

Noora heard footsteps—she was coming—and pulled back into the dimness of her room. She sank to the floor and held her breath. From under the window, she could see the *sidr* tree, thirsty under the glaring sun. And then Shamsa sauntered past, made sure to stop by the window and throw a sidelong glance of achievement , just in case Noora was looking. And Noora was.

It was a brief stop, but it served its purpose: "I have him and you don't!" Noora could almost see the words form on her lips, rosy with self-confidence. "I have him and you don't." It was a simple truth that terrified Noora. Later, as on every night, Noora would toss and fidget on her bed, wonder whether it was the heat lingering in her palms that kept her up or the noise coming from the other side of the wall. She would hop off the bed and run her hands along the crumbly gypsum, hoping to feel some dryness trapped in its surface. But it was always moist, the scent of chalk heavy in it. What was the use of it? It didn't trap the coolness, nor did it keep the noise out. All those whispers and stifled giggles were the sounds that made Noora's heart beat with dread.

Shamsa turned and walked back to her room, and Noora rested her head on her folded knees. Was she so naïve, so brainless, to believe that things would stay the same with the *arbab* forever? He was a man, after all. And he had to do what men were supposed to do: keep his true feelings locked away. For a man to speak of his desires or insecurities was a weakness. That much, she knew. Hadn't Sager behaved in the same way? Kept his feelings bottled up always? Not a tear had trickled from his eyes as he gave her away.

And Rashid, too! Noora tried to think of some breeze of an emotion that had settled on his face. He always spoke of his feelings, but now, she finally understood that all that talk was not real. Only words—sweet words, big words, but empty words—mouthed so that he could touch her. And how foolish she had been to let him.

Noora sighed. The words of men, none of them meant anything. Now Jassem was showing her that he could control his feelings like a man, too, keep them inside. Only her father did not act that way. He had let his passions snap like an old piece of rope tired of tying things in place. But then, he was mad. That's why.

She hugged her knees and began rocking. Every time she dipped forward she felt her thoughts twist into a tangle. She remembered the matchmakers. They had insisted she keep her husband happy. "If he doesn't want you, he can kick you out," Gulsom had warned. Where did that leave her? What if Jassem decided he did not want her anymore, took her room away and sent her to wander the streets? Would the Bedouins from the distant sands kidnap her and turn her into a slave?

Yaqoota had gone into detailed descriptions of how they chose their victims. "First, they check if you're all alone. Then they wait for you in the shadows." At this point, Yaqoota's eyes always pulsed with trepidation. "And then, when you don't expect it, three men surround you and stuff you in a sack. You don't have a chance of escape because you'll faint even before you can scream."

Every time she swayed back, Noora felt her head touch the wall, *tap, tap, tap*. But she would not stop. Her mind was choking with that fearful thought. There was her head, held tight in that sack. She could smell the stink of stale dust and old sweat rubbing off its rough yarn. No one would miss her if the Bedouins kidnapped her. After all, she had no family to protect her, to ask after her, to search for her if she disappeared. *Tap, tap, tap*. And another sound, too.

The knock on her door was light. Still, it jolted her. Was it Jassem coming to tell her to pack her things and go? She hurried to the door and opened it, saw Hamad standing in the glare, his arms clasped behind him. "What do you want?" she snapped. "Don't you know everyone is asleep?"

"Shh," he said, stepping back and looking around nervously. "Not so loud." His arms fell to his side, and she saw the white garment in his hand. "This suit will protect my father from jellyfish stings when he goes for the Big Dive. They say your stitches are strong, and I need to make sure the seams don't come undone." He spoke quickly, urgently.

"And how do you know I can do that?" She was annoyed at his intrusion. She was trying to think of a way of escape once those Bedouins abducted her, and before she could do that she had to pass through all that fear, with her head held so tight she could not loosen it from the sack. Now she would have to start all over, from the beginning, when she gets kidnapped.

"All of Wadeema knows you sew the best," Hamad said. "But if you can't do it, just tell me."

She expected him to turn around and leave. But he did not. How cheeky he was! She drew her *shayla* tight over her nose to embarrass him. Still he would not budge, and he kept staring at her under a sun that cast a straw-colored halo around his loosely turbaned head.

"Don't you know you are not supposed to come in here," Noora said. "Look at you, tiptoeing to my door, like a thief, to talk to me. What if someone sees you here?"

"I know, I know, but look, all the shutters and doors are closed. Everyone is asleep. I just need you to sew this."

"Yes but—"

"I'm not being sneaky coming at this time. It's the only time I can ask you to do this. If Jassem knew, or even Lateefa, they would refuse. They'd tell me to take it to the tailor." He shuffled on his feet. "I promised my father I would get this done. But I don't have the money to take it to a tailor."

Noora eased her grip on the *shayla* but kept watching him closely. Was he telling the truth? His hair was a mass of strings hugging his neck from under his *ghitra*. He had an ancient scar that cut a clean gap on the corner of his right eyebrow. And there was another scar, too, just like hers, under the left side of the chin. She was surprised she had never noticed either of them before. One on the right, one on the left. Strangely, they seemed to balance his face.

"You see," Hamad said. "My mother . . . well, her knuckles don't bend. They're as hard as a goat's hoof." He fiddled with the garment. "She just can't make a strong stitch anymore."

Finally he was showing some hesitation, and Noora pulled the garment out of his hands. It was faded by the sun and eaten by the sea. "Even if I stitch all those rips, there will be more," she said, rubbing the fabric between her fingers. She pointed at the area that was to cover the back of the legs. "This doesn't just need strong stitching at the seams. It needs big patches to cover these faded bits." Under the arms, the fabric was sadder than her flowered red dress of the mountains. "And here, look."

"You can't do it."

Noora watched the blood crawl into his ears, paint them so red under the sun that they looked as if they might pop. Now she was sure he was embarrassed, regretting having asked in the first place. She watched his head lower, only slightly. But his eyes remained fixed to her face, full of that same desperation she remembered seeing on the boat, all those months ago, when the wind had lifted that sheet.

He was about to leave. As he reached out for the garment, Noora held it tight. "It's all right," she said. "I'll do it."

Noora snuck her arms under the mattress, pulled out the body-suit, and fluffed it open. She smiled at her handiwork. Not only had she repaired the rips and strengthened the seams, but she had replaced large sections of it, using the extra white bits of cotton fabric she had collected from the dresses she'd made for all those village women. And now the bodysuit looked set, reinforced with shining new triangles and squares. *No jellyfish stings can get through it*, she thought.

It had taken her a whole week to stitch and patch the bodysuit. She had kept it hidden and had stolen the moments for sewing, when she was sure she would not be disturbed. If Shamsa saw what she was doing, she would surely make a big, embarrassing problem, and that was the last thing Noora needed at this point.

She had even kept Hamad's visit a secret from Yaqoota, who had asked her the day before whether Hamad had come to see her. It wasn't that she didn't trust Yaqoota, but her voice was so loud. And Noora had told her as much, which had upset her, too.

Walls had ears, and Yaqoota still hadn't learned to lower her voice when she spoke. "Why didn't he come to see you?"

"I don't know why and I don't care," Noora had whispered, hoping Yaqoota would do the same.

Instead, Yaqoota's voice came out in a blast. "But he told me he wanted to see you, to talk to you about something."

"And why do you care?" Noora hissed.

Yaqoota shrugged but would not speak softly. "I am just asking. And what's wrong with you, anyway? Why are you suddenly chomping your insides?"

Noora raised her hands. "Look, forget me. Just don't talk so loud."

"Loud?"

A shriek! Yaqoota's up-and-down voice was exasperating. Why couldn't she learn to speak softly, like everyone else? "Yes, loud."

"And why are you acting so snotty," Yaqoota said, "as if you're the favorite of the house?" Yaqoota pointed her nose up. "Snotty, snotty, snotty." Then, with demure steps, she tiptoed out of the room.

From that time, Yaqoota had stopped talking to Noora. But Noora wasn't too concerned. *A few days of sulking and she will be all right*, she thought. She lay the bodysuit on the bed and ran her palm along the creases to flatten them, frowning at the bits of the old fabric that snuck their tired threads here and there. It was not as perfect as she would have liked; it wasn't one clean piece of newness. Still, it could not be helped.

How would Hamad's eyes look when she handed it to him? Would they sparkle with silent approval? Would he notice? Ever since she had decided to fix the bodysuit, he seemed to be in the house more often, delivering this, picking up that. She had even spotted his shadow outside her window during the resting hours. Twice!

Whenever they came face-to-face, crossing the courtyard or in some other part of the house, they would both let their eyes look to the ground—at least she did. And somehow, she saw him in her mind, and she always wondered whether he saw her, too, in his own mind. Or maybe he opened his eyes when she looked down. And those were the thoughts that circled in her head, like mischievous fish, chasing one another's tails. The thoughts would not stop until she shook them away, slapped her cheeks for being so silly. She was acting as if she were committed to some guilty secret.

Noora drew lines with her fingers on the bodysuit and folded it into a neat square. Then she smoothed it again. Another week or two and the divers would be sailing away. And Jassem, too, off to India for trade. Deep inside, she felt some relief, but not enough to wipe away her anxiety at her shaky position in the household. She lifted the mattress and slid the folded garment under it. Later, she would try to send a silent message to Hamad, let him know that the bodysuit was ready.

28

Noora sat in front of the three large trunks that lined the wall of Lateefa's room. Brass studs, hammered into the thick wood, festooned the lids and sides. She ran her fingers over the arrangement—triangles put together to make stars—and, once more, in her most casual voice, asked, "Where are you going, *Ommi* Lateefa?"

And Lateefa's impatient answer was the same. "We, my child, we!" Her usual restraint was ruffled as she sat to one side in front of a smaller tin chest. Some new restlessness kept her rocking back and forth. "Well, what are you waiting for?" she said. "Open that middle trunk, take out my things. Let's pack."

Noora lifted the handle and pulled open the trunk. There were Lateefa's clothes, the same dresses, *thoubs*, *abayas*, and burkas they had packed and unpacked the day before, and for days before that, too.

"Take only one dress, the rest must be *thoubs*," she instructed. Lateefa preferred to wear loose, cotton *thoubs* in the hot weather. With its wide sleeves, from shoulder to waist, the garment was much more efficient at trapping breezes. "No, no, not in the middle, more to the right side," she said, as Noora placed a sky-blue *thoub* with yellow dots into the trunk. Lateefa blew an irritated puff into her burka. "Take it out, take it out. It is not folded neatly enough. Fold it again."

Noora did as she was told.

"All right, that's better," Lateefa said. "Now, that *abaya*."

The *abaya* was harder to fold. The fabric floated out like a flyaway tent. As she placed it on the ground, to wrap it as best she could, she felt Lateefa's scrutinizing eyes ready to pick on any mistake she might make. Those eyes seemed to follow her all the time, everywhere she went. The divers would be leaving soon, and Noora hadn't even been able to nod a direction to Hamad as to where she could leave the bodysuit for him to pick up. Whenever she faced him, she always worried that Lateefa was watching, and her neck would freeze and her eyes would fix ahead to some invisible point.

"Now, the burkas," Lateefa said, handing Noora an old strip of fabric. "Stack them on top of each other and wrap them in this. I don't want the indigo to seep out and color my clothes." She paused briefly before losing her patience once again. "Pah! Just take everything out, take it out! We'll pack later."

The next morning, Noora found out why they were packing, but not before breakfast. As Jassem and his wives settled around the breakfast mat, Shamsa hinted that she was pregnant. Again.

"Ah, I can't eat," Shamsa complained, stroking her stomach with glee. "I don't know what it is, but something is blocking my appetite. I feel nauseous." It was the same act every morning. Shamsa was giving Lateefa and Jassem hope, trying to put in their minds that the child would come through her. Shamsa sighed and wedged her hand under her *shayla* to neaten her flawless fringe. Was Noora the only person who noticed her smugness? Clinging to her wrist was another bangle. This one was flat, with a turquoise dot set in its gold filigree.

"Are you feeling sick, dear?" Lateefa mumbled. She hadn't quite finished munching her breakfast.

"A little," Shamsa said, and Noora wanted to see some ugliness in her parted lips, but there was none. They were as vibrant as the petals of a desert flower after an unexpected rain.

Lateefa touched Shamsa's head. "I think it's the weather, dear," she said.

"Have you packed my things?" Jassem asked Lateefa.

Lateefa closed her eyes solemnly. "That I am about to do."

"Well, Lateefa knows, but I suppose I had better tell the rest of you," he said. "I'm not going to India anymore."

Noora's eyes widened, and she opened her mouth to ask why when she felt the yolk of the egg she was eating dribble down the side of her chin—a warning to hold her tongue. She was not in a position to be so bold.

"Instead, I'm going to go to Leema. The rest of you will go to Om Al-Sanam, stay the summer there." He nodded his head wisely. "You will get more drafts in the *barasti* huts out there than over here."

Lateefa agreed with him. "Yes, much cooler, out there in the open desert."

"I don't need to tell you this, but this trip, the Big Dive . . .

well, it's going to be the last. It's costing too much, and let's be honest, there are simply no more pearls in the sea."

The last dive? No more pearls in the sea? There was not a hint of regret in his voice, not one thought for the divers and their families. Noora remembered Jassem's conversation with *noukhada* Hilal: all that money advanced to the divers, and now they would not be able to pay it back. What would they do? How would they feed their children? Noora pictured the divers roaming Leema's tight streets, begging for *ardees*, just like that madman.

Jassem's voice trailed back. "So I've decided not to waste money on the Big Dive, open other roads. The way to go is trade."

"The way to go is trade," Lateefa repeated, with a sober nod of her head.

"Yes, trade. Not just with India or Africa. But right here, in our own town, in Leema." Jassem rubbed his palms. "So many *Inglesis* roaming around, with so much money and so many goods. I must make friends with them so that we can buy and sell from one another." He leaned back and moved his tongue along the inside of his mouth, clicking away what egg and bread remained stuck to his gums. "Maybe I'm telling you more than you ought to know, being women and all, but it's good for you to understand a little about the world."

"Yes, trade is the way to go," Lateefa repeated one more time.

29

They set out under the violet of the dawn sky. Walking in the sand was not the same as climbing mountains, and no matter how lightly Noora stepped, the sand seeped into her slippers and settled between her toes. Again and again, she paused to shake her feet and let the sand trickle out, until Lateefa scolded her. "Walk on, walk on. Don't fall behind."

It was better to walk barefoot. Noora pulled off her slippers and caught up with Hamad and Yaqoota, who strode along the side of Lateefa's donkey. They were on their way to Om Al-Sanam, a desert where the dunes rose as the gentle camel humps it was named after. They would be staying there the full summer, far from the sticky heat of the coast.

Noora watched Lateefa's hips sway on a donkey that looked too small to carry her. Every now and then, it objected, pausing to shake its head, only to be whipped with a soft reed and

clicked back into a trot with a twist of her tongue. Secured behind her was her tin travel chest, filled with everything she
might need out in the dunes. Everyone else's belongings were
wrapped in small bundles of cloth. If Shamsa had been with
them, there might have been two travel chests, but Shamsa had
asked for permission to stay with her family, and Jassem had
agreed.

Noora was pleased she wouldn't have to deal with Shamsa's
moods and sneers. At the same time, she was bothered that both
Shamsa and Jassem would be staying at Leema for the summer.
So much time! Shamsa could poison Jassem's thoughts against
her, mold Jassem's mind however she wanted, establish her position in the household.

Noora wondered whether they were all thinking of the same
thing. It was hard to see Yaqoota's face, swallowed in its darkness by the plum sky. And Hamad, she tried to catch some appreciation in his face (after all, she'd managed to deliver the
bodysuit without being spotted just two days before), but he
would not look at her; he only stared straight ahead. He was
probably thinking of his father, left to sea on this same day
with the other divers, to search for those pearls.

"It will be better for us all out in those cool, white dunes
of Om Al-Sanam," Lateefa said. She sounded unperturbed,
her voice as soft as the plods of their feet on the sand. "There
the air will be dry, instead of all that humidity by the sea that
makes my blood curdle."

Noora watched her lean back with ease, holding on to the
chest, as the donkey struggled up a dune larger than the rest.
Its hooves dipped deep into the sand so that the tips of Lateefa's
slippers skimmed the surface. Her mind seemed empty of worries. Didn't she see Shamsa as a threat as well? She had closed

her eyes with clear-headed approval when Jassem had told her that Shamsa would be going to her family.

Such thoughts toppled on one another in Noora's head, till she decided to put her slippers back on. At least there would be the distraction of trapped sand caking her toes.

The first arrow of light pierced the sky, and Noora squinted at the cluster of *barasti* huts that made up the settlement. There were other people there as well, families from Leema who had come for the same reason: to get away from the sticky, salty heat of the sea. There were goats, chickens, donkeys, and a couple of camels, too.

Noora welcomed the noise and movement after their walk under the silence of sky and sand. The scent of freshly baked bread in thick puddles of ghee wafted into the air, and children scampered out of one *barasti* and into another. The flat-roofed palm-frond huts were scattered randomly in a large dip between the dunes, about twenty, all in all. Jassem's two huts stood at the end of the settlement, just under a gathering of three upright palm trees.

Hamad had brought everything they needed beforehand: pots and pans, cushions, flour, dates, rice, coffee, tea, goats, and chickens.

"There's a well over there," Lateefa said, pointing ahead, "with water as cool as a winter's rain."

Noora could not see it and wondered how anyone could find anything in such a vast expanse of shifting swells and hollows.

Lateefa quickly ordered the organization of the sleeping arrangements. She would take the first *barasti* (the one with the wind tower made of sack cloth). Noora would share the second hut with Yaqoota. A wooden ladder led to Hamad's sleeping quarters. It was a palm-frond platform on four wooden stilts situated a little distance away, as was proper.

As the rays rose higher into the sky, the heat blasted out of the sand. They had unpacked, cooked and eaten lunch, and now Noora staggered into her hut. In the dimness, she rested her eyes from the sun's glare and slumped loose-limbed next to Yaqoota on the woven palm mats that covered the soft sand.

The sweat clung to her hairline, and she pinned her face to the elongated gaps in the palm-frond walls, waiting for that mysterious breeze to wriggle through one wall and out the other. And then it came. A tired breath that was certainly drier but just as hot as the air by the sea. "So hot," she said.

Yaqoota spat out her response. "Hot is hot, whether you're here or there. Hot . . . is . . . hot." They were her first words since they had left Wadeema, and her tone was as dry as the desert they were sitting in the middle of.

"What are you so upset at me for?" Noora asked.

"Hmph. You should know."

"Oh? And what if I don't know?"

"You know everything—especially how to keep secrets."

"There are no secrets to keep."

"Just tell me the truth. That's all I want. Then I'll know whether you're my friend or not."

"What truth?"

"Humph."

"If you're talking about Hamad, he didn't come to see me as you think he did."

"If you say so."

30

In the desert, the sun seems much bigger and somehow rounder and brighter. It washes the color out of the sky and blanches the dunes. Only in the late afternoons does the sun forgive, calling back its strongest rays to be stored for the next day. That's when Noora wandered into the mass of humps that surrounded them.

Along with the vast emptiness of the desert came a strange informality. She could leave the huts and head in whichever direction she wished. Not that there was much difference, since every rising dune looked the same. Still, she liked that she could do that. Now, she sat on the edge of a lofty hill and burrowed her feet into the sand, watching a group of girls tumble down the slope.

"Come on," shouted a little girl wearing a canary-yellow dress. "Swim down with us. Race us." She was one of the older girls, perhaps seven or eight. She was climbing up the hill toward Noora, her shoulder-length hair crumpling into tangles as it began loosening out of her plaits.

Noora smiled at her. "I'll get all messy. And look at your hair! Here, let me fix it."

The girl pulled away. "It's only sand," she said. "You just shake it off, like this." She waggled her head and, finally, her plaits fell open. "Come on, let's go."

Noora shook her head and wished Yaqoota was with her. They would have giggled and swam down the dune without a second thought. How stubborn that slave girl was! Ten days of sulking in Wadeema and another ten since they had arrived at Om Al-Sanam, and still Yaqoota refused to shake away her hurt. And now it was too late for Noora to confess that she had been right all along. That would just lead to more suspicion in the future. No, Noora decided, she must stick to her story. The girl was pulling her arm. "All right, all right," Noora said. "What's your name anyway?"

"Afra."

Noora grinned and secured her *shayla* around her head. "You're going to make me messy, too," she said, lying on her stomach.

"Arms out, straight in front of you," ordered Afra.

Noora did what she was told.

"Now swim!"

Noora clamped her eyes and mouth shut and, headfirst, slid down the dune. Sand everywhere! It trickled into her nostrils and seeped into her ears, snuck into her *shayla* and collected in her dress. Every time the sand tried to swallow her, she tossed it to the side with broad strokes. She was swimming, faster and faster. She could see the world slide past, even though her eyes were closed. Only at the bottom did she let the sand drown her.

And then she heard the mothers call their children back to the *barastis*. Noora did not open her eyes, just flipped onto her back and opened her arms and legs like a star, listening to the children's hollers as they rushed back home.

What an exhilarating feeling! That plunge down the dune seemed to free her after all those months in Wadeema of watching how she talked and walked. She yawned and stretched her arms tight to the fingers, lengthened her feet to a point. She stayed that way for a long time before relaxing her limbs. And that's when she felt a darkness creep over her face. She snapped open her eyes to find Hamad standing over her with crossed arms. She sat up instantly and squinted.

"What cheek you have," she scolded. The sun was behind him, and she shifted to one side so that she could see his face better, find out whether he was smirking. "What nerve, coming out of nowhere like that . . . like a, like a . . ."

"Like a thief?"

She shook her head and frowned.

"Like a ghost?" He grinned.

"Worse than a ghost! The rudest . . . most disrespectful of . . . of . . ." Again, the word would not fall off the tip of her tongue. Her *shayla* had somehow twisted around her neck, and, as she loosened it, she felt the sand plop out of it. What a mess she was!

"Well, this ghost just came down to thank you for the lovely work you did with that bodysuit. My father kept asking me which tailor I took it to, and every time I had to disappear, pretend someone was calling me or needing me urgently."

"Well, I'm sure that wasn't so hard for you," Noora said, "seeing as you are so talented at disappearing and appearing." She stood up and shook free the rest of the sand from her dress, brushed off the grains that caked her face, all the while half-listening to Hamad thank her once more.

"I feel I have to do something for you in return," he said. "What can I do?"

"Nothing," Noora said. "Just don't make problems."

31

The dunes sped along with her till she left them behind and soared into the sky. Even though she tightened it on her head and secured it under her arms, her *shayla* ballooned and flattened—again and again. Noora could not get enough of the swing. She heard the tired pieces of rope grate the leaning palm they were slung over, but she just kept going higher. How liberating it felt! She always arrived before the children to enjoy it on her own. "Hamad fixed it for us." That's what Afra had told her. But Noora knew better. As the afternoon air raced over her face, she smiled. She knew he had hung the swing for her.

There he was, like every afternoon, crouched on the top of the dune, watching her. And she let him. She would not slow down because caution did not fit with the reckless informality of swinging. He was rewrapping his *ghitra* now, a graceful flick of his arm, which she trapped in her mind with a quick twist of her head. And the ease of his gesture surprised her once more, as did everything else about him lately.

Something was happening. Hamad was changing. No longer did his shoulders creep up to his neck with frustration. Nor did his mouth pout with that angry sulk she had gotten used to seeing in Wadeema. And his eyes . . . those unfathomable eyes no longer glanced at the ground. Hamad kept them open, let the sun burnish them russet.

Perhaps it was the informality of not having walls to box you in. Maybe it was because Jassem wasn't with them. Perhaps it was all that emptiness around them. Whatever the reason, every move Hamad made exuded an ease that was not there before.

The children were coming. She heard their voices before they appeared at the top of the dune. Noora slowed down. Her turn on the swing was coming to an end. She watched the girls huddle around Hamad and drag him down the slope, their excited squeals begging him to "hang another swing, please."

His legs, lithe as a deer's, sank into the sand in broad strides, and Noora felt her cheeks light up like hot coals. She blamed it on the swinging and kept watching. "He's like my brother." That's what she whispered under her breath as the swing swayed to a halt. She called him that, too, "Brother Hamad," as was appropriate.

She didn't feel as if she was breaking any rules by meeting him at the palms every afternoon, which is what they called the broad dip from which a cluster of six palm trees sprouted. After all, they were always surrounded by children, and adults keeping an eye on the children made it all right. And no one seemed to care, anyway. Neither Lateefa, who floated out of one hut and into the other with a smile on her face, as if the desert arid-ity had dried the grumbles out of her speech, nor Yaqoota, who remained in her unending bad humor. They never asked where Noora went every afternoon or whom she saw.

"I don't have any more rope," Hamad objected once they had reached the swing. "Besides, there's only one bent tree. The others are straight. You tell me, girls, where would I hang another swing?"

"Next to the first one, next to the first one," the girls pleaded. "Pleeease!"

And there was Afra's voice, always bolder than the rest. "You must make us at least three more," she commanded. "Fit them next to each other. We will fetch you all the rope you need."

Hamad laughed again, and this time Noora joined him while Afra scrunched her nose at them in confusion.

"You must have been just like Afra," Hamad said to Noora as they settled to watch the girls. "So cheeky, so bold."

"I don't know." Noora shrugged her shoulders. "Maybe . . . a long time ago."

"You know, sister, if we don't watch them, make sure every girl gets her turn on that swing, Afra wouldn't give anyone a chance," Hamad said. "Look at her. There she goes again."

She certainly had the bullying of the rich in her. Afra was hugging the swing to her canary-yellow dress with one arm and pushing a plump girl, older and taller than she, out of the way. "It'll fall if you sit on it," she screamed. "You're too fat."

Noora put on her strict voice. "It's her turn. She hasn't sat on it yet. Give it to her."

Afra kicked the sand and dropped the swing, rooted her fists to her hips, and warned the girl, "Not very long, though. If it breaks, the rest of us won't get another turn."

Noora nodded her satisfaction. Wasn't that why they were there, to keep a vigilant supervision over the girls?

Noora wasn't sure what she enjoyed more, the swinging or her conversations with Hamad. He let her say what she wanted. And she did, with an abandon that surprised her. Under the saffron sun of afternoon, Noora spoke of her childhood in the mountains, her mother's fatal illness, her father's disappearance, and Sager's selling her off. And when she thought she might have said too much, she would look into his eyes and sigh, content to spot the shine in them that encouraged her. And then she'd have no regrets that she had said too much.

He spoke, too, but his words came out like the waves of the sea. He would talk a little, hold back a little, then say some more. His voice could be the sea's soft ripples on a still day or the firm slaps on shore when the tide rolls in with a strong wind.

"I don't want to answer to anyone, brother Hamad. I don't want to be afraid," she told him one afternoon. She had hopped off the swing as soon as she saw him approach, even though the children hadn't arrived yet.

He joined her under the palms and said, "I know what that is like." There were his eyes, his sun-struck eyes, assuring her that she was safe to let out all that troubled her. She sat hugging her knees, the cushioning of the warm sand around her burrowed feet.

"How would you know?" Noora said. "You are a man. You can do what you want, go wherever you please. You can decide what to do with your life." She let out a hopeless sigh. "Me? I belong to Jassem, and he decides my fate. All I can do is wait and see what will happen."

He nodded. "True, sister, but don't think I am completely free here. To live the way you want, man or woman, you need money. And I don't have any."

"But my hus— Jassem . . . well, he pays you."

"Coins," said Hamad. "He promised to take me with him when he traveled for trade, teach me how to become a merchant. That was four years ago. And still, nothing."

She wasn't in the mood to talk about her husband. "You don't need him, brother Hamad," she said. "You can go and work for someone else. As I said, *masha' Allah*, you can manage to do anything if you really wanted it."

"I bet the same goes for you."

"Hmm." She smiled and pulled her feet out of the sand, straightened them in front of her and leaned back, supporting herself on her hands. A soft breeze teased the branches of the palm above them, and she watched the ripples of sunlight dance on her feet.

Hamad said, "How about if I told you that ever since I was a child I have wanted something so badly that I was sure it would happen."

"And?"

"It didn't." Hamad blinked at the sun, and Noora was intrigued. She waited for him to tell her more, but he didn't. Instead, he looked down at his feet and followed the movement of a black beetle with a humped back that was beginning to climb onto his large toe.

"Well, why didn't it happen?" she asked.

He shook the beetle off his foot and took a deep breath. And Noora knew that the biggest wave was about to spill on the shore.

"There's a shop in the souk," he began. "It's got all those things I wanted to own as a child: the stone that pulls the diver down, the cotton bodysuit that protects him from jellyfish stings, the wooden nose-clips, the leather finger stalls, the basket, and that sharp scoop—you know, the one divers use to pull out the oyster from its shell. And I always dreamed of owning them." He paused and his lips curled down toward his chin. "I don't go by that shop anymore," he said. "You see, sister Noora, it reminds me of my shame." He sighed. "All those bits and pieces remind me of my uselessness."

"Shame? Uselessness?" What was he talking about?

He flicked the sand with his toes. "You see, I have always wanted to be a diver. When I was a boy, I kept dreaming the same thing. I was on this small boat on choppy water, on a cloudless day, under a scorching sun. It was always full of tired divers." Hamad wasn't blinking at the sun anymore. Instead, his eyes remained fixed, defiant, against the afternoon rays. Then he sneered. "It's a boat of neglect, you see. Why I wanted to be on it, I don't know." He raised his brows. "No hope in it; it might as well sink. But then, something happens in this dream of mine."

"What, brother Hamad, what?"

Hamad snorted. "I become the hero! As the divers give up, I take one last plunge into the dark, dark deep. Under I stay for ninety-seven, ninety-eight, ninety-nine counts—so much longer than any other diver could stay without breath. Then, just as I am taken for dead, I come back up." Hamad did a pretend-gasp for air and raised his arms with victory. "The divers cheer and clap for me, the champion, as I hand them the biggest pearl they have ever seen. 'Hamad has saved us,' they cry." Although he was laughing, his chin would not stop twitching.

Noora was laughing as well, even though she knew she shouldn't. An unfulfilled dream is like spilled milk on dry earth. It sinks instantly and leaves a useless patch to remind you that you can never taste it.

"What a sweet tale," he said, and halted the laugh with a sharp snap of his fingers. "All it took was one dive for that dream to disappear. You see, sister, the sea has eaten my father's health. His eyes are foggy, his skin is like ripped leather, and his bones—well, you can hear those bones crack every time he bends. I have always wanted to save him from all that, and I was always sure I could, sort of turn into that hero in my dreams, the one who would find those riches—to save the whole family, really."

Should she change the subject? Yes, no, yes, no? She decided not to. Maybe he would feel better, the way she felt better when she spoke of something that hurt.

"Two summers ago, I was ready," Hamad said. "I had been practicing hundreds of times holding my breath in the shallows of Wadeema. Then, once we were out, I stood on the edge of that boat. I remember I was right next to my father, scanning the water for jellyfish. When I saw none, I didn't even bother pulling on my bodysuit. My father told me not to sink deeper than him." Hamad deepened his voice. " 'Don't think you can beat the sea,' he said to me. And I was just nodding at him. I couldn't wait to get in! I'd spotted a dark patch at the bottom—a rock. And I thought, that's it. The oysters must be clinging to it. Waiting for me.

"Then I locked my nostrils with the nose-clip and filled my lungs with air. And I sank after the divers. Down, down, down, we went. And then I got panicked. I couldn't tell which of the divers my father was. The water stung my eyes and I wanted to rub them. But I didn't dare. I was terrified I might mix up the ropes. Right hand to take me down, left hand for up. You see, there were two of them, one attached to the weight that was pulling me down, the other clasped to my left hand—my lifeline. One tug and the hauler on the boat knows he must pull me up."

The air felt thin and Noora breathed deeply. What was it like with all that water pressing on him, not allowing him to breathe? She lapped the perspiration that had gathered over her lips with her tongue and waited for the rest.

"I remember wondering how I was going to collect the oysters if I had this fear of freeing my hands from the rope. And that's when my problem began." Hamad paused and pulled his feet out of the sand, took his time as he folded them under him. And Noora wanted to scream at him to go on, tell her what had happened next.

As if guessing what was on her mind, he said, "Pain, like you wouldn't believe—all the way inside my ears and under my eyes. I shook my head, but that didn't help. I tried to pop my ears, but the pain only grew worse." He cringed and pressed his ears. "It began dribbling into the sides of my neck and throbbing. Argh! Such a throb, behind my eyeballs, everywhere!"

She could hear the children's voices from behind the dune and felt irritated at the coming intrusion. She was under the water with Hamad, sharing his pain. She leaned closer. She had to know what he did next.

Hamad clapped his hands. Noora winced and pulled back.

"I tried to slow down," he said, "but that stone was speeding into the deep, pulling me with it. I was so scared. I was kicking and forgetting to yank the rope, and all the time this horrible pain. The water was so thick around me, it was swallowing me."

The children were at the top of the dune now, calling to Noora and Hamad. She ignored them. "Tell me, tell me quick," she urged. "What did you do?"

"I could have drowned right then, but *Allah*, He was merciful. I must have been struggling so hard that the hauler understood I was in deep trouble." He turned toward the children and watched them slide down the dune. As usual, Afra was in the lead. "When I popped up on the surface, I was like a dying fish, belly up and struggling to breathe."

32

Early one morning Noora peeked through Lateefa's *barasti* and saw her rummaging through her trunk. One by one, Noora watched her pull out the *thoubs*, *abayas*, and *serwals*. "Where is it?" Lateefa muttered loudly.

Noora entered and was about to ask what she was looking for when Yaqoota pushed her way past her. "I can't find it anywhere, *Ommi* Lateefa," she said.

"We probably didn't bring it then," Lateefa said. "Your fault for not reminding me."

"My fault?" Yaqoota objected, and for a moment Noora was caught off guard by that high-pitched squeal she had not heard for so long. Yaqoota lifted an accusing finger, sharp as a spear, and froze it at the tip of Noora's nose. "It was her! Not me, *Ommi* Lateefa. She's the one who packed your travel chest. She's the one who forgot your mirror."

"It doesn't matter who packed, Yaqoota," said Lateefa, quietly. "You should know to check what is in the chest, even after it has been packed. Noora is new in our house. She doesn't know the things I need."

Yaqoota scrunched her nose. "But you're the one who told her what to pack."

"Shh, child! No need to make a storm about this."

"But you have your mirror," Noora said. "It's right over there, in the corner by your perfumes."

Yaqoota waved her arms in the air like an octopus. "Not that one," she said. "That one is sooo small she has to hold it sooo far to see her face properly."

"My eyes," Lateefa explained. "I can't see so well if it's too close. And it's too small anyway. Even if I hold it back, I can see only this part." She tapped the side of her forehead. "Or this part." She touched the opposite side. "It's the bigger mirror I need, the one with the bronze handle and colored, glass bits stuck in it."

Noora pretended to understand the urgency with a bob of her head.

"I must have it," Lateefa insisted.

And Noora nodded some more.

Lateefa threw a casual wave at Noora. "You must go and get it for me."

"I'll go," said Yaqoota, jumping to her feet. "I can get your mirror."

Lateefa shook her head. "No, I want you to stay here in case I need anything. Noora can go." She paused. "And Hamad, too—he knows the way, and can watch out for her in case there is any danger."

"Danger? She was born in the mountains, *Ommi* Lateefa, where snakes jump at you from under every stone! Green snakes, black snakes, striped snakes, spotted snakes." Yaqoota's laugh was full of the venom of those same snakes. "She can handle any danger that comes her way. She can even scare bandits away just by messing her hair and waving her arms like a madwoman."

"Shush, you insolent girl. If it's not Shamsa, it's you. Why can't you treat Noora like your sister?"

"Different color," Yaqoota sang. "When you are lighter, you think the darker one has no brains, can't see or understand." She turned to Noora. "Isn't that right, sisss . . . sissster?"

"Enough! Noora is a wife of the *arbab*." Lateefa's eyes bulged out from behind her burka, two shiny pebbles, the anger in them held firm. "She will be the mother to his children one day. You must respect her when you talk to her."

Yaqoota scowled and stormed out of the hut.

"Ehh . . . Bin-Surour!" called Lateefa.

"He is like my brother and we are going to talk a lot on our walk to Wadeema." Noora repeated the whisper again and again. And yet she felt a gush of restlessness speed through her like a flash flood through a *wadi*—a flash flood that uprooted bushes, ripped trees, even washed away whole sections of the gorge. She breathed deeply to slow her thumping heart. *It's the heat*, she thought.

"Why this, why that? You always spend too much time thinking about things." That's what Hamad had told Noora one time. And she had said that she liked to understand better and make a list of her options, so she wouldn't have to decide on something there and then. Now she had a new list of everything she had to do before setting off for Wadeema.

She would wear her better dress and cover it with the blue *thoub* with the delicate floral spray of embroidery on the chest. Just right. Of course, all the layers of clothing would have to be incensed so that the trail of *ood* peelings and musk could waft out with her every move. She would polish clean her teeth with a *neem* tree twig, wash her hair and twist it into two plaits, keep it neat with a stroke of jasmine oil, dab a dot of amber essence behind each ear. And naturally, there was the kohl—always the kohl.

She walked out of the hut tapping one finger on the others, counting, until the noon's sharp rays dazzled her, made her forget where she was going and what she needed to do. Then she remembered the pouch of red argil in her pocket. That's what she had to do first, wash her hair. She hopped over the scalding sand and crouched in the shade behind the huts.

As she emptied the powdered clay into her hair, she heard the rustle of fronds as Yaqoota entered the hut, puffing and grunting, in hurried steps that seemed to carry her in circles. She was like a caged wildcat, and her intensity infected Noora as she rubbed the stickiness out of her scalp.

All that urgency! They became like creatures of the desert, like the nervous jerboas always hopping out of danger, like the tiny ginger ants that ran so swiftly you couldn't see their spindly legs touch the ground, like those sand fish she sometimes spotted diving into the dunes quicker than the wind's lift of fine granules. They were so at home in the velvety mounds where there was nothing hard to bash into. *It's the heat*, she thought. The heat demanded that it be that way.

Only Lateefa remained unaffected. Cool as the moon glow, she carried a sedate smile that tightened the dips under her eyes. Lately, whenever she spoke to Noora, her words were like droplets of pure honey, sweet with only a slight bite in the aftertaste.

Why? Noora thought, and heard her heart thump louder. Why was that mirror so important to Lateefa? They had already spent half the hot months at Om Al-Sanam. Why couldn't Lateefa wait till they returned to Wadeema? It wasn't the distance that bothered Noora. Wadeema was not so far, so she and Hamad could easily be back by sunset. It was something else.

A hush mingled with the heat as Noora tipped the earthen jug over her head to soak her scalp. Yaqoota's march had halted and there was no noise coming out of Lateefa's *barasti*. Noora shrugged away the urge to investigate since she had to hurry. She rinsed a few more times, till the water ran clear.

33

They stopped to rest on the slope of a high dune. Even though she was thirsty, Noora would not guzzle the water. She lifted the burka just enough to sneak in the water skin to her pouted lips. And then she let a little of it slip down the sides of her lips, like the dew of dawn along the petals of a flower that was waking up to morning's light. She could have tossed the date Hamad handed her into her mouth, but she didn't. Instead, she held it just under her burka and nibbled it, letting the tiny bites rest on her tongue, all the while conscious of the subtle roll of her mouth. There was deliberation to her every move, a careful design to bring out all the femininity that was in her. And Hamad was watching her, watching and pretending he wasn't.

Every time she looked up at him, he blinked away the discreet desire in his eyes and glazed them, fixing them to some distant bush behind her. Such were the little games that set off the flutters in her heart. She could go on and on, knowing he was observing every tiny gesture she made.

Now she wanted him to drown in the deep wells of her kohl-lined eyes. She tilted her head just enough for the sun to fall through the slits of her burka. And then she stayed that way. She would not blink, only let her eyes take in all that light, let the green in them grow as bright as emeralds.

That sun! A blood-red ball cradled in a broad smile of cloud. So bold! It was daring her to go on. She adjusted her *abaya* and *shayla* with a light stroke to let more of her forehead show, pictured her olive skin turn radiant under its ruby rays. And that's when a sudden gust lifted the covers off her head. They slithered along her back to settle around her hips. This was not one of her little flirtations. It was the wind playing its naughty tricks once again, just as it had done on that boat, all that time ago.

Hamad was watching her intently now. No longer did his eyes dart away. Without the familiar feel of cloth on her head, she was overcome by a peculiar timidity. Feeling exposed, she quickly pulled the covers back up just as a whirring, muffled growl broke the hush of the desert.

The sound traveled along the rolling dunes as a dull rumble. The veins in Hamad's neck expanded as he craned his neck east to west, north to south, in an attempt to guess where it was coming from. It was hard to tell and, finally, he lifted a handful of sand and let it seep through his fingers. "There," he said, pointing east.

Before Noora could respond, he yanked her wrist and pulled her up the dune. His palm was moist and she was surprised by the strength in it. Somehow, that strength did not fit with the agility of his lean build. They crouched behind the clumps of unruly grasses that crowned the crest and waited, like hunters stalking their prey. "There, sister, do you see it?" Hamad said, pointing ahead.

Noora watched the plume of dust rise some distance away. Then the Jeep came into sight. It was the color of dusty leaves with a growl louder than its size. Like a rolling wave, it slid into another depression and disappeared.

As the Jeep drew closer to them, they dipped their heads lower, even though they knew they were well camouflaged behind the bushes. Finally, it stopped on a level dune just below them, its sputtering engine falling silent like the breath of an exhausted camel.

Two men and a woman jumped out. When they spoke, the words fell out of pursed lips in soft plops that sounded like dripping water.

"*Inglesis!*" Hamad whispered.

Noora nodded. Jassem had told her all about them. They had come to search for *bitrole*—a sticky, black oil, hidden deep under the sand, which was meant to make life easy. They lived in army barracks in the salt flats outside Wadeema and, every now and then, drove in the same shape and color of Jeep along the shore.

Noora had spotted them through the window of the men's *majlis*. One time they had wandered so close to that window that she could see their eyes, like bright marbles with every color of the sky and sea in them. But they were always men. This time, there was a woman, too.

Noora was taken aback by her dress. It wasn't the print of giant flowers of sunshine yellow; it was the shape, which was nothing like the loose dresses that kissed her own ankles with every step. This dress—the *Inglesi* dress—curved along the woman's ribs and bunched at the waist. From there, it flared into an umbrella that stopped short just below the knees. There were her exposed legs, pale and lucid, just like the lizards that clung to the roof of her room in Wadeema.

Noora's eyes snuck back to Hamad. Lying on his stomach, propped up on his elbows, he was watching the English people intently. The sun's red glow had settled evenly in his ears, and she expected him to voice some disapproval at the exhibition of bare skin. After all, there was none of the modesty that guided their ways.

"Shameless!" That's what she expected him to say when he opened his mouth.

But he didn't. Instead, he whispered, "That's the box that makes reflections of things."

Noora curled her lips with puzzlement and looked back. Indeed, there was a compact piece of metal as large as her two palms put together. One of the men was fixing it on three metal legs.

"See it, sister? It's called a camera," Hamad said.

Noora watched the man glue the side of his face to the box and waited. When nothing happened, her gaze drifted back to the woman, whose age, although young, Noora could not guess. Her gold tresses were as thin as silk threads, and even though the breeze was light, it lifted each string as easily as it did the fine desert sand. She was stroking the other man on his shoulder now, laughing so heartily, so naturally, that Noora's mouth unlatched with astonishment at the casualness of the woman's gestures.

He laughed, too, and threw an arm around her shoulder, squeezing her bare arm with the tips of his fingers before flattening his hand into a generous palm that followed the giant flowers of sunshine yellow that hugged her waist. He stroked those flowers so hard Noora thought he might want to wipe them away.

They did not seem to care that there was another man present, even when that man removed his face from the camera, looked over his shoulder at them, and shouted some more popping words through his puckered lips.

Was he telling them off? Noora waited for the couple to separate, as was correct in the company of someone else. Instead, they cackled and hugged each other. He pulled her tight to his chest. And then the woman lifted her face and smiled at him, unflustered, to bond her mouth to his.

Noora gawked at those mouths. Stuck together like that! She felt confused and uncomfortable, and yet she was unable to look away. Was Hamad watching, too, or was he still scrutinizing the camera? She did not dare look at him. Only when she heard him grunt did she drop her face into her elbows. It was time to pull away. With a quick swivel, she sat up and rowed her way down the dune.

34

A heightened vigor touched Noora as she poked through Lateefa's trunk, searching for the mirror. Was that a kiss, the way their tongues met like that? She felt like a child trying to understand a difficult word.

Hamad was standing at Lateefa's doorway, waiting. She knew he was thinking about it, too. From the moment she had slid down the dune, they had walked the rest of the way in silence, embarrassed by what they had seen—or at least she knew she was. How clumsy she had been, like those camels with their legs tied so they couldn't wander too far. She had tripped twice over the hem of her dress in the deep sand when she had tried to walk faster, as if getting to Wadeema would wipe away her discomfort. And her hands! She wasn't sure what to do with them. When she swung them, they gathered too much momentum, and when she clutched them to her chest, they molded too tightly to her skin. Nothing felt right on that walk.

That kiss! Was it something she could talk about? She and Hamad were comfortable speaking about so many things. Still, Noora had long decided to hold back what she thought was too intimate, like her experience with Rashid. And now, the kiss. She could not chase it out of her mind. As she scraped the inside of the trunk, trying to feel the hard handle of the mirror through the clothes, she imagined those tongues entwined like mating snakes.

"It's the way they do things." Hamad had moved closer, and now his voice was a murmur hovering just above her head.

Bent over the trunk and on her knees, Noora felt her hands hesitate in the middle of the fluff of garments. His breath was falling warm on her neck. She picked up the sound of three discreet sniffs and closed her eyes, imagined he was catching the whiff of the amber oil that she had dotted behind her ears. It was a quick three sniffs, but she savored them before opening her eyes and turning to face him.

Hamad straightened up and looked away to hide his embarrassment, but the blush had already settled in his ears and was still there when he looked back. He cleared his throat and said, "That's how they kiss. I have seen it before . . . kissing like that when no one is watching, when they are alone."

"But they weren't alone, brother. There was another man with them."

"In front of their own people, it's okay."

Noora frowned and drummed her fingers on her crossed arms. He should have told her earlier, then she could have shrugged that English kiss away. Instead, he had let her walk all that way feeling uncomfortable, stumbling and tripping with uneasiness.

"Well, did you find the mirror?" he asked.

"No."

Hamad retreated to the doorway, and while he waited, Noora took her time finding the mirror with a leisurely shuffle from one trunk to the next. Even from that distance, she felt his touch—without his having to touch her. It was a pretend touch, of course. He was like a tender spirit that enveloped her skin, its warmth a lingering encouragement to a desire that felt so natural she could see only the good in it.

When she reached the last trunk and still could not find the mirror, she scanned the rectangular room as if seeing it for the first time. Still so many places to look. Her eyes ran lazily along the colored crystal bottles and bowls that decorated the room. They sat on onion-shaped alcoves carved into the walls. Since it wasn't being used, Lateefa's mattress was rolled and stacked under the four-poster bed in the corner. The bed was covered with *takyas*, large cushions decorated with silk borders and squares of a red, green, and blue patchwork. She would have to move those to see if the mirror was under them.

Overlooking its heaviness from being stuffed with all that cotton, she plucked the first *takya* off the bed. Immediately it slipped out of her fingers. "It's all right," she said, as Hamad hurried to help her.

They reached down at the same time and hit their foreheads so hard Noora felt the pain shoot down the side of her neck.

"Ow!"

"Arkh!"

Hamad's head felt like wood. She flopped back and pressed her palm to her forehead, knowing that it would bruise.

Hamad was on his knees and by her side instantly. "Are you all right?"

Noora didn't answer. Thoughts of how she would explain the bruise to Lateefa raced through her mind. What would she say? The *takya* was too heavy? A bruise caused by a cushion sounded absurd, and she began giggling.

She could see Hamad was concerned, but the more he stared into her face with those grim eyes, the harder it was to stifle her chuckles. And when she noticed Hamad's shoulders shudder, infected by her glee, she finally let go.

She couldn't remember ever having laughed so loudly. Tears streamed down her face, and she thought of the kohl spilling out and streaking her cheeks. As the stitches of hilarity bit into her stomach, she thought of how puffed her eyes would look at the end of her laughing fit. Better! Then Lateefa would assume she couldn't stop weeping from the pain! After what seemed an eternity of merriment, she couldn't remember what had set her off in that way to begin with. All she noticed was that she was leaning forward, propped up on an elbow, her aching forehead close to Hamad's.

His laugh began to melt into a soft titter. His breath began to blow hot. Noora sniffed the tears away and wiped the runny kohl from under her eyes. Still, that steaming breath—so near, so thick she felt she could slice it with a knife.

And then he leaned closer. She felt his *ghitra* brush her cheek. And on her bruise, he placed his lips and held them there.

It seemed right, even though she knew it was wrong, and Noora closed her eyes.

35

Somewhere along their walk back to Om Al-Sanam, they stopped calling each other brother and sister.

The sun's last pink glow sank into the horizon just as Noora slipped into Lateefa's *barasti*, hoping she could drop off the mirror and go. But Lateefa was waiting for her, legs stretched straight in front of her, rubbing her knees.

"*Masha' Allah*, you're back, and with the mirror, too!" said the older woman.

Noora nodded, thankful for the lantern's weak flame, which cast broad shadows in all the right places, but still Noora would not tidy away the strand of hair she had purposely pulled out of her plaits. From under her *abaya* it spilled thick as a horse's tail over the bruise she was trying to hide.

"Well, where did you find it?" Lateefa asked.

"On one of the shelves," Noora mumbled. She had to get out as soon as she could. Her mind was like a twirling dust storm, filled with so much sand that it was hard to see clearly. Too many questions might make her nervous, make her say the wrong thing.

She handed Lateefa the mirror, but as she turned to leave, Lateefa clutched her wrist and pulled her back. "Wait," she said. "Tell me all about your journey."

Noora went limp as a thirsty flower. Her tongue felt thick, as if it were weighed down in a mouth full of clay. Would she be able to speak?

"Sit with me a little and tell me all about it."

Her knees wobbled as she sank onto crossed legs. The silence that followed did not help, and she felt the rush of tiny tremors along the length of her arms.

"You're shivering," Lateefa observed. "You must be exhausted with that long walk." And then Lateefa did exactly what Noora feared. Lateefa reached out to touch her head, flung the horse's tail out of Noora's eyes, and settled her prying eyes on the bruise. "What happened to your head?" she asked.

Noora gulped and mumbled, "Knocked it."

"Yes, yes, knocked it. A little accident, I think." Lateefa nodded with knowledge. "On the door, I think."

"Mmm, yes, the door."

"So easy to do that. It has happened to me, so many times."

Noora looked down and twiddled her fingers in her lap, tried to remember when she last saw the careful older woman bump into a door or knock herself on any other piece of furniture. There was a studied consistency to Lateefa's movements, from her calculated slides off the bed in the mornings to the way she leaned so thoroughly onto her knees whenever she got up. She even plucked her dress up to her shins before taking those tiny footsteps that carried her from one part of the house to the other. No! Lateefa could never knock her head on the door!

Noora looked back up at Lateefa, an unruffled queen, her eyes half-closed with self-assurance. There was a calmness that varnished her lids. And her silence! Why wasn't she asking more questions? Lateefa's silence disturbed Noora the most.

That night the moon was a mighty ball of light. It seeped through the gaps in the palm-frond walls and spat patterns on the ground, distorted squares and jagged lines that Noora broke as she hopped in silent agitation from one end of the hut to the other. A doomed chicken running away from the ax, that's what she thought of. A panicked chicken, unable to reason, in an aimless flutter. That's what she was.

She paused over Yaqoota, sleeping hard and heavy even though it was an airless night. Yaqoota's hums of inhalations and groans of exhalations made Noora's mouth curl with scorn. Yaqoota had none of her worries.

Her tongue felt heavy in her mouth in the stillness of the night, and she began to walk up and down again. Had Lateefa smelled the scent of lovemaking on her skin? Noora had been thorough in washing it away. She had emptied three earthen jars over her head, made sure the water ran the length of her body, under her arms, behind her knees, and in that most secret of places.

She stopped pacing once more and the palm-frond wall rustled as she leaned on it. She thought of Hamad, and the details of what had happened swam in her head like spiraling tadpoles in a pond.

Hamad had pulled away after that kiss to her forehead, as if waiting for her to slap him or storm out of the room. Instead, she had remained passive, feeling her eyes turn into bottomless pools on which floated a silent willingness.

He had hugged her awkwardly, and then leaned away once more.

And that's when she should have stopped him. After all, he was giving her a chance to change her mind. When she didn't, everything else had followed. It had felt so right, even though she knew it was wrong.

There was no clumsiness in his next embrace. Hamad had seized her back into his arms and held her tight. She could not move, and yet she did not feel trapped. She had felt safe as he molded his body to hers with his head burrowed in the nest of her neck. No man had ever held her that way. And the shivers of desire had swallowed her whole.

Noora let the palm-frond wall grate her back as she slid to the ground. She had to give him up! With that thought the thuds in her ribs grew forceful. She gasped to swallow air that was growing so thick it seemed intent on choking her. She turned her head and glued her face to a gap in the palm-frond wall, breathing deeply. There was the moon, a silver face, radiant with serenity.

She yearned to have him near her, to feel his touch. A tremor of fear ran along the length of her spine. Even though she knew it was wrong, she wanted him again.

36

It seemed Lateefa had forgotten most of her important possessions at Wadeema. Noora grew accustomed to seeing her delve into her travel chest, every few days, in search of this or that. Then Lateefa would puff into her burka and shake her head with disbelief. "Now, why didn't I bring that orange *thoub* with me? It's so light, so cool for this weather," or "I don't know why my kohl is burning my eyes. I think it's gone bad." And then she would send Hamad and Noora to pick up whatever it was that she urgently needed. "You must go. You must go right away," she would insist. This time Lateefa had accidentally spilled her henna in the sand.

"How much henna does she need?" Hamad asked as he watched Noora empty the greenish powder into a small bottle.

"I don't know," Noora said. "At least two handfuls to make sure she can cover all those white roots, to make sure she gets her hair nice and red."

"Maybe you had better put four handfuls, just to make sure she doesn't send us back."

"I'm sure she will find something else she has misplaced," Noora said, frowning. "Why do you think she keeps missing things and sending us to get them?"

Hamad shrugged. "I don't know. I guess she is becoming forgetful." He leaned back on a *takya*, stretched his arms over his head, and yawned. "When they get old, they begin to forget."

"She's not that old," Noora said, shaking her head. "No, there's something else. She has become so nice to me, bringing me milk before I sleep, sitting with me to chat, letting me use her perfumes. Saffron, amber, sandalwood, rose, all those essences, I mean, they are so expensive." She paused. "It's just not like her."

Hamad yawned again. "Why do you always worry so much? We are together, aren't we? That's all that matters."

She stopped pouring the henna and looked up at him. "Is it?" she asked. He seemed so unconcerned, stretched on the *takya* like that. So at ease. Seeing him that way brewed a rumble in her chest. "Is that all you can think of, that we are together? Don't you think of my position? I know I can't stop thinking of it. Soon, Jassem will be back. Then what will you do?" Her voice was shaking now. "What will we do?"

He was by her side within moments. "Easy, easy," he cooed, stroking her head gently. "Let me take care of us." He began nibbling on her neck. "Come on," he mumbled, "finish pouring the henna so I can hold you."

"No!" Noora elbowed him away.

"Why?"

"I'm not comfortable."

Hamad pulled back and let out a defeated sigh.

"Look," she explained. "I am very worried. Something doesn't feel right. Maybe it's better if we finish this now."

Hamad's jaw dropped. "Finish what?"

"Us! Finish us. There's no point."

"What are you talking about? I want to be with you always."

"Really?"

"Yes, really. Divorce Jassem and marry me."

There was sincerity in his eyes, but Noora shook her head at the impossibility of his suggestion. How simple he was.

"It can happen, really happen," he insisted.

"Divorce Jassem? And who said he would agree?"

"We'll think of something. We'll make him agree."

"We, we, we, we," Noora mocked the earnestness in his voice before letting out a hopeless groan. "As if we matter, as if we can pick what we want." Her voice had turned shrill, and she paused to swallow some control back into it. Then, with a forced patience, she continued, "I am a woman—a married woman—and you are a man—a poor man. We are not in a position to make choices. Don't you agree?"

"Don't you agree?" Hamad mimicked the adult-speaking-to-children tone she had used. Then he stared deep into her eyes and said, "I have plans, you know. I do think and plan. I'm not stupid." He paused. "I am planning to dive again."

Noora's eyes fluttered with disbelief. "Dive?"

"Dive, you know, dive. I think I can do it. I know there is a special pearl down there for me to find. I know it."

"But you have tried it, and it didn't work." She crossed her arms. "And what about your ears?"

"Don't worry about that. I can bear the pain."

His head was bobbing up and down, so eager, so determined, that Noora felt sorry for the desperation that was overtaking him. Still, she had to shake the silliness out of him. He was speaking nonsense. "Wake up, Hamad, wake up," she said.

"I can do it, I tell you."

"Wake up," Noora repeated. "There won't be any more dives." She flung her arms into the air, shouted, "No more! This is the last dive!"

Noora drummed her fingers on her thigh and stared at the henna, poured into three small bottles and wrapped into a knotted bundle, ready to be delivered to Lateefa. Hamad was outside in the courtyard. She could hear him, marching back and forth from one end of the house to the other.

Why did she have to open her big mouth? Why couldn't she have let him find out from someone else? She heard the slaps of his feet at the door—he was back—and his breath, too. Exhausted wheezes, as if he had just run to Leema and back.

She patted the mat she was sitting on. Like an obedient child, he entered and slumped next to her. She ran her hand up his spine, along the line of perspiration on his dishdasha, till her fingers cupped his neck and pulled his head to rest on the flat of her chest. It felt like a rock that was heavy with age, so old it was ready to crumble.

Noora clasped his hand, a limp piece of flesh that could be molded into any shape. Lifeless! So she pinched it with her fingers and rubbed it with her palms, squeezed it hard and stroked it with her thumb. She had to keep touching him, touch some soul back into him. Slowly, his passion returned and he wrapped her in his arms, holding her so tight she felt an over-powering desire to throw away all her modesty.

She had never gone bare. It was an unnecessary embarrass-ment, a not-done thing she was always grateful for whenever she was with Jassem. Having before been too shy with Hamad, she now yearned for the feeling of skin on skin. He must have felt the same, for he loosened his embrace and they lifted their clothes up together. She watched his dishdasha fly to one side as she wriggled out of her *serwal* and peeled off her dress and rolled it into a bundle, which she dropped just behind her head.

Before she had time to dwell on her nakedness, he had eased her onto the mat and taken her whole. She belonged to him, ev-ery little bit of her. She clamped her lips and shut her eyes tight for fear of losing control. But the tears slipped out and snuck down her cheeks. And the whimpers of passion squeezed out of her throat anyway: tiny twitters of some morning bird, as she trembled with rapture.

It was only when Hamad rolled onto his side that she be-came aware of her rapid breathing. She did not try to pacify her pounding heart. Nor did she wipe away the film of perspira-tion that clung to her face; she just crossed her arms over her chest and grinned at the ceiling, seeing nothing till the flicker of a lizard's tail slid into her view. It had been there all along, and she had not noticed it. Noora wondered whether it was the same lizard that used to cling to the ceiling when she was under Jassem, whether it had somehow scuttled across the courtyard into Lateefa's room to watch another kind of lovemaking. Did it recognize her as the same person?

The chill of a sharp puff of air blew through the open doorway. Noora reached behind her head and lifted her dress, fluffed it over her chest. Next to her, Hamad moaned. She rolled her head toward him and watched him as he lay on his back, fast asleep. Peace had softened the clamp of anxiety that had gripped his jaw earlier. There was a glimmer of his front teeth through his parted lips. He seemed as vulnerable as a child, and a gush of tenderness soaked her eyes, and tremors of guilt dried her throat, remorse at having upset him earlier, hurting him like that.

It was getting late. "Come on, wake up," she said, prodding Hamad on his arm.

He started. "Hmm? What happened?"

"Come on, get up. We have to go."

She wanted to get back to Om Al-Sanam so that she could unfurl all that had just taken place. Never had she felt such an outpouring of passion. She wanted to recall every discreet touch and caress, every mighty shudder and release. She wanted to take every small detail of their intimacy and think about it on her own. Until the next time.

37

Hamad's shadow was breaking the light that spilled through Noora's window. He was like a spirit lost in someone else's world, unable to touch her, aggravated in its own existence. And so, this spirit, Hamad's spirit in that shadow, hovered and tried to remain as close to her as it could.

Of course, there were always the fleeting glances that trapped her eyes whenever she came face-to-face with him. His eyes seemed to have stared at the sun for so long that they had swallowed its burn. She was sure he couldn't sleep. How could he, when he knew she was sharing her bed with Jassem?

It had been a full sixteen days and nights since they had returned to Wadeema, and Jassem visited her on most evenings with renewed passion. And under his weight, she would mourn the joy she had lost. And her eyes would water. And Jassem's vigor would rise at the emotion she was showing.

"There's no need to cry," he would gasp. "I am back now."

That angered her, and she felt frustrated at having lost the brief happiness she had shared with Hamad.

Noora heard the rooster crow and propped herself up on her elbows. Still dark outside, still quiet, and yet her heart throbbed with anxiety as she wondered whether she would feel all right on this day. But then the dizziness drifted to her head like a thick haze and settled between her ears. She fell back onto the mattress and closed her eyes, breathed deep, and tried to ignore the familiar pinch of nausea that dried her mouth.

It was no use. She tumbled off the bed and staggered to the washroom. She coughed quietly and whispered under her breath, "It'll go, it'll go." She hoped no one could hear her retch. After all, the nausea hit her only once a day, always just before dawn. As she crawled back to the bed, Noora tried to count the number of times she had been sick: seven times in as many days.

It was by late morning that Noora's dizziness began to subside, only to be replaced by a weakness that settled in her joints. It was a particularly sticky day, and as the household hushed after lunch, Noora crossed over to the men's *majlis* to chase away her fatigue. The breeze came from the sea just after the summer, and it was the wind tower in the men's *majlis* that caught it best.

She lay on the mat under the wind tower and raised her legs into a tent. She could hear the pigeons roosted on the beams in the hollow of the wind tower. Their shuddering coos and flutters calmed her, and she rested her palms on her stomach, rubbed them in circles as her eyes grew heavy and she drifted into slumber.

She was not sure how long she had been asleep when she became aware that someone was standing over her. Heavy, heavy head—she refused to open her eyes, as that would just chase the sleep away. She covered her face with her *shayla* and rolled toward the wall. "Whatever you want can wait till later," she mumbled, guessing it was Yaqoota. "Leave me to sleep for now."

"It's me," said Hamad.

Noora pulled off her *shayla* and sat up. "What are you doing? The house isn't empty, you know. Everyone's here."

"I must talk to you." Although he spoke calmly, there was a warble of urgency in his voice. "We haven't talked since we got back."

"Talk?" Her eyes were still blurry with sleep. Yet her gaze drifted to the open inner doorway and immediately a panic seized her. He hadn't even bothered to close the door. Anyone could have spotted him entering. "What are you doing?" she hissed. "Why is the door open?" All those times when they had roamed the house as if they were husband and wife, all those times and they hadn't been caught. That didn't mean they wouldn't be discovered now. She jumped up, startling the roosting pigeons into flaps of alarm, and swung the door closed, leaving just a tiny crack from which she could look through to the courtyard.

"It's all right," Hamad whispered. "They are all asleep." He yanked her hand to his lips and kissed it.

Noora would not turn to face him, keeping her eyes glued to the gap. The kitchen door was ajar, and she squinted, trying to pick up any movement in its dimness. Only when she was sure they were safe did she turn to scold him. "What were you thinking, sneaking in like this?"

"I have a plan."

"What plan?" she asked, looking back through the gap. She had to be absolutely sure.

"Look at me," Hamad said, and twisted her shoulders so that she was finally facing him. He placed his lips on her forehead. "I miss you so much, and I haven't seen you alone, and when I think of that ugly, fat Jass—"

"What plan?" she insisted. She was anxious to send him out again.

"Don't you miss me?" he asked.

She watched those eyes, watery with hope, and sighed. "Of course I do, but we both knew it would not last." She did not want to encourage him.

"But we were so happy. Why wouldn't you want it to last?"

Hamad the dreamer, she thought. Her lips curled into a half-smile and she shook her head. "You can't be always happy. That's not how the world works." She felt they were someone else's words, but she continued anyway. "We were lucky we got a chance at being happy, and even luckier that no one caught us." She sighed. "Now, well . . . we have the memory. We will have to live with that."

"I didn't know you would give up so quickly."

"It is not about giving up."

"It is."

"It's not."

"Yes, it is," he insisted, his voice rising higher.

"Shh." Noora wanted to scream her frustration, but instead she just rolled her eyes. Again, he was being careless, getting worked up and letting his voice rise like that. He wasn't thinking of her, how vulnerable she was when he put her in such a position. Images floated into her head: images of Jassem, the wives, and even Yaqoota, finding out their secret. They would certainly throw her out into the street. "Keep your voice low," she whispered. "Now, what is your plan?"

He took a deep breath and began, "Well, the most important thing is that we be together. And every time I think of you with that big, round, ugly man—"

"Enough! I don't want to hear about the ugly man. I want to hear the plan." She could hear the chants of the fishermen on the shore as they hauled in their drift-net. The village was awake.

"Well, to be together—that's the thing," Hamad said, as if he had made some important discovery. Next, he paused and scrunched his nose, looked at the roof, searching for something, and Noora wondered whether he was making up his plan right there and then. She wanted to shake him. But then he spoke. "I don't like what I have become," Hamad said. "Spineless! Not able to make decisions. Remember that time, when you first arrived, when we brought you from your mountains? That beggar in Leema's souk?"

Noora coaxed him to speak faster with rapid bobs of her head. The household was waking up. She could hear the ringing of the brass coffee mortar. Yaqoota was in the kitchen grinding the beans.

"I saw the way you looked at me when Jassem beat that beggar. And it was because I did nothing. But I wanted to do something, really I did."

"But you didn't."

"No, I didn't."

"Well, what could you have done?" She sighed. "You would have lost your job."

"Exactly what I thought at the time. But what job is this, a measly five rupiahs every month? That's enough to buy me a basket of dates." He blew a mocking puff into the air and shook his head, repeating, "A basket of dates, that's it. This job isn't taking me anywhere."

Noora shrugged. She could see no solution. "Well, what are you going to do?"

"Leave. And take you with me."

Noora lost patience. Once again, he was being foolish. "You can leave if you want, but I am not leaving," she said matter-of-factly. "I'm not happy here, but I have a place to live in. I have a bed to sleep in, my own room. I have food and water. I have security. Out there, I would have nothing."

"No, no, no, you will have everything with me. We will start our life with money in our pockets."

"Money? Is it going to fall from the sky or are you going to dig and find it?" She shooed him out with a flick of the fingers, but Hamad just crossed his arms and smiled.

"It's right here," he said, twisting his forefinger to the ground. "Right here."

"Where? There's a secret hole in the ground under me with all your saved rupiahs?"

"The trick is to get that money. It's a bit risky and not completely honest . . . but then it becomes honest."

Noora lost all patience. She began to jostle him toward the outer door. "It is time for you to go," she said. "This is too dangerous, having you here like this. I don't have time for all these little words that do not make sense."

Her hands were prodding his ribs, and he giggled and twisted out of her grip. When she tried to push him again, he clutched her wrists and said, "The pearls! That's what I am talking about. Just a teeny handful. Jassem won't miss them."

How many people knew about Jassem's hidden pearls? "That's stealing."

"Borrowing."

"Stealing! We would have to get his keys and steal them."

"Just for a short while. Then we will use them to start off and give him their worth later."

Noora shook her head and tried to free her wrists, but he held them firm.

"Think of it," he begged. "Me and you, together, always."

"Let go of my wrists," she snapped through clenched teeth.

Hamad released his grip so quickly that her arms swung back with such force she heard a loud pop in her shoulders. She flinched and marched to the other side of the room. There, she faced the wall and composed herself, before turning back to him. Hamad remained standing by the outer door. He seemed unsure whether to approach her or to wait for her to say something. He was giving her a choice, a second chance at happiness.

The pigeons were settling back on the beams, and she listened to their flutters and coos, and then, from the kitchen, came Yaqoota's syrupy voice breaking into a song that, under any other circumstances, Noora would have enjoyed listening to. Now it sounded more like a warning of the risk she was taking by being alone with Hamad.

"They are waking up," she whispered, with a nod toward the inner door. "You'd better go."

38

"This is what they do with the nacre," Jassem said, his hand unfurling to reveal a handful of shiny, white buttons. He lifted one of them and bit on it. "See? Top quality, so strong it doesn't even break when I bite it." He had called his three wives to his room for one of his rare, important talks. And this talk was about buttons and change.

Noora felt her eyes broaden with concentration. She and Shamsa were sitting like attentive students on either side of Lateefa in the middle of the room, facing Jassem and his cupboard. But Noora was only half listening to his words. Her head felt as if it were clogged with a wet rag, heavy with betrayal. Hamad had wanted to take those pearls, and she had refused to join him. Jassem was her husband, and she had betrayed him. And there was the cupboard behind Jassem, and in it were the pearls. She could see her reflection, a perplexed blur, in its smooth, rosewood veneer. And if that wasn't enough, that wet rag in her head was beginning to clump with a queasiness that was all too familiar.

Lateefa picked a button out of Jassem's palm carefully, as if it might burn a hole in her fingers, as if it were a piece of hot coal. "And this little thing will open new possibilities?" she asked, pulling it close to her eyes for a thorough scrutiny. "I don't know about this." Her voice was thick with suspicion. "I am not sure if I trust them, those *Inglesis* with their green eyes and all."

"True." Shamsa chuckled, plucking another button out of Jassem's open hand. "Anyone with green eyes is as cunning as a cat, not to be trusted."

Those words were intended for Noora, of course, but before she could answer, Jassem threw in a grunt and an impatient series of nods. "Yes, yes," he said, "but that is not the point. The point is to establish a relationship with these English people, so that when they want to trade in more things, bigger ventures, they choose me. It's not the buttons I am interested in. It is making sure those *Inglesis* know I am an honest and efficient businessman."

Perspiration gleamed on his passionate face, and Noora followed his spectacles as they inched down his nose. Once they had settled at the tip, he would not push them up. He had more to say, more lessons to teach his wives. "You must start observing things with the sweeping vision of men, not the narrow outlook of women," he said. "Open your minds and see what this all means. With this button venture, I am opening big possibilities for the future. The English will be leading the future, and I will be right there by their side."

Lateefa grunted. She still seemed unconvinced. "Here, feel it," she said, popping a button into Noora's fingers. "Just think, if we start using these buttons, you won't have to sew over and over the same place to make your cloth-and-thread buttons anymore."

Jassem tilted his head toward Noora, his eyes hovering over his clinging spectacles. He still would not push them back, and although she couldn't understand why, she was impatient for him to flick a finger and settle them in the right place. He seemed to be waiting for her to say something, and Noora guessed he wanted her to show that she was as excited about his talk as he was. "What about these shells and the nacre?" She asked the first question that came to her mind and followed it with another. "Where are you going to get so many from?" She paused, before adding quickly, "And how?"

"Hoo ho," he sang, and let loose a blustering clap. Then he took a deep breath and, finally, shoved his spectacles back. "Now that there won't be any more diving, my boats can go and get those shells." He snaked his arms in the thick air, mimicking the rises and dips of a sailing boat. "Off to the mountains they will go. Off to Nassayem, and all those other mountain-and-sea villages, where those large shells cling to the rocks."

Shamsa's eyes brightened with mischief. "Ah, isn't that where the mountain goats live? Isn't that where you got Noora from?"

This time Noora did not attempt to answer her. A weakness was beginning to fall over her like a heavy blanket. Her face was hot and her mouth parched. She wanted to rush to the well and quench her thirst, but the dread of fainting kept her rooted in place, that and the heaviness of the wet rag in her head.

"We will bring those shells back to Wadeema and scrape off the barnacles and algae," Jassem continued. He shook the buttons in the cave of his clasped palms and listened to their clicks, smiled at the promised fortune they would bring. "Then we will wash those shells and pack them in crates to sell to the English." He chuckled. "Clean shells with shiny nacre inside. Off they'll go, to the English company in Bombay, to make buttons. Our own nacre buttons to be sold to the rest of the world."

As he ranted on about opportunity, hope, and the river of wealth that would soon be flowing to his doorstep, Noora thought about Hamad. Wasn't that what Hamad wanted? And yet, Hamad had chosen to steal. She had not spoken to him since he'd snuck up on her in the men's *majlis*. Would he go ahead with his plan, or was it just talk? Noora's eyes traveled along the vines that crept up the sides of the cupboard to rest at the sculpted urns at the top. The keys to both the cupboard and the metal safe within were hidden behind those urns.

Suddenly, she was overpowered by an urge to warn Jassem to move his keys somewhere else, so that no thief could find them. A clammy chill settled on the nape of her neck and her lips unclamped. She might have spoken had she not noticed the abrupt stillness that surrounded her. Then Jassem jarred her with a thunderous voice. "What are you staring at?" The crisp rasp of his dishdasha was as sharp as the swab of a blade on stone as he twisted to look over his shoulder.

Noora shook her head, and through the strobes of her rapid blinks, there were the questioning faces of Lateefa and Shamsa, leaning toward her.

"You are as white as the nacre," Lateefa said, and reached out to touch Noora's forehead, flattening the seeds of perspiration that lined her forehead. "Are you sick?"

"Why is she so drenched? It's not that hot," Shamsa said, and for the first time Noora heard a lilt in Shamsa's voice that sounded like concern—or alarm.

Noora fanned her face quickly and gasped for air. "I can't breathe," she panted, and as she leaned to get up, she felt Lateefa's firm grip on her wrist pulling her back down. And Noora was thankful for that, for the room was starting to spin and dim with the speed of a spiraling storm of dirt.

And then Lateefa began touching her. Noora was not sure why. And she could not ask, for she was busy fighting the tug that was pulling her eyelids closed. Everything felt exaggerated. Lateefa's arm sliding down along her back was as heavy as a bloated water skin, and Lateefa's hands as they patted her waist were as sharp as the slaps of a sandal. Finally, Lateefa's palm slid onto her stomach. And there it remained for a moment that Noora was sure was brief but felt as sluggish as the lift of the morning mist in her mountains.

"Too much meat on a woman or too little can mean only one thing," Lateefa said, her words sounding warped, thick, stretched. "And you, dear daughter, have got too little for my liking."

Noora's eyes burned as she forced them to stay open in the swirl of scattering shadows that were enclosing her. She could see Lateefa leaning back, captured the disbelief in her eyes, and finally fell under the spell of her bobbing burka as the older woman uttered, "You're pregnant."

It could not be! That's what the tiny voice in Noora's head screamed. She had to run away, as fast as she could. With all the strength she could gather, she sprang up. And that's when she felt her limbs grow floppy and her chest sway to the side. That's when her head spun and she collapsed. That's when the darkness swallowed the light completely.

39

Noora woke up in a haze and tried to sit up, only to feel Lateefa's arms press her shoulders back into the mattress. With the weight of her shame, her tongue tripped into a stutter of meaningless babbles before she could hear the words that made sense, the ones she could understand. "It just happened on its own . . ." It was a feeble utterance of remorse. "I don't . . ."

"Don't talk," Lateefa ordered.

Was that the snarl of a wild dog grating the back of Lateefa's throat? The older woman loomed above her and she seemed to have grown in size. Noora watched her raise her arms high up above her head, expanding them just as an eagle spreads its wings in a show of might. And Noora was in her shadow like a cringing mouse, the truth of what had passed swallowing her as surely as quicksand.

She was pregnant. The signs had been there for so long and she hadn't even guessed the cause. And now she was feeling hot and cold, her body drenched in a freeze and thaw, as she waited for Lateefa to strike her. Lateefa's arms remained over her head as Noora strained to keep her eyes open. She had to see what would happen next. Would Lateefa slap her or would she claw her fingers into Noora's face, scratch it till she drew rivers of blood that would leave behind marks to stay with her always as a reminder of her deceit? She was ready to receive either, for she deserved it and much more.

But Lateefa did neither. Instead, she relaxed her hands behind her head and untied the knot of her burka. Then she slid it off her face, revealing inky smudges imprinted on her cheeks from the indigo-stained cotton that lined the inside of her mask. It was a rare moment for Noora, a kind of privilege, seeing Lateefa's naked face, which beamed a most puzzling smile. Her thin lips spread so high that her short nose flattened into her cheeks, pushing those dark, blue smudges farther up, as if they might empty into the hollow pools under her eyes. Not a hint of anger blemished that smile. It was a smile of pure joy.

Noora's head lightened and the room darkened, and she sank into a nervous sleep filled with ugly dreams. Her next waking moment began with the squish and drip of water. When she opened her eyes, she saw that Lateefa was still sitting next to her, squeezing the liquid out of a wet cloth and into a bowl.

"Ham—"

"Shh," Lateefa said, quickly placing her finger on Noora's lips. "Enough silly talk. Don't think of anything, except getting better. Rest, my dear, rest. Don't try to talk." She placed the wet cloth on Noora's forehead. "You are feverish, and now we have to make you better. You have to get strong again. We don't want that fever to affect our baby." She lifted a bowl of chicken broth and placed it to Noora's lips. "We won't get ourselves strong unless we nourish ourselves."

A yelp cut the stillness between them just as Noora was about to sip the broth, and it sounded as if it were coming out of a deep well. So shrill she thought it was Yaqoota, but the pain in that voice was not Yaqoota's. "Who's that?" she whispered.

Lateefa closed her eyes and said, "It's Shamsa—just ignore her. She is upset about the baby." A series of clicks ricocheted in Lateefa's mouth. "So selfish, that one, you would think she'd be happy that the *arbab* is finally going to have a child." She let out a raspy sigh, thick with the pleasure of a purring cat. "Finally, you have made Jassem's dream come true, all our dreams. A child! Finally, the blessing of Jassem's child."

With those words, the broth slid down Noora's throat the wrong way, and she fell into a fit of violent coughs that splattered the bed. Through teary eyes, she watched Lateefa quickly place the bowl on the floor, and with the skill of a healer of many years, she scooped Noora into a sitting position and began thumping her back.

Noora regained her breath, even though her chest felt bruised. Her head fell into a weary spin again, and she slumped back into the mattress, confused, wondering whether she was dreaming, whether she had imagined it, or whether Lateefa had really said that the child was Jassem's. She turned her head to one side and caught the dwindling sunlight, a sprawling river of amber, streaming into her room through the window. Even that gentle light hurt her eyes.

"You have been in and out of sleep all day, talking nonsense," Lateefa said, nodding. "You're feverish, and you didn't know what you were saying—all silly things, of course—so don't talk anymore."

Noora tried to focus on the flecks of dust that swam in the light as the questions flitted in her mind like moths fluttering toward a fire. What were the silly things she had uttered? Had she mentioned Hamad? She yearned to know, but getting too close to that blaze could burn her.

So she remained silent and let Lateefa help her sit up once again. Noora sipped her broth, and when Shamsa's choked sniffles seeped through the wall, she began slurping. Anything to cover the sound of those muffled sobs.

The door creaked open and a shaft of light pierced the dimness. Lateefa plodded across the room and placed her palm on Noora's head. "It is gone," she said, sighing with relief. "A whole week of fever, you had us so worried. We thought you were losing your mind with all that kicking and mumbling, as if you had so many important things to say."

Noora was still weary after the yoyo of hot and cold that she had endured. Her breath was shallow and her mind a cave of confusion. The only thought that seeped through, clear as running water, was that she was pregnant, and the weight of it kept her pinned to her bed as surely as if there sat a heavy boulder on her chest.

Lateefa lapped a cloth into a bowl of buttermilk and turmeric. It was the same mixture she had used to bring Noora's fever down, and now, as before, she squeezed the cloth with a devotion that was quite new, one that Noora had never seen in the older woman. The room remained heavy with the smell of spiced old milk, and Noora shook her head as Lateefa lifted the cloth toward her forehead.

"But it will bring your fever down," Lateefa said.

"Fever's finished," whispered Noora. "No more, please."

Lateefa paused with the cloth in her hand and chuckled. "All right, if you don't want anymore, that's fine. But there is something that I'm sure you do want." From her pocket, she pulled two halves of a lime. Suddenly, Noora felt her breath quicken and her mouth drool. Sifting through her jumbled thoughts, she remembered her frenzied calls to satisfy her craving for the sour taste of limes. She sucked the flesh greedily, and as her lips pursed under its tartness, she thought of Jassem and his belt-tightening tales of his precious limes. He had been in her dreams, too, or were they her waking moments?

While she was feverish, in and out of sleep, she remembered seeing him at the door, more than once, asking in a low voice whether she was getting better. She was sure there were lines of worry on his forehead. It was another first for Noora, seeing her husband, the man with the lion's growl, meowing a timid cat's fears.

As Lateefa tiptoed out of the room, Noora relished the lime. Her secret seemed safe. Otherwise, Lateefa and Jassem would not have been so accommodating, so concerned, and, dare she believe it, so loving. She peeled the inside of the lime with her teeth and chewed the pulp. It was bitter and sharp at the same time. Just what she wanted, just what she needed for now, until she could think more clearly, until she could understand her new position in the household.

40

Noora broke half of a pomegranate and felt the sting of its juice spit into her eyes. Immediately, Lateefa wiped it off by flinging a wet cloth on her face before Noora got a chance to blink.

"It's all right, *Ommi* Lateefa," said Noora, trying to keep the irritation out of her voice. A full month had passed since she'd recovered from her fever, and still Lateefa hovered over her like a bee protecting its honey.

The pomegranate was almost as sour as the limes she daily devoured, and it suited her fine. As the ruby pips exploded in Noora's mouth, she watched Lateefa neaten the bed she was lying on. That is what the older woman did these days whenever she felt her hands grow idle, since it was another way of fussing over Noora.

"Don't swallow the pips," Lateefa instructed. "Just put them back into the tray. They are too hard on the stomach."

Noora spat the pulp out with an exaggerated *whoosh* and fixed Lateefa with a stare of confrontation.

The older woman continued with a kind smile, "With pregnancy, the mood goes up and down all the time. What to do? But you must know that you can talk to me whenever you want, tell me what bothers you, and I will try to do my best to help you."

It was the invitation Noora was looking for, and she did not hesitate. "I'm so tired of staying in this room, so tired of all this attention you are giving me. I haven't walked out in the courtyard for so long." She was whining like a dog begging for food. "Why can't I go out and walk, just walk, that's all."

"Pah! What talk! The sun is too hot for you."

"But it is cooler now. Anyway, I can go out when the sun sets in the early evening or late at night. I don't mind."

Lateefa refused once again, this time with a determined shake of the head. "It is for your own good that you stay indoors and rest. Outside, there are germs that could be brought in by anyone: Yaqoota, Shamsa, even our husband."

And Hamad, too? Noora wanted to ask but thought better not to. Where was he?

"In your state, you will pick the germs up, just like that," said Lateefa, and her fingers joined in a thunderous snap aimed to establish her authority, to show that she was in control of Noora's pregnancy.

Defiance rose in Noora like the sudden heave of a wave at the start of a storm. "I'm not asking for much," she said. "I only want to exercise a little." She rose and dangled her legs to the side of the bed. "I think I will go and walk outside a little right now."

Lateefa crossed her arms and, slanting her head to one

side, shot a fierce look at Noora. "I don't think you should," she said.

Noora slid off the bed.

"Do not go out," Lateefa warned.

Noora continued to disobey the older woman. She flung her *shayla* over her head and took a few steps toward the door. She was about to slide the door's thick, wooden latch when Lateefa spoke again. "Don't let your head grow big just because you're having our husband's child." There was the rumble of a storm sitting at the back of her throat. "When I say you should rest, you should listen to me."

The wood rasped as Noora dragged the latch slowly to one side.

"Don't forget that I set the rhythm of this house," Lateefa continued, "and to set the rhythm of the house, I have to know everything. And believe me when I tell you, I do."

Noora hesitated. The door was unlatched, all she had to do was pull it open and take that tiny step out. Then she'd be in the light. Then she would have won. But victory seemed already behind her, in Lateefa's voice, which was filled with all the colors of confidence and authority.

"I know things," the older woman said, "and you would be wise to listen to me when I tell you to."

What was Lateefa saying? Did she know that it was Hamad's child swimming in her womb? All the fears Noora had been stifling emerged. Terror shot into her limbs and the clammy pricks of dread sped to her fingers. Her hands stiffened and she dropped them to her side. She had to step back from this confrontation. Lateefa's threats seemed real.

She remained facing the door as she tried to churn up some poise. "Look, I don't want to upset you," Noora began, trying to blow into her voice as much of the carefree breeze of good humor as she could without sounding as if she were backing down. "I just want to exercise my legs." She swung round and stepped back to the bed. Then she decided to look deep into the older woman's eyes, since it was the only way to catch the truth. Surely, everything would be reflected in the tiny sparks of those eyes!

But Lateefa would not allow it. As Noora dove into the slits of her burka, she saw nothing but an expansive grin that shrank Lateefa's eyes into seeds, sitting on a pair of hollow crescents as crinkled as rotten fruit.

Late that night, Noora resisted sleep. She did not want to dream. In her dreams, there was always that horrible sense of trying to get somewhere but not being able to. Steps on a cloud that could carry her weight would dissolve into mist; gravel on a mountain she was climbing would slip under her feet. She always felt trapped in her dreams, either falling to nowhere or climbing to nothing. Those dreams, so many of them, wrapped themselves around her like sticky ocean weeds.

Sleep tugged at her eyelids. She got up and tiptoed to the door. She was as silent as a breeze as she entered the forbidden courtyard and snuck into the shadows of the arcade that rose over the house *majlis*. There, she stood very still and tried to find peace by staring ahead, but there was a cloud in her mind, filled with dreaded questions that tripped over one another. It had been there from the moment Lateefa had crushed her resolve. Noora had avoided it, hoping it would disperse. But now, in the stillness of the night, every fear and doubt tumbled out.

Did Lateefa really know her secret? And if she did, how

would she have found out? Could it be the villagers setting Lateefa's mind along a trail of suspicion? And there was another possibility, too. And it was the one that filled Noora with the biggest terror of all. What had happened during her illness?

She tried to recall every detail of that feverish week. She remembered her throbbing head and limbs, clogged with weariness. There were the sips of chicken broth, the tiny mouthfuls of water, the heavy scent of Lateefa's mix of buttermilk and turmeric on her body.

Lateefa said she had tossed, punched, and kicked while she slept under the heat of fever. Had she spoken, too? Noora shook her head. She was sure all the sounds she made, all those shrieks of alarm, had been in her head. In her waking moments, her voice rose above her lazy heartbeat in random mumbles that were entwined so tightly she could not understand them. Her tongue had been full of the gasp and quiver of a fish out of water. What damage could it have uttered?

Noora breathed deeply, again and again. She was sick of her pitiful state. As she felt the crisp air clear her head, she dared to imagine another life, one that would take her far away from Lateefa's tyrannical authority. Perhaps Hamad was right. Perhaps he should steal those pearls. And then they could escape together.

It was a thought that immediately overwhelmed her. There was hope in it. There was boldness in it. She dragged her feet on the ground, feeling an urgent need to move, wanting to wipe away the wretchedness that plagued her. She began with a few quiet steps, here and there, remaining in the dark. But it was not long before she exposed the length of her, a rebellious shadow under the glittering half-moon, marching silently in full view.

Her tummy was still small, and with the weakness and nausea past her, she felt strong enough to run away from this oppressive household. She would travel, cross the seas to India, and bring up her child alongside Hamad as he quickly grew rich.

While the house slept, Noora rushed from one side of the courtyard to the other and back again, intent on erasing that pathetic creature she had become. She was like a thief looking to get caught. She dug her heels into the sand till the flash of defiance filled her with a crazed thrill. How easy it all was. How clear the picture of that other life was. She could see herself, sitting by his side on a mat under a leaning palm with her infant lying on her lap as she rocked it to sleep. She could feel Hamad's light breath blowing away the humidity that settled on the nape of her neck. There was her mouth, slackening into a gentle smile, and there were her eyes, a pair of glossy olives, lulled half-shut in an arc of fulfillment.

It was a pleasing reverie, cut short only by a spike of pain in her lower back that prompted her to stop. That is when Noora noticed that she was breathless and a dull ache had settled in her calves. Her heart was racing, too. And it made her sad to realize that all the agility and endurance that she had possessed when she lived in the mountains was now gone. Her steps were sluggish now, and she wondered how she would survive a two- or three-month voyage over rough seas and into an unfamiliar land where people spoke a strange language.

As the pain in her back subsided, she thought more about the risk involved in such a move. She was tempted to shrug away the whole plan that had formed so haphazardly in her mind. But Noora was fed up with the voiceless coward she had become.

Tomorrow, I will find Hamad, she resolved. Where was he anyway? She paused and looked up at the sky, as if she might find him there. Ever since her illness, Hamad had disappeared, and she had not had the nerve to ask his whereabouts. Tomorrow, that would have to change. Tomorrow, she would ask Yaqoota.

41

It was one thing to decide what she had to do and quite another to act on it.

First, she had to catch Yaqoota in a moment of gentle contemplation so that the noisy slave would not shout out her secret to the whole house. And that was proving difficult. Right from the start of Noora's pregnancy, Yaqoota had shrugged away her temper and ill feelings toward Noora and now shared Lateefa's and Jassem's unending thrill and anticipation. The slave grabbed any chance she had to fuss over Noora. She squealed and sang all day.

Noora decided she had to give her time to grow bored and calm down. By day, she followed Lateefa's rule and remained captive in the room. But at night, Noora rebelled and stole into the courtyard where, as any lost Arab might, she gazed at the starry sky to find guidance. Night after night, she looked out for some sign in the stars' flickering light, but she only noticed the passing of time as the moon swelled and shrank.

Then, one morning, as Noora sat combing her hair, Yaqoota burst into her room and declared, "Shamsa is leaving."

The comb was stuck in a knot, and Noora left it where it was, dangling. She stood up and walked to the wall to listen. There was shuffling and clattering on the other side. It was true: Shamsa was packing.

Noora grabbed her *shayla* and draped it over her head. She was about to walk out of the room when Yaqoota clutched her arm. "Where are you going?" she asked.

"To see Shamsa, to see why—" And Noora stopped. Why was she going to see Shamsa? Why did she care? Even though Shamsa had never uttered a kind word to her, Noora felt a sense of grief and betrayal that surged thick as the spurt of blood out of a deep wound. No matter how catty they had been to each other, Noora felt there was a bond they shared, just by being in a marriage not of their choice. She had to do something. "Maybe she needs help packing," she said.

"I don't think she does, not from you anyway," Yaqoota said. "After all, it's because of you that she's going!" She wagged her head. "Shamsa said to the *arbab*, 'I want to be with my family; I miss them.' Hoo!" Yaqoota's brows wiggled, and she leaned toward Noora and whispered, "She said that it would be just for a while, and then she will be back. But we know better, don't we? She'll never be back. She will stay in the nest of her house, sitting on her failure like a chicken on a broken egg."

"Why now?" Noora asked.

"Why now?" Yaqoota mocked. "Look at you! Soon your tummy will be so big you won't be able to see your feet."

Noora clasped the base of her belly, as if it might fall if she did not.

"What are you now?" Yaqoota continued. "Six months in or so? Safe! That is what you are. Shamsa waited this long to make sure there was no chance of your losing the baby."

Noora frowned and began stroking the sides of her tummy. "And the *arbab* agreed?" She remembered how angry Jassem had been the last time Shamsa had gone to visit her family.

Yaqoota shrugged. "He doesn't seem to mind."

Noora frowned. "Well, maybe I should just go and say good-bye,"

"She'll spit on you if you do," Yaqoota said, with a chuckle. "Just think. You won; she lost. Be happy." She peered out through the window.

Noora felt none of Yaqoota's glee. Instead, gloom, dark as a moonless night, shrouded her mind. A woman's place in a household could be determined only by what she could provide. And Shamsa, it seemed, had nothing to give. Shamsa had first fled with Noora's arrival, and now she was fleeing again with this pregnancy.

"He's here, the old man is here," Yaqoota said, and skipped to the door on one foot, and then the other, before slipping out of the room.

Noora held the door ajar and looked out just as the group outside quickly disposed of the customary greetings. Lateefa and Jassem were asking Shamsa's father to rest and have coffee, but he insisted that he was in a hurry. The old man had brought two men with him to carry his daughter's belongings.

And then Shamsa walked out fully veiled. There was none of her usual blaze of hysterics, only quiet words of farewell. She held her head high and stooped slightly for Lateefa's embrace. And Lateefa wrapped her with all the tenderness of a mother to her child.

As Jassem kissed Shamsa on her forehead, Noora noticed Juma's thin fingers creep onto his daughter's shoulder and squeeze it. It was a tiny gesture but was so full of meaning. That was a pinch of support, and suddenly Noora envied her.

Shamsa was returning to her family, a rich family who loved her enough to take her back. And she, Noora, had no family or home she could go back to. She had to stay where she was, under Lateefa's bullying hand, a hand that could crush her with the simplest touch. And Noora wondered who the real winner was.

Noora could not watch anymore. She pulled off her *shayla* and untangled the comb from her hair. She climbed onto the bed and, dangling her legs over the side, began swinging them. The rest of her remained as rigid as a tree trunk as she listened to the front door open and Shamsa leave.

She should have felt victorious. She had won. Instead, Noora felt defeated, trapped in the possibility that Lateefa knew of her secret affair with Hamad. Her swinging legs were gaining momentum. There was nothing she could do but follow Lateefa's "advice," as the older woman called it. And that's what she had been doing. She kept her objections behind clenched lips whenever Lateefa fussed over her and spent her days in her room, just as Lateefa had "advised" her to. Noora's only respite came when the house slept and she skulked into the courtyard trying to find some inspiration, some hope, or a solution in the stars.

The days were cooler now. She did not sweat as she continued to swing her legs back and forth. The moist sea air wafted through the bars of her window easily, and now it carried the voices of other men entering the house and Jassem's, too, so full of vigor, calling out his orders to them to seal the wind towers.

"We have to hurry," he was saying. "It's coming today or to-morrow at the latest."

Of course he was talking of the rain. For the past few days, there had been so much rain talk in the household. But Noora could not share that excitement. She knew that even the rain would not be able to wash away the gloom she felt.

Noora swung her legs harder and with her next kick in the air came another kick. She squeaked with surprise at the sharpness of it and pressed her hands to her stomach. There was urgency in it. That kick seemed to be hurrying her on to take some action. Was her baby telling her that it was strong enough to be carried away—somewhere else?

Before she could think more, the door swung open and La-teefa entered, followed closely by Jassem. Noora crossed her arms in a huff. Now there would be two bees buzzing over her: Lateefa spewing out the frequent reminders of what she must do and what she mustn't and Jassem grunting his approval.

She ignored the drone of their fussing and placed her hand on her stomach and waited, waited for the next kick. When nothing happened, she began to wonder whether the baby was telling her something else. Perhaps she should be thinking about it, its security instead of her own.

Lateefa clapped for attention, and Noora flinched. "Don't swing your legs like that." She lifted her finger in a strict wag. "It will make the blood slip to your toes instead of nourishing the baby." Her voice was as annoying as a mosquito in still air. "And why aren't you lying down more? Every time I walk in, you are sitting up like a watchman."

"Yes, you must lie down," Jassem added, his voice brimming with so much concern that Noora felt she must listen to him. She stretched out on the bed and caught his approving nod as he explained, "You see, sweet wife, the weight of you sitting up all the time will make you short."

Lateefa slapped his arm with a tender giggle. "Nothing to do with that, husband. It's so that the child can get a firm grip in its mother's womb."

He hung his head awkwardly and mumbled something under his breath. Noora watched him as he tried to wipe away the embarrassment with a cough. He had allowed himself to sink into women's matters, and now he needed to change the subject. "You must listen to your mother Lateefa, Noora. She is only thinking of you and our child. When that child is born, *insha' Allah*, with God's will, I will give it everything." He had regained his confidence, though his voice croaked under the surges of emotion that were beginning to brew in him. "Think, woman, think. This child, our child, will have all those things you've never had."

Noora sat up straight. Suddenly she was interested. "Like what will it have?" she asked.

"Everything! All that I own. And before that, all the opportunity you could hope for it." He coughed softly. "I will bring a tutor, an Indian tutor, to educate the child in English and mathematics. And science, too. This child will be armed with knowledge, ready for the new days to come, days full of promise, because it won't be long before the oil starts bringing riches to this land."

He paused and let his eyes drift along the wall behind Noora, as if seeing the spectacular pink and violet streaks of a sunrise bloated with promise. And Noora followed his eyes to make sure she didn't miss any details of what he was saying.

"And I'll be ahead, ready for all that's coming," Jassem continued. "Why do you think I am building relations with the

English people? They will be drawing our beginnings. And I will be right there with them."

"Enough, enough," Lateefa interrupted. "You are getting her all excited for nothing. It's all early still." She turned to Noora and continued, "Now remember, no swinging those legs."

Noora did not hear her. How could she when her head was bursting with Jassem's magical words? He was painting a bright future, splashing all the colors of good prospects. She kept her eyes fixed to Jassem's, looked through his spectacles and sank into the expectation that glittered in them. There was truth in there, too, as sharp as a ray of light. Noora felt hope seep to her tummy, and she shuddered as it warmed the tiny limbs of her unborn baby.

42

How beautiful Jassem's words were. Throughout that day and for the many days that followed, all that he had said rolled in Noora's head like gentle waves, lifting her aspirations with every rise and spreading security with every dip, in an open and mild sea.

She was sure Jassem had meant every word. She had spotted the earnestness in his voice from the moment he had opened his mouth; his promises had caused her to drop her defenses and they had numbed the alert that tingled at the tip of her ready tongue. And now, along with a smile, she carried his thoughts with her as she drifted into the courtyard and flopped onto her back in the dancing night-shadow of the *sidr* tree. Its leaves rustled above her head and the cool air that caressed her face reminded her of time's passing. Soon, her tummy would spread so big that she would have to waddle like a duck.

There was the moon, a thin sliver that shied away in a blanket of sky peppered with countless stars. Just as she did every night, she watched them, those flickering stars. On this night, they seemed to have taken away the moon's silver glow. She wanted them to point her in the right direction, but this time the thought of running away did not fully occupy her mind. This time she was looking for another kind of guidance. She searched for some order in the stars and found it in one group that seemed to belong together as a family of sorts, forming what looked like the peak of a mountain.

At the crest, the stars beamed a steady and sure light, establishing their place in the cluster, just as Lateefa had established her place in the household. At the bottom, the stars were so fragile they seemed to be dying and they reminded her of Shamsa. And then, in the middle, in the body of that flickering mountain, the stars were erratic. They twinkled and dimmed, again and again, confused as to what they wanted to do, needed to do—just as she was.

She placed her palm onto her belly and stroked it. "Our child," she whispered, but there was none of the confidence that Jassem's voice had exuded. "Our child," she said again, slightly louder. This time her voice wobbled with guilt at her deceit.

Noora rounded her eyes wide till the inky sky swallowed the stars within it. Blackness! How could she bring a child into Jassem's life that wasn't his, grant this child the gift of his generosity? She pictured a leech, fat with the blood of someone else. So, too, was her child, to be nurtured and groomed, nourished and educated, through someone else's wealth and kindness.

She closed her eyes and buried her cheek in the sand. Up and down she rubbed her cheek, felt the rough bits of tiny, white coral chafe her skin till it burned. She didn't care. She deserved it, the pain, and more. She would keep rubbing her face till it bled. But she stopped short—there was a noise.

It came from the animal enclosure in the corner of the house by the men's *majlis*. She heard the scratch and ruffle of fabric over the flaps of the chickens' wings and the shuffles of the goats' hooves.

Was it a thief? Noora sat up and spat out the grains that had slipped through her lips. There was a shadow marching toward her. She was about to wake up the household with a scream, but then she recognized that shadow. At once, she wished it were a thief.

Hamad didn't bother to creep under the cover of the arcade. He was crossing the courtyard like a fearless camel. His feet dug deep into the sand, indifferent to what they trampled on.

Noora jumped up. She wanted to scold him for not thinking of the position he was putting her in. She wanted to push him back into the dark. But he was by her side already, clutching her wrist and pulling her to her room.

He pushed the door open with his leg and yanked her in. The lamp blazed, dangling on a nail in the wall by the window, and she could see the surge of his breath balloon his chest. His brows knotted in a frown and he swallowed her with his stare.

Noora stiffened and held her breath tight. Only when he spun around to peer out the window did she slacken, puffing out all the air that she had held.

"Safe," Hamad said. "Safe so far, but we don't have a lot of time."

She had mistaken his urgency for anger. She shook the tension out of her neck and inhaled some control into her voice before whispering, "What are you doing here so late? How did you get in?"

"I managed," he said. His eyes remained focused on the courtyard. "Now, come on, don't waste time. Hurry."

"Keep your voice down," she whispered. "And what are you talking about, anyway?" Noora's heart was racing. Even though she was comforted by knowing that Shamsa was not on the other side of the wall to hear them, there were the others. She had to get him out of her room. "Tell me what you want and leave," she ordered.

He snapped his head back at her. "What do you mean? Did you think I would leave you in this horrid place? Come on now, pack quickly, and carry only what you need. And let's go."

"Where?"

"Away, to a better future."

"I can't," Noora said, and let her hand slip to her stomach. For the first time, she felt she had to protect the baby that was being formed inside her. "Where have you been, anyway? You disappeared. I was sick, near to dying, and you disappeared."

"I was made to disappear. I was told not to come back. I was told I wasn't needed anymore."

"Who told you? My husband?"

"No, not your husband," he muttered, and dug into his pocket, pulling out a knotted bundle. "Anyway, it doesn't matter." His fingers fiddled to open the knot. "What matters is that it is done. Look."

There they were: a handful of pearls cupped in his thieving hand.

"We are all set," Hamad said, and he pushed the pearls closer to her face. In the dimness, they looked gray. Noora tried to pick out the shine in them, but all she could see was another shame Hamad was asking her to share.

"We don't have all night," he said. "I have planned everything."

But Noora could not hear him. The thuds in her chest were deafening in an air that had stopped moving, and all she could think about was that he wanted her to become a fugitive. She would never be able to come back to Wadeema or even return to her mountains. She would have to live in exile forever.

"We will hide in Leema for a few days," Hamad continued, "till the British steamer can take us over to—"

Finally she cut him off. "You did it," she whispered. "You really did it."

He scrunched his nose. "For us," Hamad said, the lilt of puzzlement dampening the bounce in his animated voice.

"I thought you had given up the idea. But you didn't. You stole them."

"Borrowed them."

"Stole them." Her voice was louder, and she tapped her mouth with her fingers to remind herself to keep it low. "How did you find the keys?"

"I managed."

"Managed, managed, managed," she croaked. "You stole them, Hamad. You stole them."

"All right, whatever you want to call it, but it's only for a little while. I will return their worth when I make money. I have told you that before. Now, come on. We have to rush."

A blast of hot air shot out of her nose. "You think you can just come and take me wherever you want, whenever you decide?" She rooted her fists to her hips and pushed out the roundness of her tummy. "And what about my situation? How can I travel with you, with this child I am carrying? You know I'm with child, don't you?"

The haste in Hamad slackened, and he slipped the pearls back into his pocket. "Is that what's worrying you?" He stepped closer to her and slowly lifted both hands to settle on her shoulders. They felt heavy, burdened, but she did not shake them off.

"You shouldn't worry about that," he continued. "The child will have a father in me and a mother in you."

Even in the lamp's weakening burn playing on his face, she could see the yearning and desire in his eyes. They were begging for her consent, her approval, her blessing. Tiny twitches teased his eyelids, but he would not blink. She felt a pinch in her heart as she watched those eyes, moistening just as a puppy's when yearning for its master's affection.

Noora could not look at him anymore. She lowered her head to her chest and rolled it from side to side, mumbling, "No, Hamad, no. I can't come with you. I have to stay here. This is my home and this is my family. When I was sick, it was *Ommi* Lateefa who healed me; it was Jassem who asked after me. So much care they gave me, *masha' Allah*, and now you want me to take from them their pearls and this child—their dream—and run away?"

"It may be their dream, but it's not their child," Hamad said. His voice was as soft as velvet. And yet Noora heard only the threat in it.

"It's hot in here," she said, wriggling out from under his hands. She paced to the door and stuck her head out. "So hot, don't you feel it?" She pulled her head back into the room, even though she dreaded what Hamad might say next. "No air," she insisted, and strode to the washroom. He followed her, and she could feel his eyes on her as she tilted the earthen jug, poured some water into her cupped hand, and splashed her face.

"Of course, you had to keep it a secret," he said, quietly, "but not with me. You don't have to pretend anything with me."

Again and again, Noora soaked her face, till the water dribbled down her neck and doused her dress. Still the heat of worry would not evaporate.

"It is my child."

There. He said it.

Noora stiffened. The secret was out, but to admit it would let loose a whole string of problems. "What are you talking about?"

"I said, I know it's my child," he said, his voice barely louder than a whisper.

"It is not your child!" She spat the words as if she had just tasted a rotten piece of meat. "It's Jassem's."

"Jassem's?" Hamad said. "If he could, he would have had at least ten by now. Hah! The whole village, no, the whole of Leema—no, no, no, the whole of India—knows he can't have children. Don't you know how many mystics and healers he's gone to see in Bombay? And each one promised him the same thing: 'This time it will work, *arbab*.'" He wagged his head. "All that money he poured into the visits and treatments. And in the end, nothing."

"Just talk, old people's talk," Noora muttered through pursed lips. "Sometimes you can be so silly, imagining the stupidest things."

"Me? Imagining the stupidest things? I don't imagine anything. I see and I understand. It is you who are blind, you who can't see that you have been played with, made to believe a lie."

"Words, words, and more words," Noora said, dabbing her wet face with her arm and mumbling into her elbow. "That's all you're good at, making up words to mix me up."

"You don't know what I'm talking about, do you?"

Now Noora turned to look at him. It seemed the color was

draining out of his face. There was alarm in his strained glare and his lips were a squiggle of puzzlement. She sneered and looked away.

"You haven't guessed, have you?" he said, his voice remaining even. "You haven't even felt that there was something very strange taking place. What, you think it was normal for us to have been together all that time, encouraged by your protecting *Ommi* Lateefa?"

"*Ommi* Lateefa is very nice to me now." Noora remained crouched by the earthen jar, hugging her knees to her chest. She didn't want to face him. So she fixed her eyes on the tiny puddles of water that had formed at her feet after all that agitated splashing. "She loves me like a real daughter."

"Lateefa saw the wild in you. She planned it all, so that you and I could be together, so that you can have a child for her and Jassem."

The shock burst out of her mouth in a yelp. Quickly, she drew in her lips as tight as she could. What was he saying? Was he making up vicious stories so that she would run away with him? She wanted to know everything—but she could not, would not, let her curiosity stray.

"Where do you think I was all this time?" he said. "She didn't want me around. She told me to go!"

"What cruelty," she said, her voice quivering with uncertainty. "How could you be so heartless to think of something like that? And anyway, if it is true, why did you go along with it?"

"I didn't . . . ," he said, and stopped. There was pain in his voice, and finally she felt it was safe to turn around and look up at him. He was frowning, and Noora could see he was struggling with what he wanted to say. He tried to speak again. This time his mouth opened, but no words came out.

Noora stood up and slowly nodded her head, "I think you had better stop making up stories. I think you'd better go now."

As she walked past him toward the door, he clutched her hand. "No," he said quickly. "Listen to me. I'm not making these things up. I didn't know Lateefa's plan at first, but then I understood. And I couldn't say anything."

Noora glowered and he let go of her hand, as if her fingers had suddenly turned into hot coals.

Hamad bent his head down. And when he spoke, it was into his chest. "You see." He paused and swallowed hard. "You see, I loved you and that is why I kept quiet, just so that I could see more and more of you."

Such simple words, so hard to utter and so filled with truth. Of that, Noora had no doubt. He was opening his heart to her. And that's what had first attracted her to him. But now she found it irritating. He was throwing away his manhood and opening his heart like a woman.

His arms hung limply by his sides, and his shoulders caved all the way to his chest. His eyes were shut tight, and Noora sensed he was waiting for her to pull him up. He was waiting for her to tap her finger under his chin and, with the soft touch of a rose petal, lift his face to hers.

When that did not happen, he began to slowly straighten up. There was none of the agility she was used to seeing in his graceful build, only the awkwardness of a rising camel, heaving the thick curve of its neck, unfurling its lanky limbs, all the while knowing it would have to stumble into a stand.

Only Hamad didn't stumble at the end of his sluggish rise, just kept his eyes closed as his begging hands floated up toward her. With fingers spread open, he kept them in midair and waited for her touch. But she was not about to give it.

"Shame on you," she hissed, shattering the stillness that clotted the air between them. Hamad's eyes snapped open and he blinked again and again, but that did not stop her. "Sneaking into my room at this late hour," she continued. "Speaking to me that way. I am a married woman, or have you forgotten that?"

"When did your heart turn to rock?" he asked. "When?" He was shaking his head now, as if trying to forget a bad dream.

"When I knew I had to think of myself, worry about myself, because no one else will do that for me."

"Listen to you, you do every filthy thing. Then you pretend you didn't." There was spite in his voice now. "I don't know who you are, what you are. Something very different from the Noora I treasured." He threw his arms in the air. "You dug a hole in the sand and filled it with your shame, thinking it will be buried forever. But the sand is soft and the wind never stops blowing. And one day . . ." He bit his lip and looked away. "You are like a . . . a . . ."

"Sand fish," she mumbled.

He did not hear her. "Why are you doing this? Why don't you want to come with me?"

"Because I don't want to bash my head," she snapped.

"What?"

"It doesn't matter."

Hamad calmed his agitation with a deep breath. "Listen," he said, turning back to face her, "they are only nice to you because of the child. Once you deliver, they will take it and bring it up the way they want to. You will have nothing to say about it."

"I don't want to hear anymore." Noora said, and plugged her ears. Still, she could hear him and he seemed intent on hurting her.

"Look what they did to Shamsa," Hamad continued. "They don't need her, so she's sent home."

"Shamsa wanted to see her family," Noora said, the defiance raging in her heart. "It was her decision to go. And she might come back. Now go."

Hamad would not go. "And what about you?" he mocked. "Where will you go once they decide they don't want you?"

This time, she did not answer. The more she spoke, the longer he would stay. His taunts could go on all night. She pressed her lobes tighter into her ears and began humming, feeling the vibration rush to her head.

Hamad tried to catch her gaze, but she focused her eyes on the floor. He tried once more, dipping down in front of her, and she swung her head toward the roof. He did not touch her, only swiveled his body around her like a cat cornering a mouse. He wanted to catch her eyes, infect them with the urgency that she knew was throbbing in his. Noora did not allow it!

She squeezed her eyes shut, and when he started to speak again, her hum grew louder and she began rotating her lobes over her ears, round and round, up and down, until all she could hear was the deafening gush of water that drowned out all the pleas, all the revelations, all the objections Hamad was making.

She felt as stubborn as a spoiled child, but she didn't care. Hamad had to understand that he must leave, that her decision had been made, that she would not be going with him.

And then the room went silent.

Her hum weakened into a moan, and she unplugged her ears. When she opened her eyes, she found him leaning by the window, facing her but not seeing her. The burning madness was gone and a sullen defeat had replaced it. He was slipping his hand into his pocket and pulling out the pouch.

She took a few careful steps toward him. He was aching; she could see it. The pain sucked his whole face into a knot. She pictured an old rope holding everything in place, keeping his skin taut—a rotting rope that could rip at any moment.

He did not speak, only opened his hand and watched her stare at the cluster of pearls.

"I think that's the best decision," Noora said, suddenly feeling wretched. "We've done enough wrong. One more wrong will not make it better. It will be easy for you to return them."

And then, that rotting rope, the one she imagined holding his face into place, snapped. Hamad stomped his foot and flung the pearls into her chest. "You take them back!"

Noora winced. She heard only the rumble in his voice; she felt only the brisk air he left behind as he stormed past her; she heard only the slaps of his feet as he stomped out of the room.

And then she picked up the playful clicks of the tumbling pearls as they bounced and bounced on the floor before rolling off.

43

amad did not try to see her again. He had stormed
out of her room and left her with the dilemma of returning the pearls. A full two weeks had passed, and
remaining in the oppressive confinement of her room, Noora
could not shape a plan of how that could be done.

She slipped her hand under the mattress and pulled out
the pouch. She undid the knot and began counting them again.
Once she made sure they were all there, all thirty-seven of
them, she tied the pouch and slid it back under the mattress
before starting her inspection.

Noora scanned the room, narrowing her eyes at the dark
corners. It was a ritual she followed daily, whenever she was
sure she would be alone. Those pearls were as slippery as
worms. After Hamad had flung them at her, she had been thorough in collecting them. And still, they continued to torment
her. Still, they continued to appear.

She bent down on her knees and ran her hand in scrupulous strokes along the weave of the palm-frond mat, flicking every snag or tear along the way. Her belly tugged at her spine, heavy as the bloated water skins she used to lug so long ago. She was about to support it when she spotted one: a rebel pearl discreetly lodged in a gap at the base of the bed's leg.

She reached out to pluck it when the door burst open and Yaqoota rushed in. "You are big enough, safe enough!" Yaqoota yelled, flinging her arms in the air. "Finally!"

"What?"

"Free, free," Yaqoota said, and then she stumbled back a step. "What are you doing down there?"

It was the first time Noora was caught on all fours, her head bent to the floor, her hips high in the air, like a cat about to rub its scent on a tree trunk. She quickly sat up, annoyed. "Why don't you knock? Must you always scream and shout? What if I were asleep?" She resented Yaqoota's continued bursting into her room whenever she wanted.

"But I have news," Yaqoota insisted.

"Well, it can wait till I've finished," Noora said, leaning over to get up and picking up the pearl in one subtle swoop.

"Well," said Yaqoota, "if you're going to be like that, I won't tell you."

As Noora shook the creases out of her dress, she pretended she didn't notice the moping Yaqoota. It took so little to make the slave girl grumpy. Her every feature ballooned. From the corners of her eyes, Noora could see Yaqoota's generous lips grow close to exploding from under her broad nose in a fierce sulk that sat solid on her bulging eyes. But Noora also knew that she could change all that just as quickly. With Noora's pregnancy, Yaqoota had become so receptive to her, so eager to get close once again. All Noora had to do was offer a little sympathy and appreciation.

"It's good of you to come, but I do need quiet at times," Noora said. "And I like to get on my knees sometimes and just stretch and stretch and stretch." She extended her arms to the ceiling. "You don't know what it is like with all this heaviness hanging on me—ah, ah, ah." She rubbed her tummy and scrunched her face to exaggerate her discomfort.

Yaqoota exhaled, and all her features deflated back into place.

Noora smiled at the result. It was all part of a decision she had recently reached for safe passage over any turbulence that might shake the peace in the household: know your people. She had decided to be clever and to weigh what she said and how.

She would allow Yaqoota to breeze in and out of her daily life, allow Yaqoota to think they were best friends. But she would be wary of their relationship. Once, not so long ago, Yaqoota had turned sour toward her, threatened to play with her insecurities. Noora vowed she would not let that happen again.

"So what is it?" Noora asked.

Yaqoota's eyes lit up. "It's all right," said Yaqoota. "You can go out now. *Ommi* Lateefa said to tell you that the danger is over and you can roam the house whenever you want."

Finally, I will be able to return the pearls, was Noora's first thought. But she wasn't about to show her relief. So she yawned and asked, "Danger?"

"The danger of losing the baby," Yaqoota said, thumping her head with the cushion of her palm. "Do I have to explain everything? Don't you know it's dangerous in the first few months? Mothers lose their babies all the time in the early months, and that is why you weren't allowed to move so much."

"Oh?" Noora raised a brow. "Is that why?"

"Of course, that is when the body decides whether it wants the baby or not."

"Hmm."

"So?" Yaqoota said. "Shall we go and look out through the door, watch the village?"

Noora was about to nod, about to skip carelessly toward the door, when a somber clarity sank to her feet, kept her rooted in place. *Must be clever*, Noora thought and yawned again to stifle her eagerness.

It seemed she was always peering at life. In her mountains, she had caught her first glimpses of Rashid through the gaps of Moza's stone hut; as a bride, she had watched her brother, Sager, through the slits of her burka as he turned away from her, rejecting her final plea; and on that boat that carried her to Wadeema, she'd peered through the rip in the partition sheet at Hamad, whose child she was now carrying. Then, there were all the other times when she caught life by looking through windows and doors, letting it all affect her own life: the *arbab*'s moods, Shamsa's tantrums, Lateefa's movements in the house—all those glimpses had sent the shivers of an uncertain future through her limbs. *Enough*, she thought.

"Or maybe we can sneak into the men's *majlis* and watch the fishermen pull in their catch," Yaqoota said, the mischief twitching at the edges of her mouth. "And what about going to the shore, splashing each other again? Remember?"

No! She would not join Yaqoota. She would stay where she was and plan the shape of her life. It was time to do that.

"Well, what do you think?"

"I don't know," Noora said. "It's so quiet here, so peaceful." She blew a casual sigh. "No, I think I'll just stay in my room . . . sew . . . maybe lie down a little."

❊ ❊ ❊

A week later, the much-anticipated rain arrived. A hard-blowing wind speared the swollen drops sidelong, and they smudged the walls of the house and pelted oblong shapes in the sand that looked like the tiny footsteps of a lame leg.

Noora lodged her head between the bars of the window and let the pelting drops splatter her face. Although the rain was late in coming, it was just enough to settle the courtyard sand, just enough to wash the dust off the *sidr* tree and rinse the walls of the house. The gush was short, but it was just enough to tug the faces of Jassem, Lateefa, and Yaqoota into cat-grins as they watched the rain from under the arcade.

Noora caught all of that through her window, for she remained faithful to her resolution: she would leave her room when she decided. All along, she had been the goat on a rope that Lateefa had led. Now she was determined to change that. For a full week, ever since Yaqoota had announced that the danger was over, Noora had collected all her stubbornness and made it her strength. It was her show of bravery, her own very special triumph.

Yaqoota let out a piercing whoop and jumped into the middle of the courtyard. Crossing an arm over her chest, she began spinning her head in dizzying circles. The rain clung to her hair like dewdrops as her *shayla* slithered down onto her shoulders.

Watching the slave girl's abandon, Noora felt no envy. Whereas Yaqoota could act like a child, Noora had decided she could not. There was a baby growing inside her, and soon she would give it birth. She could feel the days drawing closer. Her stomach kept growing and expanding. Mothers acted differently. Mothers had responsibilities.

Jassem and Lateefa remained under the arcade watching Yaqoota's frenzied dance. They were smiling and making quiet comments to each other. Noora glimpsed them briefly before closing her eyes against the pelting drops. The rain brought newness. It brought cleanliness. It washed past sins away. The rain would make her life better.

A ray of light pierced the clouds and spread on Noora's face. When she opened her eyes, Yaqoota was slowing down along with the dwindling drops, stumbling into small, random steps as she tried to stand still in her whirling world. Then the rain stopped. And Yaqoota tumbled to the ground and surrendered to the spinning sky.

And there was Noora's baby, circling the inside of her hardened tummy. It twisted and stretched, sluggish as the trickle of thick honey. With its every move, Noora was convinced it was carving a bond between them. It was telling her that they were one.

And then it kicked. And Noora yelped with delight.

44

The rain came and the rain went. It was quick, but somehow, in that short precious spell, it splashed some boldness into Noora. The effect persisted as Noora stuck to her resolution for another three days, after which time she decided it was long enough to prove her point. She pushed open her door and breezed into the middle of the courtyard. She craved the warmth of the sun, and flinging her head up to the sky, she squinted at the blue tinge that lingered in the early morning light.

"It is a morning of light today, *masha' Allah*, clean light after that beautiful rain." Lateefa's voice came from one side of the house. Noora had not noticed her. She turned and spotted Lateefa sitting in the indigo shade of the arcade that stretched over the kitchen and family *majlis*. "I saw you peeking through the window to watch the rain," Lateefa continued. "Why didn't you come out and join us?"

"I was scared of catching cold," Noora said.

"No, that wouldn't have happened if you had stood by my side, safe and dry, under the arcade." She had a metal tray heaped with dusty rice grains in front of her. "Come, come," Lateefa said, patting the palm-frond mat. "Sit next to me while I clean the rice."

Noora hobbled toward Lateefa and sank in one quick move onto folded knees.

"No, no," Lateefa said. "Don't bend down so quickly. If you sit like that, all the blood will get trapped behind your knees. Let the blood move freely." She rocked the air with a swaying hand.

That incessant badgering! Lateefa's was a tender scold, delivered with the soft touch of silk. And yet Noora had to breathe deep to smother the blaze of frustration that prickled her cheeks. She wanted to make a face and stick her tongue out. But it would not do to act unwisely. After all, Noora had decided to be clever. So she loosened her legs and extended them.

Lateefa returned to her rice, separating the tiny black stones and clumps of dirt from the grains, flicking them to one side with rapid taps of her index finger. "We have to make sure we get them all out before we can cook the rice," she said, pausing to grin at Noora. "Otherwise, one hard crunch and that will be the end of my teeth."

It was an invitation for Noora to join her in this quiet mother-daughter chore. Or was it wife-wife? Whichever it was, Noora would not. Instead, she leaned back onto the prop of her elbows and tilted her head to the side. Then, with the cool-cool glance of a lazy snake, she gazed up at Lateefa.

The older woman had returned her attention to the tray in front of her, her eyes resting in tranquil arcs. There was

serenity in her face, an unruffled peace that came with un-
questioned authority. Everything seemed to be going her way.

The more Noora watched her, the more grew a desire to
shake her, to agitate her self-assurance. "You know, you worry
so much, *Ommi* Lateefa," Noora said. "All this time, you come
and fuss over me, but really all is well. *Masha' Allah*, I've been
eating the chicken you bring me every day. I have been drink-
ing the milk. I've been resting. The baby's growing fine. I'm
fine. My stomach is as strong as a drum." She patted it. "In
short, there is nothing to be scared of."

Lateefa said, "Anything I tell you is for your own good, for
your own protection. You should know that by now."

"But the danger's over, remember?" Noora's tongue flicked
with sarcasm. "Isn't that what you told Yaqoota to tell me? Isn't
that why I can leave the room now to walk around as I please?
Danger's over, but maybe there is another danger I have to
watch out for?"

"Danger's over, danger's over," the older woman began in a
mutter under her breath that led to a chuckle deep in her chest.
"You were always one full of adventure. I spotted that in you
right from the start." She nodded and tapped the side of her
burka. "It was all in your eyes."

"Adventure? Is that what you saw in my eyes?"

"That . . . and other things."

There was the smack of bitterness on Noora's tongue, which
tasted like old tea. "Oh? And what else did you see in my eyes?"
she said.

Lateefa did not look up. She kept her eyes fixed on the rice
as she shaped it into a mound. "The thick green of those eyes,
ah, they hide so much—just like when you boil sugar. So thick

and sticky you can't see the tiny granules anymore. Of course, the sugar is still there, and it is still sweet. But it has just been swallowed by this new"—she paused, and her forehead creased as she searched for the right word—"thing . . . Yes, sugar, boiled thick, looks different but still the same." She nodded briskly and her eyes lit up in silent self-congratulation.

Noora wasn't in the mood for Lateefa's embellished images that went round in circles. "Too much sugar can make you sick." She let the tip of her tongue rest between her teeth. She was ready to bite.

Lateefa chuckled again. "Ah ha ha, you have got the wild in you, girl. But I am going to tame it." She looked up at Noora. "It may take a while, but in the end, you will be as sweet as honey." She spoke in her usual rose-petal softness, with a touch of the thorn on the stem.

"You still didn't tell me what you saw in my eyes," Noora persisted.

"Well, I'm not sure how to answer that. I'd describe it if I could. But I saw restlessness, some impulsiveness. And other things. Yes, I saw everything—all that you were capable of."

The fury moved about in Noora like agitated bubbles in boiling water, and it kept her from cowering under the drips of Lateefa's carefully chosen words. All her fears of what Lateefa might reveal evaporated. Noora sat up. Her lips fell open and the words fell out. "Are we talking about my pregnancy?"

The older woman would not say more; she only scraped any runaway grains into her growing hill of rice.

"My pregnancy, are we talking about that?" Noora insisted.

The older woman paused and looked up. It was a brief look but had the force of a door slamming shut. And then Noora knew.

It was the confirmation she was looking for. And it made her shudder. There was nothing more to be said. She wanted to run back to her room. She wanted to flop onto her bed and bury her face in her arms, and weep and weep and weep. It took all her strength to resist the impulse. After all, she had decided to be strong.

Forcing down a mammoth gulp, Noora stayed where she was, sitting straight-backed, feeling only a slight tremble at the edge of her mouth. The stillness between them was heavy, sliced only by the clicks and scrapes of Lateefa's finger shooting the dirt out of the rice.

Finally, Lateefa spoke. "So quiet here today with everyone out of the house. Jassem is at the shop in Leema, Shamsa moved out, and Yaqoota, even that fool has disappeared." She tipped her head toward the men's *majlis*. "She must be out there, lazing about by the shore." She sighed. "Everyone out . . . or gone." She was trying her hardest to turn the rice into a mountain. "Out or gone." When the grains kept dribbling down, refusing to form a peak, she slapped them flat. "Even Hamad, he's gone."

Just as Noora felt she had retrieved her poise, Lateefa ruffled her again.

"Gone," Lateefa repeated. "Left!"

Noora felt her lips quiver with vulnerability. Still, she held herself rigid, said nothing so that she would not fall into what might be another trap.

"Don't you want to know where he went?" Lateefa asked. The rasp of her voice was as sharp as a saw on wood.

"No," Noora answered, a little too quickly for her liking. "What do I care?"

But Lateefa told her anyway. "Gone to India, booked himself a passage and *pfooh!*" She blew out the last word, as if Hamad had been a blustering gust that had wafted into the house and out of it again. "I don't know what the fool is planning to do. His father came and told our husband that he was going to find work elsewhere." She scoffed. "Ungrateful boy—didn't even tell us himself, didn't even come to say good-bye. And after all that we offered him." She raised her finger like a scolding parent. "But you just wait. He will be back and begging for work, and we won't take him." She snickered. "He'll end up a coolie in Leema, carry this, pick up that. And then he might go mad with hunger and become just like that ghastly beggar—remember him, all dirt and disease clinging to his face? And the head, twirly-twirly with madness? Mmm . . ." She nodded, obviously satisfied with the life she had just drawn for Hamad. "Of course, it doesn't really matter, does it?"

"Of course it doesn't matter," Noora confirmed, surprised at how even her voice sounded. With this renewed steadiness, she shuffled toward the tray and said, "Let me help you, that way you will finish quicker."

"Ahh . . ." Lateefa purred her pleasure and tilted her head to the side. "Working together, now that's what makes an agreeable household. That was another thing I saw in your eyes: intelligence." She released a smile so generous it lifted the sag of her chin. "I think we should leave the house for a bit, go visiting. Certainly, your belly is big enough to fight off any jealous eyes that may fall on it. What do you say to that?"

"If you think it's all right, then yes."

"I do, I really do," Lateefa said. "Why don't we go tomorrow, visit my friend Atheeja. It will be good for you to get out a little. We can go together and take Yaqoota along, too. That would be nice, won't it?"

Noora nodded and thought of the pearls she still had to return. "It would be very nice," she said.

She should have jumped up, run across to Jassem's room, and returned those pearls as soon as Lateefa and Yaqoota left. Instead, Noora remained lying on her bed feigning fatigue, which had been her excuse for not joining them. And for a long time, after their voices had faded into the streets of Wadeema, she stayed where she was till she fell asleep and entered a dream overflowing with Lateefa.

She was behind Lateefa, who strolled across a sea of sand. Every now and then, the older woman would look over her shoulder with half-closed eyes, as if making sure Noora continued to follow her. There was a smile there, too, more of a pinch on the side of her mouth. It was discreet, yet it was filled with Lateefa's typical self-assurance.

Step by careful step, Lateefa walked on, her feet leaving behind footprints for Noora to step into. Oh those feet, round and plump, leading her along. And there were Noora's feet, long and curious as a fox's snout, stepping into Lateefa's footprints, one foolish step at a time.

Noora awoke in a sweat, stapled to the mattress, to the voice of the muezzin. She fought against the numbness that weighed her limbs down as she staggered to the washroom. Crouched by the earthen jug, Noora poured water over her hands—three times on the right hand and three times on the left. Her movements were slow and uncoordinated as she performed her ablutions for the afternoon prayer. The three cold splashes to her face dribbled down her chin and sank into her dress.

That treacherous Lateefa! Hardly the gentle mother she pretended to be. The poison that lingered on her tongue was always hidden in sweet words and unfinished sentences. The thought left an ugly taste in Noora's mouth, as if she were chewing a mush of rice, onions, fish, and bananas all in one go. She spat and rinsed her mouth—three times.

And then there was Hamad. Gone. Noora wondered how it was possible to feel loneliness and relief at the same time. She blew an irritated honk and slapped the water in the final three rinses for prayer onto her feet, first the right, then the left.

Noora caught a glimpse of her long shadow behind her, pushing her along, as she made her way to the door and nudged it open. The street was empty save for the familiar sounds that seeped through the *barastis*: the muffled voices of women, the whine of an infant or two, the clang of pots and pans, those persistent cat howls floating out of some hidden street.

She stepped out and turned toward the sea. There were the little girls and boys of Wadeema, doing what they did every afternoon. As she watched them hopping and rolling, tumbling and running by the shore, the sudden flutters and cries of a flock of seagulls, flapping low over her head, made her start. Her eyes followed them as they flew toward the sea. That is when she spotted the sun, herding the last of the day's rays back into its round form. Soon, it would sink into the horizon.

The urgency hit her sharp as a smack on the face—she had wasted so much time. Now her shadow dragged as she hastened to her room and pulled out the pouch of pearls from under the mattress. From the kitchen, she grabbed a rag to serve as a good excuse that she was cleaning in case anyone caught her, and she entered Jassem's room.

She placed the pearls on the ground and looked up. *It was easy*, she thought. The keys were at the top of the cupboard, so all she had to do was pick them up, unlock the cupboard and safe, and then put them back. Simple.

She flung the rag to the ground and placed three *takyas*, one on top of the other, to the side of the cupboard. Once she was perched on top, her baby stirred and she dropped her left hand to her navel. Her other hand groped the top of the cupboard. When she did not feel the metal of the keys, she extended her arm farther, scraping and stroking blindly. Still nothing.

Noora rose onto her toes for a look. The keys were neither at the far corners nor lodged behind the sculpted urns that sat on either side.

She shook away the horror that was beginning to grip her and unleashed a frantic search, all the while cursing her stupidity in delaying the return of the pearls. Her arms burrowed under the mattress; she shook the *takyas* and pillows and checked what was behind them; she flipped the corners of the carpet, with its dizzying patterns that curled into each other. Fabric, weave, and stuffing was all she could feel. So she stopped and scanned the room for other possible hiding places. She was certain the keys had been moved elsewhere to dodge burglars.

There were the shelved alcoves: three broad domes carved deep into the thick wall that faced the door. On them were various decorative vases and plates. She moved each carefully, but no keys sat behind them. She flung the *takyas* to the other side of the room and made another tower so that she could reach the decorative plaster screens above the door and windows. One by one, she poked her fingers into the recesses of the carvings of pots of flowers and into the squares and triangles that made up the geometric borders. As her frustration grew, so, too, did the movement in her belly. Her baby was wriggling and twisting like sand pouring out of a tight fist.

Finally, she stepped down. The light was dimming, and soon she would have to fetch the hurricane lamp. She had to hurry if she wanted to search Lateefa's bedroom, too. She quickly neatened Jassem's room, and just as she leaned over to pick up the pearls, her baby launched a big kick that surprised her into leaning heavily onto the side of the cupboard. She heard the cupboard groan. And something else, too—the plunk of sliding metal.

Her eyes rounded with anticipation, and in a flash she was pushing the cupboard with all her strength. It budged slightly and the wedged keys slipped to the ground.

And then her head was stuck to the side of the cupboard at an awkward angle while her hand tunneled through the gap. And Noora felt her baby swim in her. She ignored it—this was no time to calm its acrobatics. Her fingers stretched taut. Her knuckles snapped. She caught the keys.

And that's when she heard the thud of wood on wood.

She held her breath and listened. Was that a door opening? With keys trapped in her fist, she hurried to steal a look into the courtyard. Satisfied that the house door had not shifted, she turned back to the cupboard. But there was the sound again: grating wood. She turned back again, only to see once more that the house door remained closed. And for a moment, she was puzzled. Until she saw it. Another door was opening. And her heart turned into a spasm of flapping wings.

There was Jassem pushing open the *majlis* door. There he was stepping into the courtyard. She was about to get caught, about to be labeled a thief. The thoughts tripped over each other in her head. He was going to lift a stern finger and point her to the street.

But he did no such thing. Jassem was lifting up his leg and slipping off his sandal. He was shaking the sand out. Now he was doing the same with his other sandal. Jassem had not seen her.

She felt the metal keys, hot as a dying coal, in her tight fist. She had to put the pearls back. Immediately.

She heard him plod across the courtyard as she unlocked the cupboard. He was calling her as she clicked open the safe, and she guessed he was by her room. Her fingers wormed through the knots of the pouches of pearls with his second call. She would not answer, would only finish her mission. With an odd thoroughness in the middle of her panic, she emptied the stolen pearls into their rightful pouch and locked both safe and cupboard.

He was coming. There was the rustle of his dishdasha, like wind through a tree, as he crossed the courtyard. Her heart was pounding. She still had to return the keys to the top of the cupboard.

The door opened with a grunt. And Noora was on her knees, her finger poked into the rag, as she rubbed the grooves of the cupboard's blossoming vines with a fierceness that pulled her face into a scowl. She was ready, armed with a storehouse of excuses for being in his room.

"What are you doing?" Jassem asked. There was the gurgle of shock and bother in his voice.

A shrill voice screamed the answer in her head: "Cleaning!" But as she turned to look up at him, she could not verbalize all those excuses she had planned to throw at him. The words tip-toed on her tongue like the sprinkling of a light rainfall as she felt her hand slacken and the rag fall to the ground.

Then she was still. Crouched in place, guilt and vulnerability kept her as rigid as a withered tree stump. The only movement came from her baby, swimming strong, like the surge of water through rocks packed tight.

"Didn't you hear me call? And why are you doing housework in your pregnant state?" He stepped close to her and squinted in the dimming light. "Look at you, flushed and sweating, like you've run to the sea and back."

She had to act. He was about to say more, but Noora rose so suddenly he stopped short. Then, with a swooping arm, she seized his hand and nestled it on her belly.

Immediately, he tried to pull it away, but Noora kept her grip firm till the baby kicked. Then it was Jassem's turn to stiffen. There was shock and hesitation in his tightened face. His eyeballs bulged, as if about to fuse with his spectacles.

"You can stroke it," Noora said, as gently as she could manage through her shallow breath and the thundering beats of her heart. "Don't worry, you won't harm it. It is strong. Move your hand to the left a bit."

Jassem's fingers trembled as he let his hand slide along to the side of her roundness.

"A little lower," she instructed.

Yes, shock and bewilderment washed over him as the churn in her stomach continued. Noora recognized something else in him, too: delight. It radiated from his face like the glimmer of the moon in an otherwise inky sky.

"It is moving so much now," Noora said.

He did not answer her, only went on exploring the movement within her belly. With lips unlatched, she could see his tongue lying limp within the cave of his mouth. He was captivated.

Noora continued to draw the map of motion on her belly, instructing him to move his hand lower or lift it higher, move it to the right or left. "I don't care what anyone tells me," she said, "about how proper it is and all. I really think you should feel it." She was quietly creating a bond between them by allowing him to enter her secret world—a woman's mysterious world, there for sharing only between women. Watching him, she knew he treasured the privilege. And she felt bold enough to add, "After all, it is your child."

He moaned, and Noora pulled in her reward of a proper lungful of air. She had averted disaster with her quick thinking. Jassem suspected nothing. She let her eyes drift to the urns that crowned the cupboard. The keys were lying safely at their base.

The baby kicked once more. Jassem flinched and Noora knew she had won a small piece of his heart.

46

oora placed one more shell in a line along the wall. There were eight altogether, each representing a month of her pregnancy. These were shells she had pulled out of the wall. Curved and chipped, yellowed with age, the shells had none of the beauty of the stones of her mountains. So she decided to create a pattern of sorts to make them look more attractive. She pulled off the necklace that clung to her neck and threaded it between the shells in a wavy line, a design she leaned back to admire, but only the glimmer of the gold filled her eye. The necklace, thick gold with a tassel at the end, was a gift from Jassem, along with a gold filigree bangle with a tiny, pink coral set in its center, which sat flat on her wrist.

Jassem was like a child with a secret toy, sneaking into her room whenever he could, always pleading with his eyes to touch her stomach. Of course, he didn't have to, as she always agreed.

It was a small kindness for the appreciation and support that she was getting in return.

Now she could hear him approach her room. He was coming to her again. She slid the necklace back over her head and waited. The door opened with a sigh, and Jassem entered and crouched next to her. He tilted his head for permission and she nodded.

His forehead puckered with concentration as he moved a cautious hand toward her belly. This affectionate frown was reserved for when they were alone. In front of Lateefa, he'd always retrieve his formal self.

"It's moving less now," Noora said.

"Mash' Allah," he said, and waited for the baby to stir.

"Look how big I am. And the baby's bigger, too. I don't think there's much room for it to move anymore. Ah, wait, there . . . lower your hand."

But Jassem didn't have time, for Lateefa's sudden bark broke his focus. He wrenched back his hand and looked over his shoulder. Lateefa had slunk into the room unnoticed, and now she was waving her finger at him.

"What do you think you are doing," she scolded, "touching a pregnant woman like that? Shame on you! Don't you know you shouldn't be prodding women's tummies?"

The embarrassment exploded in Jassem's face. He stood up quickly and fidgeted. His eyes darted around the room, like a caged animal searching for an open door.

A panic washed over Noora as she watched him. He wanted to leave the room without answering. He wanted to flee. She sprang up and shifted in front of him, to face Lateefa. "It's nothing," she said to the older woman.

"Pah!"

"He only wants to feel the baby move."

"Feel the baby move?" Lateefa scoffed. "There are customs we have to follow. Pregnancy is a woman's business. Men should have nothing to do with it. Our husband should not be a part of it. What, you have suddenly decided to make up your own rules now?"

"My father touched my mother's belly every day when she was pregnant with my brothers." That was Noora's answer. She did not waver, even though she was making it up. "I saw it and there's nothing to it."

"Maybe where you're from, up there where the goats run wild," Lateefa said. Her voice was filled with the crackle of gravel on glass. "But here, we have our ways. Even our goats know where they can run and where they can walk. Even our goats understand the rules."

"What harm is there?" Noora persisted.

"Harm? Well . . . ," Lateefa said. "Well . . . that's not the point, is it?" Lateefa was faltering, and Noora was about to prod on, when Jassem cut her off.

"Stop it, women, stop it both of you," he said. He had remained standing behind Noora but now stepped between his two wives. "I won't have you arguing and fighting like cats in my house."

"But it's her," Noora said, as Lateefa turned away from them and walked toward the door. "She is always putting blame on me, making me feel everything I do is wrong."

Lateefa grunted and folded her arms tight over her ribs. She had coiled into the corner of the room, and with a pained swivel of her head, she looked down at the ground. It was a poor-me pose; it was a take-my-side pose.

"Nothing I do is good enough for her," Noora continued.

Jassem twisted back to Noora and whispered, "I know, I know." Then his voice grew louder, more stern. "Not the way to talk about our Lateefa. She's older than you are, and you should know to show some respect."

"That's all I ask for, some respect," said a meek-voiced Lateefa.

"Respect, that's all. Do you understand?" Jassem said, still speaking to Noora but looking at Lateefa. And then his hand snuck behind his back and groped the air. And Noora understood. She had stood up for him and he wanted to show his gratitude. So she slipped her hand into his. But she felt more—so much more—in his steady grip. It was a warm, protective squeeze, with just the right amount of pressure to make her feel special. "So do we agree?" he said. "No more fighting?"

"We agree," said Lateefa.

"Yes, we agree," said Noora.

47

O f course, Noora knew that that would not be the end
of it. Lateefa would be looking for retribution. And it
came, three days later, with Lateefa's declaration that
Shamsa had asked for a divorce and Jassem had agreed.

Noora gasped. It was an important piece of news and very
unexpected. They had just settled around the lunch mat, under the arcade that hung over the kitchen and family room, and
were waiting for Jassem to join them.

"Well, why are you so surprised?" Lateefa said, before
stretching out her foot to squish the tiny, orange ants that always arrived with the scent of a meal. Those that did not meet
an instant death writhed to escape with whichever part of their
bodies they could. "I was sure she would do that," Lateefa continued. "You see, her pride was injured."

Of course, Noora knew it wasn't uncommon for a woman to
ask for a divorce. What puzzled her was that Jassem was agree-

ing to it. Almost two years since she'd first set foot in Leema, and still the memory remained as clear as rinsed glass. How angry he was at Shamsa's abandonment even then! His hurt pride had bubbled like boiling water as he carried it through the market. Along the way, he had poured it on the unsuspecting madman. It had taken no more than a dagger look to make Shamsa's loose tongue twist back into her mouth, harmless as a snake coiled in a frozen pit. He had made it clear that Shamsa belonged to him. And yet, now, he was setting her free so quickly. None of it made sense.

Lateefa caught her thoughts. "It is surprising, I must say," she said. "Why did our husband agree?" She retrieved her foot out of the ant slaughter and brushed off the few victims that clung to her big toe. "Pah! We don't really have to worry about her. Less food to cook." She reached out for a piece of radish and, tilting up her burka, tossed it into her mouth.

How harsh of her to speak that way! Noora felt she needed to defend Shamsa, even though, through all their days together, they had been rivals. Still, they'd shared something: the lack of choice. Weren't they both thrown under the same roof and into a life not of their selection? But then, wasn't that the fate of all young women? Something in Noora, an emptiness, expanded in what space was left in her belly as she struggled to find a sympathetic remembrance. When she could not, she said, "I thought you liked her."

"Hmm . . ." Lateefa let the muffled crunch of teeth on radish fill the silent space between them before speaking. "I suppose our husband is relieved that she chose to leave on her own. I mean, why would she stay? What's the point in the end? You see, unlike you, she has a rich family that wants her. Unlike you, she really does not need the security of this house."

A croaky groan lingered at the back of Lateefa's throat. "Yes, I suppose there's no reason to keep her."

No point in keeping her? Noora thought of Hamad and his warning. Was she next? "Well, I suppose it is just like me. Once I deliver this child, you won't need me anymore." That's what Noora was thinking. She realized that her thoughts had fallen out of her mouth only when Lateefa shrieked and the disintegrated radish splattered into her burka and bounced back to dribble down her mouth.

"Jaaassem!" Lateefa cried. "Come and listen to what this ungrateful woman is saying about us."

Noora's hands turned into butterfly wings as she tried to calm the older woman's unexpected outburst. All the while, she resisted the urge to reach out and twist the burka off Lateefa's face, see what was behind it. Was this genuine hurt or, as she suspected, another of Lateefa's tricks for sympathy?

"Shame on you," Lateefa cried, thumping her chest. "What do you think we are, monsters? Jaaassem!"

"What is it?" Jassem's call flew out of his room.

"Come, come and listen to what she thinks of us," Lateefa cried, with a voice filled with the wail of a grieving mother.

As Jassem rushed across the courtyard, Lateefa began blinking hard to break the solid glaze that sat on her eyes. But as always with sly tears, they took their time.

"What happened?" demanded Jassem. "Didn't we agree to stop these cat fights?"

"You didn't hear what she said," said Lateefa. "It hurt me so. You didn't hear what she thinks of us. She said . . . she said . . ." And she paused, while a much-desired tear grew in the corner of her right eye. There it lingered, until she squeezed it out with a forced wink.

The panic rushed up Noora's spine in waves of prickly heat as she watched Lateefa's silent tear's sluggish journey down her cheek and into the half-moon pouch beneath her eye. There it stopped. There it dried. Lateefa wiped it anyway.

"She said we are cruel, that we would throw her out of the house once the baby is born," said Lateefa.

"Is that true, is that what you think of us?" Jassem asked.

Fury, merciless as a rockslide, rumbled in Noora. Lateefa could twist words all she wanted, but she would not cower. Right there and then, Noora decided she could twist words, too. "Of course not," she said. "You are my family, my life."

"And why would you say what you said if you didn't mean it?" Jassem asked.

"It's just . . ." And here, Noora paused and gathered all her fears, let them flood her mind. And quickly, her eyes began to moisten. It is so easy when you have a real reason. "*Ommi* Lateefa doesn't understand how things get muddled up in the head when you are pregnant. You feel like you're angry and happy at the same time. You say things without really thinking, so many silly things. And well, what can I say?" She did not need to wink; her first tear plopped heavy as a dewdrop into her lap. Then another and another. "I mean, of course I didn't mean what I said. You must believe me." In between sniffles, she caught glimpses of Lateefa's tilted head. Was there puzzlement behind that burka? Noora didn't have time to ponder, for she was immersed in this new tactic of playing with words. It was a trick mastered by Lateefa, and Noora was finally giving it a go. "And I don't blame *Ommi* Lateefa for reacting that way," she continued. "How would she know what's going on inside me? After all, she has never been pregnant."

"Enough, enough, enough," Jassem said. "It's not good for you to get so worked up."

"Yes, enough, enough," Lateefa repeated, her voice sharp with impatience. "Maybe I did overreact a little. I don't want you upsetting yourself. After all, you need the strength. The day is coming, very soon. You'll be giving Jassem his most desired dream, and he will always be grateful to you, as will I."

Noora calmed down her snivels with deep and noisy inhalations.

But Lateefa had not finished. "Of course, once that child comes, you'll be able to rest, finally. Leave everything to me. I will take care of it."

She was twisting words again, this time twirling them tighter than a sailor's knot. "No!"

"See, husband?" said Lateefa. "That's her problem. She has no trust in me."

Jassem grunted.

"It is my child," Noora said, taken aback by the warble that had suddenly sprung to the back of her throat. She had felt so confident playing the role of the distraught younger wife, and now there was this strange emotion surging through her. And her face! Now there were real tears rolling down, full of the spattering sting of sea spray.

"Look, it's all early, and everything will work out," Jassem said.

"No, no, no, you see, it's different," Noora said, taking raucous gulps of air. "A mother always knows what's best for her child. *Ommi* Lateefa has never felt a child growing in her stomach. So she doesn't know. It's . . . it's—"

"How ridiculous you are sometimes," Lateefa interrupted.

Noora continued despite Lateefa's disdain. "It's hard to explain, but that child is a part of me." She was regaining an even breath, the heat of her outburst slightly conquered.

"Part of us, too," Lateefa said, with a snotty jiggle of the head.

"Yes, but growing in me." Now she felt ready as a mother cat, ready to hiss and scratch. But Jassem stopped her short.

"And made by me," he said.

Noora looked up at him, puzzled and irritated at his disruption in the middle of this test of wills between her and Lateefa. She shook her head and frowned. What had he just said? And then it struck her. And there was Lateefa, looking up at him, too, her eyes as dark and lifeless as ash. Lateefa could spill her secret right there and then. And the thought shook the fear back into Noora.

"What?" he said.

They looked down and mumbled at the same time, "Nothing, nothing."

"Well, let's eat then," he said, and he called Yaqoota to bring their lunch.

While they waited, only the soft coos of roosting pigeons broke the silence that hung over the house. While they waited, Noora tried to understand why, just moments ago, Lateefa had had a chance to reveal her secret and didn't. Why?

Yaqoota placed the tray in the middle of the mat. As they burrowed their hands into the rice and rubbed free the fish from bone, Noora remained eagle-eyed with Lateefa. She tried to catch some hint in the older woman's eyes, but Lateefa kept them fixed on the tray. And then Noora felt her biggest fear melt away as she realized her secret would always remain so.

Lateefa never intended to let it out, only threatened. After all, what would she say? What could she say? And, more impor-

THE SAND FISH {333}

tant, would Jassem believe her? Such tales! Certainly, he would take them for what they were: tales of spite and jealousy. Hadn't Lateefa been showing a lot of jealousy recently? *It is all falling into a neat pattern, like the scales on the fish I am now skinning,* she thought happily.

She ate with a greedy appetite. Food had never been so tasty. Of course, there was still that argument they were having, she and Lateefa. It had remained unresolved. She smiled anyway. When that confrontation came, she would be ready.

But it came right away. And Noora was not ready.

Halfway through their meal, Lateefa took her time in shaping the next ball of rice that would enter her mouth. And then she sighed, twice, making sure the second sigh sounded somehow more burdened than the first. "I think there is no point going round and round." She released a third sigh, this one filled with anguish. "This is your child—we all know that—in the body-part of things, the carrying-part of things." She nodded and paused, for her ball of rice was ready to be devoured. She tilted her burka up and dropped it into her mouth. The mask fell back in place and moved to the rhythm of her chomps. "I think," she continued, with mouth full, "we have to look at the important things here, don't you agree, husband?"

Jassem grunted.

"Most important of all is that once it is born, it will belong to all of us, so that we can give it everything together."

Noora's mouth fell open to object, but Lateefa cut her off.

"Shh . . . shh . . . Listen to me. We will pour all our love, dear. We will share it. Don't you think that's fair, to share it, hmm? As it grows, it will learn more from its father, Jassem, and from me than it will from you. After all, you are just a child yourself, with none of the wisdom or blessings that we have had."

"I can give it other things," Noora said. "I can give it love."

"Yes, yes, yes, of course you can. But I think the best thing is that I will be with you always as you do that, to make sure this child follows the good way, the right way. My foot and your foot making the same prints, how beautiful is that?"

Jassem nodded and mumbled, "That's very beautiful."

Lateefa flipped her palms to the sky. "May this child be born healthy, *insha' Allah*. May this child be graced with wisdom, *insha' Allah*. May this child follow the moral way, *insha' Allah*. God be blessed for all that He has given us."

"Amen," said Jassem.

48

So that's how it was to be: she and Lateefa making the same footprints. Wasn't that what Lateefa had said? Wasn't that what Noora had dreamed a while back?

Noora squinted at the afternoon sky, an oppressive glare of white that seemed to have sucked in the air. Only the clucks of the baby chickens broke the still air. Jassem had brought them to nourish her after the delivery so that she could recover her strength quickly, and there were so many of them running about behind the mesh enclosure.

"Rain's coming." She was thinking it but found out she'd spoken it.

"Rain? Are you crazy?" Yaqoota had just walked out of the kitchen with a load of dirty trays for washing by the well. "No rain comes at this time, only heat and humidity." She sniffed the air, thick with the scent of the sea. "It's going to be a sticky summer."

Noora moaned and breathed deeply with another rolling contraction, but she wasn't going to say anything. Then Lateefa would rush the midwife over to the house. Three times she'd done that and, every time, Noora had had to listen to a detailed account of what she had to do and what to expect. There was pain, obviously, and, most probably, a long and exhausting labor. But the last time the midwife had hurried to their house, she had mentioned death, too.

"So many die," she had said, rubbing Noora's tummy to check the position of the baby. "It starts fine, but then . . ." She had shaken her head at this point. "Then . . . we lose the poor mother, and we never know why. In the end, it's all in God's hands." She had paused a long time before shrugging her sadness to the side to lift up Noora's legs to give them a rough shake. "But not you, *insha' Allah*, not you. You are young and strong, and everything seems fine." She had slid Noora's legs down and grunted at Lateefa. "Still too early, not ready yet."

"But soon?" Lateefa had asked.

"Very soon."

"You must come right away when it's time."

"Well, haven't I done that every time you've called me? Of course, I will come immediately. And I'll stay on, too, just as we agreed, for a full forty days after. She will need the help, especially as there aren't any other women in this house who'd know what to do."

"Pah!"

"Yes, yes, yes," the midwife had said. "You may think you know what to do. But you know only in your head, not with your hands. When to give her the raw egg and garlic mix to speed the delivery, when to walk her and when to sit her on that sack of warmed sand, how to hug her, hold her, rub her, support her . . ."

"All right, all right, all right," Lateefa had said. "But I'll be there just the same."

So that's how it was to be. Lateefa in the room with them so that she could touch the baby first, so that she could take control right from the start.

Noora cradled her tummy and shambled back into her room, pausing over the wooden, rocking crib next to her bed. Piled in the middle of the mattress was a circle of clean sand, to be changed every time it got dirty, and stacked at the base of the crib, along with the long, cotton wrap, were the tiny, white gowns, eight of them, that Noora had sewn for the baby. Yes, everything was in place for its arrival.

She climbed onto her bed and eased into the mattress, tried to forget what was sitting on the chest in the corner of the room. But what if something had gone missing? With sudden alarm, she sat up to check.

On the ground, a black stone, to flatten her tummy after the birth, sat next to the sack of sand that was to prop her up into position during the delivery. She began counting the items on the chest. There were the scissors and thread, twisted many times over itself for thickness, to cut and tie the umbilical cord. There was the disinfecting *yas* powder to dab on the navel and the bowl of water with cotton next to it to clean the baby immediately after the birth.

Yes, everything was in place for the delivery, even the salt. She cringed. Oh, that chunk of salt—the size of an egg—that was to heal the rawness of her insides right after the delivery. The burn of it! A sudden fatigue overwhelmed her and she slackened back into her bed.

49

She was stuck in a dream.

Her feet sank deep as she staggered up a massive hill in a vast desert of undulating, golden dunes. The faster she climbed, the deeper the sand shifted around her ankles, and those velvety caresses trapped her calves till she slumped with exhaustion.

That's when she spotted the sand fish—that haunting sand fish—at the top of the hill, its head raised to the sky, taking in all that sun. It did not sink, just stayed where it was. After all, that's where it belonged.

Then the ground shook around her. The pounding stomps of a figure hurried past her; man or woman, she could not tell, for this figure was swathed in layers of cloth as it headed for the sand fish.

She gathered her strength and uprooted a foot. Then the other, and up she went, suddenly so spry, so alert, in a tiptoe scurry over the steep slope. All the while, she kept staring at the figure's feet, plump with spite, closing in on the sand fish.

She was crying. It was crying.

The foot rose and came crashing down. But the sand fish had vanished, leaving behind only the twirl of its body print on the face of the sand. A little distance away, it emerged.

It was crying. She was crying.

The foot was raised high once more, a shadow over her head. She dove again, wriggling her body, feeling another wriggle inside. But the quake was above her and burrowing through.

She was crying. She was crying.

She flapped her arms and kicked her legs, swam deeper and deeper, till she could swim no more. All those tears were clumping the sand, turning it into gobs of mud. Even the foot was struggling.

Soggy mud, sticky mud, heavy mud.

She was crying, sodden and damp. The wetness seeped out of her eyes, her face, her body. The wetness was everywhere.

Noora awoke in a shudder, her head still hazy with sleep, breathless from that dismal dream. So quiet, so still, so dark, save for the dwindling flame of the hurricane lamp hanging on a nail in the wall. The shriek of a mynah broke her daze. *A morning bird at night?* She tried to piece the logic of it just as she heard it flutter away, and the room blanched in a bolt of lightning. There was a puddle around her.

It was happening. It was coming.

The thought sent tremors through her just as a ripping spasm gripped her insides. Her scream was swallowed by the growling sky.

Rain was coming. It was coming.

The pain subsided. She gasped for breath, but her head was

brimming with the fear of knowing that the next contraction would be worse. Why was she alone? Where was Lateefa? What should she do? Where was the midwife? What had she said? "Walk, walk, walk!"

Noora stumbled off the bed only to double over as another gnarled wave traveled through her body. Was it signaling the beginning of a life or the end? What had the midwife said? "It's all in God's hands, whether you live or die." Would she die?

There was no time to think. Her labor started following a furious pace, rushing with the dash of the thunderstorm. She squatted. What had that midwife said? "Sit, sit, sit on the sack and hold on to me!" There was no time to grab the sack, so she clutched the bedpost and became one with the bursting clouds.

She roared with the storm, howled with the wind, screamed with the smacks of thunder. Her tears fell like the pelting raindrops, and when the hail came and knocked on the roof, that signaled the last stage of delivery.

And then she could not think anymore.

50

❦

S o quiet now. How quickly you calmed down."

 She paused and glanced over her shoulder, through the door, at the fit of panic in the courtyard. The hurricane lamps jerked like bright yellow fish on the surface of a black sea. There were stomps filled with the squish and slop of wet sand. Round and round, back and forth, they paced with urgent voices: concern in Jassem's, agitation in Lateefa's, madness in Yaqoota's.

"What should we do? What should we do first?" said Lateefa.

Noora turned back to her baby. "You hear her? That's the one who barged in just moments after you were born." She patted flat the shock of black hair and guided the dampened piece of cotton round the face, along its gurgling mouth and into the dips of those eyes, struggling to stay open. "Did you see her?"

"The midwife, we have got to get the midwife immediately!" cried Lateefa.

"Do you remember her? Did you see how she rushed in, stood there not knowing what to do, before she ran out again? She had wanted to touch you before me. But she arrived too late. I touched you first, remember that."

"We have to wait till this rain stops a little," said Jassem.

"Wooo," wailed Yaqoota. "If we don't hurry, she'll die, the baby will die."

"Don't listen to them," Noora whispered to her child. "Nothing will happen to you. You are blessed, *masha' Allah*, you're blessed." She dabbed the baby's feet—a boy—with the last piece of cotton, her hand still shaking with this delicate task. How fragile he was: the soft spot at the top of his head, the racing breath in his tummy, the curl of his spine, the tiny limbs that would not stay still, those twitching fingers that were already groping the air. How had she managed to wipe him clean without hurting him? Then again, how had she managed at all?

Perhaps it was that life-giving storm. She could still see the blinding flashes of light. She could still hear the rumble of the inky sky, the claps of thunder, that wet-wet hiss of rain, and, finally, the chaotic clatter of the hailstones. All that noise had chased the fear out of her. The sky had ripped open when everyone had given up on the blessing of rain. It had opened up for her and thrown buckets of hope and aspiration. The thunderstorm had rushed her along its hastening rhythm. How urgent, how hurried it was! After all, it was there for one thing only: to be her partner in delivery. Only now was it tapering off to a light drizzle. Why would it stay longer once its task was finished?

The exhaustion washed over her and she willed it away. "You're blessed," Noora whispered again and began securing him in the long swathe of cotton. "You will not face what I had to. You will not make my mistakes." The baby attempted to raise his drowsy eyelids, managed halfway before giving up with a yawn. "Just a little bit longer, and then I'll lay you down to sleep."

There was an argument outside, but this time Noora did not look up.

"Go now," Lateefa ordered.

"Nooo," cried Yaqoota, and Noora imagined those fleshy lips tightening into an unbending loop.

"All wrapped now." Noora lifted the baby and stepped softly to the crib.

"Go and get her, I said. We need her here now!"

"Do you hear her? That's her again. You have to be careful with her. One thing you should know is that she likes to play with words. I've learned to do that, and soon you must, too."

"I'm not going out in the dark, *Ommi* Lateefa," Yaqoota wailed. "The Bedouins will kidnap me . . . And you'll never see me again!"

"I'll go." That was Jassem.

"Don't be silly. This is a woman's job, a woman's concern. Yaqoota will go."

"I will not!" cried Yaqoota.

"You will!"

"Don't listen to them. One thing you should learn early is that in the end they're only good at talking." She rocked her son in her arms, sang softly, "That's all it is. Just talk, only talk, just talk."

Outside, there was the shuffle of a struggle. Someone was pulling; someone was resisting. There was a rip; there was a thud.

"Ooo!" screamed Yaqoota. "Did you break your leg?"

Could it be that the woman with careful steps had slipped?

There was a moment of silence before Lateefa hooted her pain. "I can't move. I need the bone setter."

"I can't go to see if she's all right. I've got you now, and, *masha'Allah*, you need me more than anyone else." She hugged him closer to her chest. "Tomorrow I'll bathe you properly, line your eyes with kohl, and put thumbprints of indigo on your forehead, cheeks, and chin to protect you from jealous eyes. Not that you need it. You see, *masha'Allah*, you're blessed."

"The baby, the baby, what's happening with the baby?" cried Lateefa. "Get the midwife! Get the bone setter!"

"Calm down," said Jassem. "I'll help you to your room, and then I'll set out with Yaqoota—so nobody kidnaps her—and bring them both here."

"Listen to me," Noora murmured, as she laid him in the crib. "In the end, this life is the better one for you."

The baby stirred and gurgled.

"Hush now, hush. Go to sleep."

Acknowledgments

I would like to thank my mother, Maryam, who possesses not only tailoring and embroidery skills, but also layers of wisdom and insight, and my father, Mohammad, for his vivid remembrances of the past. I am blessed to have them.

I am fortunate to have my three brothers, Sameer, Anwar, and Shehab, who carry an unceasing goodwill toward me. I am also lucky to have their wives, Souad, Cyma, and Lamees, who have become the sisters I never had.

My appreciation goes to my special friend, Ali Khalifa, who was with me right from the start when the novel was no more than an idea. With his flashes of inspiration and intuition, he was happy to guide me through the many drafts as the manuscript turned from raw to polished.

I am extremely grateful to all the people who opened their hearts to give me an authentic sense of the past lifestyles of this region. In particular, I would like to thank the daughter and granddaughter of a pearl merchant, May and Fatma Bilgaizi, for their warmth and honest recollections. A sincere thank you goes to my aunt, Amna, for her sharp memory and vivid ponderings, and Maryam Al-Hashemi for sharing the painful details of past childbirths. A warm mention must go to my grandmother, fondly nicknamed Mama-Hintain, or second-mother, who, during my childhood, told tales as precious as gems. Although she has passed away, her bedtime stories of *jinn*, witches, love, and marriage live on in my mind.

I am indebted to my friends Mimi Raad and Lina Matta, who immediately fell in love with my protagonist. I thank them for their valuable remarks, diligence, and all the time they spent examining every detail.

My gratitude goes to my agent, Emile Khoury, for believing in this novel and introducing me to the HarperCollins family, which has been so kind to me in its supervision and support. My sincere appreciation goes to my editor, Stephanie Fraser, for her professional guidance and keen observations.

My thanks to Ali Jaber for his infecting enthusiasm and to Samer Hamza, Aliyya Al-Khalidi, Susan Ehtisham, Aileen Mehra, Mike Mirolla, Monica Daniels, and Kawkab Bin-Hafez for taking the time to read my early drafts and to give their comments.

Finally, I am grateful to all my nephews and nieces: Ali, Mohammad, Omar, Ahmad, Maryam, Noora, Soraya, Faye, Maha, Jude, and Mansour. Thank you for bouncing into my work time to provide those much-needed breaks.

Turn the page

FOR MORE ABOUT MAHA GARGASH,
DUBAI, AND THE WRITING OF
The Sand Fish.

Meet Maha Gargash

I was born in Dubai to a prominent business family, with parents who have always believed that knowledge, experience, and a strong sense of being are the vital elements of personal fulfillment. These values were not spoken of, only understood with every year of growth. They are values that helped me tremendously when I was studying in America and, years later, in London.

America was an eye-opener. Upon first arriving, I was struck by the vastness of it. The highways felt like they would go on forever, and underground parking lots had a sinister mood about them (no doubt because of all the movies I had watched in which they were the most convenient place to carry out a murder). It puzzled me that children would address their parents as if they were in the same peer group and that teachers insisted I do away with the formality of calling them sir or ma'am and use their first names—John, Mary—as if we were best friends. I felt the only sensible thing I could do was to resist this new attitude of informality. As a result, that first year I suffered from culture shock. It was only by the second year that I realized my folly and started to change my approach, supposing that adapting, even temporarily, is always a good thing. From then on, I managed exceptionally well, and even regretted leaving America, where I had made wonderful friends and had exceptional teachers who had taught me to think and express myself.

With my degree in television and radio, I returned to Dubai and, straightaway, joined Dubai Radio and Television to pursue my interest in documentaries. It was a field that provided extensive travel opportunities and opened many doors. I directed a number of documentaries that remain to this day noteworthy resources about various aspects of Emirati culture. During the making of these programs, I traveled to all corners of the Emirates, and the experiences I had are precious, to say the least. I filmed nimble-fingered older women weaving a little girl's hair into wings to make up the traditional *shoongi* hairstyle, tracked a lone traveler and his camel in the middle of an empty desert while he recited the *tarij*—verses that follow the plod of the camel's movement and serve to while away the long, lonely hours in the middle of the dunes—and recorded a group of musicians assembling a traditional drum, chanting together as they stretched the hide over its frame.

Working on these documentaries was very similar to writing this book in that the effort involved me fully in a long and detailed process that, once finished, brought an inner satisfaction and a mountain of experience.

My next project was a little different from the documentaries. This was a cultural television program that consisted of long features on art, culture, nature, and unique people and communities from all over the world. Our team was small, and as a result, I ended up not just directing but also researching, scripting, and presenting. The program aired for five seasons, with features on topics such as India's ancient science of Ayurveda, a man who had purchased an island paradise in the Seychelles in 1962 for a mere ten thousand pounds sterling, and the khat plant, which sits at the core of social life in the Yemen and imparts a state of euphoria and stimulation when chewed and stored in the corner of the mouth.

For this program, I visited more than forty countries, which have all left invaluable impressions in my mind. I can still trace the beauty of the Simian Mountains of Ethiopia, take in the fragrance of pristine dawns at the bottom of the world in New Zealand, feel the thunderous power of the Nile as it crashes through a six-meter gorge in Uganda's Murchison Falls National Park, recall with awe the sight of the seventy-five saker and peregrine falcons soaring over Pakistan's mighty Hindu Kush, as a part of a UAE government program designed to increase their population in the wild. Traveling as I did, my senses were sharpened, and my desire grew to learn more and to probe for more.

A Past I Cherish

In my mind, I could see this book long before I began writing. There was the big, open sky, the salty gulf waters, the scorching sun, and a boat—it was a pearling dhow, and my imaginings led me to put characters on it. I thought of a young male hero onboard this dhow, the hardship he would endure, the feats he would accomplish, and the hope that would reside in his heart.

Historically, pearl divers lived harsh lives. On diving voyages, under an unforgiving sun, they lived for months on the overcrowded dhow. They were fed very little, and, due their constant diving and a lack of vitamins, the health of their eyes, ears, and lungs suffered. Most would take advances from the owner of the boat in order to provide for their families during the months they were at sea. If their seasonal catch was not enough to cover their advances, they were in debt to the owner at the start of the next season, when they would have to get another advance. The more I discovered, the more I was convinced that pearling must be the backdrop to my story.

I began a period of intense research, logging all the minute details that I felt must be included in the novel. When I interviewed surviving divers, I was surprised to find them less than keen to share their feelings about those trying times. One old man, with eyes full of the milk of disease, said to me, "Those days were so full of misery, I prefer to forget them."

No matter. I still felt I had enough material to create a wonderful book and began writing with so much passion that it took me six months to notice that my story was not moving forward. There were no plot twists and my characters had no attributes that would make them memorable. My project was turning into a detailed textbook—very handy, I might add—for people interested in pearling. Those first twenty chapters, written with so much gusto, went straight into the bin as it dawned on me that what was missing was the essential ingredient: detailed knowledge of a personal kind.

After some thought, I felt that it would be more interesting to tell the story through the eyes of a young woman. And not just any woman. Noora, my protagonist, grows up in isolation, uncultivated and wild. Having established this background, I posed the question: What would happen if this carefree and self-reliant young woman were forced into a life of restrictions? And the answer came in a number of possibilities, which became the basis for this novel.

The United Arab Emirates has gone through a fast and impressive transformation. In fact, change came to this young nation so quickly that we Emiratis have had little time to reflect on it. That is why I decided to set my novel in the past, choosing the 1950s because that is when it became clear that the old lifestyle would soon disappear.

It was in the 1930s, with the worldwide economic depression and the Japanese discovery of cultured pearls, that the pearling industry, which the communities of the Arabian Gulf depended on, dwindled. By the 1950s, save for a few foolhardy merchants who insisted on carrying out "one more voyage," it was clear that the pearling industry would not recover—and the people of the region watched and waited to see where the black oil they had heard about would lead them. What change would it bring?

The oil brought opportunity, prosperity, education, and health care, in what can only be described as a grand transformation—a plunge into modernity whereby people quickly put the past behind them and looked to the future. Today, the United Arab Emirates is one of the most desirable countries to live in. It is a tax haven and boasts an impressive infrastructure. The lifestyle is comfortable and the population cosmopolitan. It holds an enviable safety record, and its policies are tolerant toward all races and religions. As a result, people of more than 190 nationalities call the United Arab Emirates home.

With all these advances, the lifestyle has shifted gears, especially in my city, Dubai. The new generation of young men and women is following a different pace in their daily lives, which are now filled with opportunity, promise, and progress. There is no time, it seems, to mull over the past—that other life their grandparents had lived. But to ignore it would be a big loss. No one has expressed this sentiment better than our late president, the visionary Sheikh Zayed Bin-Sultan Al-Nahyan: "A people that does not understand its past and does not draw the correct lessons from it will not be able to deal with the challenges of the present and the future."

Historically, the Emirati culture is an oral one. Our traditions, feelings, and morals were passed on from one generation to the next through storytelling and poetry. Therefore, there is a very real danger of losing the fine details of former lifestyles with the passing away of those who lived it. Today, not enough is recorded about our past, and what is displayed and documented in museums across the country gives facts but no personal accounts.

Luckily, my work as a film director specializing in documentaries gave me access to the societies portrayed in the book. To capture the feel of those years of deprivation before the wealth that came with oil, I conducted rigorous interviews with numerous elders, whose memories make up much of what is described in the book. It was the women who had the most poignant tales. Because I am an Emirati woman myself, they opened their hearts to me and revealed not only the intricate details of their day-to-day lives but also their hopes and desires, their fears and aspirations. Some of the interviewees were my family members, including my parents and aunt. During the process of collecting information, I realized that it was not enough to be able to imagine their lives. I had to be able to see, smell, hear, taste, and touch that world.

To write this book, I spent much time researching architecture and town structure, pearl diving, Arabian dhows, Arabian trading routes, women's costume, fabrics, jewelry, makeup, and sewing techniques. To describe the settings, I explored the topography of the land and traveled to abandoned homes set high in the mountains as well as the skeletons of homesteads by the sea. I wanted to give the reader a true sense of the surroundings. Through phrasing that was simple and spare, I attempted to reflect the barrenness of the external landscape, where heat was endured, scarcity tolerated, and rain celebrated.

I feel *The Sand Fish* makes an appealing read in that it is a depiction of a very specific time and lifestyle mixed with universal feelings and understandings of love, jealousy, friendship, and survival. I was interested not in the grand scheme of things in the greater world but rather in a tiny slice of life and how big it looms in my protagonist's mind. My aim was to provide an emotional setting for the novel by showing what is going on through Noora's emotional filter. She is a third wife stuck in a household of schemes. I wanted the reader to get caught up in this ride, to get inside Noora's head and see the world the way she sees it.

The novel is Noora's journey to self-discovery. Her small world in the house by the sea is dependent on intricacies of conversation: what to say and what not to say, the sweet words that carry ulterior motives, the psychological games that are played even at the most basic level. Her steps toward intimacy with Hamad are all very playful at first, but at the same time very dangerous, with a shadow of impending doom hanging over her every action.

Although beautiful, intelligent, and fiery, Noora is a different kind of heroine. She has little choice and no opportunity, so it would have been unrealistic to give her great ambitions. In her poverty-stricken situation, it is enough that she is able to cope—not a heroic action by Western standards, but by coping she was able to gain the upper hand, winning small battles in the midst of the shifting relationships of the household she becomes part of.

Under an Amber Sun

There was a time when you could see the sand change in color and texture just by traveling short distances. That has all changed now. Dubai has grown to become an exciting city that attracts visitors from all over the world. They come for the lavish resorts, trendy restaurants, and grand shopping malls. Often, there is so much to do that it's easy to overlook the culture of Dubai—and beyond.

Dubai

DUBAI CREEK
Dubai Creek, an inlet of water, was the main element that established Dubai's commercial position. Dubai's pearling industry and trade with India and Africa were based primarily on expe-

ditions in the creek. It divides the city into two parts: Bur Deira and Bur Dubai. People used to use the *abra*, a small rowing boat, to cross from one side to the other, a practice that continues to this day. Although the boats are now motorized, the *abra* remains the best way to appreciate the hum and throb of the city.

BASTAKIYA

Bastakiya is one of the most charming historic neighborhoods of Dubai. Linked to each other in rows are some of city's oldest homes, which go back to the 1890s, built by Dubai's prosperous residents. The houses are made up of two floors and are designed to combat the hot and humid climate. From every home rise eye-catching wind towers. The wind tower is an ingenious method of fanning. It takes wind from any direction, funnels it through the house, and, according to the tower's depth and height, accelerates it up to five times over.

SHEIKH SAEED AL-MAKTOUM HOUSE

Dating back to 1896, Sheikh Saeed Al-Maktoum House was not just the residence of the former ruler of Dubai but also the seat of local government and a place of dialogue for political and social issues. Vaulted, high-beamed ceilings, arched doorways, and sculpted window overhangs characterize this historic building. Today, it houses an impressive collection of photographs of old Dubai.

AL-AHMADIYA SCHOOL

Built in 1912, this is Dubai's first semiformal school. Set deep on all four sides, the rooms are arranged under a covered arcade, and in the middle of the building is a sandy courtyard, which was the arena for morning assemblies as well as a playground for the students. Al-Ahmadiya is located in Deira and remains close to the hearts of all those who studied there.

Gold Souk

Thick necklaces, earrings, and bangles hang in shop after shop, all in rich gold. Located in the heart of Deira, the Gold Souk consists of more than three hundred retailers that deal almost exclusively in jewelry. Trade grew in its tight streets during the 1940s due to Dubai's free trade policies, which encouraged entrepreneurs from India and Iran to set up their stores. Today, by some estimates, more than twenty-five tons of gold are present at any given time in the souk.

The National Bank of Dubai Pearl Museum

It is a collection not to be missed. The world's largest collection of natural pearls sits in heaps under glass at the National Bank headquarters building. The pearls belonged to the late Sultan Al-Owais, a businessman, poet, and philanthropist, who donated them to the people of the Emirates under the custodianship of the bank. He had a wish that the pearls should be available to remind people what life was like before the discovery of oil. Some of the most exquisite pearls, of perfect roundness and luster, can be seen at this museum.

Beyond Dubai

Abu Dhabi: Sheikh Zayed Mosque

The Sheikh Zayed Mosque in Abu Dhabi is the third-largest mosque in the world. It is named after the father of the nation, the late president Sheikh Zayed Bin-Sultan Al-Nahyan, who is buried adjacent to it. The mosque can accommodate 40,000 worshippers and has set some world records. With more than two million knots and weighing forty-five tons, the world's largest carpet is housed here. It took 1,200 weavers from Iran two years to create it. The mosque is a stunning feat of architecture, with an assembly of soaring minarets and grand domes all in brilliant white marble.

SHARJAH: BAIT AL-NABOODAH

The Bait Al-Naboodah in Sharjah is no ordinary home. Its size and luxurious detail indicate that it belonged to a rich family. There are columns with granite bases from India and wood from Zanzibar. The rooms are typical of Gulf-Arab houses. They are long and rectangular, with high ceilings; their width follows the length of the roof beams. Windows are small to let in just the right amount of light and prevent excess heat. It is a handsome house, stylish in its simplicity and always a pleasure to visit.

LIWA

Located on the edge of the Empty Quarter, Liwa is far but well worth the trip to enjoy the serenity of one of the world's most beautiful desert landscapes. Here exists a vastness so profound it's overwhelming. Liwa is called the desert of deserts, where the dunes are as high as mountains. The descents are nearly vertical, and if one slides down in a Jeep, the sight of the hollow below is both nerve-racking and exciting.

SHEES VILLAGE

The best time to visit the mountains of the Emirates is after a rainfall. That is when the dust is washed away and the earth's deep hues of red, brown, and purple are at their most vivid. A particularly scenic route of deep ravines and palm groves cuts through Fujairah's mountains, ending at an enchanting village called Shees. Here is a small community living in isolation on tight, stonewalled terraces that trap runaround breezes. What makes this place so special is its natural setting and the availability of water from natural springs.